IN THE PALACE OF THE *CHAMA*. . . .

Without question, the guards of Vediaster had led Terril, Tammad, and Cinnan to a room in the palace, telling them they would be summoned when the leader, the *Chama*, was free to see them.

Perhaps, thought Terril, their mission would prove easier than they had assumed. Yet why hadn't they even been asked who they were and what their business was?

Even as this tendril of worry brushed her mind, Terril felt an overwhelming wave of exhaustion sweep over her. Vaguely, she wondered why Tammad was sitting and staring and blinking slowly at nothing, why Cinnan was struggling to rise with no success.

And then Terril ceased even to wonder, as a humming chant lulled her, stealing all strength, all will, all consciousness. . . .

SHARON GREEN
has written:

The Terrilian series

   THE WARRIOR WITHIN
   THE WARRIOR ENCHAINED
   THE WARRIOR REARMED
   THE WARRIOR CHALLENGED

The Jalav Amazon Warrior Series

   THE CRYSTALS OF MIDA
   AN OATH TO MIDA
   CHOSEN OF MIDA
   THE WILL OF THE GODS
   TO BATTLE THE GODS

The Diana Santee Series

   MIND GUEST
   GATEWAY TO XANADU

THE WARRIOR CHALLENGED

Sharon Green

DAW BOOKS, INC.
DONALD A. WOLLHEIM, PUBLISHER

1633 Broadway, New York, NY 10019

DAW Book Collectors No. 681.

First Printing, August 1986

1 2 3 4 5 6 7 8 9

PRINTED IN U.S.A.

1

I sat on the carpet fur among the cushions, my eyes closed, feeling the faint, unimaginative sadness brush at me. As sadness it was no more than mild regret, about as compelling as having missed that dull meeting you had decided to go to, but then forgot about. I sighed at the thin-bloodedness of the sadness, then shook my head.

"That wouldn't be enough to get a blink out of a chronic hysteric," I told him without opening my eyes. "Try it again, and this time make me cry."

A surge of annoyance and frustration daggered through the weakling sadness, strong enough to make me flinch if I hadn't been guarding against it, and then he made a sound that was half growl and half vexation.

"Should it be your wish to weep, *wenda*, there are other means of achieving that," he said in that dangerous, deep-voiced way of his. "As my efforts in this manner fail to please you, it shall likely soon become my duty to fetch a switch."

"Threatening the teacher isn't allowed," I answered with a laugh, finally opening my eyes to look at him. Tammad lay stretched out on the carpeting not far from me, one big leg bent comfortably at the knee, the rest of his giant body not as relaxed as it should have been. His swordbelt was conspicuous by its absence, leaving him nothing but the green *haddin*

5

he wore wrapped around his loins, and his leather wristbands. His blond-haired head was crammed full with feelings of rebellion and resentment, feelings he wasn't used to experiencing without being able to do something about them, and his blue eyes said his threat had been only half joking. Tammad was getting impatient with his progess—or lack of it—and was having trouble controlling that impatience.

"If this isn't working out it's only because you're not trying hard enough," I told him with feigned calm. Tammad loved me, I knew he did, but if he decided to look around for something to punish me for, he would not have to look very far. I'd only gotten my empathetic ability back a couple of days earlier, but I'd spent a good deal of that time experimenting with the changes I'd noticed. Tammad didn't like the idea of my experimenting, and if he found out about it I'd really be in for it.

"If this isn't working out, it's only because you're not trying hard enough," I told him as his pretty blue eyes, looked annoyed; I was trying to sound firm and teacher-like instead of nervous. "And if you're scandalized over being taught by a woman instead of another man, you have only yourself to blame. Len was perfectly willing to put you through these exercises, but he couldn't do it with his head splitting apart. Which was *your* doing.'

"A doing which I truly regret," Tammad said with a sigh, accepted-guilt now flowing through his mind. "To give pain to one attempting to aid you is not an action of honor, even should that action be involuntary, as mine was. I continue to have no understanding as to why it should have occurred."

"That's because you can't see yourself from the outside," I said, immediately soothing the ache I could feel in him as I pushed the skirt of my gown aside so I could crawl to him. "Your entire life has been aimed at being better than the other men around you, toward making yourself their leader. A leader dominates, always, and that's what you were doing to Len when he tried to teach you. He can do something you can't, but you weren't about to allow that to keep you from being *denday* over him. Len isn't strong enough to block your

6

output without shielding, and if he shields he can't teach you. If he doesn't shield—well, he ends up with the kind of headache he did end up with. He knows you weren't doing it on purpose, but he also knows that doesn't make any difference. He doesn't have the strength to fend you off and teach you at the same time, so you're stuck with me."

"A *wenda* who does indeed have the necessary strength," he murmured, putting those big hands to my sides to pull me down closer to him. "For teaching as well as other, more pleasurable pursuits."

"Indeed, *hamak*," I murmured in Rimilian, Tammad's language, putting my hands to his face. "This *wenda* shall ever have strength for her beloved, for he is her *sadendrak*, the one who gives meaning to her life in all things. Perhaps a short rest would now be advisable, to conserve the strength of one who learns, for other, more pleasurable pursuits."

I leaned down to put my lips on his, feeling again that I would never get enough of him no matter what, and he wasted no time putting his hand behind my head and returning the kiss. I could feel the growl of desire beginning in him, just as it usually did when he looked at me or put his hands on me, but then the heavy calm swirled into his mind, the calm he used as both a shield and a control over his own emotions. He took full pleasure out of the kiss we shared, but when it was over he simply lifted me away from his chest.

"As this one must learn, best would be that we continue with the lessons," he said, his light eyes showing the calm behind them, his mind firmly made up. "As I must depart soon to join the *Chamd* Rellis for a meal, we must leave other things for another time. For what reason were you displeased with my efforts?"

"If you had made the effort, I wouldn't be displeased," I muttered, staring at him darkly from where I sat on the carpeting, hating the way he could ignore me as I'd never been able to ignore him. "Does Rellis mean more to you than I do?"

"The *Chamd* Rellis is our host, *wenda*," he answered gently with only the hint of a grin in his eyes, one hand

7

stroking my arm. "To refuse the invitation of one's host to a meal, or even to appear later than the appointed time, is to give insult to one who has given hospitality. That you find great joy in squirming beneath me is known to me, yet were you given such joy when we awoke, and will be given the same again later. Might Rellis not be given a small portion of the attention which is rightfully yours, in return for the welcome we have had in his house?"

The grin had by that time spread to his face, most likely due to the way I was blushing I wouldn't have described my enjoyment quite the way he had, and it was enough to make me back off in embarrassment—just the way he'd wanted me to do. I was learning that he didn't have to hand out orders to make me obey him, and the revelation was less of an interesting discovery than a nasty surprise.

"I'm thinking about hating you," I stated as I leaned both arms on his chest to look straight down at him, trying to put a growl in my voice. "I'm also thinking about raping you."

"Should you find it possible, you have my permission to do so," he came back with a broadened grin and a chuckle, his eyes shining. "I am now aware that you would find the first as difficult to achieve as the second. Are you prepared as yet to discuss the reason for your displeasure with my efforts to learn?"

"I'll be glad to discuss my reasons," I agreed with annoyance, wishing I *could* find a way to rape that big hulk of a warrior. "Your efforts were unacceptable because they didn't have any—" I quickly lowered my face to his shoulder, sank my teeth into it hard enough for him to feel, then raised my head to his startled outrage and finished, "—bite."

"Perhaps, woman, it would be best if I were to fetch a switch after all," he growled angrily. The look in his eyes hardened as he began projecting that deadly promise effect, but I'd been expecting it and was already shielding.

"There, *that's* what you were missing!" I pounced, my pointing finger startling him out of the anger. "You have enough strength to project any emotion you like, but the only ones that get that strength are the emotions of violence. You have to learn to push behind the others just as you do with anger and outrage; otherwise you're wasting your time."

"I dislike your manner of evoking the reactions you seek," he grumbled, bringing one hand up to rub at his bitten shoulder, his eyes still displeased with me but lacking that you've-had-it outrage which usually means I'm in trouble. "How am I to put strength behind those feelings which normally have no strength of their own?"

"All emotions have strength of their own," I retorted, leaning down again to kiss the place where I'd bitten, at the same time using pain control. There hadn't been that much pain to begin with, but kissing-it-to-make-it-better takes on new meaning when a Prime empath indulges in it, something that made Tammad chuckle again.

"An emotion doesn't have to be strong to have strength," I continued, looking down into his eyes as I toyed with the blond hair on the unbelievably broad chest I rested against. "What you gave me for sadness was this," and I replayed the faint regret, "when you should have given me this." I reshaped the emotion and brushed him with it, the feeling of loss that one has been expecting yet nevertheless deeply regrets. "Or this," I added, making the loss unexpected and moving, the sort to bring tears to your eyes. Then I changed it to an opportunity gone that might have been more than worthwhile if it had been acted on, and the broad body under me squirmed in discomfort, the swirling calm trying ineffectively to block me out. "When you're sending an emotion, don't try to imagine it, *feel* it. Let it touch you before sending it on its way, even if it's an emotion a *l'lenda* doesn't usually allow himself to feel. If a person doesn't believe the emotion you're projecting he won't feel it the way you want him to, so you have to make it *real*. The more real it is to the two of you, the more it will be felt."

"There are no emotions a *l'lenda* refuses to feel," he corrected, reaching up to brush a strand of hair from my shoulder. "Should a man refuse to allow himself to feel, soon he will become no man at all. Merely do I find difficulty with this—sending—you attempt to teach."

"You're not finding difficulty with it," I corrected in turn, producing a sharpened look in the blue eyes watching me. "When someone says they're having trouble with something, that usually means they're trying but not making it. You, on the other hand, are not making it because you're not trying. You think what I'm teaching you is dishonorable."

"Indeed do I feel it dishonorable," he grudged, not happy with the admission but not wanting to lie. "I continue to feel that to invade the being of another is completely lacking in honor, yet was I given this—gift—without having been consulted. I must learn the control of it so that I do not intrude without being aware of it."

Only two days earlier, when I had regained my empathetic abilities after thinking they were gone forever, my brother empath Len Phillips had discovered that Tammad, the man who had banded me, was a strong, natural empath himself. Tammad was trying to hide the bitterness he felt, the deep-down despair that something like that had to happen to *him*, and I knew exactly how he felt. Asking, *Why me?* had filled a large portion of my self-dialogue in the months just past, and knowing it had to be *someone* didn't do a damned thing to make acceptance easier.

"There are other reasons to learn that you should like better," I said, putting my hand to his face as I let my compassion touch him so that I might share his pain. "Once you have the control you need, you not only won't intrude accidently, the choice will be entirely yours whether you intrude at all. And don't forget that if Len's guess is right, most of the men on this world are empaths. If you happen to run into one who can control the ability, you won't be at a disadvantage. Learning control will be just like getting better with a sword. There's nothing dishonorable about getting better with a sword, is there?"

"No, *hama*, there is nothing dishonorable in increasing one's ability with a sword," he agreed with a soft smile, accepting not so much what I'd said as the reason I'd said it.

He knew as well as I that he would have to come to terms with his doubts by himself, but I'd also wanted him to know I was there to help him, to make the time as easy and acceptable as possible. He did know that now, in a way untalented people could never experience, and when I touched him with the love I felt, he fumbled briefly to copy the emotion and send it back to me before drawing me closer for another kiss. There was no desire in that kiss, only the sort of pure love we had touched each other with, and when I raised my head to look at him again, we were both smiling.

"And that's another benefit in learning control," I said, spreading my hands out to enjoy the hard-muscled feel of his shoulders and arms. "You can tell someone you love them even in a crowd of people, and no one else has to know about it. Or, at least, *I* can do that. You still haven't learned to narrow your projection enough. If anyone else had been in this room a minute ago, they would have felt awfully well loved. Your projection was fat."

"Fat!" he repeated in mock outrage, his eyes twinkling as he shook his head at me. "I show the woman the size of my love, and she deems it overfleshed! I shall be certain to bring a switch when I return."

"Don't you dare!" I laughed, knowing this time he was doing nothing more than teasing me, and then it came to me that that might be just the time I'd been looking for to ask him about the strange urge I'd had lately. I didn't know what his reaction would be, but I'd known from the first that even the asking would have to be carefully timed.

"I think I had best be on my way now," he said before I could get my request phrased just right, stretching where he lay. "Sit up now, *hama*, so that I might rise and retrieve my sword."

"Tammad, wait," I blurted, reluctant to let the opportunity slip away. "There's something I want to ask you first."

"My answer is what it was, *wenda*," he said with a grin, reaching one big hand out to stroke my bottom. "When I return I will give you the joy you crave."

"That's not what I meant," I protested, upset all over again

11

at the new blush I could feel in my cheeks. I also wanted to push his stroking hand away from my bottom, but that was something I knew he'd never allow. "What I want to know is if you would be willing to teach me something in return for what I'm teaching you. A trade of skills, so to speak, so that both of us will benefit."

"It pleases me that you wish to learn, Terril," he said, and I could feel the strong approval in his mind. "There are, however, those who are far more qualified than I to teach cooking and such. Best would be that you await the return to our city, where there are sufficient *wendaa* to teach you what. . . ."

"You don't understand—" I interrupted, forcing myself to get the words out before I lost my nerve. "Oh, I do want to learn how to cook and do other things for you, but first I'd like to learn how to—use a sword."

I mumbled the last three words, so I wasn't sure he heard me, especially since there was no immediate reaction. Those blue, blue eyes stared at me for a long minute, the mind behind them practically motionless with surprise, and then he was fighting hard to keep laughter from erupting.

"So you would learn the use of a sword," he said, his hand back to moving in a circle over my bottom, his voice even and his eyes studying me, just as though he were seriously considering my proposal. "And what would you do with such a skill once you had acquired it?"

"I—don't know," I admitted, wishing I could make him stop touching me like that so that I could think. "Please don't laugh at me, *hamak*, it really means a lot to me. Couldn't you find a—smaller sword that you could teach me how to use?"

"Indeed would you require a smaller sword than mine," he said, grinning as he remembered the time I discovered I couldn't even lift his sword. "Perhaps it would be best if I were to consider your request for a time before voicing a decision. And should you truly wish this thing, you also may take a time to consider how best to please me. A man who is pleased will often allow the things his *wenda* asks."

I began to protest that I'd been offering a trade, not asking a favor, but even if he hadn't moved me aside so that he could stand up, the words would never have gotten said. When I'd accepted Tammad's bands I'd also been agreeing to do things his way, the way everyone else on that world did them. That meant that whatever help I gave him was due him, just as his love and protection were due me. If I wanted anything above the basics of food, shelter, clothing and protection, I had to ask for it in the way he wanted to be asked. The thought of wheedling a man for something I wanted was so humiliating I didn't know how the women of that world could do it, but I knew well enough that they did. I'd agreed to try doing things Tammad's way without anyone twisting my arm, but to wheedle and beg—!

"It is a thing you must become accustomed to, *hama*, should you truly wish what you have asked for," Tammad said, interrupting my thoughts as he reached down to lift me to my feet, obviously knowing what I was feeling. "Should you find yourself unable to act so, we will merely allow memory of so— unusual a request to slip from us, and speak no more upon it. I will return when the meal with Rellis is done."

He leaned down to kiss me then, impossibly tall and impossibly broad, and then, as he had already replaced his swordbelt, he simply left. I stood in the middle of the large blue and white room, the high-arched windows behind me, and tried to keep remembering how much I loved that overgrown barbarian. I did love him, I really did, but sometimes he made me so mad I could spit!

"Damn him!" I muttered with what was nearly a growl, my hands clenched to furious fists at my sides, the anger filling my mind so completely I was almost to the point of projecting it. He was trying to make me obey him again, and I was angry because I couldn't see a way to get out of it.

I turned and started toward the windows, stopped abruptly as I changed my mind, turned toward the stack of furs Tammad and I used as a bed, changed my mind again, then furiously kicked at one of the white pillows on the carpet-fur. He hadn't laughed aloud because he hadn't wanted to insult me, but that didn't mean Tammad didn't consider my asking to learn how to use a sword comical. He also didn't approve of something that ridiculous, but he didn't want to hurt me by coming up with a flat no. That was why he'd said he'd think about it, to give me the chance to back out on my own—with a little help from him. He'd told me I had to convince him to agree, all the while knowing how humiliating I'd find doing something like that, fully expecting me to find it impossible. When I discovered I couldn't wheedle and beg he'd let me forget all about the silliness I'd asked for, and that would be the end of an awkward situation—without his having to refuse. He had it all neatly tied and wrapped—which was what made me so absolutely furious.

I couldn't have been seething more than five minutes before a knock came at the door, a knock that lacked the arrogance of the usual knockers on that world. There were no slaves in Rellis's house so I wondered who it could be, then remembered my own lunch date. Still mired in bottomless distress I strode to the door and yanked it open, to see the two faces I'd expected. Garth looked curious, but Len seemed ready to cringe back with shield locked tight.

"Is it safe to come in?" Len asked more diffidently than was usual for him, his handsome face wearing a wary expression. "If you've changed your mind, we can come back some other time."

"It's safe to come in only if you're female," I returned, staring him straight in the eye. "If you're male, you have to take your chances."

Len moved his wary expression to Garth, but Garth was already looking at Len, both of their glances asking the same question. Lenham Phillips, a brother empath from Central, and Garth R'Hem Solohr, Colonel of Kabras from Alderan, were trying to decide just how much they'd risk if they did come in, and their uneasy hesitation lightened some small part of the anger I was still feeling. The two Amalgamation men had given me nothing but trouble from the first day they'd set foot on Rimilia, but the last couple of days seemed to have changed all that. They were the ones who had been helping me and keeping Tammad from finding out, and sharing the secret had apparently drawn us all together.

"I have a better idea," Garth said after the heavy hesitation, trying hard to lighten the mood. "Since the food trays have been delivered here to the bathing room, we don't have to go in. Terry can come out."

"I always knew the military mind was good for something," Len put in as he brightened, giving Garth an amused look. "For a minute I was afraid we were going to have to turn female. How about it, Terry? The food's getting cold."

They were both turned to me expectantly, trying to talk me into it without words, and truthfully I was in no mood for my own company. I took a deep breath which didn't do a damned thing to make me feel better, then nodded my head. The two of them immediately stepped aside to let me by, then followed after me.

The bathing room had a large pool surrounded by an area of uncarpeted marble, the same sort of arched windows the bedroom had letting in what seemed like miles of sunshine and warmth. Two well-stuffed trays had been brought and left on two small tables not far from the marble, but walking up to one of them and looking down at what it held showed me I was in no mood to eat.

"He said no," Len guessed from not too far behind me, his mind sharing and commiserating with my upset. "Was it a final no, or did he leave room for argument?"

"He didn't say no," I grumbled, turning around to look at them. "He said he'd think about it, and while he's thinking about it I'm supposed to coax him a little. If I don't coax him, *then* the answer will be no."

Len shielded immediately and looked down at the carpeting, but Garth didn't know how to shield. He put one broad hand to his face and turned away, but the delighted amusement he felt just about flamed out of him. I'd expected them to react that way, and how nice they weren't disappointing me!

"I'm going to throw this food at the first one of you who laughs out loud," I warned them, glaring back and forth between Garth's dark-haired head and Len's light-haired one, my fists planted on my hips. "There's nothing funny about this and you ought to know it!"

"Come on, Terry, lighten up," Garth said, fighting to keep his face straight as he looked at me over his shoulder. "You know we all expected him to refuse immediately, so you're still ahead of the game."

"And if you need any coaxing practice, you know you can count on us," Len put in in a very solemn way, which immediately caused Garth to break up in laughter. A second later Len was joining him, the two of them laughing like a couple of *virenjj*, totally ignoring my disgusted stare. Briefly I toyed with the idea of carrying through on my threat, then gave it up and simply turned away. Len and Garth were really enjoying themselves, but I was starting to get depressed.

"I don't understand why you're so upset," Len said after a minute, his laughter eased down to chuckling "What's the difference between doing what you usually do with Tammad, and coaxing him? The end result will be the same, and if you don't mind that then what's the big deal?"

I turned my head to look at him, seeing the *haddinn* and swordbelt both he and Garth wore, realizing that they really didn't understand completely. Or maybe they were just seeing it from the wrong side of the fence.

"If you don't know why I'm upset, then why did you laugh?" I asked in turn, including them both in the question. "Tammad knows exactly how humiliated I'd feel wheedling him for something and so do you, otherwise you wouldn't have laughed. How would you two have enjoyed wheedling someone for those swords you're so proud of? And how well would you do learning to use them, if you'd had to get them in that particular way?"

"I think I preferred you as an unreasonable brat," Len answered wryly, his tone matching Garth's look of discomfort. "Being cooly logical and reasonable makes you difficult to argue with."

"But, Terry, you're not a man," Garth protested, less able to understand than Len. "What would be absolutely demoralizing for us shouldn't be nearly that bad for you. And maybe learning to use a sword isn't as important as you think it is. What will happen if you don't learn?"

"I don't know what will happen," I answered glumly, turning away to seat myself among the blue and white cushions the room held. "I don't even really understand why I should need to learn something that—violent and senseless. There's just no confusion to the feeling: I *do* need to learn it."

"But you don't even know if you can depend on this new ability of yours," Garth said, following me over to the cushions to crouch beside me, the disturbance in his mind reflected in his eyes. "It's making you believe you need to do something without giving you any reasons for the belief. What if you're misinterpreting the whole thing?"

"Then I'd be making a fool out of myself for nothing," I answered with a shrug, feeling the annoyance and frustration rising inside me again. "But you have no idea how strong the feeling is, practically to the level of compulsion. You called it a new ability; Garth, I'm not even sure it is! What am I going to do?"

"The first thing you have to do is stop putting out that static," Len interrupted before Garth could say anything, coming over to seat himself to my left with an expression of mild pain on his face. "It was a lot worse when we first got here, and you're starting to slide back to it again. The power behind it is so much higher now— Terry, you're going to have to learn to control yourself a good deal better than you have."

"I don't want to learn to control myself," I muttered, with rebellion added to what Len called static, my eyes drawn down to the small-linked bronze chains around my wrists, two of the five that made me Tammad's. "I don't want to control myself, I don't want to be stronger, and I don't want anything to do with new abilities. Why can't it all just leave me alone!"

"It won't leave you alone," Len pursued, his voice relentless despite the strain in it, his mind fighting against the urge to shield itself from my output. "Your abilities are growing both in size and strength, and you can't pretend they aren't. All you can do is learn to control them, before someone gets hurt. Like me, for instance."

I looked up to see the sweat on his face and the tension in his body, outward signs of the way he was trying to fight me off without using his shield. When I purposely moved into his mind he flinched, expecting more pain, then relaxed with a sigh when he felt the soothing of pain control instead. I hadn't wanted to hurt Len, but that seemed to be all my increased abilities were good for. Hurting people and making me feel like a fool.

"Stop pouting," Garth said, holding his sword out of the way as he changed his crouch to a sitting position, his gray eyes annoyed. "Very few are born with everything in life; most of us have to work hard to earn whatever we have. Since you have more than most, you should be feeling grateful instead of resentful. You're not an infant, Terry; stop acting like one."

"I'll act like anything I please," I replied with all the surliness I was feeling, tired of trying to be reasonable. It isn't possible to be reasonable when you're constantly surrounded by infuriating unreason, and I was discovering I resented Garth's lack of jealousy. Almost everyone around him was an empath, either active or latent, but Garth didn't feel left out. He knew the problems of being an empath, understood them from having seen them, and was inordinately pleased that they weren't *his* problems. I envied the sure self-acceptance that was his, and wished I could figure out how he did it.

"Well, *I* feel like acting like someone about to eat," Len put in, rising to his feet then heading toward one of the trays. "How are Tammad's lessons coming, Terry? I'll bet he's taking it easier with you than he did with me."

"He's not," I denied with a headshake, looking down at my wristbands again, ignoring the small sound of vexation that came from Garth before he rose to join Len at the tray. "He's trying to stop himself from feeling insulted over having to take lessons from a woman, but it keeps getting away from him. If I couldn't filter it out I'd have the same headache you had, and that would be the end of the lessons. If Tammad thought he was hurting me, he'd refuse to let it continue.''

''I wish to hell I could figure out how you do that filtering,'' Len said with heavy frustration in both mind and voice, bringing back a bowl of fried meat strips to the place he'd taken earlier. ''You said it's like letting down a thin curtain, but I can't detect it when you use it. Do you get it the way you get the shield you showed me how to form?''

''No,'' I said, moving the bottom of my gown aside so that I might stroke the bands on my ankles. ''It came when I needed it, just the way it did when I was struggling with that intruder in the resting place of the sword of Gerleth. If I need it it forms, but I can't form it if I don't need it. Do you want to try needing it?''

''I have to think about that,'' Len muttered, a glance confirming the unease his mind was evincing, his hand just holding a meat strip without his seeing it. ''It didn't form when I needed it with Tammad, so there's no reason to believe it will against you. Maybe there's a trigger for it that we don't know about.''

''That's a very pretty gown you're wearing, Terry,'' Garth said suddenly, only a small portion of his attention on the meat chunks and vegetables he'd brought back. ''You really do look good in pink, which is probably why Tammad enjoys seeing you in it. When are you going to tell him about the experimenting we've been doing, the experimenting you've *had* to do to find the limits of your new abilities?''

Garth had kept most of his question casual, tying it into his easy observation about my gown, but there was nothing casual about the alertness in his mind or the look in his gray eyes. I found I was staring at him intently, the distress in my mind so suddenly intensified that I had to fight to keep it inside, and Len choked where he sat to my left, then waved a hand at Garth.

''Give me a break, will you?'' he gasped, putting one hand to his head even though his shield had formed almost immediately. "If you're going to do that to her, how about warning me first? If you were trying to find out if I could form that filter curtain, the answer is no."

"I'm sorry, Len, I didn't mean to cause you pain," Garth apologized, but his eyes hadn't moved from my face. "I was just testing a theory I had, and the test turned out positive. It looks like Terry is worried again over her relationship with Tammad, afraid of what he'll do if he finds out her abilities have increased. Don't you think it's about time you learned to trust him, Terry?"

"I do trust him," I came back, trying not to sound as defensive as I felt, uncomfortably aware of Len's gaze joining Garth's. "I'll tell him what we've been doing, as soon as I find the right time."

"Terry, take your hand away from the band around your throat," Len said with a sigh, his blue eyes filled with sadness. "I don't even have to open my shield to know Garth's right. You've been stroking and playing with the other four bands as if trying to memorize them against a time they'll be gone, and now you're holding the fifth band as if you had to defend it. You're obviously afraid Tammad will unband you if he finds out your abilities have increased, but I don't understand why."

I hadn't realized I was holding the fifth band, and Len's pointing it out was faintly embarrassing as well as upsetting. I dropped my hand to my lap, found that my fingers went immediately to a wrist band, and suddenly discovered I was losing all vestige of control.

"Why do you keep asking me these questions?" I flared at Len, then sent the same to Garth. "I have no idea what Tammad will do if he finds out about the increase, but I'm still afraid! Are you silly enough to think only untalented people hate and fear Primes? If you are you're in for a shock, but I can't handle the thought of a shock like that. I'm too much of a coward."

I turned away from them to stretch out on my stomach on the carpet fur, hugging a pillow to me with all the strength of the agitation I felt. I did trust Tammad, as much as I loved him, but expecting the impossible from people only leads to horrible disappointment. Tammad had accepted more insanity on my behalf than almost anyone else would have found possible, but how much could he be expected to take? This new thing I was now able to do—would that be the final straw?

"Come on, Terry, it's not all that bad," Len said after something of a hesitation, and I knew he'd exchanged significant looks with Garth; I could hear the overheartiness in his voice even if I couldn't reach his shielded mind. "*We* got used to the idea without any trouble."

"And Len and I had reason to do just the opposite," Garth quickly agreed, his tone urging belief even though his mind worried over what I'd said. "If it was all that bad, would we have helped you with your experimenting?"

"You helped me because you were feeling guilty," I pointed out, staring at the bright, sunshiny windows. "Tammad punished me because of what you two told him, and it bothered you afterward that it took me as long as it did to stop crying. You volunteered to help because it made you feel better, and you stuck with it because you got curious. How would you like to run into that particular talent without it being a carefully controlled experiment? Do I hear any volunteers for that?"

All I heard at that point was a thick silence, which wasn't particularly surprising. Still holding the pillow I turned around and sat up, then looked directly at my two lunch guests.

"Well?" I prompted, seeing how they couldn't quite make eye contact with me. "You both had a taste of that talent before I got it under control and strengthened. Which of you great, big, strong, newly made *l'lendaa* wants to try it again?"

"Now, Terry," Garth began in a soothing way, and, "Come on, Terry," Len said with calm urging, both sets of eyes worried, and that really annoyed me.

"Now, Terry, come on, Terry," I mimicked, letting them see how disgusted I felt. "Can't you two find anything else to say? One of you is braced and just short of cringing, and the other refuses to drop the protection of his shield. You're so

21

unimpressed with my new abilities that you don't even argue with me anymore. One frown and you both jump like frightened birds.''

"That's not fair!" Len protested with heat while Garth colored in embarrassed resentment. "We weren't arguing with you just for the fun of it! We were trying to make you see how Tammad really felt about you! Now that you know he loves you, what's there to argue about?''

"If you're trying to suggest we're afraid of you, you're wrong,'' Garth growled, his anger glowing in his eyes, displacing the hesitancy his mind had trembled with. "Len and I might have a good deal of respect for your talent, but we're not afraid of it—because we've learned to have the same amount of respect for you. What you did to us that day *was* an accident; we've learned you're not into doing it on purpose just for the fun of it. Or at least I have.''

His angry gray eyes moved to Len, and Len didn't need to be unshielded to know what he was thinking. Garth was facing me without protection while Len wasn't, and Garth was right in believing that that was making things worse. If one of my own didn't trust me—

"What has fear or respect got to do with anything?'' Len demanded, trying to disguise embarrassment behind indignation. "It's not my fault I don't have the strength of a Prime to fend off her output! You can't afford to criticize until you know how it feels, Garth. Do you remember what you went through during sword practice yesterday, when that big ape kept pounding on your weapon until he broke through your guard and floored you? It's a lot like that, only it's my head that gets pounded on. I didn't see you throwing away your sword, so what's wrong with keeping my shield up?''

"Garth kept his sword up only while he was under attack, Len,'' I pointed out, wondering how I could sound so calm when I felt so rotten inside. "You've been shielding a lot lately, only I hadn't really noticed it sooner. Have you been under attack all that often then?''

"It's that static you're leaking,'' Len nearly begged, one hand out to me, blue eyes filled with tragedy—but shield still firmly in place. "You know I don't like walking around shielded, Terry, but you're not giving me a choice! It's either that or develop a permanent headache. How can I make you believe me?"

"What—if I told you I could get through that shield, Len?" I said suddenly without really meaning to, almost as surprised to hear the words as Garth. "What—if I said your shield was good against nothing *but* the static?"

"That's ridiculous," Len laughed, but uneasiness turned the laughter uneven. "You know you can't get through my shield. You've tried it before, more than once, and you haven't been able to do it."

"Not since the change," I said, the words soft and easy to match the strange floating I seemed to be in the middle of. I felt nothing but a mild curiosity as I reached out to a no-longer smiling Len with my mind, coming up very close to his shield. Round and shining that shield was, at first seeming as unbreachable as it always had—and then I saw the key. The shield was solid if looked at from a distance, but very close up I could see the spaces between it, the spaces I could slip through. I had to thin myself to do it, more than I'd known was possible, and then Len's mind was before me, shivering and filled with a terrible fear. He *was* afraid of me, horribly afraid, and when I sent calm and reassurance to soothe him, panic flamed instead. He dropped the bowl of meat strips with a strangled shout, fought his way spasmodically to his feet, then ran out of the room. He'd had trouble wrenching the door open, but none slamming it closed behind him. I could have followed his desperate run through the halls for quite a distance, but I didn't. Despite the way the floating was holding me up and bracing me, I put my face into the pillow I was holding and tried to stop living.

"Poor Len," Garth muttered after a minute, both voice and mind shaken. "He really is afraid. What did you do to him, Terry?"

"I reached through his shield," I answered with my face just above the pillow, not understanding why I was responding. "I couldn't do it before but I can now, and he hated the

23

invasion. The same way he hates me. The way Tammad will hate me if he finds out.''

"Terry, what's wrong with you?" Garth demanded, suddenly concerned as his hand came to my face. "You sound like you're in a trance! Snap out of it!"

His hand shook my face and then both hands were on my shoulders, shaking me hard enough to rattle my teeth. The floating had helped me break through Len's shield, but it didn't seem to be strong enough to resist physical assault. It left me as abruptly as it had come, substituting sight of Garth's worried face, and suddenly I could *feel* what I'd done.

"No, no, I didn't do that," I begged, grabbing at the Kabran's arm in a way that stopped the shaking. "Please, Garth, don't be afraid of me! I didn't do that! I was imagining it, lying, making it up! You don't have to be afraid of me, really you don't!"

I had scrambled onto my knees and had captured one of Garth's hands in both of mine, the terror turning my heartbeat to a deafening thud, the desperation choking my voice. Garth was staring at me with such dismay that my thudding heart nearly stopped; he was paying no attention to the way I was crushing his hand, and then he was pulling me to him one-armed, holding me even tighter than I was holding him.

"No, Terry, no, it's all right," he said hurriedly, repeating the words over and over, his arm holding me tightly to him, his mind pouring out compassion and a determination to soothe. I was shivering hard against him, tasting the panic Len had almost drowned in, miles beyond being able to control myself. I had done it again, and I just couldn't stand it.

It took quite a while before Garth was able to calm me down, before he was able to coax me into turning his hand loose. The warmth of his body had finally been able to melt the ice around mine, but the ice turned out to be the only thing holding me upright. I slumped against Garth's shoulder, wishing I had fainted, wishing I could stop my mind from thinking ever again.

"Are you all right now?" he asked quietly and gently, his voice nearly a murmur, looking down at me in a way I could feel.

"I'm just great," I answered dully, shoulder-deep in depression and slipping lower by the minute. "Now there's another category to add to the list of all things new and wonderful. I think I'll kill myself."

"If you jumped out a window, you'd probably discover you can fly," he said with gentle teasing, his arm tightening around me as his free hand stroked my hair. "Or levitate, which is not exactly the same thing."

"How can you joke about it?" I demanded, appalled at the thought, pushing away from his chest to stare at him. "Now there are two things I have to try to hide, and Len will never come within half a mile of me again!"

"Three things," he corrected, reaching out to brush the hair out of my eyes. "And Len was upset, but he'll calm down and come back. Until he does, why don't we talk about what's been happening?"

"If you've gone crazy, don't expect me to join you," I answered, not understanding how his gray eyes could look—and be!—so calm. "The last thing I want to do is go into it all over again."

"Now let's see," he mused, pretending he hadn't heard what I'd said, locking his hands behind his head as he lay down on the carpeting. "The first of the three is the ability you're not sure about, but we'll count it anyway: the—*feeling*—you get that certain things have to be done. Have you had that feeling about more than learning swordwork?"

"No," I said to his gray-eyed gaze, wondering why I wasn't simply ignoring him. "Isn't once enough?"

"We'll put a question mark next to that one, but we'll leave it on the list," Garth decided, still not hearing anything he didn't want to hear. "The second entry is this newest thing you've developed, the ability to get through Len's shield. Does that mean you can look through your own shield? And also work through it?"

"How should I know?" I demanded in exasperation, but the

emotion was more for myself. Now that Garth had raised the questions, I found myself suddenly curious.

"Well, we'll give you a little time to look into that," he very generously allowed, just short of grinning. "The third item is the ability you've been practicing, the ability to change people's characters. It's something you can do even if they're braced against it and resisting, probably because of your increased strength."

"The character change is no more than the end result of changing the emotional outlook," I corrected, moving uncomfortably where I sat. "Since your actions always reflect your feelings, changing your feelings changes your actions. If I sat here pulling my hair out, for instance, you'd have to change the insane maelstrom of my feelings before you could get me to stop. You feel up to trying it?"

I wasn't really starting to cry, but Garth didn't have to be an empath to be aware of the wide-eyed desolation I was looking at him with. He sat up immediately and pulled me to him again, and held me as tightly as I needed to be held.

"Now, don't go back to feeling that way," he soothed, rocking me gently. "You don't have to face this alone, I'm right here to help you. I don't hate you, I'm not afraid of you, and I *will* help."

"How?" I demanded, not arguing but needing the reassurance. "I don't know what's happening to me, or why it's happening so fast! Unless you can think of a way to stop it, how can you help?"

"Maybe I can help you accept the fact that it's not something that can—or should—be stopped," he answered, only dimly aware of the pleasure he was feeling at the way I clung to him. "Maybe I can help you understand that you owe it to yourself to be the very best you can be, in whatever you do. Trying to deny your abilities means you're trying to deny yourself, Terry, and that's wrong. You must always be proud of what you are, and that will help you to be proud of what you do—and do things to make yourself proud."

"How am I supposed to be proud of chaos?" I asked,

feeling tired but fractionally less upset. "Things are coming at me too fast, and I just can't handle them."

"You still don't want to handle them," Garth corrected, gently but refusing to be argued with. "Of course things are coming fast, how else did you expect them to come? When a baby learns to walk, the first steps take the longest; once they do come, though, everything else follows with blinding speed. Striding, hopping, running, climbing—and falling down. There's no shame in falling down, girl, only in refusing to pick yourself up again."

"You think my new abilities are normal developments?" I asked with a frown, leaning back again so that I might see him. "How could they be *normal* developments? I didn't only just become an empath."

"In a manner of speaking, you did," he said, one finger scratching at his cheek as his mind worked. "I hadn't looked at it that way before we began talking, but now it seems obvious. Before the blank time you spent recovering from the storm damage, you used almost nothing of your abilities even when you were awakened. You began stretching your mental muscles here on Rimilia, but if physical development takes time, why shouldn't mental? You were hurt by the thunderstorm and the battle you had with that intruder, but once the hurt was healed you were developed enough to go on to bigger and better things. Now you're ready to hop, skip, jump—and maybe even fly."

"Flying you can forget about," I told him firmly, but couldn't help matching his grin. What he'd said made a strange kind of sense, and also fit in with my own wondering thoughts on the subject. Empaths on Central were taught to use their abilities, but only up to a certain point and were definitely discouraged from experimenting. It wasn't even possible to think about experimenting unless you knew there was something to experiment with, and being unawakened— which was the way empaths lived on Central—meant the very memory of the talent had been taken away. My people had evidently worked hard to keep me tied up tight, but now I was beginning to slip the leash.

"I don't think I really blame Central for trying to limit their empaths," I said after a pause, losing the grin Garth had helped me find. "If what I've been running into is a sample of what we're capable of, they have a right to be frightened."

"Garbage!" he snorted, riveting my attention to him—and away from my wristbands. "They have the right to demand that you obey their laws, but not to cripple you because of a *suspicion* you might not. You don't back away in fear from something you don't understand, you try to understand it so you won't fear it. And some people won't fear it even if they don't understand—like Tammad, for instance."

Those gray eyes were staring straight at me again, obviously not having missed the place my attention had wandered to. I deliberately put my right hand around my left wrist, letting the feel and presence of the band soak into me, its hard strength helping me to ask what had to be asked.

"How do you know?" I put to him, this time challenging him for solid facts rather than empty reassurance. "Len is an *empath* and he was afraid. What makes you think Tammad won't be?"

"Simply the fact that I know Tammad," he answered with a shrug, his mind showing not the least doubt. "You know he never really understood your talent, but when was he ever afraid of it? How many times did he take a switch to you for what you did, no matter *what* anyone else thought about your 'power'? Or are you worried that now that he can appreciate what you're capable of, now's the time the fear will start?"

"Why shouldn't it?" I asked, beginning to feel defeated. "Len never used to be afraid of me, but now. . . ."

"But now he is," Garth interrupted, annoyed again. "It would help if you were able to read the reasons behind an emotion, not just the emotion itself. Sure Len's afraid, but not of you. He's fascinated by your new abilities and would love to have them himself, but he saw what you went through before you developed them, and is now afraid he doesn't have the strength to go through the same thing without breaking. He's also afraid he won't have a choice about going through it, and that's something that has him just about talking to himself. Would Tammad feel the same way? Is there any sort of challenge you can possibly think of that Tammad would be afraid to face?"

"When he's even planning to take on the entire Amalgamation and intends winning?" I asked, delight and relief seeping into me around the fading doubt. "That would be the day. Oh, Garth! Do you really think it'll be all right?"

"I'm positive it will," he said with a grin, patting the hand I'd put on his arm. "Especially if you decide you need some coaxing practice."

"Damn it, I almost forgot about that," I said with the mind-equivalent of falling to the earth and squishing, the delight instantly evaporating. "I still have to figure out how to get around that."

"You can get around it—maybe—by telling Tammad what we've been doing," Garth said, and again his tone wasn't allowing any argument. "The longer you put it off, the harder it will be."

"I know, I know," I grumbled, and then I looked at him again. "You think there's a chance that telling Tammad *why* I want to learn to use a sword—as far as I can say why— *won't* change his mind? You think he'd still make me—coax him?"

"I may be wrong, but that's what I think," he agreed, this time looking faintly frustrated. "I don't know if I can explain this, you're obviously not male. On Central or Alderan, training a woman to do a man's job doesn't mean a thing; most of those jobs could even be done by a trained panith, and no one would notice the difference. Here on Rimilia though, being a warrior, a *l'lenda*, is a thing to take pride in, something a man has to work hard to achieve, something he has to be willing to risk his life for. No woman could ever hope to match a Rimilian *l'lenda* in sword skill, and training her to it could be looked on as demeaning that skill. It's a man's thing, and not for women to get involved in."

"Then you think he won't say yes no matter what I do," I said, oddly relieved despite my confusion. "But that doesn't explain why you said. . . ."

"I'm coming to that," Garth interrupted, holding up a hand and waggling it at me. "Because swordplay is a man's thing, Tammad might ordinarily refuse—but he loves you very much. He wants to make you happy by giving you whatever he can—if you really want it. It won't take him long to see you don't really want it."

"But of course I want it," I protested, confused now as well as annoyed. "I told you how strong that feeling is, so strong that I can't ignore it. Why would I have asked if I didn't really want it?"

"You asked because the feeling was that strong," Garth sighed, running the hand he'd waved through his long, dark hair. "You're very female, Terry, and a highly sensitive empath, and you think of swordwork as violent and senseless— you said so yourself. The feeling you have doesn't give you a reason for learning it, only the conviction you must, so you're unconsciously looking for a way around the need. By hating the idea of coaxing Tammad, you found that way."

I pronounced an unladylike word and punched the pillow I'd dropped earlier, just about the only reactions I could think of to what Garth had said. I'd heard the same thing from Gay King under other circumstances, but this time I couldn't argue the point. Despite the roundabout niceties Garth had used, his explanation suggested I was a wimp.

"It sure is a good thing you respect me and my talent," I muttered after á minute, looking up at him darkly. "If you didn't, you might say something to get me mad."

"Oh, I'd never do that," Garth said with a headshake, his grin wider than ever. "If I did then Tammad would notice, and I'd have to face *him*. If you're looking for someone I both respect *and* fear, don't bother looking any farther. With him I don't have to wonder what might happen to me. I know."

"You can't distract me that easily," I said with impatience, still glaring at him. "You may feel normal fear at the thought of facing Tammad, but you're not afraid of him. Now that you've told me exactly what I am, tell me what I can do to change it."

"Changing is your job, not mine," he denied, looking around on the carpet fur for the bowl of meat and vegetables he'd dropped, finding all of the meat and most of the vegetables still in it. "My job is giving tactical advice and eating, the second of which I now intend getting on to with enthusiasm so I'll have enough strength to do the first. If you're waiting to learn the right technique, just keep watching."

"How can you just sit there and stuff your face when I still don't know what to do?" I demanded, feeling his appreciation of the food he ate—and his amusement. "All you've really said is that maybe Tammad will teach me to use a sword if I tell him why I want to learn, and maybe he won't. And if he does decide to teach me, maybe he won't make me coax him, but you think he will. If he understands why I want to learn, why would he still make me coax him?"

"Men on this world are taught that nothing of value is gotten in life without paying a price for it," he mumbled around a sloppy mouthful, more of his attention on the food than on me. "The price has to mean something to the one paying it, has to be more than a gesture, otherwise it buys nothing but its own value. If you're not willing to pay that sort of price you won't get what you think you want, even if someone decides to let you have it. If Tammad does it at all he'll do it the right way, and your price will be paid in full. If you decide you really want it."

He looked straight at me with those gray eyes again before going back to his food, and only then did I begin to understand that Len and Garth were being taught more of Rimilian ways than how to use a sword. What he'd said to me was probably something not usually said to a woman, as most women would have no need to know about it. Paying a price for something was obviously one aspect of the Rimilian code of honor, and women weren't expected to have anything to do with honor.

When Garth's eyes left me I rose silently to my feet, then walked around the bathing pool to stare sightlessly out of a window. The trouble with a code of honor was that it was horribly habit-forming, like a dangerous drug; once you got a taste of it you found yourself lured to other aspects of it, wondering if you could handle it under real pressure. Calling it a stupid waste of time is one way of admitting you don't have what it takes to cut it, and I wasn't ready to admit a defeat like that. I closed one fist around a handful of sheer white curtain, knowing that refusing to admit it didn't negate a defeat, but I wasn't beaten yet. I might end up beaten, but I refused to anticipate an end before it reached me. I wanted to win—if I could just figure out what it was I was fighting for—and against.

I wasn't very good company for the next couple of hours, but Garth didn't seem to mind. He made a considerable dent in the contents of both food trays, then lay down among the cushions simply to watch me. I became aware of that along with the humming in his mind, the sort of humming Rimilian men usually did when they looked at me. But Garth wasn't Rimilian, not originally at any rate, and I wasn't used to getting that sort of hum from him. It was enough to bring my attention back to my lunch guest, and when he saw my eyes on him he grinned.

"Tammad ought to be getting back soon," he observed, raising the goblet of wine he'd poured to sip from it. "Have you made any decisions yet?"

"Dozens," I answered, pulling my eyes away from him and trying to do the same with my mind. "If I can manage to stick with even one of them, I might be able to accomplish something."

"Why don't you stop wandering around the room like a lost soul and take it easy?" he asked, his amusement rising again. "If you keep up that pacing for very much longer, you won't have the strength to coax Tammad even if you decide that that's what you want to do."

"Is that what's you got you turned on?" I demanded as I jerked around to face him, suddenly understanding the reason for the hum. "Are you expecting him to let you watch?"

"I don't have to watch," he said with a grin, still sipping at the wine. "Just knowing what he'll make you do is enough. Some day I'll have a woman of my own, and I'll do the same thing with her. What he'll be teaching you is that no matter how strong you get, he'll still be the boss. On this world, men always are."

"Are they really," I said, straightening where I stood, the anger threatening to fill me completely. "Would you like a dissenting opinion on that?"

The fact that I hadn't raised my voice erased Garth's grin and replaced it with a narrow-eyed, wary look, but I didn't get the chance to tell myself that whatever I did to him he more than deserved. The door to the hall chose that minute to open, and the one opening it was Tammad.

"Ah, Tammad, you're back!" Garth called out at sight of him, rising quickly to his feet with relief flooding his mind. "How did the meal go?"

"Rellis has no doubts concerning the wisdom in joining our efforts against the Amalgamation," the big Rimilian answered as he closed the door behind him. "He wishes to hear further upon the matter which is primarily your province, therefore shall you soon be summoned to speak with him. It will be necessary that Lenham translate for you, yet do I see that he has already departed. Where has he gone?"

"I'm not sure, so I'd better go look for him," Garth said, finishing his wine in a single swallow before returning the goblet to the tray it came from. "It would be rude to make Rellis wait."

If Tammad hadn't already moved away from the door, he would have been in definite danger of being run down despite the fact that Garth wasn't his giant size. He got a quick nod and smile and then Garth was gone, getting out while the getting was good. Garth still wasn't really afraid of me, but he had more sense than to hang around after getting me mad.

"For what reason does the Garth R'Hem Solohr act so strangely?" I was suddenly asked, the words turning my attention to the frown that accompanied them. "For what reason was his leave-taking so hurried, and for what reason had Lenham already gone?"

Those blue eyes were reflecting the abrupt suspicion behind them, the suspicion that there might be a matter of duty to be attended to. Tammad considered it his duty to punish me when I did things he didn't approve of, usually things that could conceivably get me hurt or killed if I did them under other circumstances. My *hamak* was trying to keep me safe and alive, but I didn't particularly care for the way he went about it.

"One of the reasons Garth left so abruptly is that I have something to tell you," I forced out, nerving myself to do what had to be done. I still didn't really understand why I could say just about anything I liked to Len and Garth, but couldn't do the same with Tammad. My fingers twisted nervously at my waist as he approached me, and I could feel the questioning coming out of the blue eyes looking down at me. The top of my head didn't even reach his chin, his giant, well-muscled body was nearly twice as wide as mine, and the sword hanging at his left side that he could handle one-handed was too heavy for me to lift even with two. I looked up at him with as little of the dismay I felt as I could manage, and blurted, "Are you afraid of me?"

I knew I'd botched it as soon as the words were out, but it was too late to call them back. Tammad was looking down at me almost blank-faced with incomprehension, his mind—wide-eyed, if a mind can be said to be wide-eyed—with total lack of understanding and the beginnings of serious concern. If that didn't mean he thought I was going crazy, no other reactions of his ever would.

"Should a man be wise, he will indeed look upon *wendaa* with a certain fear," he answered slowly after a very long minute, carefully choosing his words. "*Wendaa* are small and usually helpless, and should a man allow this truth to slip from him, he may easily, although inadvertently, cause them harm. To feel such a fear and guard against its loss is the duty of a man, for no true man would wish to harm his *wenda*. Is this what you sought to speak to me of?"

His mind was now cautiously trying to approach mine, a habit he'd picked up in the last couple of days. When an empath looks at someone, he or she looks with mind as well as eyes, and Tammad was as much of an empath as I—or Len.

"No," I answered, looking down from his stare even as I stopped his fumbling, mostly untrained probe from reaching me. "For the last couple of days I've been—experimenting—with my returned abilities. Len and Garth have been helping me."

"I see," he said, the words a good deal more neutral than his inner response. His first reaction, anger, was being held down, temporarily put to one side; he wanted to know what was going on, and why everyone was acting so strangely. His second reaction, annoyance, was just as sharp as the anger, but wasn't being controlled as well; he hadn't liked my keeping him from my mind, and really wanted to say something about it. "This—experimenting you have done. Why was I not told of it sooner?"

"I—had to know what there was to tell, before I could tell anyone anything," I answered, keeping my eyes from him as I began to move around the room again. "There have been some—changes in my abilities, and some—additions."

"Changes of what sort?" he asked, and the concern was there again, overriding everything else. "Were you given harm through the power of that storm after all?"

"I suppose that depends on how you look at it," I said, feeling the cool marble under my bare feet as I stepped onto it from the carpet fur. "My abilities are stronger now, much stronger than they were, and they're spreading out to allow me to do other things. Len and Garth were helping me learn to control all of it, both of them acting as subjects. Len's mind is stronger and better trained than Garth's, but we discovered that that made no difference. He couldn't resist me any more than Garth could, and maybe not even as well. Len left early because we found that I could get through his shield, and he was—upset; Garth left as quickly as he did because he said something just before you came in that got me angry, and he thought I was about to—"

I broke off the jumble of words and just stood looking down into the marble bathing pool, unfortunately having no trouble feeling the whirling agitation in the mind only a few feet behind me. Tammad was nearly as upset as I was, which was really a feat.

"Garth felt you were about to touch him in some manner," Tammad said after a moment, the whirling of his thoughts again slowing his speech. "Was his concern well founded? Were you indeed about to touch him?"

The questions had been quietly put, more gentleness than harshness in them, almost as though they were a casual attempt at information-gathering. I would have felt better if I could have reached into his mind to confirm that, but his agitation wasn't letting me do it. I turned my head reluctantly to look at him, seeing the outward calm he usually wore like a skin, wondering how I was going to answer those questions. I'd really wanted to do something to get even with Garth for what he'd said, but would I have actually gone through with it? I opened my mouth, found nothing inspired coming out, so I closed it again. I felt like an idiot just standing there moving my lips like a wooden dummy, but I was saved from further embarrassment by a knock at the door.

At first Tammad seemed determined to ignore the knock in favor of waiting for my answer, but then he did something I'd never seen him do before. He sent his mind to find out who was at the door, the action seeming more automatic than carefully thought out and done deliberately. He was faintly startled when he reached that other mind, but I couldn't tell if he was startled at what he'd done, or at finding that our caller was a deeply disturbed Dallan. The big barbarian turned away from me with a frown, and strode to the door to open it.

"Tammad, I have come to ask for your assistance and that of Terril," Dallan said immediately, his pretty blue eyes showing his concern. "The guard has searched everywhere, but they have been able to find nothing. Cinnan is beside himself."

"They have still found nothing?" Tammad asked, stepping back to let Dallan enter the room. Dallan was just as impossibly big as Tammad, his hair as blond, his eyes as blue. Most Rimilian men were the same, blond, blue-eyed and big, but Dallan was also *drin* of Gerleth, prince to his father Rellis's *Chamd*. Dallan had an older brother, Seddan, but Seddan was still being kept close to bed by the healers.

"I, too, find it difficult to believe," Dallan agreed, so distracted that he didn't even look my way. "I had not thought there were that many places in this house where a *wenda* might hide. Clearly, anger gives them cunning as well as strength."

"Wendaa!" Tammad said with a growl of annoyance, shaking his head. I didn't know what they were talking about, but since Dallan's request for help had included me, there was no reason to stay in the dark.

"Who is it that you discuss?" I asked, walking forward away from the bathing pool, speaking Rimilian so that Dallan would understand me. "Who has been lost that you now attempt to find?"

"My cousin Aesnil again feels herself unjustly put upon," Dallan answered, giving me something of a smile to go with the automatic hum in his mind that started as soon as his eyes touched me. "She has done so well in putting her short time of slavery from her memory, that this morning she attempted to disobey Cinnan. He, of course, refused to allow her disobedience and strapped her for it, and when the punishment was done she fled their apartment in tears. He allowed her a short time to herself before seeking her, however found himself unable to discover her whereabouts before his presence was required at the meal with my father. He then set the guard to searching in his stead, yet have they been as unsuccessful as he."

"Perhaps he has earned such lack of success," I suggested, thrilled that now I had something else to add to my distress. "Had he not found it so necessary to strap her, he would now find it unnecessary to search."

"You would have had him overlook his duty?" Dallan asked with brows raised, surprised that I would question so obvious and necessary a thing. "Aesnil remains as arrogant as ever, and should Cinnan stay his hand from her punishment, those in Grelana will suffer when she resumes her place there as *Chama*. Have you so soon forgotten what we all of us had at her hands?''

I shook my head at his calm, sober question, not likely to ever forget what Aesnil had done to us. Dallan, her own cousin, had been declared a servant-slave in her palace, his brother Seddan declared a *vendra* and sent to the *vendra ralle*, the arena, to fight for his life. Tammad and Cinnan had also been sent to the *ralle*, and I—I had been forced to act as her secret weapon against her *dendayy*, threatened with being thrown to the wild male slaves to keep me in line. No, I wasn't likely to forget what Aesnil had done to me—but I also remembered that she was the one who had escaped from Grelana with me.

''It may perhaps prove true that Cinnan has indeed erred in his punishment of her,'' Tammad said, looking down at me rather than over at Dallan. ''Should this be so, how is he to learn of it and make amends while the girl remains unfound? An exchange of words is impossible when one must exchange words with oneself.''

The calm he felt was now shielding his mind as well, but behind that calm I could feel the electric outlines of his continuing agitation. If we stayed in that room we'd be right back to our previous discussion, and that was something I wanted to avoid. A flash of annoyance touched me as I realized I was being forced to obey him in two different ways, but I also couldn't argue with the truth in what he'd said. Aesnil did need to be found, before she did something foolish.

''Very well, I will assist you all in searching for her,'' I grudged, wanting them to know I wasn't happy about it. ''The doing should not prove overly difficult.''

Both men nodded to show their approval of my agreement, and we left to begin the search. I really didn't expect it to take long to find her, but what we found was something else entirely.

Aesnil had disappeared from Gerleth, and she hadn't gone alone.

2

"How is one to take the word of a *seetar*?" Cinnan demanded, so upset that all he could do was pace back and forth across the room. "How is a *seetar* to know what occurs in the world of men?"

"The ability of *seetarr* was discovered by us when we searched for Terril among the Hamarda," Tammad said for the third time, trying to convince Cinnan with calm and patience. "With Lenham's aid, we found that my own *seetar* was able to follow Terril across the sand, and thence to Aesnil's palace in Grelana. Do you doubt that we were able to find Terril?"

"No, certainly not," Cinnan denied with a gesture of dismissal, but the gesture referred only to finding, not to believing. "I continue to find difficulty in understanding not how a *seetar* may follow, but how it may speak of what occurs about it. How is such a thing possible?"

"I know not," Tammad admitted with a sigh, then his eyes came to me where I sat. "The woman has great facility with *seetarr*, and perhaps her own words will aid our understanding."

All the eyes in the room came to me then, most of them questioning. Tammad, Cinnan, and I were in Rellis's entertaining room, and the *Chamd* and his son Dallan were there

39

with us. We all sat relaxing against cushions in the gold, red and marble room, goblets in our hands, all, that is, except for Cinnan. He carried his goblet of *drishnak* around with him, the same drink all the men had. I was the only one drinking a gentle golden wine, something I wasn't quite as happy about as I'd once been.

"The *seetar* whose mind I touched was yours, Cinnan," I explained, privately wondering how much good the explanation would do. "His concern for Aesnil is yours, as it is from your mind that he took it. He felt surprise at her appearance in the stabling cavern without you, displeasure that the sweets he had had from the two of you in the past days were not forthcoming, then curiosity as to what she was about. He was indignant that she chose another mount rather than taking her place behind you upon his own back, then saddened that she rode away without once having greeted him. That he felt no worry concerning her well-being indicated that she was accompanied, an indication confirmed by the disappearance of two further *seetarr*. The—discussion I held with your *seetar* was a good deal less clear than the manner in which I present it to you, yet am I certain of the interpretation I have made. The word you have is mine, not that of a *seetar*."

"She would not have ridden from me in such a way," Cinnan said, also repeating himself for the third or fourth time, his face and eyes stubborn. "The love we found together could not have been put aside so easily by her, as though it were naught. The *seetar* is clearly mistaken."

"There is no mistake," I said as if it were a memorized speech, feeling the annoyance and frustration rising higher and higher in me. Cinnan was so frantic with worry that he was all but broadcasting, forcing me to keep my shield tightly closed, which may have been a good thing. He was barely making a token effort to acknowledge my presence among all those important *l'lendaa* as it was, and had just about called me a liar. Tammad wasn't likely to get insulted on my behalf, not with the sympathy and compassion fairly oozing out of him for Cinnan's loss, but my own reactions were another story. It was that damned concept of honor, that habit-forming drug that was coming at me from yet another slant. Cinnan wouldn't have spoken to me like that if I'd been a man, but what did he have to worry about with a mere *wenda*?

"Cinnan, three *seetarr* have indeed been taken," Rellis told him gently, rising to his feet to console the younger man. "Also are two serving *wendaa* gone from the house, none knowing to where. Had my niece remained behind, we would surely by now have found her. It is a virtual certainty that Aesnil departed in company with the two missing *wendaa*."

"Where might three *wendaa* have gone to alone?" Cinnan demanded, finding nothing but further wildness in the truth he could no longer deny. "Who will there be to protect them upon such a journey, to hunt for them, to guide them? How did they dare to depart alone, and where have they gone?"

"They have gone to where Aesnil meant to go when we fled Grelana," I said suddenly without knowing I was going to say it. "They have gone to Vediaster."

The news was greeted with staring silence by everyone in the room, most especially by me. I could feel their eyes on me as a physical weight, but I was too busy closing a fist in the carpet fur and watching my hand holding the goblet tremble, to have attention to waste on stares. I wasn't guessing about where Aesnil had gone, I *knew*, just as surely as if she had told me about it before leaving. The knowledge was a compulsion, like the compulsion about learning how to use a sword, and I had no more idea where the second conviction had come from than I had about the first.

"What leads you to believe such a thing, *wenda*?" Tammad asked in the deep silence, his voice calm and gentle. "Was it gotten from the *seetar* along with the rest?"

"No," I said, still not up to looking around, not with the way I could feel those stares. "No, this is a thing I know in—another manner, yet am I just as certain. Aesnil has gone to Vediaster."

"To a land ruled and run by *wendaa*," Cinnan said, distaste strong in his voice. "To a place where females dare to take to themselves the calling of warrior. I shall not allow Aesnil to remain among ones such as they, for she is not of their sort. I will ride after her and find her, else shall I not return."

"You shall not have to ride alone, Cinnan," Dallan told him, rising to his feet as his father had done a few minutes earlier. "I will ride with you, and we will find my cousin together."

"Your presence will be most welcome, *drin* Dallan," Cinnan answered with warm gratitude, moving across the carpet fur to clap Dallan on the shoulder. "As will be the presence of your blade."

"I believe I, too, will accompany you," Tammad said slowly, thoughtfully. "I must continue with the task I have undertaken to protect our people, yet are the directions many in which the task has already taken me. The road to Vediaster may be looked upon as no more than another direction."

"Tammad, my friend, you, too, are most welcome," Cinnan said, watching with a relieved smile as the big barbarian also rose to join everyone else. "Should we somehow lose the trail, your *wenda* may be of some aid in rediscovering it. Should you mean for her to accompany us."

"You are correct in assuming I mean exactly that," Tammad reassured the other big man, his hand going to his shoulder. "I have given my word that she shall not again be allowed to leave my side, and she may indeed prove to be of some assistance. As the day is nearly gone, let us depart with the new light."

"No," I said as Cinnan and Dallan agreed with Tammad, Rellis also nodding in approval, but none of them heard me. I was about as important in that gathering as a piece of furniture, the sort of furniture you put something down on without even looking, knowing it will be right where you expect it to be. I raised my voice and repeated, "No!" and the second time it got through to them.

"It would be foolish to depart sooner, Terril," Dallan said with partial attention, speaking for them all. "When the new day begins, we shall begin as well."

"That is not what I was referring to," I said at once, before they could go back to their terribly important planning, getting to my feet to make it unanimous. "My disagreement referred to my presence, which will be absent from your distinguished company. I have no desire to join you, therefore shall I remain behind. My loss will be devastating, I know, yet are you *l'lendaa* and surely able to bear up beneath so terrible a load. You have my good wishes for your endeavor, though I scarcely believe you will find them necessary. Success, as always, will certainly be yours."

I put my goblet of golden wine down on one of the small tables the room held, not bothering to drain it first, ignoring the thick silence I moved through. I knew I was being stared at for a third time, but I really didn't care; they'd made it abundantly clear that I wasn't one of them, that I wasn't good enough to be one of them, so I'd made my answer just as clear. I was a Prime Xenomediator of the Centran Amalgamation, and I was damned if I'd be treated like a piece of furniture. I then walked to the door, opened it, and simply left.

When I got back to the apartment I shared with Tammad, a servant was there lighting the candles against the approaching darkness. She carried an enclosed candle that supplied the flame she passed around, and also had a bag over her shoulder that contained fresh candles to replace any that had burned all the way down. The bedroom had already been taken care of before my arrival, and the bathing room was quickly finished up. The girl smiled to me on her way out and I started to return the smile mechanically, but even that feeble gesture was lost to me when her opening of the door to the hall showed I'd been followed from Rellis's entertaining room. The expression on Tammad's face reflected his usual calm, but his mind was back to whirling behind that calm. I turned away from him and walked to the center of the room, and didn't turn back even when I heard the door close.

"How long a trip do you think it will be?" I asked, looking at one candle flame that was destined to grow brighter as soon as it got darker. "You'll probably find it hard to believe, but I'll miss you."

"I truly have no doubt of that, *wenda*," he said with a sign, slowly moving across the carpet fur toward me. "And it has come to me that we have not as yet completed the discussion earlier begun between us. Clearly is it necessary that the matter be seen to."

"There's very little that needs seeing to," I said with a shrug, uncomfortably aware of how close he stood behind me. "I'll be careful with my experimenting while you're gone, and probably won't even leave these rooms very often. How long do you think it will be before you get back?"

"*Wenda*, there is a great deal remaining to be seen to," he argued, holding the tops of my arms, his deep voice fractionally less gentle. "This—experimenting you have done with Lenham and Garth has not been good for you, and there will be no more of it."

I tried to turn around to disagree with him, but the hands on my arms were already directing me toward the room's mound of cushions with a firmness that brooked no refusal, as if to insist we get more comfortable before the fight started. When we got there Tammad sat and pulled me into his lap, so that our faces were almost on the same level.

"You must hear my words, *hama*, for I have been greatly disturbed by what has been told me," he said, serious blue eyes looking straight at me while one big hand smoothed my hair. "I had thought having Lenham and Garth near you would be an easing for you in your new place, a last tie to the old which would assist in your acceptance of the new. In believing this I have, instead, caused you harm."

"Tammad, that's not true!" I began, putting my hands to the bare chest I sat so near, but his hand tightened at the back of my neck as he shook his head.

"Terril, it is no other thing than truth," he maintained, the sadness in his eyes replaced with determination. "I had thought the two men of your worlds well along the road toward learning proper behavior, yet is this patently not so. Your request for their assistance should have first been discussed with me, to learn if such a thing had my approval. Neither of them even spoke of the doing afterward.''

"But that was because I asked them not to!'' I protested, deliberately refraining from mentioning that Len and Garth had volunteered to help, not merely agreed when I asked. I hadn't asked, but I didn't want to get them into more trouble.

"It matters not that you requested such a thing of them,'' he said, shaking his shaggy blond head again. "It was their duty to speak first with me, for I am the man to whom you belong. Such decisions are mine alone to make.''

"No,'' I said with a headshake of my own, unable to take my eyes from his face, my voice suddenly without strength. I wasn't trying to argue what he's said, and he was well aware of it; what I was trying to deny was the entire concept, the very thought that he would do that to me, but he wasn't allowing denial.

"It may be looked upon in no other way, my *sadendra*,'' he said, the sadness returned but the determination still firm. "You are my belonging, my *wenda*, and your obedience to me must be complete. To have allowed you time to accept this was also an error, one which will not be continued. You will perform no further experimentation, and in fact are forbidden even to speak with Lenham and Garth ever again.''

"You can't mean that!'' I whispered, so deeply shocked that my mind felt numb and cold, my hands like wood on the chest I still held them against. "Tammad, please don't say that, you know I can't. . . .''

"But you shall, *wenda*,' he interrupted, his calm, even voice so remorseless that it made me want to shiver. "The pain and distress given you by cause of your power has already been far too great; I will not allow there to be more. To be accepted and desired as an ordinary *wenda* was your deepest wish; it is this wish I mean to see granted you.''

"But I'm not just an ordinary woman,'' I protested wide-eyed, so confused I was growing dizzy. "I'm a Prime and getting stronger so quickly that I don't know what's happening! And Len and Garth! I can't just. . . .''

"You shall," he repeated, interrupting again, those blue, blue eyes refusing to release me. "Though it was surely not done by intention, Lenham and Garth are the cause of your present upset. They look upon you not as a woman but as a Prime, and are able to deny you nothing. In their minds you stand as *l'lenda* to them, one to be looked up to and obeyed. This has led you to expect the same from all men, and brings you distress when you fail to receive it. You shall not receive this from men, Terril, for you are not *l'lenda* and never shall be. You are *wenda*, and must now learn to accept the place."

What he was saying was so insane and unreal that I *couldn't* accept it, not the least, smallest part. He believed it completely and was determined to go through with it, but I couldn't let him do that to me. I wanted to be his, with every part of my mind and body, but not as a slave!

"You're wrong in everything you've said," I got out, looking down from his eyes and starting to get out of his lap. "Just give me a minute to straighten my thoughts, and I'll prove to you that. . . ."

"You will prove nothing, Terril," he denied, refusing to let me move away from him, frighteningly still wrapped in that calm. "Does my error lie in the insult you felt when Cinnan failed to give you thanks for your presence on the search? One does not thank another man's *wenda* for accompanying him where he goes, yet you felt the lack as insult, a thing made clear by your parting words. Or perhaps my error lies in the fact that Lenham and, to a lesser extent, Garth, have come to fear you, and therefore have led you to believe I would do the same? Are these the things in which I am mistaken?"

I looked up at him again with the chill back and spreading, his hand on my arm and his arm around my waist two metal bands of irresistible strength, finding myself immediately recaptured by his light blue stare. I *had* wanted to have nothing more to do with my abilities, and it *had* bothered me deeply that Len feared me and Tammad might do the same, and I *had* been feeling insulted over the way the men were treating me, but—

"I can't obey you completely and be nothing more than another woman," I whispered, still whirling with confusion that spun out thin tendrils of fear. "Tammad, please, if you really love me you won't ask me that. There are times when I wish it were possible to have nothing more to do with my talent, but that only happens when I'm tired from the fight to control and understand it. When I'm not tired I know better than to wish for such a thing, because my talent can't be ignored or forgotten about. I want to live with you and never leave you, but it has to be in a way we both can accept. If you ask me to give up using my abilities and be something I'm not, it will destroy everything we have together."

"*Hama*, I shall not allow anything to destroy what we have together." He immediately soothed me, drawing me close to lean against his chest, the hilt of his sword brushing my right side as he did so. "And I would not demand that you cease being what you are, for that cannot be done. You will use your power when I find it necessary for you to do so, and in the interim you will continue with my teaching. As for asking you to obey me and being no more than another *wenda*— Terril, those are things I would not and do not ask, nor would any true man. These are things I *shall* have from you, as my due, for I am the man to whom you belong. You have not been given the choice of obeying, for such a choice would be difficult and demeaning for you to make. There is no choice before you; you *shall* obey."

I tried to shake my head in denial of that terrible calm and rock-hard decision but his arms tightened around me, holding me against him exactly as he wished. I wasn't being asked to obey him—I was being told that I would, no arguments, buts, excuses, or exceptions. I struggled against that warm, broad body, fighting to get loose, but how was I supposed to fight against strength like his? I squirmed wildly, but even that didn't dent his calm.

"Your upset now is great, I know, yet shall it soon pass," he said, trying to send a portion of his calm to soothe my desperate panting and struggle. "You now believe you face a terrible fate, yet shall it prove to be more pleasurable than

47

terrible, more delightful than confining. The burdens will
be gone from your shoulders, and your heart will be light
with song. All decisions of weight and upset will be mine to
make, and your lot no more than to give me your love. Is
this too great a thing I ask, that you give me your love?''

I tried to look up at him and found that I could, discovered
that he was letting me do it. But there was something else
that was happening, something I could feel although not
understand or fight back against, something that was taking
me over. I hadn't cried in a while, hadn't really wanted to
cry, but his last words and that sudden, terrible feeling had
brought the tears out to roll slowly down my cheeks.

"Please don't do this to me," I begged, the sobs already
beginning to shake me, feeling so terribly, terribly small in
the circle of those mighty arms. "I don't know what you're
doing to me, but you have to stop it! You have to!"

"*Wenda*, I do no more than reassure you of my love," he
said with gentle sadness, wiping at my tears before cradling
me in his arms again. "Do you not feel the same love for me,
the same burning desire I have ever felt for you?"

As he said the words I *did* feel it, the bottomless, insatiable
need to have him again, to be held in his arms and kissed
fiercely, to belong to him with every part of me. My tears
increased as I shook my head yet again, trying to beg him to
stop, but he would not. His hands were already moving
slowly over me, his mind clearing to the growl of desire, his
eyes demanding my very soul. In an instant I no longer sat in
his lap but lay on the carpet fur beside him, his lips brushing
mine, his hand moving up beneath my gown to slide to my
thigh. I put my own hands to the broadness of his shoulders,
shuddering at what his stroking touch was doing to me,
closing my eyes to stop the useless flow of tears. I had to fight
him but I couldn't, couldn't and was rapidly reaching the
point where I didn't want to, couldn't even remember why I
had to. He was so strong and hard under my hands, stronger
and harder even than the fur-covered marble floor I lay on,
warmer even than the fur carpeting itself. His lips came to my
lips again and I accepted them hungrily, moving against his

hands even as I tried to touch all of him with mine, whimpering when his swordbelt and *haddin* kept me from it. His mind chuckled but his lips refused to leave mine, one broad fist going to my hair to hold me still. Whatever was done would be done the way *he* wanted it, and allowing me my way wasn't what he wanted.

By the time he let me up long enough to pull my gown off, I was almost in tears again. I struggled out of the wretched thing as quickly as possible and lay back down on the carpet fur, then had to wait while he slowly removed his swordbelt and *haddin*. His eyes touched me all over as he rid himself of encumbrance, as slowly as his hands had moved, as thoroughly as he had taken my kiss. I burned so terribly that I wanted to writhe where I lay, moaning for what I knew he would soon give me, certain I would die before he decided he had tortured me enough. I closed my eyes and tossed my head back and forth, holding to the fur to either side of my body, and then he was lying down beside me again to take me in his arms.

"Do you doubt that you are mine, *hama*?" he asked very softly, his hands on me setting the flames to leaping and crackling. "Are you able to oppose my will?"

"No," I whispered with a violent headshake, knowing I spoke the absolute truth, clutching at him with a frenzy beyond my control. "I am yours beyond doubt and denial, *hamak*. Take me now, I beg you to take me now!"

"You have only to ask, *sadendra* mine," he answered, his mind glowing with the pleasure of my having spoken to him in Rimilian. "You shall never find the need to do more than ask."

In no more than a heartbeat he was thrusting inside me, gathering me to him and taking my lips even as he began to stroke deep. I held to him as he took my soul, mindless with the joy he gave, trying to make him know that I never wanted him to stop. It went on for a time that was just short of forever, to that place of total fulfillment and shuddering ecstasy, and then, when awareness returned though the glow still remained, I looked up to see him crouching beside me. I hadn't even completely come out of it yet, but he had already replaced his *haddin* and swordbelt.

"I go now to speak further with Cinnan and Dallan, concerning the journey we begin tomorrow," he said, one wide hand smoothing back my sweat-soaked hair. "Rest yourself now and regather your strength, then plan what you do not care to leave behind you. When I return we will take a meal, and you may ask for what you wish then."

He went to one knee and gave me a quick but very definite kiss, his mind thoroughly appreciating me, and then he was up and striding toward the door and out. By the time I was able to do more than just lie there on the carpet fur he was long gone, but by then my mind was beginning to creak back to functioning. I rolled to my side and forced myself to sitting, put my head in my hands to ease the dizziness, then managed to wonder what the hell he had done to me.

After another couple of minutes I was able to get unsteadily to my feet, but I didn't even look toward my discarded gown. The first thing I needed was in a silver pitcher on one of the side tables, a light, pretty wine I had come to enjoy. I stumbled over to it, tried to get as much of the wine as possible into the cup, then held the cup in two trembling hands. I had always been told that wine wasn't made to be gulped, but the fools who had told me that had certainly never experienced what I'd just been through. I gulped down everything I'd poured into the silver cup, closed my eyes and took a deep breath, and only then felt ready to try standing without leaning or holding on.

"I don't believe it," I muttered to myself, grateful for the way the wine was starting to force my blood into moving again. "I absolutely and completely don't believe it."

The small, wavery image in the silver goblet I still held didn't believe it either, and I was glad there were two of us. Somehow—some *how*—Tammad had overwhelmed me with his mind, a mind that wasn't anywhere near as strong as mine. How the hell had he done it?

The same way he did it the last time, the wavery silver image answered, sounding smug and know-it-all. You tried to force him into taking you back to the embassy, and he nearly blew your circuits. This time he refused to let you disobey him.

That's stupid, I retorted with ridicule, not quite up to gesturing such nonsense aside. Last time he used the strength of anger and outrage. This time he wasn't even annoyed. And wouldn't I have felt him attacking? Why didn't I understand what he was doing until it was way too late? And what happened to my filter curtain and my shield? Why didn't one of them activate to bail me out?

If *you* didn't know you needed help, how do you expect unreasoning defenses to have known it? the image sneered, just short of laughing at me. He isn't of Centran stock, you know, so why does his talent have to be like yours? Even identical twins have differences, and he got you with one of the differences.

There's got to be a defense against it, I came back with more desperation than certainty. There's got to be a way to keep him from doing that to me. I can't spend the rest of my life being nothing more than a—a—

Rug? the image suggested helpfully with a snicker, and that absolutely finished it. I threw the goblet across the room with every ounce of strength I'd recouped, then sank down to the carpet fur with my hands in my hair.

"I just had an argument with a reflection," I said out loud, wondering if that's what it felt like to lose your mind. "And I don't even think I won. What am I going to do?"

This time there were no answers handily available, which wasn't quite as comforting as it should have been. I didn't know if I would rather be crazy, or forced to do everything Tammad's way. He loved me so much he was even going to protect me from thinking for myself.

By the time Tammad came back, I hadn't so much pulled myself together as scraped the scattered shards into some semblance of neatness. After I'd gotten into my gown again, it suddenly came to me that I'd been told I was going after Aesnil whether I wanted to or not, and definitely not as one of the chief searchers. Something inside me laughed hollowly

51

at that, with nothing resembling real amusement. There would be trouble if I went, certified and guaranteed, but what good would it do just saying I "knew" it? Lately I was beginning to know a lot of things, and one of them was that whoever said "knowledge is power" was an idiot.

Tammad was followed into the bathing room by a servant carrying a tray, and once she had made her delivery he closed the door behind her. I sat calmly and cooly among the room's cushions, my legs folded modestly to my left, my hand holding the silver goblet I'd retrieved and refilled, my mind closed tight behind the heaviest shield I could buffer up. Garth had wondered if I could work through my own shield the way I'd worked through Len's, and so had I. If it did turn out to be possible, I'd find it out some other time.

"I see you have bathed, *hama*," he observed, walking over to investigate what was on the tray the woman had brought. "Once we have eaten I, too, shall bathe, and then we may see to giving one another further joy. For what reason did you not greet my return as you usually do?"

He turned around to look directly at me then, his question decorated with just the right hint of faint disappointment; not criticism, mind, just disappointment. He did it so well that I wondered briefly what full mind control could possibly do to improve it.

"If you don't mind, I'm in the middle of getting stinking drunk," I said, raising the goblet to illustrate my point. "Right after that I intend killing myself, so don't waste your time waiting for the answers to any questions."

"You may not kill yourself, *hama*, for you have not asked my permission to do so," he retorted, a faint grin touching his face and eyes, knowing damned well there hadn't been enough wine left in the apartment to make a child drunk. "For what reason did you not greet my return as has become usual with you?"

"I can't decide whether to jump out the window or to drown myself," I mused, firmly refusing to remember what Garth had said about jumping. "What about poison? Maybe I can find some poison."

"Perhaps one of these dishes here has been poisoned," he suggested, beginning to get into the spirit of the thing. "Come and join me for the meal, and we may investigate the matter together."

"I don't want to die with you," I said, looking down into what was left in my silver goblet. "I may not be able to live without you, but I don't want to die with you."

There was silence for a moment after that, and then he was crouching down in front of me to put a gentle hand to my face.

"Do you find life as my woman so intolerable, then?" he asked softly, the words faintly tinged with hurt. "Have I brought you too great an amount of pain to bear?"

"Stop that!" I snapped, startling him, sending my glare directly into those innocent blue eyes. "When I said I wanted you to see me as clearly as you see others, I didn't mean I wanted to be manipulated! Haven't you done enough to me for one day?"

"Truly do you sound as though you had been beaten, *wenda*," he said with a dryness that surely covered annoyance, taking his hand back to hang the arm on one broad thigh. "As you seem to feel the need so greatly, perhaps it would be best to grant it to you."

"Not all beatings have to be physical," I muttered, swallowing the urge to back away from that hardened stare. "How would you like it if I did the same thing to you?"

"Would you attempt such a thing?" he asked in turn, the words now very soft, opposing the look in his eyes. "Would you seek to do to me what the Garth R'Hem Solohr feared you would do to him?"

"Certainly," I answered after trying not to swallow very hard. "Then I could stop wasting time looking for ways to kill myself. It would be taken care of without my having to lift a finger."

"Indeed," he said with a nod, his grin strong. "Indeed would the matter be quickly seen to. For what reason do you upset yourself now? For what reason do you not wait till the horrors of your new life have been experienced before agonizing over them?"

"I like to get started with things as quickly as possible," I replied, not caring much for his version of humor. "You don't seem to think I'll have any problem, but you're not looking at it from where I'm standing. I won't be able to do it, you know."

"Have no fear, all necessary doings will be mine," he reassured me, the grin still strong. "Have you thought upon what you will need on the journey?"

"Tammad, I don't want to go to Vediaster," I said, trying to make him understand how serious I was without projecting the feeling. "If I do go, something will—happen."

Oh, good, I thought, watching him frown faintly with lack of understanding. *Such detailed description and flowing verbiage is guaranteed to make him see your side of it.*

"What sort of thing do you believe will occur, *wenda*?" he asked, working at sounding reasonable. "That Vediaster is ruled over by *wendaa* should not disturb you, for you, too, are *wenda*. *L'lendaa* are not encouraged to visit there, yet are they allowed to do so and also to depart in peace. There will be danger for neither you nor we. What is it that disturbs you?"

"I really wish I could tell you," I answered, frustrated over having nothing more than a stupid *feeling*. "You'll just have to leave me behind."

"*Wenda*, such a thing might have been possible had you not spoken as you did earlier in Rellis's chamber," he said, more reproof than regret in the eyes that looked down at me. "Your words were a challenge to my authority over you, and therefore may not be allowed to stand. You shall not be left behind."

"Damn it, if you go alone there won't be any trouble!" I nearly shouted, rising to my knees in response to the way he'd straightened and headed back to the food tray. "If I go with you, *something* will happen!"

"Indeed," he said without turning to look at me, reaching to the pitcher of wine the tray held. "What will occur is your learning full obedience. What things do you wish to bring with you upon the journey?''

"I don't own anything *to* bring with me," I answered with the fuming anger I felt, filled up to *there* with frustration and upset. "I don't own one single thing on this world, and my posessions equal my value, which is just the way you want it. The only problem is, you won't regret it nearly as much as I will."

I sat back down on the carpeting turned away from him, one knee up with elbow resting on it, hand to head. Hints, hints and more damned hints, but nothing solid but a *feeling!* If I hadn't been so angry I would have begun feeling frightened, that and sick to my stomach. *Something* unpleasant was going to happen, but what?

"Terril, when one fears a certain thing, justifiably or unjustifiably, all other things about that central object take on a reflection of the fear it generates," Tammad said from not too far behind me, his voice filled with compassion. "You fear the life which will be yours beside me, and therefore do you begin to fear all occurrences in that life. I shall not allow harm to come to you, *hama*, and for that you have my word."

When his big hand touched my shoulder I twisted around and grasped his arm two-handed, really needing to put my face to it. He'd be hurt because of that promise, I knew he'd be hurt, and I had to do something about it.

"*Hamak*, please!" I nearly begged, strangling his arm with the hold I had on it. "When are you going to teach me how to use a sword?"

"*Hama*, I have not yet given my agreement to do so," he came back, his voice suddenly very neutral. "Is this the sole manner in which you wish to ask for the thing?"

I hesitated briefly before looking up at him, but using my eyes didn't tell me anything I didn't already know. The man I'd been banded by wore no particular expression, neither encouraging nor discouraging. Neutrality is at times a very fine trait, but I suddenly noticed that he also wasn't making any promises.

"Doesn't it matter to you that now I know I have to learn swordwork because of you?" I asked, reflecting that the more upset I got, the more answers I seemed to get. Maybe if I got hysterical, which wasn't, at that point, too farfetched a possibiity, I'd know it all. "Don't you want to be as safe as you promised I would be?"

"To wish to learn sword skill in order to protect your *hamak* is a fine and noble motivation, *wenda*," he allowed, a twinkling in his eyes despite the continued sobriety of his expression. "There is, however, your *hamak*'s permission first to be obtained, which may perhaps be gotten by pleasing him. Do you mean to please him?"

That's a good question, I thought, still looking up at him. I'd just discovered that the reason I needed swordwork was to protect my beloved, but my beloved, a true *l'lenda*, considered that too funny for words. It so happened I did too, especially since Cinnan and Dallan would be with us, but none of that answered the question. Tammad thought it was funny, but I *knew*; was I going to let something terrible happen to him because I was too good to bend a little?

"It so happens I do intend pleasing him," I replied with a sniff, finally letting his arm go. "What do I have to do first?"

"That, *wenda*, should be fairly obvious," he said, straightening up and raising to his lips the goblet he was carrying, probably to hide a grin. "You have not yet greeted my return in the manner which has grown usual with you."

He spent some time swallowing the wine he'd taken, but why he wasn't choking was beyond me. He knew damned well I'd have to drop my shield to give him his greeting, and that would put me at his mercy again—if I couldn't figure out what he was doing and how to stop it. He didn't seem willing to discuss what he'd done to me; was that because he was hiding something—or because he didn't understand it himself?

"Now, how could I have forgotten to greet you?" I asked in a murmur, deciding to go for broke. It was time to answer a previously asked question, and also time to dent some of that nauseatingly thick smugness my *hamak* was wrapped in. For the first time I made the effort to really look at the inside of my shield, just as I'd looked at the outside of Len's. At first there was nothing, no single crack or crevice, nothing that would allow the faintest breath in or out—and then it came to me that I was looking at it wrong. Len's shield was the way mine had been before the trouble, adequate for the purpose but full of spaces if you looked at it properly. Mine lacked those spaces—but that didn't mean I couldn't go *around* it. "Around" wasn't the right word any more than "spaces" was, but that was the closest I could come to verbalizing something that could only be felt. My shield had no spaces, but I *could* go around it.

It felt odd reaching around with my shield still in place, as though I were reaching out with a hand that didn't move from my side—yet could still get to and grasp anything in normal range. An invisible hand it was, or an emotion invisible to another empath, to someone who was watching closely for my shield to drop. Rather than becoming aware of my unshielded mind, Tammad felt instead the bodiless kiss I had taken to giving him in greeting, the sensation that was interpreted as having a pair of lips pressed to his. He started when he felt that unexpected sensation, and then he was frowning down at me.

"What have you done, *wenda*?" he demanded, his annoyance and outrage deliberately pushing at my shield. "You could not have touched me as you are."

"The wise teacher makes sure to stay a few steps ahead of her student," I commented, drawing my knees up to hug them with my arms. "I told you my abilities were growing stronger and spreading. Didn't you enjoy your greeting?"

"Ever shall I find joy in the greeting of my *wenda*," he said as he stared down at me, his annoyance so high that his voice had nearly become a growl. He seemed to want to say something else, but rather than do so he turned abruptly and went back to the tray, lifted the pitcher, then took his time pouring more wine. When he finished his task and turned back to me, he was well in control of himself again.

"There is a thing you perhaps fail to comprehend, *hama*,"

57

he said, the words as smooth as his expression. "When a man bands a *wenda* she is then completely his, to be touched and used by him as thoroughly as he wishes. No *wenda* is permitted to keep herself from her *memabrak*, the man who has banded her, in any manner whatsoever. Should you truly wish to please me, you must also do the same."

His blue eyes were full of satisfaction as he sipped from his refilled goblet, the satisfaction of knowing he would win no matter what I did. If I obeyed him I would be unshielded, if I disobeyed he could forget about teaching me to use a sword. There were definite disadvantages in being paired with a strong, intelligent leader of men, I could see, but I really had no choice. It was annoying that he was making it so hard for me to protect him, but I wasn't about to give up just because he was a stubborn barbarian. I could be stubborn too, and I had to learn to counter whatever it was he'd done to me at some time or other. I would have preferred later to sooner, but it wasn't working out that way.

"Of course no woman should keep herself from her *memabrak*," I agreed after only a slight hesitation, dropping my shield even as I rose to my feet. "What else may I do to please you, *humak*?"

"You may now join me in our meal," he answered, the grin returning when he let his eyes and mind brush me. The hum of interest in his mind was always so strong that it intimidated me somehow, making me feel small and weak and very vulnerable despite the fact that I knew he would never hurt me. Or, rather, that he would never hurt me voluntarily. Sometimes when he made love to me he lost control of himself; although he never caused any serious damage, it was enough to remind a woman of the price she sometimes had to pay for being mindless enough to get involved with a barbarian in the first place.

I walked over to him near the tray, joined him in deciding what we both wanted to eat, then carried one of the chosen bowls as we took them back to the cushions. Every step of the way I was aware of his attention on me, the hum in his mind that could turn to a growl at any time, his very close proximity without the least touch of his hand. He was brushing me with his restrained desire, forcing me to feel it, getting me ready for what he'd want after the meal. He knew I lost control when he did that to me, that I became aware of the soft fur under my feet, the silken gown draping my otherwise bare body, the five bronze, small-linked chains that were the bands he'd put me in. Soon those things would focus on and highlight my own desire, and control of my abilities would be completely beyond me.

"Do not sit yet, *hama*," he directed, breaking into my thoughts just as we reached the cushions. "First I would have you remove that gown, so that I might look upon all of the woman who is mine."

I could feel his eyes on me as I bent to put my bowl on the carpet fur, but I didn't dare look up. Without the gown I would be totally naked, in a room where anyone could walk in at any time. Most people knocked before entering a bathing room, but not everyone and not every time. He was trying to fluster me, and was unfortunately doing a damned good job of it. It took very little time to slip out of the gown and put it aside, and then I stood in nothing but my bands.

"How lovely a woman is in the sight of a man," he said softly, this time drawing my eyes to him. He had removed his swordbelt and seated himself among the cushions, his goblet on a small, low table not far from his left hand, the bowl he'd chosen in his right. He sat cross-legged as he looked up at me, and that light-blue stare conveyed the absolute sense of possession all Rimilian males felt when they looked at their women.

"Come and sit beside me, *hama*, so that we may share our meal as always," he said, patting the fur to his immediate right after shifting the bowl to his left hand. "And you may also, if you wish, speak of what you would have of me."

I retrieved my bowl and sat down where he'd indicated, my right side to his right thigh, angled to face him, legs together and bent to the left. I was also very busy cursing him out, silently but nevertheless vitriolically. He had made me strip naked while he remained clothed, and that was the way I was supposed to ask for lessons in sword use? I was a woman, nothing but a lowly *wenda*, and he was going to make sure I understood that fact in every fiber of my being.

I had chosen spiced fish cubes and he a meat and cooked vegetables concoction, and there was silence while we fed ourselves and each other. When I put a fish cube in his mouth, he took it with the feeling of being given what was his anyway; when he fed me some of the meat and vegetables, he was sharing what was also his, what he generously gave to one who had none of her own. The emotions were a little blurry around the edges and too wide and full to be accidental or natural, but that doesn't mean he wasn't really feeling them. Tammad was magnifying what he considered the truth, helping me out to make sure I didn't miss it. He didn't want me confused about who and what I was, where I stood and what was expected of me. I'd been spoiled up till then, allowed to believe as I liked, but now that was over.

We shared another two bowls of food, then two after that, and every once in a while Tammad gave me his goblet to drink from. The wine was soft and golden rather than hot and tawny like *drishnak*, suitable for a woman as the strong, spicy *drishnak* was not. By the end of the meal I was gritting my mental teeth, fighting to resist his deliberate propaganda, but I was finding it harder and harder going. I *was* a woman and I *did* belong to him, and standing up to him had always been so damned difficult. When I sipped from his goblet, taking wine with his permission, something inside me wanted to throw up its hands and walk away in defeat.

"Now that we have had our meal, we may spend a time speaking together," he said, taking his goblet back after my last swallow, then stretching out among the cushions on his rightside. "Was there any matter you wished to discuss?"

The eyes watching me were open and innocent, the mind behind them comfortable and patient. He was more than aware of what I was feeling, and had no intentions of letting me regain my self-possession before pressing the point of sword lessons. I was female, and had to be taught how silly I was for wanting something that was strictly for men.

"*Hamak*, I would—have you teach me the use of a sword," I got out with difficulty, looking down from his eyes, knowing why I was speaking Rimilian. I was a Rimilian woman asking something of a *l'lenda*, and that was the only language suitable. Both of my hands were on my bare right thigh, and the embarrassment was so severe it was painful.

"*Hama*, I would give you all that I might, yet am I far from convinced of the necessity for such a thing," he answered, also in Rimilian, his deep voice grave with the weight of a decision that just might *have* to be no. "You must speak to me of the reasons you feel such a need, and also urge my belief. No *wenda* of our city has ever asked the same."

The gentle reproof in his voice was making it worse for me, telling me I wasn't being the best woman to him I could possibly be. I loved him so much I *wanted* to be the best woman possible for him, which meant he was pitting my own feelings against me. I was being made to feel that what I wanted was wrong, but the feeling wasn't coming from him. I looked up hesitantly to find that he had turned to his back in the fur, a cushion under his head, his goblet put aside. He held his arms out to me, telling me to come closer, and I was so eager to obey that I nearly forgot our conversation. I put my hands on him as he drew me close to his chest, and then he simply waited. With his warm, hard flesh under my hands it took me a minute to remember what he was waiting for, and another minute after that to force myself not to say to hell with it and begin kissing him all over.

"*Hamak*, I must learn sword use for I feel that I must," I said, haltingly, looking down into the eyes that looked up at me. "There is a—a feeling—that I have, that will not let me rest; it whispers to me constantly. You have my word that I will do my utmost to keep from shaming you."

"I have no doubt of that, *hama*," he said, using one hand to slowly stroke my hair. "And yet must I be sure that this—need—you feel would not interfere with what other duties I set you. Are you able to reassure me of this?"

Reassure him. He was holding me and stroking my hair and making sure I could feel the hum in his mind, and I was

supposed to *reassure* him. I'd never heard it called that
before, and also discovered that what it was called didn't
make much difference. He wanted to be coaxed and I was
going to have to do it—without a single guarantee of success.
I still had the choice of forgetting about it, but that was one
choice I didn't care to make.

"Surely you know, beloved, that I would never neglect
you," I murmured, leaning down to put my lips to his face,
then gently work my way to his ear and neck. "Please,
Tammad, I ask a very great deal, I know, yet are you one of
the few strong enough to be asked such a thing. Other men
would merely laugh and refuse, but you—you have the strength
and understanding to do more than simply reject my need.
You are a man among men, and may do as others cannot."

The dialogue was making me queasy, as was the wheedling
tone I was using, and kissing him that way was making me
want him more. Aside from that, though, things weren't
going as badly as I'd thought they would. Tammad was a
Rimilian *l'lenda*, and Rimilian warriors were used to letting
themselves be coaxed into things by their women. I could feel
his sudden realization that what I'd said was beginning to
sway him, and decided to press my advantage as far as
possible.

"Ah, *hamak*, my respect for you is boundless," I purred,
letting him feel how much I was enjoying running my hands
over him. "To take on the burden of instructing one who is
so helpless and weak! Truly is that an undertaking for a man
with capabilities far beyond those of others. You are strong,
and brave, and generous, and— Oh!"

I'd cried out involuntarily at the sudden, unexpected sensation, a sensation that was completely nonphysical in origin,
no other thing than physical in application. Both of his hands
were on my back, holding me to him, but just as I hadn't
used lips to give him his kiss, he hadn't used a hand to touch
me in his favorite place. He'd been looking for a way to
distract me from saying what was obviously getting through
to him, and it seemed as though he'd found it.

"Ah, you felt my caress, then?" he said with surprised

satisfaction, really very pleased with himself. "My progress clearly continues and improves, just as you wished. Are you not pleased as well?"

"Indeed, *hamak*, I am greatly pleased," I gasped out, finding it impossible not to try pulling away from him, finding the pulling away just as impossible. Slowly, clumsily, but very definitely, he was touching me, exactly the sort of touching he was trying for.

"It was not my intention to interrupt you, *hama*," he said, his hands also moving slowly over my back, under my hair. "Please continue with the thought already begun."

"The thought," I echoed, trying to remember what I'd been saying, my hands already closed tight on his arms. Oh yes, swordwork, a sword that cut rather than only pierced, a sword worn to the side in a sheath rather than under a— "The feeling—the feeling will not let me rest, *hamak*," I babbled, beginning to feel dizzy and even more aware of how naked I was. "It is for your sake that I seek such a thing, only for your sake. For your safety, for your touch, for your love— Ohhh!"

I lost it entirely, then, squirming up to bury my fists in his hair so that I might kiss him wildly and madly. He had apparently paid attention to what he was receiving at some time when he made love to me, and that's just what I was feeling then, that he was prepared and beginning to make love to me. The sensation of the first touch of his flesh to mine was what I had, that and no more, and I knew I couldn't live without more. I moaned and begged as I kissed him, dying for him, and he wasted no time giving me what I begged for.

3

The early morning was dim and chilly, especially in the stabling cave where the *seetarr* were kept. The torches on the walls were low from having burned all night, and that seemed to add to the lack of warmth. I hugged myself against that chill, then had to admit its source was more inner than outer. I'd been given a new sort of *imad* and *caldin* to wear, in place of the gowns of my former, temporary wardrobe, and another set was already packed in with Tammad's things. My *memabrak* had bought me the long-sleeved, blouse-like *imadd* and ankle-length, full-skirted *caldinn* for the upcoming trip, both articles of clothing warmly made against the cooler air we would find higher in the mountains. He had also bought me a pair of lined, soft-leather foot coverings, but those were just then also packed away. They would be given to me when I needed them, when my *memabrak* decided I needed them; until then I walked barefoot on the smooth rock floor of the cavern, simply hugging myself against the chill.

"Tammad, *aldana*," Dallan called softly in greeting as we neared him, his voice both hollow and muffled in the large cavern. "I have myself only just arrived, yet has Cinnan been here for some time. Did he ride alone, he would already be gone."

"Though one might wish it otherwise, one cannot follow a trail one is unable to see," the barbarian answered, his mind throbbing with sympathy for Cinnan. "Let us ready our *seetarr* as quickly as we may, so that the man need not agonize the longer."

"Most certainly," agreed Dallan immediately, also feeling the sympathy strongly, then they both turned to what had to be done. Neither one spoke to me or even looked in my direction, but that didn't mean they weren't aware of me. Tammad, especially, was very aware of me where I stood, about ten feet back in the shadow between torches, hugging myself and looking down at my still-bare feet.

The night before, our "conversations" had continued the way the first had begun, with the barbarian being pleased and me barely in control of any language whatsoever. After giving me what I had begged for he'd had me bathe him, then he'd given me a few lessons of a kind other than mental. His body was mostly healed from the terrible whipping he'd been given by the intruder, but the remaining scars and ridges upset me out of even more control. I didn't want him to be hurt again so I'd kept trying to ask my favor, but he hadn't wanted to be asked. By the time he'd carried me to the bed furs, I'd been as limp as a rag and totally beyond speech.

Earlier the next morning I'd awakened before him, to lie in the furs and stare into the darkness. Tammad had refused to believe what I'd said about my going to Vediaster, but I knew it wasn't something that could be avoided by disbelief. He also had refused to listen to a request to learn swordwork, and that was a request he could put off indefinitely, especially during a trip when there would be very little time or opportunity for that. At first I hadn't known what to do, and then it had come to me that both of my major problems could be solved with a single effort, the effort to stay behind. My avoiding the trip would keep the three men who were going safe, and while Tammad was gone I would be able to find *someone* to teach me swordwork, with the help of my talent if necessary. Rellis felt he owed me a favor for saving Dallan's life by ending the intruder, and there was sure to be something I could do with that. If I hid out somewhere with my shield closed tight until the three were gone, and then told Rellis I'd been too afraid at the thought of Vediaster to let myself be taken with them, everything ought to turn out just fine. I'd known Tammad would be angry with me when he got back, but I'd preferred the thought of him angry to the thought of him hurt.

Once I'd made my decision I'd slipped quietly out of the furs, tiptoed through the darkness into the bathing room to find my gown, then had gone toward the door to the hall. It was difficult seeing well with all the candles blown out, and I'd been groping for the door when a big hand closed about my arm. My heart had almost stopped still from the fright, but that was only the beginning of it. Behind the shield of deep, deep calm Tammad had rigidly imposed on himself had been his anger, an anger he'd let me feel once it was no longer necessary to stand hunter-still in the darkness. He'd waited to find out if I really had been trying to sneak out of the apartment, and once he'd known for sure he'd punished me for trying to disobey him.

"*Aldana, wenda.*" Dallan's voice came, bringing me back to the stabling cave. He was leading his two *seetarr*, the first a saddle animal with a pack animal behind, and he'd stopped a couple of feet away from me. "I give you greeting for this fine new day, Terril."

"I thank you for your greeting, Dallan," I answered, looking up at him with very little enthusiasm. "Please allow me to return it, for it seems only fitting to do so with one who is able to find approval of a day such as this."

"You find the look of this day unacceptable?" he asked, raising his brows with a surprise he wasn't feeling. Dallan was teasing me, and knew without doubt that I knew it. "I had not thought you would prefer clouds and rain."

"My preferences matter not in the least upon any matter one would care to cite," I informed him, in no mood for even the gentlest of teasing. "The sole point of satisfaction now remaining to me is that soon you will no longer consider this day quite so fine."

"Of what do you speak, *wenda*?" he asked, narrowing his eyes as his amusement faded. "What is it that you anticipate?"

"I?" I asked, raising my brows as he had and with just as little real surprise. "I am no more than a *wenda*, no more than the belonging of one of true worth. In what manner might I anticipate doings concerning *l'lendaa*?"

Exasperation touched him then, the sort that straightened *l'lendaa* to their full height to look down at you with hard blue eyes, but I wasn't in the mood to be intimidated. I was in the mood to be scared stiff, but that wouldn't have done me any more good than trying to run away had.

"As you seem so well aware of your true place in our world, perhaps you would care to reconsider the response you have given me," Dallan said, still keeping his voice low. "Or would you prefer that I speak with Tammad concerning your behavior?"

"Speak with him or not as you will," I retorted, making sure I avoided Dallan's eyes. "You may be sure, however, that *I* shall not speak with him, for I no longer feel the least concern over what may become of that beast. Nor those who call themselves brother to him."

"I had thought, Terril, that you and I were also *helid*," he said, using the Rimilian word for a very close, non-blood, non-sexual, relationship. "Have I given you insult with either word or deed?"

I looked up at him then, his features more clearly illuminated by the dying torches than mine, and saw the sober face of truth looking down. Dallan was asking me not to take my mad at Tammad out on him, which was a reasonable enough request for anyone in the mood *to* be reasonable. The only trouble was, to that point being reasonable had gotten me nowhere, and I was tired of wasting the time and effort.

"You ask me to speak to you of my misgivings so that you, too, may have opportunity to give me insult?" I said, noticing that my question brought back some small part of his amusement. "I am not that much *helid* to you, Dallan."

"I gave you no insult, *wenda*," came another voice, one I was more than eager to forget. Tammad had his own *seetarr* ready, and had brought them over beside Dallan's. "Merely did I weigh your words and find them unsubstantiated, and

67

then did I strap you for disobedience. Insult was neither thought upon nor given."

That damned calm was back in his mind, the calm he usually moved through life with, the calm he used in place of the true shield he didn't seem able to form, the calm I didn't have to look up to his face to see. This time it wasn't covering anything but more calm, but even if it had been I wouldn't have been in the least interested. The strapping he'd given me had been very short, but he'd made sure it would hurt; I wasn't going to be allowed to disobey him, and that's all he cared about. For my own part I didn't even care about that much anymore, and was beginning to hope I'd get killed. He'd be sorry then that he hadn't listened to me.

"What words of hers did you find unsubstantiated, Tammad?" Dallan asked when it was clear I would be neither looking at nor speaking to the big barbarian. "Perhaps Cinnan and I should hear them as well."

"The woman wishes to remain behind, Dallan," Tammad said with a sigh of long-suffering patience, his calm faintly rippled with annoyance. "She has been told that she will be taught proper obedience upon this journey, therefore does she seek to avoid making it. She has said that her presence will bring us ill; is such a contention to be credited when we ride to Vediaster? Perhaps in another city her fears might well be justified, yet in Vediaster?"

"I see the difficulty," Dallan admitted with his own sigh, one that tried to disguise the fact that he had already switched sides. "In a city of *l'lendaa* there might well be some number who would stand against you for the possession of a green-eyed, dark-haired *wenda* such as Terril; in Vediaster there is unlikely to be even the thought of such a thing. The *wendaa* who rule it would not allow such thoughts."

"Exactly," the barbarian agreed, his annoyance gone. "I have never myself visited that city, yet have I heard of it from others. The woman fears naught save the wailing dark."

Dallan shrugged without adding anything, trying to catch my eye to let me know he'd been as open-minded as possible, but that was his opinion. Mine was that I'd get more positive, intelligent response by looking for it in the stone of the cave floor.

With all packing and conversations taken care of, I was herded along between the two men as they went to where Cinnan waited for us. The third Rimilian was dressed the way Tammad and Dallan were, which surprisingly wasn't in their usual *haddinn*. Under their swordbelts all three men wore tight cloth pants like the leather pants Dallan had worn as a servant-slave in Aesnil's palace, pants that had a good deal of stretch and were made of the same cloth as my *imad* and *caldin*. Tammad had a tight, long-sleeved shirt and short, lined boots to go with the pants, but both shirt and boots had been packed away for use at another time, probably the same thing the other two men had done with their accessories. Cinnan's pants were gold, Tammad's tan, and Dallan's blue; both sets of my *imadd* and *caldinn* were of a lovely, delicate pink.

"Dallan, Tammad, I give you greeting for this new day," Cinnan said warmly as we came up to him. "I had not thought you would be prepared so early to depart. You both have my thanks."

"Thanks are unnecessary, Cinnan," the barbarian said with a shake of his head, dismissing Cinnan's almost-pathetic gratitude. "There is a question I would ask one final time, however: you both continue to feel it wiser that we leave our followers behind rather than have them accompany us? We three alone will be a more effective force?"

"We three alone will cause the *wendaa* in Vediaster less distress," Dallan said, Cinnan's firm nod supporting the statement. "We would not wish them to believe we ride in conquest, and cause them to send their females against us in defense of their city. We go to retrieve a *wenda*, not to slay hordes of them."

"Indeed," said Cinnan, his mind as confident as Dallan's. "Were we to ride against them we would certainly be victorious, therefore do we refrain from causing them fright."

How chivalrous, I thought as Tammad nodded his own agreement, now completely convinced. The tall, generous

l'lendaa of this area magnanimously allowed the poor little
females to believe themselves safe due to the strength of their
own swordarms, chuckling indulgently all the while. It came
to me then to wonder why *l'lendaa* from another area, not
quite as generous with an entire city and its surrounding
countryside at stake, hadn't already ridden in and defeated
those poor, helpless women. Remembering the pair of twin
male slaves brought as a gift to Aesnil by the ambassador of
Vediaster, the two big, beautiful men whose minds had been
so full of fear and cringing that slaves were all they would
ever be for the rest of their lives, I would have enjoyed
asking about previous invasion attempts. I really did want to
ask the question, but the three big, strong men I accompanied
had already dismissed the subject, and were too busy leading
their *seetarr* out of the stabling cavern to be bothered. I was
herded along with the rest of the animals before the question
could even be framed.

Outside the cavern the rising sun was already beginning to
warm the air, and a small crowd was there to see us off.
Rellis and a recovering Seddan, among others, said good-bye
to Dallan; Loddar and Kennan and a dozen others wished
Tammad a swift journey, and Cinnan's men confidently assured
him that he would soon be returning with Aesnil on his saddle
fur, holding to him with the deep love he had made her feel. I
tried to find Len and Garth in the crowd, checked again when
I couldn't, then remembered that the barbarian had forbidden
me to see them ever again. I stood alone in the middle of all
those friendly, chatting people, an island of silence in a sea of
conversations and laughter, and looked down at the flagstones
of the courtyard. Tammad said no and Len and Garth obeyed
him, and I was already beginning my new life. A bright new
life, full of all the hope and promise and love I'd told it
would have, as deeply satisfying as anyone could ask. The
flagstones were rough and hard under my bare feet, but I had
long since become used to walking barefoot. People can
become used to anything, if they're kept at it long enough.

The good-byes and good wishes lasted until we rode away
from them, Cinnan in the lead, Tammad and Dallan together

behind him. I, of course, was on the saddle fur behind the barbarian, my arms around his body as I'd been ordered to keep them. The saddle fur was a lot softer than the saddle itself would have been, but I was still in a good deal of discomfort from the punishment I'd been given. The discomfort was meant to be an extension of that punishment, an object lesson on the consequences of disobedience, and I'd been forbidden to use pain control to make the time any easier. I tried to tell myself I wouldn't have used pain control anyway, would have preferred feeling the pain to help myself remember that I didn't care about that beast any longer, but after only a few minutes gave up the effort. It hurt to sit and ride like that, hurt in a way that was terribly humiliating, but I wasn't being allowed to avoid the sensations. I was being made to feel them and learn from them even if I didn't want to. I was a banded *wenda* being taught to obey her *l'lenda*.

Depression is a funny emotion; it can be weak enough to simply sour a good mood, or strong enough to cause suicide or murder. It makes you very aware of the grim things happening around you, but lets you ignore anything pleasant; events are never neutral under its sway, only dim, bad, or dreadful. We rode away from Dallan's house back up to the mountain road Aesnil and I had been caught on during our escape attempt, followed the road to the turnoff for Vediaster, then followed that new road. It was narrow enough to cause us to ride single file for quite a way, surrounded by the rock of the mountain, the trail leading gently but definitely upward. Cinnan's mount moved eagerly forward, somehow almost smelling Aesnil's previous passage from the very air we moved through, but no one asked me about it. Cinnan, up ahead, already knew where the search was taking him, and Dallan, bringing up the rear, was simply enjoying the ride and the pretty day. The barbarian I held to was busy with his own thoughts, was enjoying the feel of my arms around him, and was faintly impatient to be where we were going. I, as opposed to the others, was simply depressed.

The higher we climbed into the mountains, the wider the trail became. With the widening came the presence of some grass and eventually a few trees, but I couldn't seem to make myself interested in the landscape. The air was pure and sweet, warmed by the sun but a good deal cooler than what I'd recently grown used to, and birds flew over us screaming out their indignation at our trespass or merely watching us curiously. The slow, swinging pace was boring and soporific, and when Cinnan pulled off the trail and stopped, it was scarcely an improvement.

"This place seems wide enough to halt for a meal," Cinnan observed, looking toward the two men who had followed him to the side of the road. "What think you?"

"The same," Dallan agreed, his casual words showing nothing of his relief. When Cinnan had kept going beyond noon Dallan had begun thinking about his stomach, but Tammad hadn't noticed. The barbarian was busy plotting and planning again, something that tended to turn him oblivious of his surroundings.

"The halt will do well for us all," he told Cinnan, reassuring the other man that they weren't merely wasting time. "When I rode in search of Terril I lacked the good sense to know this of my own self, needing the words of others to calm my haste. The woman is in no danger, Cinnan, merely does she journey as we do. When we find her, you will see the thing for yourself."

"Indeed," said Cinnan with a heavy nod, dismounting as he worked to believe what he had been told. "There is little danger in these mountains for those upon *seetarr*, and once beyond them there will be *l'lendaa* to give what aid might become necessary, and then the *wendaa* of Vediaster. Aesnil will not be harmed."

"Before she is found," qualified Dallan with a chuckle, also dismounting. "Afterward I feel sure you will speak to her, Cinnan, concerning the foolishness of a woman running from her *memabrak* and the responsibilities which are hers. My cousin seems greatly in need of a speaking to."

"Indeed," Cinnan said again, but this time he didn't add to the single word. Dallan's comment had done more to distract him than the barbarian's reassurances, something

Tammad knew and didn't mind in the least. He chuckled quietly as he slid from his mount and then turned to lift me down, a chuckle that anticipated what Aesnil would get once they caught up with her. As soon as I was on my feet he went to see what Cinnan was already digging out of one of the packs, leaving me alone to move painfully on the thin, stony grass. I was stiff and aching from the ride, more so than I had been that morning, but that was the way I was supposed to be. It was all part of my punishment to teach me to be a good little girl.

Once I was sure my legs would hold me, I walked as far from the road as possible, right up to the side of the mountain looming so high above us. The grass was slightly thicker there with fewer stones, and the angled sunlight was thick as well. I lay down facing the brownish rock, on my left side in the grass, ignoring the thoughts of comfort coming from the barbarian's mount. I'd already told him I wanted no comfort, but he refused to leave me alone. He cared about me and could feel the shape and motion of my thoughts, and kept trying to pull me out of the depression. But realizing that the only one really concerned about me was a *seetar* simply pushed me further down into it.

I lay in relative peace and quiet for a while, aware of the casual conversation exchanged among the men but not really listening to it, and then my solitude was ended. A pair of feet walked up to me through the grass, and a minute later a hand touched my arm.

"Why have you not yet come to me for your food, *hama*?" the barbarian asked, his hand warm on my arm even through the sleeve. "We must soon resume our journey."

"I don't want anything to eat," I told him, making sure my mind didn't move toward his. "I'm afraid I'm not feeling very well, but it should pass after a while."

"You are not ill, *wenda*," he said, moving his hand to stroke my hair. "Merely do you feel the punishment you were given for disobedience. The ache will indeed pass, yet not, I hope, the lesson."

"No, the lesson isn't likely to leave me very quickly," I

73

agreed, ignoring the hand on my hair. "Especially since it was a lesson I asked for. I wanted you so much I didn't stop to ask what I'd be getting, but you're certainly helping me to find out. From now on I plan on doing a lot of thinking before deciding I want something."

"What do you speak of, *wenda*?" he said, his confusion touched only lightly with disturbance. "What is it you mean to ask for?"

"I ask for nothing, *memabrak*," I answered, reverting to Rimilian as I sat up away from his hand. "Should it be your wish that I take a meal, I will certainly do so."

"There—is no need if you have not the desire for it, *hama*," he said, his voice a shade more unsure as I stared at the brownish stone in front of me. For the first time that morning he deliberately tried approaching me with his thoughts, but there was nothing out of place for him to find. Every one of my emotions was sealed up and unmoving, and he was far too new at what he was doing to separate and interpret them. I wasn't resisting him in the slightest, but there was nothing inside me for him to touch.

"Perhaps—you would do well to merely rest till we ride again," he said at last, upset and frustrated at not being able to find something he couldn't even define to himself. "I will summon you when your presence is required."

I had the impression he was about to reach out to touch me again with his hand, but the touch never came. Instead he straightened and walked away, and a minute later there was more low-voiced conversation. I simply lay down again on my side, and stared at weather-browned rock.

After a while I was called over to the *seetarr*, lifted to my place on the saddle fur, and our trip was resumed. I'd been able to feel a sort of curiosity in the minds of all three of the men when I'd rejoined them, but I hadn't cared what they were curious about and hadn't even looked at them. The road kept going upward and we followed the road, the minds of the others working while mine seemed bogged down in the mud. You were a damned fool and now you're paying for it, something inside me kept saying, paying for it the way every damned fool should. You decided you're a big girl now, too big to keep running away from commitments, so you made the commitment your gonads screamed for and now you're stuck with it. You can't run away and you can't change it, and you sure as hell can't live with it. There's not much of anything you *can* do, and you know it. Even if you shed a stream of tears it won't help, because no one cares. I knew the something was right, that even I didn't care, just like the browned, weathered rock all around.

"So, Terril, your *memabrak* tells us you mean to learn the doings of a woman of this world." Dallan's voice came suddenly from my right, pleased approval beside lighthearted interest. "As that is your wish, I shall myself begin your lessons with a dish unknown to all save my family. I must have your word that you will speak of it to no other, of course, for its preparation is to be a secret between us. Will you give me your word?"

"You may have what you wish, *drin* Dallan," I answered, looking at nothing but the broad back I sat behind. "I will, of course, do as you say."

"Of course," he echoed, the approval and interest gone elsewhere, a familiar-seeming frustration and disturbance fighting to fill his mind. "When we make camp for the darkness, we will begin."

No other answer seemed necessary, but it came to me that three minds seemed to be waiting for one anyway. Even Cinnan had apparently listened to the very brief conversation, but the browned rock and I didn't care.

As we rode higher and the light got lower, the temperature started going down. It still wasn't as cold as it would have been if we'd been going over the top of the mountain instead of through a relatively low pass, but after the warmth of the rest of the country we'd passed through, the difference felt extreme. By the time sundown came and we found a place for the night, the men had already pulled their shirts on and my feet felt numb. There was very little more than stones and rock all around, and I was given my new ankle-highs as soon as the barbarian took me from the saddle fur. I put them on without saying anything, then walked back and forth a few times until my legs and back stopped aching so much and my feet felt less wooden.

The three *l'lendaa* took their *seetarr* to the left of our camping place to tie and hobble them and relieve them of their burdens, but Dallan left his two to the others and came back almost immediately with wood for a fire. He built the fire then went back to his packs, and this time returned with meat and a pot and vegetables and all sorts of things. When he gestured to me I joined him at the fire, then started doing things at his direction. Every once in a while he tried teasing me, then finally gave it up.

By the time the meal was ready it was full dark, the camp was completely set up, and we needed to sit near the fire to keep from shivering. Three *camtahh* were now standing away from the road near the mountain wall, one for each of the men. I served out the thick stew I'd made according to direction into four wooden bowls, and wondered which of the three small tents I'd be sent to.

"This dish of yours seems quite interesting, Dallan," Cinnan said as he took a bowl and sniffed at its contents, his brows rising in approval. "Likely the *wendu* had a great deal to do with the manner in which its aroma takes one, yet does it appear interesting."

"I do not recall it ever being quite this tasty," Dallan said thoughtfully after sampling the contents of his own bowl. "Surely was it somehow improved in its preparation. What think you, Tammad?"

"It cannot be as enticing as it appears," the barbarian said with a frown, reaching for the third bowl. "I have seen many dishes which appear quite savory, few which taste the same." He fell silent while taking a small bite of the stew, took a second, larger one with strong surprise, then looked again at Dallan. "It is excellent, my friend, truly excellent! Confess now, the doing was primarily yours."

"I did little more than supervise," Dallan said with a laugh of enjoyment, crouching nearer to the fire with his bowl. "The actual doing was Terril's alone, a *wenda* who will clearly require little teaching before becoming a woman like no other. You are a fortunate man, Tammad, truly fortunate.''

"Indeed," said Cinnan with enthusiasm, but whatever else he said was lost after that. I had left the fire after doing the last thing required of me, and had by then reached the *seetarr*. It was terribly cold away from the fire, and dark enough to make the footing treacherous, but I couldn't hold back any longer. I had to have *someone* to share my misery with, or it would explode and break me to pieces.

The barbarian's *seetar* knew I was coming, and rumbled softly in encouragement until I reached him. Once I was there he lowered his giant head to my shoulder, pushing me up against his great black body so that I might share his warmth, his mind immediately putting out soothing thoughts. He didn't know what was bothering me, didn't understand anything beyond the fact that I *was* bothered, but that didn't keep him from trying to comfort me. As I pressed my cheek to his soft, sleek hide and held him as far around as I could, I wondered just how many times he *had* comforted me since I'd come to that world. He'd been my first friend, the only one who had never judged me or tried to make me do things his way, the only one who had always been concerned with nothing but my happiness. He didn't understand why I couldn't seem to find that happiness, but that was because he didn't know me for the damned fool I was.

"I had thought as much," a quiet voice said from behind me, a voice that startled two of the other *seetarr*. "When my *wenda* takes herself from the sight of men, there is but a single place she may be found. How is it possible for a man to feel jealousy toward a *seetar*?"

"Forgive me, *memabrak*." I said at once, pushing away from the big black body I didn't want to leave, turning to face the large dark shadow standing so near. "You sought to tell me which of your brothers you would have me give pleasure to. Speak his name, and I will go to him."

"His name is Tammad," the barbarian answered with a growl, and then his hand was wrapped around my arm. "I see there must again be words between us, for I cannot bear this. Come with me.''

The hand around my arm pulled me away from the *seetarr* and back toward the fire, leaving rumblings and bellowings behind us. My friend didn't like having me pulling away from him before he could comfort me, not even by his owner, and he wasn't leaving his unhappiness in doubt. If he hadn't been well tied and hobbled, he might have tried to follow us.

''Tammad, what occurs?'' Cinnan demanded as we reached the fire, his big body standing and frowning into the darkness. ''What has disturbed the *seetarr*?''

''They wish to give challenge for the possession of a *wenda*,'' the barbarian answered, his voice as sour as his thoughts, pushing me down next to the warmth. ''A *wenda* who has learned to be perfectly obedient.''

''Obedient,'' Dallan echoed, heavy distaste in his mind. ''May we ask what her obedience entailed?''

''She requested the name of which of my brothers I meant to give her to for the darkness,'' was the answer while I tried to warm up enough to stop shivering. I didn't know what they were so upset about, but if all they were going to do was carry on a conversation with each other, I could have stayed with the *seetarr*.

''She had cause for such a question, had she not, my friend?'' Cinnan asked, turning near the fire to face the barbarian. ''Also do I believe that her request was in no manner a refusal.''

''She has become as all *wendaa* should be, Tammad,'' Dallan observed, also turning where he stood. ''For what reason are you disturbed and dissatisfied?''

''I am not disturbed and dissatisfied,'' the barbarian said through his teeth, his mind seething, and then he blurted, ''She calls me *memabrak*.''

''For what reason should she not?'' Dallan asked, sounding calm and totally reasonable. ''Are you not her *memabrak*, the one who has banded her?''

''Certainly,'' the barbarian answered, trying for a calm to match Dallan's. ''And yet—''

"And as she now obeys you without question, you may indeed give her to Dallan or myself to warm our furs," Cinnan put in, now adopting the calm the barbarian wanted. "Which of us will it be, Tammad?"

"No!" the barbarian snapped as his mind jangled, but then he caught himself with an almost-audible snap. "That is, I would be honored were either of you to accept the use of my *wenda*, however there is something of a difficulty," he said as he backtracked, his mind whirling madly. "The difficulty is—that is, seems to be—rather, appears very much like—"

"Yes?" Cinnan prompted pleasantly, helping out when the barbarian fell silent, the muddle of his thoughts rising to a clamor. I wasn't looking at any of them, only at the fire, wishing I could climb into the middle of it.

"If there is a difficulty, we would assist with it, my friend," Dallan said, sounding somewhat less—amused than Cinnan. "Just as you would not hesitate to assist us."

"The difficulty," Tammad repeated, still horribly at a loss, and then he seemed to give up. "The difficulty is that she prefers the company of a *seetar* to mine. That she calls me *memabrak* rather than *hamak* or *sadendrak* as she formerly did. That the shine is gone from her, the vibrant glow which was my beloved. She now obeys me as I demand, and in doing so is no longer with me. One full day of complete obedience, and I cannot bear it; I must surely be going mad!"

"Do not despair, brother," Cinnan said very quietly, moving from the fire to gently clap the barbarian on the shoulder. "The difference in the woman is so great that I was drawn from my distraction because of it. There is indeed something amiss, and we would do well to discover it."

"What is amiss is that this is no longer Terril we see," Dallan said, more in practical questioning than in pure sympathy. "As you said, Tammad, there is no longer a glow about her, no longer the sense of being in the presence of one of unusual strength. She is as lovely and desirable as ever, yet has she become—ordinary."

"Ordinary," the barbarian echoed, filled again with that whirling disturbance. "And yet, this is what she had wished to be, what I sought to help her become. For what reason are we neither of us pleased?''

''The *wenda*'s lack of pleasure is likely due to her seeking to be what she is not,'' Dallan answered, his voice and mind very serious. ''Yours, however, more likely stems from having mistaken your own desires. I have no doubt that you have had many *wendaa*, most of them eager to be in your bands. For what reason did you fail to keep them there?''

There was no more of an answer than an increase in mental whirling, an answer Dallan couldn't make much use of, but he had always been exceptionally good at getting things from silences.

''You see,'' he said, just as though the barbarian had spoken. ''You made no effort to keep those others in your bands, for you sought not the ordinary but its opposite. Many men wish no more than a soft, loving, eager and obedient *wenda*; you are not one such as that.''

''You speak the truth, brother,'' the barbarian said with a sigh, still not over his upset but finally calming down. ''It most certainly is not an ordinary *wenda* that I desire, and now I am aware of what must be done.''

It took him no more than two steps to reach me, and then he crouched down to my left.

''Hear me, *hama*, for I wish to speak of an error that I have made,'' he said, putting his right arm around me. ''I was mistaken in demanding complete obedience from you, for such a thing does indeed make you other than that which I wish you to be. You no longer need be concerned with obedience, for I shall no longer demand it.''

His words were warm and eager, his mind filled with excited anticipation, and his arm tightened the least little bit, as though he expected me to turn to him and throw my arms around him. I kept watching the leaping, crackling fire, and nodded very slightly.

''I thank you for your consideration of me, *memabrak*,'' I said, wishing I had a coat or a fur to put around me. ''When you have decided upon what degree of obedience you wish from me, merely inform me and I will, of course, see to it.''

"What is it you speak of now, woman?" he demanded, disappointment bringing him anger. "I have said you no longer need be absolutely obedient. For what reason do you remain so—distant and strange?"

"At first I was informed that I must be completely obedient," I said, forcing the words out against a vast reluctance. "When I failed, I was punished to teach me my error. Now that I have become completely obedient, I am told that you wish me to be otherwise. As I have no desire to be punished again, you must tell me what you wish and exactly how disobedient I am to be. Am I to obey you only in the mornings and evenings? Only through midday? On alternate days or perhaps every third or fourth day? Is the decision to be mine, or am I to disobey only at the direction of another? Speak to me, *memabrak*, and tell your *wenda* exactly what you wish."

I ended up looking directly at him, the anger rising in me so swiftly that it was totally out of control, blazing at him through mind and eyes. The expression he wore was pure confusion, shock and dismay, a very accurate sampling of what he was feeling. The next strongest emotion in him was guilt, brought about by the realization that his error hadn't been what he'd thought it was.

"You attempt to berate me for my foolishness," he began, "and you are correct in feeling wronged, however. . . ."

"Wronged!" I repeated, getting more outraged by the minute. "I sought to keep you safe from harm, and you gave me punishment for the effort! I sought to merge my life with yours, and you thrust me behind you! I fought to accept and control what rises roaring within me for *your* sake, and you dismissed my struggle with disbelief and insult! Insult. Never will you know the true meaning of insult till you must face it without the presence of a sword and the strength to ease it. The fault for all of this, however, is not yours but mine. It was I who wished to belong to you, and now I do. The more fool, I."

I stood up and walked away from both him and the fire, passing between a very silent Cinnan and Dallan, feeling the weight of all their eyes and minds but refusing to let any of it touch me. I didn't *have* to let any of it touch me, none of them was strong enough to force their will on mine, not even working together. That, of course, was the key to stopping what Tammad had done to me with his mind, not *wanting* it to affect me. He had overwhelmed me because I'd loved him so much I had wanted to deny him nothing, and that's exactly what you get out of a softheaded attitude like that. Nothing.

Without really paying attention to what I was doing, I picked out one of the *camtahh* and entered it. Once I was through the roofed-over verandah and in the tent flaps I could stand straight again, but what I wanted couldn't be reached by standing up. I got down on my hands and knees in the absolute darkness, crawled and groped around for the sleeping furs I knew would be there, then pulled one to me when I found it. Getting angry had chased some of the chill away, but not enough to make the fur unnecessary. I didn't know whose tent I'd crawled into, and I didn't care. I simply wrapped myself in the fur and sat staring into the darkness.

Not many minutes passed before I heard a sound from the verandah, and then the tent flaps were pushed aside. Tammad came in holding a candle, shielding its flame with one hand, then turned once he was inside to reach to one of the tent braces. He let a few drops of hot wax fall onto the brace before setting the candle on it, then was able to leave the candle knowing it would stand where it had been put. He sat himself down about three feet away from me with half a sigh and half a grunt, then looked at me bleakly.

"Truly must a man be bereft to insist upon a woman of pride, spirit, and strength," he said, the disgust in his eyes and mind more than clear. "What difficulty I face is self-chosen difficulty, for there are many *wendaa* indeed I might have had in your place. And it was not my intention to give you insult."

"Of course not," I agreed, nodding at him. "All you were trying to do was drive me crazy. Please accept my congratulations on your success."

"Enough, *wenda*," he growled, annoyance flaring in him.

"Your tongue has already stripped the skin from my flesh. I will not allow the taking of the flesh as well. I attempt to speak words of apology."

"And what if I don't want to hear those words?" I asked, pulling the fur more closely about me, seriously meaning what I'd said. "What if I honor the commitment I've made to be your belonging, but do nothing beyond that? You can't touch any part of the inner me if I don't allow it; what if I refuse to allow it?"

"Have I truly given you that much hurt?" he asked, his light eyes filled with sadness and pain. "The punishment I gave was my duty as I saw it, and would not be withdrawn even were it possible. As for the rest—I had not meant to bind you to strangling, nor did I mean to give insult with disbelief. Should you make the effort to see it so, I, too, was given insult. It was clearly understood between us that my word would bind you, yet were my wishes thrown aside the moment it suited you. The decision was yours that I would accept your protection, whether I desired it or no."

The lines of the disagreement were suddenly a lot less clear-cut than they had been a few minutes earlier, but I wasn't about to let him talk me out of my mad. He was really good at that, shifting the ground under my feet, but this time I wasn't going to let him do it.

"Weren't you doing the same thing to me?" I demanded, straightening where I sat. "Did you consider *my* wishes in anything you did? How would you like it if *I* laughed and refused when *you* offered protection? It would make you feel pretty cheap and small, now wouldn't it?"

"Protection of a man's *wenda* is his duty, Terril," he answered very gently, still looking down at me with that same expression. "It matters not in what manner you accept the offer, only is the manner in which I discharge the duty to be considered. Should you wish to laugh you may do so; still shall I protect you with all the skill and determination at my command. Do you mean to contend that you did not disobey me, and therefore should not have been punished?"

"I—was trying to do what was best for everyone involved," I maintained, upset to realize that being laughed at *wouldn't* have bothered him. "You made the plans and included me in them, and not once was I consulted, not by any of you. If you three can do it, why can't I?"

"You have no need to be told the reason, for you already know it," he said with such true, easy calm that I wanted to avoid those light eyes pinning me with a stare. "We who are *l'lendaa* see to decisions such as that, and have no need to consult with what *wendaa* may be involved. Speak to me truly, Terril: are you *l'lenda* yourself, or a lovely, desirable, beloved *wenda*?"

"What's wrong with being both?" I demanded, hating the way he described a woman for the way it made me want to be like that. "You said you couldn't stand my being absolutely obedient, so you don't see anything wrong with it either. You want me to be both."

"No, *wenda*," he disagreed, even more gentle than he had been, a faint, fond smile curving his lips. "You were wise to show me the foolishness of what I had demanded, for to be such a thing would make you no longer yourself, no longer the woman I love so deeply. You must be what you are, yet does that continue to mean a *wenda*, one who must nevertheless be as obedient as possible to the man to whom she belongs. I have no doubt that you shall continue to require punishment, yet shall that punishment never be given for speaking the truth as you did earlier. No more shall it bring you than my apologies, for having wronged the woman I love."

"I hate you!" I cried, thrusting the fur away so that I might throw myself on him and beat at his face with my fists. I did hate him, desperately, for making everything turn out the way *he* wanted it to, for the fact that a real *l'lenda* didn't need anyone else's agreement in order to be that thing—and for forcing me to know how terribly I still loved him. I didn't want to be nothing but a *wenda*, but at the same time I wanted to be nothing other than *his wenda*, nothing but the beloved of a man who could apologize when he found he'd been wrong. I screamed and threw myself at him, raging at the way he'd pulled me back to him so easily, but he didn't even have to unfold his legs to defend himself from my attack. Before my fists could touch him my wrists were in his hands, and then they were behind my back and I was being pulled up against him.

"You feel no hatred, my beloved, no more than do I," he said, looking down into my eyes as I struggled uselessly against his strength. "No more than unhappiness touches you, and for that I am indeed responsible. I will strive to the utmost to remove that unhappiness, for never should it have been allowed to approach you."

He put one hand to my hair then bent his head to kiss me, at the same time touching my mind with his love. His lips were so soft and warm against mine, nothing to really fight against, nothing to hate or resent. He kissed me gently, lovingly, tenderly, this barbarian who could have crushed me to broken bones with only a fraction of his limitless strength. I suddenly found my arms were around his neck and I was kissing him back, but not with the more pristine emotions. I wanted him as much as I always did, with both body and mind, and when he realized that he chuckled.

"It's not funny, you beast," I murmured, pressing myself to his body as I kissed his face. "And I do hate you—for always winning."

"Are not my victories yours as well, *hama sadendra*?" he asked, letting his hands move over me. "First you must eat, and then I shall give you the joy I am able to feel that you desire."

"I forgot about eating," I said with annoyance, but his mention of food reminded me just how hungry I was. "But while we're at it, shouldn't we also move to your own *camtah*?"

"*Wenda*, we are already in my *camtah*," he said with a grin, moving me back off his lap so that he might get himself ready to leave the tent. "Which other of those we ride with would have set out two sets of sleeping furs?"

He gestured just before moving through the tent flaps, and I turned my head to see that he was right. The fur I'd taken to put around myself was his, but mine were spread out just beyond that. It annoyed me that I'd gone straight to *his* tent even when I was furious with him, but something inside me was smugly satisfied. I crawled over and retrieved the fur I'd dropped, wrapped it around me and sat where I'd been, then decided that I didn't much care for this "something inside me." Having part of me be totally on Tammad's side struck me as the basest sort of betrayal, and I'd have to see what I could do to get rid of it permanently.

A minute later Tammad was back, with the fourth bowl of stew that had been kept warm by the fire. I took the bowl and raised the scoop to my lips, took a good mouthful of the stew—then just looked at the crouching barbarian until I'd managed to swallow it.

"That was awful," I got out at last, seeing his grin at the face I was making. "I thought you three said it was so wonderful?"

"We deemed it wonderful to give pleasure to *you, wenda,*" he answered, still clearly amused. "Each of us was able to feel your great unhappiness, and wished to give you a thing to be proud of. For us your effort was filled with true excellence, for we measured the desire behind the effort rather than the doing itself."

"You all lied to make me feel better," I accused, but the accusation brought only a silly smile and a feeling of true warmth. "Thank you for doing something that—foolish."

"To give others pleasure is never foolish, *hama,*" he said with an answering smile, no least feeling of insult in him at being accused of lying. "Finish quickly, now, so that I may give pleasure to another."

"And of course take nothing for yourself," I agreed with a laugh, then went back to the awful stew. It wasn't absolutely awful, just badly seasoned and a little overcooked, but that put it way out of the running as far as regular Rimilian cooking went. It annoyed me that I hadn't been able to get it right even with Dallan right there to help, and I made the decision to try just a little harder next time. After that the bowl was taken away from me, and all the following decisions were made by someone absolutely determined to give someone else pleasure.

4

I carried both sets of furs out of the *camtah* the next morning, already having folded them, wishing I was wearing them instead of simply carrying them. It was cold at that early hour, really cold, and everyone was feeling it. I, however, was also feeling something else, and for the life of me couldn't understand why.

"Hai, calmly, good beast, calmly," I suddenly heard from over near the *seetarr*, Dallan's voice struggling to be soothing. The pack animal he was working on had rumbled warningly with a good deal of anger, and even *l'lendaa* walked carefully in the presence of an angry *seetar*. I headed over there to see what was going on, but was stopped before I could reach Dallan.

"Come no closer, *wenda*," he warned me, giving the angry *seetar* all his attention, but nevertheless knowing I was there. "I have not the faintest notion what ails this beast, therefore are you to remain well away from him."

"I have no need to approach the nearer," I told Dallan, having stopped beside the barbarian's giant black mount to put a hand to his sleek neck while he nuzzled at my hair. "The *seetar* is in discomfort from the last pack strap tightened, and wishes to be eased. I will soothe him, and then you may adjust the strap."

I touched the angry animal with my mind, letting him feel

88

more clearly the concern being put out by the man holding his lead so carefully, and he seemed to calm down almost immediately. His previous anger began puzzling him then, knowing as he did that the man he served would have adjusted the strap at the least sign of discomfort on his part, just as he had already done any number of times before. Dallan hesitated very briefly, his mind almost as puzzled as the *seetar*'s, then he immediately fixed the strap while the beast stood quietly and allowed it. As soon as that was done, he left the *seetar* to stop in front of me.

"What occurs here?" he demanded, dubiously eyeing the way the head of Tammad's mount rose above mine with a soft rumble of warning meant to tell him to watch himself. "That *seetar* is one I have used as a pack beast ever since it was fully grown. For what reason would it come so near to being enraged with me, and for what reason does Tammad's beast believe I would mean you harm? Why are the *seetarr* suddenly so strange?"

"The *seetarr* are not alone in being strange," I said, automatically calming the big black standing over me as first Cinnan and then Tammad came to join our discussion. They'd seen what went on and had heard Dallan's question, and were wearing frowns almost identical to his.

"What disturbs you, *hama*?" Tammad asked, looking down at me with real concern. "I am able to feel your disturbance, yet cannot make out the nature of it."

"What disturbs me is that the depression I struggled beneath all of yesterday has again returned," I told him, putting one hand to my head. "That there is no reason for such a feeling is more disturbing still, and I find myself growing angered at the same time. Perhaps what *I* feel is in some manner being passed to the *seetarr*."

"That may perhaps be so," he mused, looking down at me thoughtfully. "Shield your mind completely, so that we may see what, if any, results there are."

"An excellent thought," I said at once, and as soon as the decision was made my shield was there, cutting me off from the minds around me. Immediately, all six of the *seetarr* seemed to settle down, that indefinable air of tension draining away like water in dry sand. The big black standing over me like a giant guardsman sighed and lowered his head, then snorted a greeting to the man who usually meant so much to him. Immediately, the depression and anger I'd been feeling began easing off, obviously about to disappear altogether. I looked up at the barbarian ruefully, feeling like an idiot for not having thought of that myself, but there was no accusation in the grin he showed me, only a sort of wryness.

"It seems I am no longer the possessor of the facility with *wendaa* which once was mine," he said, putting a gentle hand to my face. "Was this not so, your disturbance would have long since been replaced with pleasure."

"Your clumsiness and ineptitude in the furs are well known among all *wendaa* who have been used by you," I agreed soberly, remembering how wild he had gotten me the night before. "The fact remains, however, that with my shield in place, I am as undisturbed as the *seetarr*. It would please me to know what occurs here."

"You, too, are no longer disturbed?" Dallan asked, rescuing me from the look I was getting from Tammad over my jocular reference to his abilities. "Then the *seetarr* were indeed unsettled through your mind. For what reason was *your* mind so unsettled?"

"I know not," I told him honestly, then thought of one possibility. "Perhaps my misgivings over this journey have now magnified to the point of affecting me and those around me without my being aware of it. I certainly continue to feel them strongly enough."

"Despite my assurances that your fears are unfounded?" Tammad asked, his expression its usual calm, but his eyes faintly annoyed. "Perhaps you had cause to feel so before we spoke, yet now. . . ."

"The woman feared to accompany us?" Cinnan interrupted, his expression disturbed. "Had I known this when I requested her presence, Tammad, I would willingly have withdrawn the request. There was little need to . . ."

"Fears must be faced if they are to be conquered, Cinnan,"

the barbarian interrupted in turn, trying to soothe the other man. "The *wenda* is now as well aware of this as we, and also must it be remembered that we may require her assistance in locating Aesnil. She does not accompany us on a whim."

"This entire matter continues to seem strange," Dallan said, staring at the barely rising sun without seeing it. "Of what did the woman's fears consist?"

"She feared that if she accompanied us there would be difficulty for us to face," the barbarian answered, now definitely annoyed. "Likely the thought of a dark-haired, green-eyed *wenda* being taken among so many strange *l'lendaa* with none save three beside her disturbed her, yet is she no more than vaguely aware of the skill possessed by the three she so easily dismisses. Are you also of the opinion that there will be those who are able to take her from my side?"

"Certainly not," Dallan said with a snort and a gesture of dismissal; then he moved his eyes back to me. "Is this the sole content of your fears, Terril? That there will be difficulty brought about by your presence?"

"Indeed, yet not for the proposed reason," I said, sending the barbarian a glance filled with my own annoyance. "Had I remained behind the difficulty would not have touched you—yet would you also not have found Aesnil. Damn!"

The last word, spoken in Centran, startled them all, but I was too furiously frustrated to care. I hadn't known I was going to say that about Aesnil until the words were out, but now that I'd said it I could feel the truth of it. If I didn't go they'd never find Aesnil, and that despite the fact that I'd never had any intention of helping them. If I kept getting these flashes of bits and pieces it would eventually drive me crazy—even if I survived whatever was ahead of me. I hugged the furs I was holding with a strength fierce enough to strangle whatever was doing that to me, then became aware of the stares from three pairs of eyes.

"And what leads you to believe, *wenda*, that my Aesnil will never be found should you not accompany us?" Cinnan asked, looking at me oddly. "She is *Chama* of Grelana, and well aware of the position. Do you believe she would forsake her people—and the man whose bands she wears—forever?''

"I—feel that she would eventually return, yet not in a manner you would wish," I said, groping for the right words. "I do not mean to upset you, Cinnan, yet what comes to me comes by itself, at its own pace and in its own time. I know of it in the same manner I know that Aesnil rides to Vediaster, yet beyond that?"

My shrug really annoyed him, his expression making me glad that my shield was tightly closed, but there was nothing any of us could do to change things. All three of the men were dissatisfied with what I'd said, and that made four of us. Standing around discussing it any more would have been a waste of time, though, so we quickly broke camp and moved on.

The only difference between that day and the day before was the presence of sleeping furs draped handily across saddles, and the fact that Tammad sat me sideways in front of him instead of astride behind him. Sitting that way let me hold my own fur around me while the barbarian kept me from falling off, and also made my legs and feet warmer. As soon as I was settled we started off with Cinnan leading again and Dallan following, and once we'd picked up the road pace, I could feel two eyes looking down at me.

"So your presence has now become necessary," the barbarian mused, his tone almost as odd as Cinnan's had been. "Had you not accompanied us, we would not be able to find Aesnil."

"Believe me, I didn't plan it that way," I assured him, moving against the two arms holding me to his chest. "I'm going to turn just a little so that I'm leaning against you with my back instead of my front. Watching where we're going might ease the monotony just a little."

"The situation is not of your choosing, yet do you seem little disturbed by it," he said, his arms tightening just a small bit to keep me from moving as I wanted to. "In truth your appearance seems one of pleasure, to find that your importance has grown so considerably."

I looked up at him then, to see those eyes on me rather than just feel them, but I couldn't quite read the expression in them.

"I hadn't looked at it that way, but I think you're right," I conceded, suddenly feeling better than I had. "Not only am I not extra baggage, we now know you three can't get along without me. Maybe the next thing I'll find out is that I don't need *l'lenda* lessons, but can give them."

I grinned at the thought, not much believing in the possibility but liking the way it sounded, then noticed that my grin wasn't being shared. My *memabrak* still wore the same expression he'd been wearing a moment ago, but now there seemed to be faint amusement behind it.

"And what were you told concerning the place of a *wenda*?" he asked, the amusement in him doing nothing to soften his stare or take the decisiveness out of his tone. "A *wenda* who is not and shall not be considered *l'lenda*?"

"It isn't *my* fault if things aren't turning out the way you want them to," I retorted, still feeling very comfortable. "I didn't make the decision to be important, it just happened, and if someone's meant to be important there's nothing you can do about it. Now, will you please loosen your hold a little so I can turn around?"

"Release my hold upon one who is meant to be so important?" he asked, brows raised high in feigned surprise. "Never would Cinnan forgive me if I were to do such a thing, and risk the one who will enable him to recover his woman. You must be kept safe, *wenda*, for the destiny which is yours."

"But I want to see where we're going," I insisted, finding it impossible to struggle while wrapped inside that fur. "Tammad, let me go."

"I shall not," he answered, and I could swear he was just short of laughing out loud. "Great importance calls for equally great strength to bear the load, therefore shall you require a good deal of rest to gather that strength. You will have that rest during this journey, *hama*, for that you have my word."

"You wouldn't!" I wailed, suddenly understanding what

he was up to, but it was much too late. Held between his arms and wrapped in a fur, all I'd get to see of what was around us would be his chest and arm and any rock or tree that rose above his shoulder. I was being punished for trying to step out of my place, and I couldn't decide if this punishment was better or worse than getting strapped. Just sitting there and staring at nothing is so *boring*.

Despite the fact that the sun rose higher and higher, the air around us kept getting colder and colder. After a while all three of the men drew their furs around them, but we didn't stop while they did it. The cold was so intense we were almost able to see our own breath, something I'd heard it was possible to do on the planet Medrin. Happily Medrin had never needed Mediating by a Prime, so I'd never had to see that for myself. The road continued upward and we followed the road, and all there was was movement and cold.

And boredom. I was furious with the barbarian for punishing me like that, but what can a normal-sized person do when an overgrown monster says no and sticks to it? Just once I'd tried looking over my shoulder instead of actually turning around, but a quiet, "*Wenda*," had put an immediate end to that idea. If I tried getting out of that particular punishment, there was always another one that could be substituted for it, one that would make the hard leather saddle I half-sat on a lot harder and more difficult to bear. So I sat between the Barbarian's supporting arms with my fur held around me, leaning against his chest, and simply sulked.

But sulking is boring too, especially when no one cares that you're sulking. There was absolutely nothing to *do*— except try to find out what was affecting my mind. I brightened immediately when I thought of that, but didn't rush into dissolving my shield. I find no attraction in depression even as an alternate to boredom, and now that I was rid of that horribly flattening emotion, I didn't care to invite it back.

The first order of business was to think about what had been happening to me; considering the fact that I neither really knew nor understood any of it, that wasn't an easy chore. I'd told Dallan that my upset over the trip might have been causing the trouble, but after thinking about it that didn't make any sense. If that were so, shielding my mind would have stopped the *seetarr* from being upset, but it wouldn't have done the same for me. I was locked inside with my fears and apprehensions, but all I felt was bored and rebellious. No, nothing inside me could have caused the depression, so where had it come from?

The only logical alternative had to be an outside source. I freed one hand from the furs and ran a finger back and forth over the soft, thick material of Tammad's shirt at rib height, trying to think of an outside source that could have been affecting me. It wasn't the people around me as none of them had been feeling depressed, and the only animals in mental reach had been the *seetarr*. It was possible the *seetarr* had been picking up my emotions and echoing them back to me in a reinforcing pattern that increased their strength, but that still didn't feel exactly right. There was something else involved, something I just wasn't seeing, something I might never see. For all I knew the mountain rock all around was doing the echoing, bouncing my output all around and intensifying it, affecting me and the *seetarr* but not the three men, two of whom were latents with correspondingly less sensitivity, and the last one who tended to shield his mind automatically with a cloud of calm. It didn't make much sense that way either, but none of what was happening made sense. As a possibility it was a definite possibility, and if it turned out to be true there was something that might keep it from happening again. The curtain that had developed when I needed it was designed to keep outside thoughts and distractions away from my working mind, but it also might be able to keep all but deliberate projections on the inside. It was definitely worth a try, and if it didn't work I could always shield again.

I worked for a few minutes at feeling a need for that curtain, then gritted my teeth and let my shield dissolve. At first I wasn't sure if my deliberate need had done the job, and then I became aware of what was being felt around me, but filtered as though through a heavy veil. Cinnan was lost in thoughts that were half anxious and half angry, Dallan was relaxed but also busy with mental exercise, and the *seetarr* were almost as bored as I was. With the curtain in place, I was protected from the world but not cut off from it the way being shielded accomplished, and apparently the world was also protected from me. The rock walls towered over us quietly, the *seetarr* were unaffected, and I felt nothing of incipient depression. The grand experiment was a success, and now I was free to look around.

At absolutely nothing. The emotions all around were about as exciting as the scenery, and that included the big barbarian who held me. He was back to plotting and planning with only a small portion of his attention set to make sure I obeyed him, his awareness of my leaning against him closed away at the back of his mind. For a minute I seriously considered experimenting to pass the time, but without Len or Garth there that wasn't a very good idea. From previous experience I knew there were less painful ways of committing suicide than tampering with involuntary volunteers, and I no longer had the depression as a goad toward permanent ending. All I had was boredom, which doesn't produce the wish for death, only the eager hope that something that exciting might happen.

More than half the morning was gone before I realized that it wasn't getting any colder, and we weren't climbing higher. In point of fact we were angled downward after a short time of moving on the level, but I hadn't noticed it sooner because I wasn't watching the road. The thought that we were now coming down out of the pass excited me, but how long can such heart-stopping excitement last? It tends to fade at the first realization that going down is just like going up as far as interesting happenings is concerned, which is to say no different at all. Time dragged and dragged and *dragged*, and falling asleep was a positively uplifting experience.

I awoke to find that the cold had definitely lessened, and we were stopping by the side of the road. Once again the sun had already passsed its zenith, but this time Dallan wasn't worrying about his stomach. All three of the men were relieved that they could get rid of the furs they'd wrapped themselves in, but being big and brave and strong was their specialty, not mine. I intended keeping my fur until I had to fight for it, or until we got back to where it was *really* warm. And then I realized that the men *were* warm, which was more than annoying; how could they be warm when I wasn't?

Tammad dismounted with the others, then came around the *seetar* to lift me down to the ground. He was feeling satisfied and again faintly amused, so I stuck my tongue out at him to let him know how *I* felt. He grinned as he put me down and his mind chuckled, showing he wasn't feeling a single trace of regret.

"Were you pleased with the punishment you were given?" he asked very softly, his right hand holding to the saddle as he looked down at me. When I shook my head with complete ill grace, he tapped me on the nose. "Should that be so, you would have been well advised to consider your actions more carefully, then. Such a show of disrespect has now earned you more of it."

"You can't mean that!" I protested, horrified at the thought of more endless hours of absolutely nothing to do. As he had already turned away I discovered that I was talking to his retreating back, so I pulled my fur tighter and hurried after him. "Tammad, please, I'll go crazy! People will start noticing if you drag a crazy woman around, and you'll never find Aesnil. She'll hear about us before we get anywhere near, and she'll hide!"

The miserable barbarian stopped short and started to laugh, real, true amusement, putting his hands to his hips as he threw his head back and roared. Cinnan and Dallan smiled as they watched him, faintly amused but not really understanding what was going on. I'd spoken in Centran rather than Rimilian, unthinkingly excluding them, but they weren't left out of it long. As soon as my sweet *memabrak* regained partial control of himself he explained what had happened then translated what I'd said, and then all three of them were busy laughing. The *seetarr* were quietly puzzled about what was going on, but I was too disgusted to care even if they went enraged. It's always been the object of my existence to become a laughing-stock.

There was a good bit of cold, unhappy-looking grass on the side of the road where we'd stopped, so I followed it back uphill away from the jolly threesome having so much fun. My thoughts were so black that they probably would have shriveled the grass if they'd been uncurtained, but I wasn't feeling depressed. Furiously embarrassed and rebellious and mad as hell, yes; depressed, no.

I stopped to stare at a section of that rocky, widened road I hadn't been allowed to look at on the way down, but I didn't get to stand there staring for long. After a couple of minutes a hand appeared over my shoulder holding a piece of *dimral*, the standard pre-cooked trail fare for those traveling on Rimilia, and I was too hungry not to take it. Breakfast had been the same *dimral* warmed in a small fire, but that had been a lot of hours earlier. I looked at the chunk before starting to eat it, then found that the meal wasn't fated to be a silent one.

"I fear, *wenda*, that you grow ever more detrimental to the behavior and thoughts of *l'lendaa*," the barbarian said, accusingly. "I should not have laughed at your words as though I had not been shown disrespect, nor should the others have found a matching amusement. The place you stand in is not the place of a proper *wenda*."

"If you're telling me I'm corrupting you, it serves you right," I said around a mouthful, looking at nothing but the meat I held. "It isn't fair punishing me again just because you can."

"The punishment will be for disrespect, not to exhibit ability, Terril," he corrected, taking a bite of his own *dimral*. "No man need accept disrespect from his woman."

"But a woman has to accept it from a man?" I countered, the disgust I'd felt earlier growing. "And don't try to tell me men are usually polite to women on this world. Being polite has nothing to do with giving respect."

"One receives respect when one is able to command it," he said with a sigh, almost as patient as he sounded. "Also must one have the ability to give punishment when that respect is not forthcoming, with a sword or with a switch.

98

When once that ability is yours, *hama*, then may you demand respect as I do.''

"You—don't think I have the ability to punish disrespect?'' I asked with sudden interest, turning slowly to look at him. "You think that not using an ability is the same as not having it?''

"Do not be foolish, *wenda*,'' he scoffed, looking down at me with that expression that translated as stern. "How often must you pit yourself against me before learning that I shall not be bested?''

"How often?'' I repeated, giving him a bright smile. "Again and again until I win—or die trying. I won't use my abilities against you unless you agree that I can—I *have* learned that anything else would be dishonorable. But if you do agree, I'm free to do anything I please—and can—until it's clear that one of us has won. If I'm the winner, you'll give me the respect I want without my having to demand it.''

"And should *I* stand victorious?'' he asked, trying to hide his renewed amusement as he looked down at me. "I, too, must have the fruits of victory, which will be no less than the following: the *wenda* who attempted to overstep herself will be taken and strapped by the man to whom she belongs, and that before the others they journey with. In their presence will she be taught humility, and then will she need to beg forgiveness from the man she wronged. Do you accept this condition?''

"But that's totally unfair!'' I protested, instantly upset to see that he fully intended collecting on his "condition'' if he won. "How am I supposed to concentrate on what I'm doing with that hanging over my head?''

"One who has the ability to accomplish a thing is able to exercise that ability no matter the attempts of others to halt him,'' he replied, still looking down at me with amusement. "Does a *l'lenda* wield his sword because he had been allowed to do so? Does he seek the permission of his *wenda* before switching her?''

"Why do you always have to be right?'' I demanded, looking up at him with all the annoyance and exasperation I was feeling. "I won't have real control over what I can do until I can do it against any and all opposition. You're absolutely and perfectly right. Now all I have to do is figure out how to accomplish that.''

"While attempting to find victory in our wager," he said finishing off the last of his *dimral*. "Perhaps such wagering would best be left to another time."

"Will you hold off on punishing me until that other time?" I asked, feeling considerably more comfortable with the thought of challenge by appointment than by spontaneous occurrence.

"Certainly not," he said with a faint grin, getting a good deal of enjoyment out of explaining the rules of the game to the novice. "One receives what one has earned, whether it be respect for abilities or punishment for disrespect. Till now you have earned no more than punishment, *wenda*."

"So it's do or die," I summed up, even more annoyed by all that enjoyment he was feeling, then took another bite of *dimral* as I shrugged. "Then we might as well get on with it. If I'm going to be punished anyway, there's no sense in not providing a real reason for it."

Some of his satisfaction thinned at that comment, but he was too filled with self-confidence to be really worried. He nodded his calm acceptance to my challenge, then turned and led the way back down to the others. Cinnan and Dallan had found rocks to sit on while they ate, and they looked up at Tammad when he stopped not far from them.

"My *wenda* has come to the decision that she would have the respect normally given only to *l'lendaa*," he announced, his tone so free of ridicule that it was the next thing to grave. "In order to justify such a desire, she will exhibit her ability to punish insolence and disrespect. She has been given my permission to touch me with her power as she wills."

Cinnan and Dallan made no vocal comments to what they'd been told, but as Tammad moved to one of the pack *seetarr* the glance they exchanged was more than eloquent. They both found the thought of my request highly amusing, about on a par with seeing a small child trying to bend a bow three times his own height. They hadn't missed the point that I'd been given *permission* to touch Tammad's mind, and as amused as they were, I was twice as furious. Although he wouldn't have looked at it that way the barbarian was cheating, trying to make me subconsciously believe that whatever happened was happening because he was allowing it. That meant it would also have to stop when he wanted it to, and would never quite get bad enough to really bother him. With restrictions like that, even unconscious ones, I'd have about as much chance at winning as that child would have to bend the bow three times his own height. But I *would* win because I *had* to win; honor and dignity demanded no less.

Even as I opened the fur I'd been holding around me and let it drop to the ground, I felt a faint surprise at the calm detachment which had flowed over me in spite of my previous anger. I should have been sputtering in outrage instead of quietly watching Tammad take another piece of *dimral* from the pack before turning away from it, trying to argue with words instead of waiting for him to establish his own ground between Cinnan and Dallan. He was going to give me enough opportunity to make an absolute fool of myself before calling a halt to the attempt, let me know finally and without argument that I had no right to anything beyond what he was willing to grant me. I watched him getting ready to sit down, and felt no doubt about what I had to do.

The first step was gathering everything I'd felt during that strapping I'd been given, the dismay and humiliation and pain and sense of being punished by someone very much stronger than myself. I'd done something like that once before to the barbarian, but I hadn't been able to put much strength into the projection or hold it for long. This time there was no lack of strength to worry about, no uncertainty or doubt as to whether I was doing the right thing; I took the punishment and sharpened its edges, then gave it to the man who refused to accord someone respect without being forced into it.

"Aiii!" he shouted in shock, dropping the meat he held and throwing himself forward to hands and knees. I'd timed the projection to match his movements exactly, and just as he'd lowered himself into contact with the grass I'd given it to him all at once. His mind had been braced against everything and anything, confidently prepared to resist any sort of attack, but he was still thinking in terms of the physical even when he knew only the mental was involved. He was sure beyond doubt that I couldn't touch or hurt him physically, and tended to forget that all too often what our minds felt was precisely what our bodies would feel.

"You have now been punished for failing to give me the respect I mean to have," I told him in Rimilian, the words so calm they should have put him to sleep. "You may not attempt to deny me again."

"May I not, *wenda*," he growled as he glared up at me, his anger rising and growing hotter when he found he could neither throw off the effects of my continuing projection nor shield his mind against it. Dallan and Cinnan stared with frowns indicating their lack of understanding as he began forcing himself to his feet, his mind determined to do something to end what was happening to him. He made it erect with his teeth bared against what he was feeling, his face red from embarrassment, and then he was moving toward me, furious and unstoppable.

Or unstoppable as far as he was concerned. I waited right where I was until he reached me, until he stretched his big hands out to grab me by the arms. He was going to shake me until I lost the concentration necessary for projection, and then he was going to collect the spoils of his victory. His furious hands came to me and began closing on my arms, and that was when I split my projection, in a way I'd never done before. Even as I kept the original projection going, I also gave him the sense of touching something so hot that skin would blister and peel and blacken if contact was made and continued. He pulled his hands away from me with a hiss, his mind clanging with shock and pure disbelief, and then he had backed two steps, hugging his hands under his arms in an effort to stop the flaming pain. He was bewildered and suddenly filled with uncertainty, his blue eyes staring at me in a very strange way, and then the determination in him surged through everything else. There was only one thing left to do, and he was going to do it.

Despite the pain he felt he reached one hand behind him, and when it came forward it was holding a dagger. I could see that he had no intentions of hurting me with it, but he was remembering the last time I'd challenged him publicly, the time I'd tried facing him with exactly that weapon. I'd been afraid of the dagger, too afraid to do more than collapse in hysterics when he'd jumped at me with a shout, but fear right then did not affect me. He grasped the hilt as tightly as he could, denying as much of the pain as possible, gathering himself to leap at me with a shout—but I was ready first.

Vertigo is a terrible affliction, one that robs people of all sense of balance, all knowledge of where the ground is and where *they* are in relation to that ground. It spins them dizzily around with the terrible fear of falling, and sends them down even when they're not sure where down is. Tammad cried out in a strangled voice, dropping the dagger as he staggered backward, his mind lost and helpless in the overpowering maelstrom, unaware of Dallan and Cinnan jumping to their feet even as he fell. The two Rimilians shouted in dismay as he collapsed, understanding nothing of what had gone on between us, and then the pain of Tammad's hitting the ground reached me. It wasn't pain I had fooled his mind into believing in, it was real pain, affecting him strongly because of the confusion and helplessness he was lost in. The detachment and calm I'd been held by broke instantly then, like a bubble, and I suddenly knew just what I had done.

"No!" I screamed, running forward to drop to my knees beside the barbarian and throw my arms around his face and head. "I didn't mean it, I didn't, please don't be hurt! Please, *hamak*, please don't be hurt!"

"Terril, you must release him or he will not be able to breathe," Dallan said from behind me, then tried gently to make me stop hugging Tammad's face to me. When he found I was holding on too tight for gentleness he switched to strength, and disengaged my arms from around the throat they clung to. Then he pulled me back through the grass despite the way I was trying to struggle, to let Cinnan crouch down on the spot where I'd been kneeling. I heard a groan as

Tammad raised his hands to his head, heard Cinnan speaking to him quietly, but paid no attention to what was being said. For the sake of a stupid bet I'd hurt the man I loved, caused him pain and hadn't given a damn that I was doing it. I was so low I didn't deserve his love, and after what I'd put him through probably no longer even had it. I put my head to the ground and hid it in my arms, already mourning the loss of something I didn't deserve to have. If I'd done anything serious to him I would kill myself, and nothing and no one would be able to stop me.

I don't know how long it was before Tammad was able to pull himself together, but the time wasn't a minute or two and both Cinnan and Dallan had to help him. I kept my mind away from all of them with my curtain in place, my back to the three as I sat with my face in my hands, too miserable to feel the cold. Why couldn't you simply have done it his way? I kept demanding of myself. Why did you have to develop delusions of pride and ruin everything? The match was too impossible for it to last very long, but why couldn't you have let it continue more than a matter of days? Is a month of happiness too useless a commodity to buy with excess baggage like overstuffed pride and a twisted joke of a sense of honor? Honor! You wouldn't know the meaning of honor if it came up and spit in your eye.

"You seem completely unhurt, my friend," Cinnan said, obviously talking to Tammad. "Perhaps it would be best if you were to rise to your feet and walk about a short while."

"Slowly and with our assistance," Dallan amended as a grunt came amid the sounds of movement. "Are you able to speak now of what occurred?"

"I am not yet sure of what occurred," the barbarian answered, sounding as though he had just been through a fight lasting hours. "The woman—gave me her concept of fitting punishment for disrespect, and when I attempted to seize her and put an end to it, I found I could not. Her flesh was more painful to touch than the flames of a cooking fire, and I could not hold to her. I then recalled her fear of weapons and thought to startle and frighten her with my dagger, yet when I made the attempt a—a great dizziness came over me, so great that I could not remain erect. All sight and sound abandoned me and in their places were a whirling and roaring, twisting me about and swallowing me. I recall naught from the time of its onset to the time it faded."

The barbarian sounded so bewildered and confused that Dallan and Cinnan said nothing, building a silence that grew larger the longer it went on. I could hear their footsteps behind me as they all walked about, trying to help Tammad shake off the last of the dizziness, feeling not the least urge to uncover my eyes and turn to look at them. That was twice now that I'd been taken over by that calm detachment, and it came to me that I no longer had to search for the control I needed to handle my abilities even under attack. The detached calm seemed to be an ability in its own right, a tool to use to get the most out of the rest of my abilities. Its existence was quite a momentous discovery—for anyone who didn't mind being totally dehumanized while under its influence. I found it horrifying and sickening, but not wanting it would not make it go away. None of it would go away, not ever, no matter how terrible it got to be. I was a monster growing more monstrous by the day, and nothing I could do would cause it to stop.

"So, *wenda*, it seems you have at last bested me," the barbarian's voice came abruptly, stronger now and more neutral than anything else. "You must allow me to offer my congratulations."

"Thank you," I answered without taking my hands from my eyes, wondering how I could continue living with everything inside me cut to ribbons by his words. "The accomplishment was certainly one to take great pride in."

"A clear demonstration of ability must ever engender pride in the doer as well as respect in observers," he said, as though he were commenting on the presence of rock all around us. "The respect you demanded is yours, *wenda*, and now it is time that we continue on."

I heard his footsteps take him away toward the *seetarr*, and really could have laughed. I'd earned the respect I'd wanted, and all I'd had to give up for it was his love. I took my hands away from my face to rub at my arms, suddenly very aware of the cold, stony grass I sat on. I'd had the respect of those around me for most of my life, but I'd never known what it felt like to be loved. To be respected is a very fine thing, but to be loved is a feeling that's nearly indescribable. To know that you mean something to someone, that his eyes will light up when you appear, that the love you feel for him is matched and returned—that if you should die it would make a difference. To die is not particularly upsetting, every-one gets to do it at one time or another, but to die all alone, with no one to care—I'd always believed that the loneli-ness would be unbearable, that there would be an awareness of it even after the brain generating the awareness of mind no longer functioned. Once again I'd gotten what I wanted, the respect I'd felt I couldn't do without, and I couldn't say I hadn't earned it. I'd earned it, all right, and everything else besides.

"We prepare to depart, Terril," Dallan said, stopping to my right with Cinnan a few steps behind him. "You had best rise to your feet now, and go to Tammad."

"I do not mean to continue on with you, Dallan," I answered, making no effort to look up at him, unsurprised by the decision I'd made without knowing it. "I will remain here a while before beginning the journey back."

"*Wenda*, you cannot remain in these mountains alone," Dallan protested, seeing nothing of the way the barbarian paused briefly in what he was doing near his pack *seetar* before continuing. He'd heard what I'd said, but he no longer cared enough even to consider arguing with me.

"And to return alone would be impossible," Cinnan added his contribution, coming forward to stand beside Dallan. "You would have no shelter and no food, no *seetar* to ride and no protection. You must continue on with us."

"I cannot," I said, still looking at nothing but their feet and legs, wishing they would hurry through their token protests and then leave me alone. There was a terrible loneliness waiting for me, but I was abruptly in something of a hurry to get started with it.

"The woman may ride with you, Dallan," the barbarian put in without turning, still completely wrapped up in what he was doing. "As you and she are *helid*, there should be little objection to the arrangement."

"You wish her to ride with me?" Dallan responded, the surprise in his voice covering all traces of the reluctance he surely felt. "For what reason is she not to remain with you?"

"Best would be that she become accustomed to being with others," the barbarian answered, finally finishing with the pack beast and moving toward his mount. "In preparation for the unbanding, of course."

He swung up into the saddle and immediately moved out toward the road, continuing on down without a single backward look. I thought of all the times I'd wanted him to do that, all the times I'd wanted him to be willing to unband me. I hadn't known it would be so easy to accomplish; all I'd had to do was want his bands with every cell in my body.

"I have no understanding of what occurs here," Cinnan said, sounding vaguely annoyed. "Ever have I considered myself a man of adequate intelligence, yet do I fail to grasp what now occurs about me. Perhaps I have been robbed of the intelligence I thought was mine."

"Should that be so, then the malady you suffer from is mine as well," Dallan returned, frowning sternly. "I, too, have no understanding of what occurs, yet do I mean to know. Up on your feet, *wenda*, and come with me. As you have been left in my charge, you will ride with me till we camp for the darkness."

"I have already said I will no longer accompany this party," I told him, finding that my right fingers had gone to my left wristband. "Do you believe he will be insulted if I retain his bands for a short while longer?"

"Terril, I cannot fathom his intent to unband you," Dallan said with puzzlement tinged with hurt, crouching so that he might put his hand to my face. "Was there a thing that passed between you which Cinnan and I are unaware of?"

"You saw what passed between us," I said, finding no comfort in the touch of his hand as I once might have. "As he said, I bested him; is it any wonder he no longer feels love for me? I have become a monster in his eyes, the monster I am in truth. Best would be that you leave me now, for monsters are well known for turning on those nearest them without provocation. I would not wish to see you harmed."

I got to my feet and walked away from his stare, back uphill to where I'd stood when I'd decided I couldn't live without respect. The sun was trying hard to warm everything beneath it, but its efforts were as weak and inadequate as mine. I'd been trying for a small taste of life beside the man I loved; I hadn't thought the taste would be quite that small.

"Terril, your words hold no meaning for us," Dallan protested, and from the sound of his voice I could tell he'd foolishly followed me. "We have no fear that you will cause us harm."

"You are fools, then," I said, turning abruptly to look at him. Dallan stood perhaps three or four feet away, Cinnan a couple of feet behind him, and with the slope of the ground neither one of them stood as high above me as he usually did. "Wise men never fail to fear monsters, and take themselves from them as quickly as possible. Would you prefer to be harmed?"

"You see yourelf as something objectionable because of the skill you exhibited?" Dallan asked, showing no insult at being called a fool. "Because of the power which was shown, we are now to consider you a monster?"

"Should that be so, you must consider us the same," Cinnan put in, coming forward to stand beside Dallan. "For what reason do you fail to show fear of *us*?"

The two of them were staring straight at me, their blue eyes showing no attempt at evasion, no indication that they weren't speaking the absolute truth. I could see that even with my shield closed, the shield I'd closed as soon as Tammad had mounted up and ridden away, but what I couldn't see was what they were getting at.

"I fail to understand the meaning of your words," I said,

looking from one to the other. "You are neither of you monsters, therefore is there scarcely a need to fear you."

"You believe there are none upon this world who fear *l'lendaa*?" Dallan asked, his tone as sober as it had been, his manner as unrelenting. "A *l'lenda* is one with skill in battle, one whose sword skill sets him apart. For what reason do you not tremble in fear against the possibility of my drawing my sword and striking you down?"

"You—would not do such a thing," I answered, upset by how grim the two of them looked. "To be *l'lenda* is to be possessed of honor, and honor would not permit the striking down of one who was unarmed. You cannot be thought of as monsters simply because of the skill you possess."

"And yet you would have us see you so for the same reason," Dallan pursued, taking a step forward. "You are a monster who might easily cause us harm, therefore are we to fear you. Strike then, monster, for we do not fear you, nor do we mean to leave you be."

"Indeed," said Cinnan, also stepping closer. "Strike, monster, and end us with your skill and power."

I looked at the two of them, trying their best to deny what I'd said, knowing they really were fools. All I had to do was lower my shield and reach out to them, and they'd know the same thing. I wanted to raise my head defiantly and show them how wrong they were, but for some reason I couldn't. I felt very small and very hurt, and I just couldn't do that to anyone again. I looked at them one last time with my fingers to my wristband, then simply and silently turned away. I meant to continue on up the trail, but a big hand came to my shoulder to stop me.

"You will not cause us harm for the same reason we would not harm you, *wenda*," Dallan said, his voice now grown softer. "As you are unarmed before us, so are we before you. You, too, have a sense of honor which disallows unprovoked attack."

"Do not speak that word to me!" I snapped, pulling away from his hand before whirling to face him. "It was the pursuit of honor which caused me to do as I did, and brought about the loss I now face! Of what use is such a thing as honor, when it brings only pain and loss?''

"It was not honor which caused your loss, sister," Dallan said, still looking at me soberly. "The true cause continues to remain beyond our understanding, yet was it certainly not honor."

"Perhaps—it was no other thing," Cinnan said slowly, his eyes focused inward with thought, one finger rubbing absently at his face. "To be defeated is no easy thing to accept, least of all for one who is *denday*. To be defeated by a woman would cut most deeply, and despite his strength Tammad is no more than a man. Perhaps his pride and sense of honor have been wounded."

"Such a possibility had not occurred to me," Dallan admitted with a frown, considering the suggestion. "Should your thought be truth, what are we to do?"

"There is naught to do," I answered before Cinnan could speak, feeling even worse than I had. "His love for me has turned to hatred, clearly shown in his intention to unband me. How great a fool I was, to thoughtlessly cause such a thing."

I looked down in misery at the band I was stroking, nearly sick to my stomach because of the stupid thing I'd done, but Dallan made a sound of annoyance.

"You must cease this wallowing in accusation and self-pity, *wenda*," he said, bringing my startled attention to a pair of equally annoyed eyes. "No matter the pleasure you derive from it, you must recall that your challenge to Tammad was accepted—and accepted with amusement. All of us have known defeat at one time or another, yet were we scarcely to be found sulking about at the audacity of the one who defeated us. One does not *dare* to find victory over another, one merely finds it; victory itself is the justification for challenge."

"And a man must truly be a fool to believe he will find victory in a battle in which another's skill far exceeds his own," Cinnan put in, looking almost as annoyed as Dallan. "The *drin* Dallan and I have both experienced your power, and in no manner would we consider accepting a challenge with the weapon of the mind. I, at least, had not at first seen the matter in such a light, yet is it all too obvious when thought upon. Despite Tammad's newly discovered abilities, he should not have thought himself able to best you.''

''Clearly has memory of the battle you fought in the resting place of the Sword escaped him,'' Dallan said with a nod of agreement. ''The strength required to best a man in such a way must truly be great, yet did he assume that his own strength was greater. Above all things a *l'lenda* must be confident, yet not to the extent of foolishness.''

''But it was not my place to humiliate him,'' I protested, beginning to feel very confused. ''His skill with a sword is far greater than mine, yet he made no effort to humiliate *me* by giving challenge in such a way. It was thoughtless and inconsiderate of me to do what he would not.''

''Did you at any time deny recognition of his skill?'' Dallan asked, still not very happy with me. ''In the absence of denial, he had no cause to give you challenge. Your skill, however, was indeed denied, therefore was challenge the sole avenue left open to you. To prove one's skill is not the same as giving deliberate humiliation.''

''Then—he had no true cause to punish me,'' I said, struggling to break free of the confusion. ''His punishment was a denial of my skill.''

''No, *wenda*, you fail to grasp the point,'' Cinnan said with a sigh of forced patience. ''As you wear Tammad's bands, it is his duty to give you punishment. Even should he know he will be struck down for it, he is bound to make the attempt. His error lay in refusing to acknowledge your skill, a skill we are all of us well aware of.''

''Then you believe I should continue to be punished, no matter the power I have exhibited,'' I said, staring at Cinnan while exasperation added to the confusion. ''You see no reason for such a doing to be discontinued.''

''Certainly not,'' Cinnan agreed, his attitude firm and without a trace of doubt. ''The skill you possess demands and merits the respect of men, yet do you continue to be *wenda*. You, too, must give respect, and obedience as well, else may you confidently look forward to punishment.''

He turned then to say something to Dallan, but I was too upset to bother listening. I turned around and wandered away from them, my mind spinning and my emotions flying in all directions at once. Rimilian men were impossible, every one of them, and I couldn't understand how they could think that way. They were willing to give me respect for my abilities, but beyond that would give nothing at all. I was a female, a *wenda*, and punishment season was always open.

I was trying to stomp through the unhappy grass, but the stones were hurting my feet and another thought suddenly came to stop my upward progress. What about Tammad? He was right to be upset with me for hurting him, but was Dallan just as right? He hadn't only accepted my challenge he'd added a side bet, and then he'd tried to win by cheating. When he lost he rode away to sulk, too put out over his defeat to even stay around and talk about it. And why had he said he was going to unband me? Was that the extent of the love I'd thought was so deep and endless?

"Come, Terril, I will explain the decision Cinnan and I have agreed on as we ride," Dallan called, looking up toward me where I stood. "We must find the reasons for Tammad's actions, and you will assist us."

"How much clearer might his actions be?" I asked, reluctantly moving downhill toward him. "He no longer wishes me in his bands."

"Should his defeat be the sole reason for this, you will be well rid of him," Dallan stated, taking my arm as I reached him, his eyes hard. "When a man feels true love for a woman, he will forgive her anything, even superiority in some matter. Should his pride be too sensitive to allow this, he is best left alone with that pride."

I was then gently propelled toward the *seetarr*, Dallan's heavy annoyance aimed elsewhere than at me. Cinnan seemed to be shaking his head in disgust, but also not with me. I bent briefly to retrieve the fur I'd dropped before continuing on to the mounts, but I was now almost as upset as I had been earlier. At some point my shield had dissolved to leave noth-

ing but the curtain, and the grim determination filling both of
the men made me very uneasy.

It wasn't long before we were back on the road, and I rode
astride in front of Dallan, the fur wrapped around me. Although the cold had begun to get a grip on me again I hadn't
wanted the fur, but Dallan had refused to let me ride without
it. His arms around me kept me in the saddle while I held to
the fur, and this time I had no trouble seeing where we were
going. Downhill was where we were going, ever downhill,
without any sign of Tammad's passage that *I* could see. I
kept having the feeling that he would keep going rather than
stop at some point, and I would never see him again. I didn't
expect things to ever be the same between us, but I couldn't
bear the thought of not seeing him a final time.

The sun was nearly gone before we found the place Tammad
had chosen for a campsite. Cinnan and Dallan had been
growing more and more annoyed the longer we had to ride,
and the sight of the barbarian's *camtah* did little to calm that
annoyance. Dallan had told me that he and Cinnan had
decided on a plan of action, and all I had to do was remember
not to interfere. He had refused to go into more detail than
that, which had added to the confusion whirling around inside
of me. I wasn't sure about how I should feel, and the closer
we got to the barbarian the more unsure I became. I'd known
where he'd stopped for some time before we reached it, but I
hadn't said anything to Dallan and Cinnan.

The two men rode their *seetarr* to a spot near Tammad's
before dismounting, and when Dallan lifted me to the ground I
had to stop near the barbarian's mount to calm his distress
and outrage. As far as the big black *seetar* was concerned, I
had no business riding anywhere but on him, and he couldn't
understand why I had. Maybe "refused to understand" would
be a more accurate phrase, but I wasn't in the mood to go
into long, involved explanations. I let him feel my apology
for upsetting him, and he accepted the apology with a small
snort of pleasure. He seemed to feel the error wouldn't be
repeated, but I couldn't say the same.

Dallan and Cinnan unburdened their *seetarr* and then

began to set up their *camtahh,* and to look at the barbarian you would believe we were all invisible. He sat in front of the fire he had built, roasting a large piece of meat, more intent on what he was doing than on what was going on around him. I stood off to one side, paying a great deal of attention to what my two traveling companions were doing, very glad that the cold wasn't nearly as bad as it had been even that morning. The fire would then have been the only really warm spot around, and although that was the place I most wanted to be, I couldn't quite find the courage to go over there.

When Dallan finished with his tent he went to the fire, glanced at the roasting meat, then settled himself on the ground with a small grunt. The barbarian was wrapped in a thick, brooding calm, and didn't come out of it until Dallan made a noise in his throat.

"The meat will soon be done," Tammad told him with an air of preoccupation, obviously ready to sink back into his mental stewing. "I trust the afternoon was as uneventful for you as it was for me?"

"Likely even more so for us," Dallan agreed with a smooth unconcern he wasn't entirely feeling. "As you mean to unband the woman and have already given her over into my care for the journey, I take it you will have no objection to her sharing my furs this darkness?"

I hadn't expected Dallan to say that, and I wanted Tammad to refuse as he had the night before, wanted him to stride over to me and pull me furiously and possessively into his arms; instead he held very still for a moment at the abrupt, unexpected question, his mind whirling with agitation, and then he shrugged.

"What objection might I have?" he asked, still staring into the fire. "Should you also wish to band her, my own bands may be returned with the new light."

My throat had been tightening up at the way he'd been ignoring me, but when I heard what he had to say I sobbed once, dropped the fur, then stumbled away into the growing darkness. He really wanted to have nothing further to do with me, didn't want to come near me again even to retrieve his bands. There was such a terrible pain inside me that I thought I would die of it, then I began to pray that I would. No matter what Dallan said it was *my* fault that he didn't want me, and I felt uglier and more grotesque than I ever had in my life. I was a monster, and no one could love a monster.

I ran a short way downhill until I was well away from the light of the fire, sobbing raggedly, then stopped to fold to the ground with the rock at my back. I'd been trying not to be such a weepy infant, trying to be as strong as possible to make my *hamak* proud, but the tears running down my cheeks were tears of pain, an agony I'd never have the strength to overcome. The ground was hard and cold and the grass stiff and damp, but I lay curled up on my side without caring about any of that. If only it was just a bad dream, my mind kept saying, if only it wasn't real. But it was real, and not a dream, and nothing would be able to change that.

"You had best return now, *wenda*," a quiet voice said out of the darkness, a calm shadow coming up to loom at the side of the road. "Dallan insists that I deliver you without bands, and now waits impatiently by the fire. Once he has banded you I will depart, and you will no longer find the need to run from my presence."

I looked up at his towering outline, hearing the deadness of his voice and feeling the same in his mind. He had absolutely no interest in doing anything other than unbanding me, no object to his entire life other than that. I closed my eyes at the stabbing I felt again in my chest, totally unable to speak, wishing I could will every organ in my body to stop functioning. Most people can continue on if their life mates are taken from them, and I knew that if I made the effort, I could, too. But I, like that small number of others, had no wish to continue on, not without the one who makes life worth living.

"Have you heard me, *wenda*?" he asked, still standing in the same place. "Let us return now so that I may be gone as soon as possible."

Gone as soon as possible. That idea was so very warming and attractive in the chilling dark. I lay huddled on the ground, the short, stiff grass stabbing at my cheek, my gaze seeking again and finding the giant dark shadow standing not far from me. Everything was growing hazy and soft around the edges, comforting like the thickest of furs, vague like the onset of drugged sleep. Farewell, my love, I will never forget you, not even in the vastness of forever. Without me your life will be full and happy; without you mine is already done.

5

"Terril, waken," the voice insisted, an accompaniment to the hands that were shaking me. "You must come awake now, *wenda*. You must return."

"Go 'way," I mumbled, moving around on something soft. I didn't want to wake up the way the voice was insisting, I wanted to do something else, but I couldn't quite remember what that something else was.

"Her mind is confused, yet it rouses," another voice said, one that sounded vastly relieved. "I cannot comprehend for what reason she has done this."

"Surely did I believe your knowledge of *wendaa* to be greater than that of a boy," the first voice returned, angry and deliberately insulting. "What man would fail to know the reason his woman attempted to take her own life?"

"The *drin* Dallan forgets that soon the woman will no longer be mine," the second voice answered stiffly, offended but trying not to show it. "She wishes to be free even of the sight of me, and for this she cannot be faulted. Replace my bands with yours, and then I will go."

"For what reason would you believe she no longer has deep feelings for you?" a third voice asked, curiosity and confusion well mixed. "I heard no words spoken to that effect."

"With one such as she, words are unnecessary," the second voice said, painful hurt hovering just beyond the edges. "She attempted to conceal her disgust and loathing at my failure, yet was I able to perceive them in her mind. So great were these feelings that she even refused to look upon me, a thing you both saw with your own eyes. She would have remained behind sooner than travel the longer in my company, and that I could not allow. I will not see her come to harm through my failure as a man."

"Should what you have said be so, then you will find little difficulty in replying to my query," the first voice said immediately, most of the anger gone from it. "For what reason has she attempted to take her own life?"

"I had not known such a thing was possible," the second voice said, a shudder of near-catastrophe in him. "Had her mind not opened to me when consciousness fled, I would not have been able to deny her will with my own. Clearly does she now find such horror in my company, that she would sooner seek death than be forced to endure it even for a short while."

"Once I knew a *wenda* who loathed the very sight of me," the first voice remarked, a musing to its tone. "So greatly did my presence outrage her that she would hurl whatever was about directly at my head whenever I appeared. Not once, however, do I recall her attempting her own life to escape me. My life she would have willingly taken—yet her own?"

"Also does it appear from the woman's face that she has wept," the third voice put in, filling the silence left by the second. "I had not known that detestation and loathing would bring tears, even to a *wenda* so lacking in fire as this one."

"Have you taken leave of your senses, man?" the second voice demanded, suddenly outraged. "To see this woman as one without fire is to see naught of the world due to blindness!"

"It was scarcely Cinnan who presented her as unspirited," the first voice said, a hardness to it now. "It was not he who declared her unable to look upon one she loathed, nor was it he who saw her search for death as the sole manner of avoiding one she detested—one she knew would soon be gone.

Clearly does one in this *camtah* consider her not only unspirited but mindless."

"Your words have no meaning," the second voice protested, his outrage mixing with confusion. "For what other reason would the woman seek her own life?"

"Perhaps for the reason that she believes her *sadendrak*'s love lost to her because of the terrible creature she has become," the first voice answered, a bleakness beside the hardness. "Perhaps for the reason that he has proven his lack of love by declaring his intention to unband her, and then attempting to do that very thing."

"Monster was the word used by her," the third voice said, painfully quiet. "So great was her horror at what she had done that she could not face any of us. Also did she declare that none could feel love for such a monster."

"It was self-loathing and self-detestation that you felt in her, my friend," the first voice said to the stunned silence in the second. "Her powers are great indeed, yet does she lack the necessary training to allow her to take pleasure from victory. The strength to face challenge is hers without doubt, yet *wendaa* are seldom taught to steel their hearts to the necessities of battle. Your defeat touched you so strongly, then, that you were unable to see this?"

"Defeat?" the second voice asked, the mind behind it whirling like a wind of destruction. "Indeed was it a defeat, yet was it even more a failure. The woman requires strength in a man, else is she unable to consider him a man. Ever before have I been able to call up the necessary strength, yet this time naught appeared save failure. What woman of strength and power would wish a man with none?"

"You castigate yourself for failing to have a power to match hers?" the first voice demanded, his incredulity nearly drowning out the painful inadequacy of the second. "Now do I truly give thanks that your new-found abilities are not mine, for what man would wish to become a fool? And one, moreover, who has taken to seeing his own beliefs as truth, rather than looking upon the world as it is?"

"You forget yourself," the second voice came back coldly,

deeply insulted. "No man may speak to me so, save with a sword in his fist."

"Sword?" echoed the first, pretending to great surprise. "One without strength of any sort would consider the use of a sword? One who is no other thing than a failure would think to face a prince and warrior?"

"The woman has ever seemed to suffer from deep feelings of inadequacy," the third voice mused, ignoring the crackling anger flashing between the other two. "Think you there is a link between the power and such feelings, one which must be watched closely to keep it from affecting a man's usual reason?"

"More does it seem a matter of misinterpretation," said the first voice, his mind immediately diving into the question. "The woman feels what others do, yet does she see those feelings in light of her own. Her difference touches her profoundly, and many of her actions seem to arise from that. Tell me: would you have ridden from her as you did had you not touched her thoughts?"

"No," the second voice admitted, a glum depression having taken the place of insult. "This new power twists me about, and although I attempt to keep myself from its use, the thing is more readily decided upon than done. More easily is it able to unman me than a life threat, and I know not how it may be conquered."

"Allowing it its way with you will not give you victory over it," the first voice said, refusing to show even a hint of compassion. "You must learn again to look upon all things as once you did, and harden your heart to necessity as she is unable to do. The woman requires the strength you deem inadequate, finding it more than sufficient for her purposes. Will you refuse her your aid?"

"For what reason must love make fools of otherwise able men?" the second voice asked, beginning to sound disgusted with itself. "Of what use is it, when it blinds a man to what occurs about him? I had thought to aid the woman by departing from her, and instead nearly drove her to self-destruction. I must apply myself to the lessons she teaches, so that I will not falter a second time. I will have the strength she demands, else shall I fall to never rise again.''

''Apparently love also causes a man to speak strangely,'' the first voice observed, clearly amused. ''You believe it likely that another failure to withstand her power will cause you to fall and never again to rise?''

''Had you felt what I did, brother, you would not find the need to ask,'' the second voice said with a rueful chuckle, now aware of how melodramatic it had just sounded. ''Never before has her power seemed so overwhelming, so undeniable. It will take a good deal to resist it, yet do I mean to do no other thing.''

''A more modest aim, yet surely more fitting to one who is *l'lenda*,'' the first voice said, and then it paused before adding, ''The *denday* Tammad seems now to have returned to himself, do you not agree, *wenda*?''

I had been lying there with my eyes closed and completely unmoving, but Dallan had had no trouble realizing that I was fully awake. The lack of surprise in Cinnan's mind showed he'd known the same, which left only the barbarian. He alone started then began to move to me, but even the loving encouragement in his mind didn't supply me with the nerve to open my eyes and look at them.

''Indeed,'' I agreed in a heavy voice, wishing I were still lying on stiff, wet grass instead of furs which gave such comfort. ''Indeed has the *denday* Tammad returned to himself.''

''And you have done the same, *hama*,'' the barbarian said, putting one hand to my face. ''For what reason do you not sit up and open your arms to me?''

''For the reason that I'm too disgusted with myself,'' I answered in Centran, turning my face to the left to escape the touch of his hand. ''I've really managed to ruin your life completely, haven't I?''

''In what manner do you believe you have brought ruin to my life?'' he asked, still sticking with Rimilian, the calm in him faintly tinged with upset but not uncertainty. ''To find and band the woman he has ever sought may scarcely be considered a man's ruin.''

"But the powers of an empath can be," I countered, turning completely onto my left side. "If I hadn't let you band me you never would have found out about your own powers, and would not now have to fight your way back to normalcy. You said you were going to unband me. Do it."

"*Wenda*, I cannot unband you," he answered, a gentle strength in the hand that followed to touch my arm. "Only the belief that you no longer cared for me allowed me to consider such a thing to begin with, and that consideration brought greater pain than I knew was possible. As I cannot leave you, will you instead attempt to leave me?"

The question was entirely neutral, the calm in his mind telling me nothing, the panic in my own mind saying it all. I tried to talk myself into it, tried to convince myself that it was for his own good, but all my life I'd been encouraged to be selfish, and I couldn't seem to break the habit. Instead of answering immediately I sat up and looked at him, then shook my head.

"I can't," I said, finding it impossible to keep from putting my fingertips to his face. "If I had any honor at all I would change the love you feel to complete indifference, then watch while you sold me to someone else and rode away. That's what I ought to do—but I can't."

"Most certainly you cannot," he agreed with a laugh, lifting me off the fur and into his lap. "It would not be possible for you to change my love to another thing, and even should it be possible, you have not my permission to do so. Such a doing would not be honor but dishonor."

"Are you again concerned with honor, *wenda*?" Dallan asked from where he sat to the left of the furs, close to the tent flaps. A single candle burned in the *camtah*, and Cinnan crouched farther to the right, beyond Tammad. The *drin* of Gerleth was staring at me in disapproval.

"For what reason should I not be concerned with honor?" I asked, switching back to Rimilian. "I know well enough how little of it there is in remaining with one who would do far better with none of my sort to plague him, and yet do I

122

nevertheless remain. Would you do the same, or would you have the courage to go?"

"I would certainly do what was best, Terril," he said, suddenly watching his words very carefully. "For you, best would be to remain with your *memabrak*, obedient to his will."

"And yet, such a best is scarcely honorable," I pursued, putting my arms as far around the barbarian as possible and laying my head on his chest, all the while continuing to hold Dallan's gaze. "I have discovered that the one I care most for in all the worlds there are would fare far better if I were not beside him. Also do I know that the power is mine to free him from his love for me. Should I use that power it will be his will to ride from me and never look back, and yet should I do so, life will no longer have meaning for me. Which will am I to obey, Dallan? Which would you obey?"

"It matters not which he would obey," came the words from the chest I lay on, so close to being a growl that the anger in the mind above was an unnecessary addition. Dallan had developed a frustrated look and hadn't known what to say, but Tammad took care of that for him. "The *drin* Dallan has not been commanded to a certain obedience, the while the *wenda* Terril has indeed been so commanded. The choice has not been given you, *wenda*, only the command. Will you obey, or will you be punished?"

Only then did I realize that his arms were around me as I held to him, circling me a good deal more firmly than I was able to accomplish. I could then also feel his eyes on me, and the way his mind had hardened. I knew I was still somewhat confused, but I should have been able to follow what was happening a lot more closely than I was.

"I cannot understand your meaning," I said, lifting my head to look up into his eyes. "After what has occurred, you cannot be speaking of punishment again. Have I not proven myself able to halt you? Have I not earned respect in the manner you demanded?"

"Indeed you have, *wenda*," he agreed, lifting one hand to smooth my hair. "The respect that was earned is yours,

freely given as was not earlier done. You have proven yourself fully able to halt me, yet do you no longer have my
permission to use the power of your mind against me. Will
you touch me so without my permission?''

He looked at me with nothing but calm, but I could feel
what was waiting behind that calm, something I had never
quite been able to stand up to. He knew I had the ability to
stop any punishment even before it began, but he had calmly
decided not to let me use that ability. It was outrageous, but
he was forcing me to obey him again!

''You miserable barbarian!'' I hissed, hitting him so hard
with a fist in the side that it actually registered faintly
somewhere at the back of his mind. ''You know I'm at
the point where I can't bring myself to touch anyone without their permission! You're cheating to make me obey
you!''

''Indeed,'' he said with a laugh filled with amusement, his
grin so wide his face was in danger of splitting. ''A man must
use what is available to him if he is to hold his own with his
wenda. Is the thought of parting from me perhaps becoming
more attractive?''

I glared at him in disgust for a minute, seriously considering what my answer should be, but I didn't have much
choice there either.

''No, it isn't,'' I said with very little grace, knowing I
would probably be stuck with that answer for the rest of my
life. ''You're a beast and I hate you, but you have me
trapped.''

''And ever shall I keep the walls of that trap unbreachable,''
he murmured, putting his hand under my chin to raise my
face. ''Without you beside me, *wenda*, I have not the will to
go on, therefore shall I never free you.''

He lowered his lips to mine, then, giving me tenderness
rather than passion, and I couldn't help but think again how
much better he would do without a monster at his side. He
could have the will to go on without me, if only *I* had the
courage. . . .

"Are we as yet prepared to take our meal?" Dallan asked in the middle of my beautiful kiss, the plaintiveness in his voice causing Tammad to raise his head with a laugh, and Cinnan to chuckle. "Should the meat not have burned itself to ashes in the fire, I will give fervent and very sincere thanks."

"And should it indeed have been burned, your saddle *seetar* will give thanks," I told him, annoyed that he'd broken things up so quickly. "Already the poor beast weeps and struggles to bear you."

"Your observation is scarcely amusing, *wenda*," he said with a stare of annoyance while Tammad and Cinnan both laughed aloud. Dallan had been eating everything in sight ever since we'd started the trip, but he was still about as far from fat as you can get. His giant frame could have carried a good deal more weight than it currently did, and he still would have been trim, hard and well muscled.

"An urgent need for a great deal of food has been mine since my time as a slave in Aesnil's palace," he went on, shifting to an injured, put-upon air of silent bravery. "The healer tells me such a happening is not unusual and will soon disappear, yet am I to cater to it the while it remains. Would you have me disobey the healer?"

"Certainly not," Cinnan said rather gravely, only his mind showing his amusement. "A man who wishes to regain his health and strength must ever obey a healer."

"Indeed," the barbarian agreed, also straight-faced, his hand on my neck beneath my hair. "We will soon be out of these mountains, therefore will it be possible to replenish our ravaged stores with little difficulty. I would, however, were I you, keep myself from that which is carried for the *seetarr*. Their understanding and compassion is most often great, yet not when they wish to feed."

"I have *not* eaten *that* great an amount," Dallan stated as he glared at all of us, annoyed again at being teased. "As the matter disturbs you all so, I shall be the first to hunt for us as soon as we are down out of this pass."

"It would be best to locate something large," I suggested,

also keeping my face expressionless. "So that there will be some meat left upon it by your return to the camp, you understand."

My comment was too much for Tammad and Cinnan. The two of them threw their heads back and roared, nearly weeping tears of laughter at the thought of Dallan's nibbling at his kill during the ride back to camp. Dallan looked at them in disgust, glared at me in disapproval, then dropped a subject he was beginning to find awkward by turning and leaving the tent.

By the time the rest of us made it outside, the meat was ready to eat. Tammad had put it aside away from the fire when he'd come after me, so it hadn't been burned after all. Dallan divided it with his knife, very deliberately taking the largest piece for himself, and the other two men spent almost as much time chuckling as eating. I'd been faintly surprised that no one had yelled at me for starting to tease Dallan and then continuing with it, but then it came to me that that had to be part of the respect I'd earned. I'd shown what I was capable of and had been given full marks for it, and was now permitted to joke with the others as though I were one of them. It felt good to have that sort of freedom, but I still didn't like what I'd had to do to earn it. I sat on the ground near the fire, my arms wrapped about me against the chill of the darkness, feeling the quiet background emotions of the others filter through the curtain over my mind. Why was it necessary to knock Rimilians down and stomp on them before they became willing to give respect? Why couldn't they just take someone's word for it the way civilized people did?

"Ah, an excellent meal," Dallan observed from where he sat, patting the material of his shirt that covered his flat middle. "I believe I shall now retire to my *camtah*. Come, *wenda*."

I looked at him blankly as he got to his feet, wondering what he was talking about, feeling the same reaction in Tammad, who sat to my left.

"For what reason do you summon my *wenda*, Dallan?" he asked, his voice puzzled. "I had thought to sit awhile by the fire before retiring to my furs, and the woman may do the same.''

"Your intentions are certainly yours to determine, Tammad," Dallan replied with pleasantness and amusement, his mind chuckling. "The woman, however, was earlier given to me for the darkness. Have you forgotten my request—and your own complete agreement to it?"

The barbarian stared up at Dallan with stunned shock, clearly remembering their earlier exchange when he thought he would be leaving forever, but I was more frantic. I didn't *want* to spend the night with Dallan, I wanted to be with Tammad, letting his arms and lips and body help me to forget the doubts I was still feeling.

"*Hamak*, tell him it was a mistake," I said at once to the barbarian, turning fast to put my hands on his arm. "Tell him it was a misunderstanding, and that I don't have to go with him. You know how I feel about that, and you said you'd think about my side of it before doing it again. Please, Tammad."

"*Hama*, I cannot," he answered heavily, speaking Centran as I had while he looked down into my eyes. "I agreed to the request which was made, and now cannot retrieve that agreement. I must honor my word, and you, too, must honor it. You must go to him and give him pleasure."

"I hate the word 'honor,' " I told him, furious that he felt bound to do such a thing to me, turning again to glare up at Dallan. He knew how I felt about being given to other men, and was deliberately trying to humiliate me.

"I believe you have been told you must accompany me, Terril," the beast said mildly, grinning as he offered me a hand. "My *camtah* will be fully warmed this darkness, and other things as well. Come, now."

I threw the barbarian a last-hope glance as I got to my feet, but his emotions told me I was wasting my time. He was disappointed that I would not be there to give *him* pleasure that night, but he was already shrugging off the disappointment with a sense of, "Well, what can you do?" Handing women around was a usual thing to those barbarians, but that didn't make me hate it any less.

Dallan lit a candle in the fire, then led the way to his *camtah*. By the time I bent through the tent flaps he was already setting the candle firmly on a brace, and then he turned to me with a grin.

"How odd that your excellent sense of humor is no longer in evidence, *wenda*," he said, looking down at me as he began to remove his swordbelt. "Have you no other amusing observations it would please you to make?"

"So you've taken me to serve you because of feelings of insult," I grumbled, finally seeing the point. "Do you also mean to take the others to your furs?"

"The others are by no means as attractive as you, *wenda*," he answered with a laugh, keeping his eyes on me as he put his sword aside. "I shall therefore allow *you* to make reparation for the group."

"And if I should refuse?" I asked, seething with the unfairness of it all. "You feel desire for me now, yet the state need not continue."

"I am aware of the fact that you are able to take the desire from me," he said with a calm nod, reaching for the bottom of his shirt to pull it off over his head. "Should one face attack, one is well within one's rights to raise a skillful defense, and I shall ever recall the time you did indeed take my desire. And yet, your *memabrak* has given me his word. Will you shame him with a refusal of either body *or* mind?"

He tossed the shirt away and simply stood looking down at me, his fingers on his hips, his blue eyes calm, his mind comfortable and completely undisturbed. He wasn't in the least afraid of what I might do to him, and that despite the fact that he'd had more than one taste of what an empath's self-defense could consist of. I suddenly began feeling very strange, an emotion I couldn't define flooding all through me, one I had, until then, felt only with Tammad. It wasn't love or anything like that, and it made me very uncomfortable.

"You know well enough that I will not shame him," I muttered, looking down at my twisting fingers at my waist.

"You may do as you will, yet shall I find only a small part of the pleasure I find with him. I have no desire to be here, and will not lie with a pretense of eagerness."

"That is only as it should be, *wenda*," he said gently, putting his hand under my chin to raise my face to him. "No man takes another man's woman with the belief that her pleasure will be as full with him as it is with her chosen. And yet do I sense an oddness here, centering about your great concern to speak the truth. Can it be you seek to shame not Tammad but me, with the intimation that I intrude between two who should be in the arms of no others save each other? Am I now to release you from your obligation, and gallantly return you to the side of your *hamak*?"

The amusement in his mind was about of the same intensity as the twinkle in his eyes, and as dim as the tent was it still wasn't too dim for him to see the sudden blush in my cheeks. I might not have been free to touch his mind, but there was nothing to keep me from trying to manipulate him with words—nothing, that is, but that damnable talent of his for seeing through to the truth of things no matter how little data he had to work with.

"I expect nothing in the way of gallantry from Rimilian beasts!" I snapped, jerking my face out of his hand. "You seek only to humiliate me in revenge for what was said of you, and I shall never forgive you for taking your revenge only upon me!"

"But I do not take revenge only upon you," he said, laughing, suddenly throwing his arms around me and bearing me down to his sleeping furs with him. "My brother Cinnan's yearning for Aesnil has given his body the belief that he has not had a woman for days without number, and seeing you sent to me was very painful for him. My brother Tammad, on the other hand, had wished to do no more than hold his *wenda*, to remove the memory of nearly having lost her. Retention of that memory will do best for him, I believe, therefore have I callously taken you from him for this darkness."

"How do you know all this?" I demanded, immediately

checking the minds of those we'd left outside. Cinnan sat moping at the fire with his mind groaning, his body so badly in need that he should have been up in flames. Tammad, however, was sunk deep in thought, and there was a definite emptiness shaping and tinging those thoughts. It was painful for me to sense him feeling that way, and I automatically began struggling against the wide arms holding me, trying to get free to go to him.

"No, *wenda*, to spare him the pain would be no service," Dallan insisted, holding me tighter against my struggles. "A man must learn to know the consequences of his actions, so that his decisions may be made on a basis of thought rather than feeling. No *denday* may act as hastily and thoughtlessly as Tammad has, a thing he has forgotten in the face of his new-found abilities. He must relearn the lesson of thought, Terril, and in such an instance you may not aid him."

"How do you know all of these things?" I asked again, staring up at his sober face, endlessly upset that he refused to release me. "Almost does it seem that you are able to read them as easily as I."

"Cinnan's state I know of from his own lips," Dallan said, his careful calm an obvious attempt to soothe me. "He spoke of Aesnil, referred obliquely to his needs, and from those things his condition became obvious. Tammad's feelings, too, were obvious, largely from the manner in which he bade you accompany me. His lack of anger and discomfort were clear to any with eyes, and am I not familiar with his thoughts upon what occurred between you and the difficulty he has had with his strengthening abilities? What need have I of your power, *wenda*, when these things are all so clear to me without it?"

Everything he said was completely logical, but something still seemed to be wrong with his explanations. I wanted to look into it further, question him more thoroughly, but the upset was growing in me instead of lessening, especially when I saw him look at me in a very strange way.

"And you, *wenda*, you, too, require this darkness with me," he said, rolling over to hold me down with his body while his hands smoothed my hair back, "You cannot deny that you continue to think upon the matter of aiding your *memabrak* by making it possible for him to leave you, and such a thing should not be. You must see for yourself what life would be, should he allow another to band you. You would not find it possible to deny that other save with your power, a doing which may now be beyond you. You have not yet grown to the height all *l'lendaa* must have—an inner height from which vantage point a warrior may see the pleasure in victory."

I began to protest what he'd said, tried to tell him as sincerely as possible that he was wrong, but he wasn't wrong and we both knew it. He used that night to show me what it would be like to belong to someone other than Tammad, what it would be like to be used by a man who was fond of me and had no intentions of hurting me, but who cared about little other than his own pleasure. Dallan had never before made me give him everything while he gave back almost nothing, but one thing I didn't let him take—I waited until he was asleep before I hid my face in my hands and shuddered.

6

When Dallan let me go the next morning, I had to swallow down the urge to run to the barbarian and throw myself into his arms. It had been a really terrible night, but even the dim gray half-light of dawn was bright enough to let me see clearly the facts of Rimilian life. If I ran to Tammad just as everything inside me screamed for me to do, my *memabrak* would probably challenge Dallan right on the spot. Tammad knew Dallan had used me before, and knew as well that I'd had pleasure from those uses; a man like Dallan was able to give an unbelievable amount of pleasure, as most Rimilian men were. If I hadn't had pleasure the night before it was only because Dallan hadn't wanted me to have it, and Rimilian men don't look kindly on other men who do that to their women. It might not matter to Tammad that Dallan had been trying to make a point, and I didn't care to take the chance.

The barbarian crouched beside the fire, prodding it into fuller life, his eyes and his surface thoughts seeing something other than the newborn flames. He was again calm but now there was something new, something hard and determined, and right in the middle of it was Tammad's thought-feeling of me. I wasn't sure I liked being in that position in his thoughts, but then he saw me and smiled, and everything else became unimportant.

"*Hama*, you are awake," he said, rising from his crouch and opening his arms to me. "Dallan, how went the darkness?"

"Acceptably," Dallan allowed from behind me as I tried not to move too quickly into those arms waiting for me. "Only once have I found naught of pleasure with this woman."

"Was she ill?" the barbarian asked in surprise, his mind automatically beginning to hum from the touch of my body against his. That that was the only explanation to occur to him was normal for a Rimilian, just as normal as asking only Dallan about how things had gone. I was glad not to have to be evasive to questions, but at the same time I was annoyed.

"The woman was not ill," Dallan answered, crouching down near the spreading blaze with a smile, to pick up a stick and a pice of *dimral* that waited to be warmed in the fire. "When the woman made Cinnan's capture possible by Aesnil's guard, my cousin was so pleased with her that she was given many gifts. One of the gifts given to her, at her own request, was the presence of her servant-slave in her new apartment, all clothing having been taken from him before he was chained hand and foot to the floor."

"Stripped and chained?" the barbarian repeated in outrage above my head, stiffening in insult by proxy. "At her *own* request?"

"Indeed," Dallan agreed, his mind beginning to chuckle. "I, a slave, was then forced to submit to my *dendaya*, which gave little of the pleasure usual in the use of a woman. To *be* taken apparently brings less to a man."

"Men are not born to be taken as *wendaa* are," the barbarian stated, still more than annoyed. "Such a thing should not have been attempted, not to speak of done. Had I known of this sooner, Terril, you would have been well punished for it."

"I had the right," I said with as much stubbornness as I could call up against the disapproval of the man who still held me, wishing I could throw something hard at Dallan's blond head to dislodge the increased amusement in it. "How often have you told me that ability provides the right?"

"And yet you felt it unfair that I punish you merely because I could," he came back, his mind sharpening noticeably. "Such was not the true reason for your punishment, yet you felt that it was and that such a reason was unfair. Does

133

the doing become less unfair when indulged in by *wendaa* rather than *l'lendaa*?''

"You're confusing me," I protested, raising my head from his cloth-covered chest to look up at his face. "I've never believed that ability provides the right, but you've always insisted on it. Now that *I'm* trying to use the same argument, you're switching sides."

"Terril, you must make the attempt to recall that speaking in your own tongue with others present is extremely ill-mannered," he scolded, looking down at me sober-faced. "I attempted to correct you in this without speaking of it in words, yet have I now found the words necessary. Will I next find it necessary to correct you as a child is corrected?"

"Do you find the answering of my question so difficult that you need to speak of other things rather than that?" I countered, feeling the flush of embarrassment in my cheeks over the way he had spoken to me. I knew it was rude to use Centran with Dallan and Cinnan around, but when I became upset it just seemed to slip out.

"*Wenda*, when first I told you that ability provides the right, you were not yet able to comprehend the entirety of the matter," he said with a sigh, rigidly keeping himself from pursuing the scolding he'd started. "As I recall, you were greatly incensed that I had taken use from you and had caused you to feel pleasure. Was I to tell you then that it was my ability as a warrior which provided the right, a right which allowed me to choose what unclaimed woman I wished? The right was one earned with skill and tempered by a knowledge of honor, yet you then knew naught of any rights save those which had been given you by others. Rights earned bring with them a balance of sorts, which most often allows one to see what is proper; rights merely given to one by others provide no such balance."

"I believe I shall cease doing anything of any sort," I answered, so confused that I wished I could lock myself away somewhere for a while, to try to get some glimmer of sense from what he'd said. I knew I was missing the point he was trying to make, and all the lessons in proper behavior I'd been getting lately were beginning to give me a headache.

"You may not cease participating in life, *hama*," he suggested with a laugh, looking down at me in amusement while Dallan chuckled. "Only through doing is it possible to learn, from those things which are done correctly, and those done in error. For now you may exercise such doing by taking a piece of *dimral*, and warming it for us in the fire."

"I find your bravery unparalleled, Tammad," Dallan commented, examining the meat he, himself, was warming. "My hunger is such that I dare not do the same as you, for burned *dimral* does little to satisfy the appetite."

"You are a cruel man, *drin* Dallan," I told him in a huff, resenting his comment, his amusement, and the deep chuckling he'd produced in Tammad. "When I have learned to cook with great skill, I shall be sure to use none of that skill for your benefit."

"One of advanced age often finds little interest in skilled cooking, *wenda*," he replied, glancing up at me with a grin. "When the time arrives, please consider yourself at liberty to disregard me as you like."

The miserable beast thought he was being clever, but worse than that the barbarian seemed to think the same. He nearly strangled trying to keep from laughing loud and hard, letting me go so that he could turn away to struggle in private. I put my fists on my hips, wasted a glare on each of them, then gave it up to go take care of our breakfast.

I managed to get the piece of *dimral* mostly warmed without doing more than singeing its edges, but that did not reduce the now-unexpressed but definitely still-present river of amusement around me. I was feeling so annoyed and put out over that that we were already back on the road before I noticed the only lack of unanimity among my traveling companions. Cinnan had stayed in his tent until the last possible moment, and had had to work at being polite when he'd given the other two men greeting for the new day. He'd then packed up fast without eating anything, and had returned to riding point wrapped in thick, self-made isolation. He'd pretended to ignore me completely, but was so intensely aware of my presence that the growl in his mind kept trying to snap out of his desperate control of it.

I was glad that my sitting behind the barbarian made it difficult for me to see Cinnan; feeling his mind was bad enough.

When the sun came up high enough to feel, it became clear that we were leaving the deeper cold of the pass behind us. It took a short while for me to realize that, however; most of my attention was on the lesson I was giving. Not long after we had gotten back on the road, my *memabrak* announced that he was falling behind in his learning, and we were wasting valuable time. The next thing I knew he was projecting sadness at me, doing better than he had a few days earlier, but more in intent than in technique. Sadness is one of the best practice emotions an empath can use; keeping it from sliding off the scale one way into indifference or the other way into grief takes a good deal of control, and control was primarily what Tammad lacked. We continued on down the road out of the pass with me trying to teach the barbarian control, and his first few hours of practice accomplished more than all the days we'd worked before that. He was determined to try and determined to succeed, and that made all the difference.

It was almost precisely midday when Cinnan pulled off the road for the lunch stop, which came as a real surprise to none of us. He'd been so miserably uncomfortable during the morning's ride that even Dallan had almost been able to feel it, and Tammad had had to grit his mental teeth at times to keep from being swept up in the emotions so often exploding at him. My curtain had helped to keep most of it away from me, but that wasn't to say I wasn't affected. Just because there's a light rain between you and a forest fire, doesn't mean you aren't going to sweat from the heat of the blaze.

"Something must be done," the barbarian said to Dallan in a soft voice as they both headed their *seetarr* toward Cinnan, who had stopped. "Even should he continue to find himself able to bear it, I cannot."

"At first I found the matter amusing," Dallan admitted, speaking just as softly "You are aware that there is but a single thing which may be done."

"I am indeed aware of that," Tammad answered with a sigh, faint regret in his mind. "I had hoped for further time before such a requirement would again become necessary, yet do we all do as we must.''

"One often grows accustomed to a matter viewed as distasteful, through more frequent indulgence in that matter," Dallan said, for some reason sounding as though he were commiserating with the barbarian. "When upset has spent itself, reason will bring to sight a clear view of the necessity.''

Tammad nodded his agreement with whatever Dallan had said, giving me the distinct feeling that this time they were the ones speaking an unknown langauge. I looked from Dallan, who rode to our right, to the broad, shirted back in front of me without any clear idea as to what they had agreed on, and tried to decide whether or not to ask. I usually dislike not knowing what's going on around me, but I'd discovered that sometimes you're better off that way. By then we were far enough off the road to stop, and Dallan and Tammad dismounted together. I had enough time to see that we were a short distance away from Cinnan before two big hands took me by the waist, and then I was being lifted off the saddle fur and down to the ground.

"I regret the necessity, *hama*, but there is a thing I must require of you," the barbarian said as soon as I was down, at the same time reaching for his shirt to pull it off over his head. "Cinnan is in great misery from his loss of Aesnil, and we must aid him."

"Indeed," said Dallan, coming around in front of Tammad's big black *seetar* in time to hear what the barbarian had said. "Tammad and I are unable to do this thing, therefore must it be you who does it."

"You wish *me* to aid Cinnan," I said, suddenly getting a suspicion of what they had meant. Cinnan could be relaxed and soothed with mind power, but I would have to be the one to do it, even if it got me upset; Dallan had no conscious power, and Tammad lacked the necessary control. I didn't really like the idea but, as had already been pointed out, there wasn't much choice. I looked back and forth between them, then asked, "You see no alternative to such a doing? You feel it would not be dishonorable?''

137

"How might it be dishonorable, *wenda*?" Dallan asked with a puzzled look, putting one hand to the *seetar* we all stood near. He had removed his shirt even before he'd joined us, which made his shrug more obvious. "Is such a thing not one of your purposes?"

"Perhaps you are correct," I allowed with a nod, trying to make myself believe that. If someone had a particular ability, using it could indeed be considered one of their purposes, even if the using wasn't especially pleasant for the user. "Cinnan requires aid, and we must aid him. All else must be overlooked for the nonce."

"*Hama*, your full understanding comes as a welcome surprise," the barbarian said, his mind really pleased with me, his smile warm and approving. "It is indeed Cinnan whom we must now consider, for we will soon be out of these mountains. He must not be made to continue on into the presence of others laboring beneath so great a disadvantage. I will take you to him upon the moment."

"I have no need to approach him more closely," I told the barbarian with a smile of my own, putting one hand to his arm as he reached toward me. "I am well able to do what must be done from here."

"You will do what must be done from here," Dallan echoed with a very odd look, while Tammad raised his brows to stare at me blankly. "You are indeed a talented woman, Terril, yet do I feel that talent such as that is beyond even you."

"There is truly little to it, Dallan," I said, wondering why they were behaving so strangely. "I have done the same with Lenham and Garth, and find a distance so small as this no obstacle. To be truthful, I am even able to do the same with a door closed between."

"Lenham and Garth must surely be possessed of talents unknown to the men of our world," Dallan said, switching his odd look to Tammad. "Never have I heard of one of us able to do the same."

"The talent, you must understand, was mine," I explained, trying to keep from sounding as though I were boasting.

"Though Lenham and Garth aided me, the doing was also mine."

"Wait, *wenda*," Tammad said suddenly, the strange stare disappearing abruptly. "The doing you speak of refers to your power. Lenham and Garth aided you in experimenting with your power, and you believe we wish the same done with Cinnan."

"Certainly," I agreed, for some reason disturbed that he'd made such statements. That was exactly what we'd been talking about, so why had he felt it necessary to restate the obvious?

"What a great relief," Dallan said with the odd look gone, exchanging a more amused one with the barbarian. "For a moment I feared for my self-esteem, thinking I might never again attempt that which others are able to do at a *distance*."

"At a distance," the barbarian repeated, grinning suddenly, and then he and Dallan were laughing, roaring out such high hilarity that tears began to start in their eyes. The laughter bent them almost double, making them pound on each other in absolute glee, the noon sun brightening their tanned, half-naked bodies. All *I* could do was stand there and watch them, wondering if they'd gone completely insane or only a little bit crazy, feeling annoyance beginning to build in me. When people start laughing without telling you what the joke is, you don't have to be paranoid to get the feeling they're laughing at you. In that instance I *knew* they were laughing at me, but I still didn't know *why*.

It took a good number of minutes before fun time was over, and that despite the fact that I stood with my arms folded staring at them coldly. I had really been tempted to make that fun time more general, by helping their laughter up to the point of causing loss of control over certain sphincter muscles, for instance, but I *had* learned something of self-control. Instead of joining in I just stood and stared, and finally they reached the point of being able to speak again.

"We ask your pardon for having laughed so, *wenda*," the barbarian said to me, his still-sparkling eyes on my face as his mind attempted to size mine up. "The misunderstanding was quite amusing, which you will see once it has been explained to you.''

"Indeed," Dallan said with a nod, wiping at his eyes with a forearm. "I have not laughed so in quite a time—nor enjoyed such a situation in even longer."

The two of them exchanged wry looks, undoubtedly remembering the last time they'd laughed together. They'd been trying to kill each other that time and the laughter hadn't been their own idea.

"And what misunderstanding are we discussing?" I asked, totally unimpressed by the apology—and the complete lack of sincerity behind it. Neither one of them was really sorry, only trying to minimize whatever damage they thought they'd caused.

"The misunderstanding is simple, *hama*," the barbarian said, moving forward a step to circle me with his arm as he looked down at me. "Thinking we referred to your power, you spoke of seeing to Cinnan from here. It is, however, another power of yours which is required, your power as a woman, which most certainly cannot be exercised from such a distance. Cinnan would need to be most exceptionally endowed for that to be possible."

Dallan chuckled and Tammad grinned, most likely because of the sudden blush I could feel in my cheeks. No wonder they'd laughed so hard, hearing me announce that I could solve all of Cinnan's problems from thirty feet away, and that I'd done that sort of thing before with Len and Garth. I unfolded my arms to put one hand over my eyes, terribly embarrassed, but then it finally came through to me just what I was feeling embarrassed about. The heat seemed to drain very quickly out of my cheeks, and I withdrew my hand so that I might look up at the barbarian.

"You have not given your word to Cinnan," I said, trying in vain not to sound accusing. "Only to me was your word given, that you would make an attempt to understand the reason I so dislike being used by others. You would not break your word to Dallan; am I so much less than he?"

"*Hama*, I continue to make an attempt to understand your

140

views," he said with a puff of compassion coming out of his mind, one that was too uneven around the edges. His arm had tightened around my shoulders, and his blue eyes looked down at me soberly. "Whenever possible I mean to consider them as my own, yet in this situation I may not do so. Any other woman of our world would find little difficulty in acceding to the desires of her *memabrak*, his urgent wish to give aid to a brother. Will you be less than they, when you are clearly so much more?"

"It is one of the purposes of a woman, Terril," Dallan urged from behind my right shoulder, his faint shadow of compassion at least real. "As we are *helid*, you may accept my assurances without question."

"To give him my body is unnecessary," I nearly begged the barbarian, putting one hand to his chest as I squinted up at him in the bright sunshine. "His difficulty may be soothed and removed with the use of my power. You need not give me to him."

"A man requires more than the removal of his difficulty, *hama*," he answered gently, stroking my hair with his free left hand. "A man requires release, and this may be obtained in only one manner. Come with me now, and this will all soon be behind us."

I tried to say something about there being another way a man alone could get the release he needed, but I felt embarrassed, and the words refused to come out. Tammad ignored my stammered protests and began leading me across the thickened grass toward Cinnan, his arm tight around my shoulders, his mind easy with the knowledge that he was doing the right thing. It came to me then that my suggestion would have been wasted breath even if I could have gotten it out; Rimilian men would undoubtedly consider the practice unnatural, especially when there was at least one woman available.

Thirty feet can be crossed awfully quickly, even when one of the two people doing the crossing is trying her best to hang back. I didn't *want* to help Cinnan with his problem that way, but I wasn't being given a choice. No matter how *I* felt about the matter, that sort of thing was normal to Rimilians, and anyone who didn't understand that was just being foolishly backward. Cinnan was sitting on the ground not far from his *seetarr*, deep in his own thoughts, but he raised his head when we stopped in front of him.

"Cinnan, my friend, I have come to ask if you would honor me," Tammad said at once, overriding my intentions to make one more try to stop it all. "My woman is not your own, yet may she perhaps prove to be something of an adequate temporary substitute."

Cinnan looked up at the barbarian in surprise, and then he moved his eyes to me, definite concern behind them. He knew as well as any of the others how I felt about being given away, and although he didn't understand it any better than they did, he was still aware of that attitude. He knew that my being given to Dallan the night before had been more of an accident than a usual Rimilian exchange, and he hadn't expected to be offered the same. His eyes examined my face carefully, the reluctance he saw disturbing him, and I could feel him trying to make himself refuse the offer. He wasn't yet honor-bound to perform the way he had been the last time, and if he pleaded indisposition his friend and brother would not be shamed. He wanted to refuse, he really did, but his need was too great.

"Tammad, my friend, the honor is mine," he said, rising from the grass in one fluid motion to put his hand to the barbarian's shoulder. "You have my thanks, and my gratitude as well."

"Thanks are unnecessary, brother," the barbarian answered, gently clapping Cinnan's shoulder, and then, with a last hug for me, he turned around and walked away. It was stupid to feel abandoned and betrayed, but that's exactly how I did feel; I wasn't Rimilian, and none of that was usual, acceptable routine to me. I stood with my head down, staring at my hands, waiting to be grabbed and mauled but instead Cinnan's hand came to my chin.

"And to you do I give even greater thanks, *wenda*" he said very softly, raising my face to make me look up at him.

"You have proven yourself able to refuse to do as your *memabrak* wishes, yet do you refuse, instead, to shame him. Had my need been less, I would not have imposed upon your reluctance."

"I am aware of that, Cinnan," I said, somewhat surprised to see the respect in his mind. He knew I could leave him hurting if I wanted to, and was very grateful that I chose not to. What he didn't seem to understand was that the choice wasn't really mine, that I couldn't face making myself even more of a monster than I already was. Being made a general community project hurt considerably less—but it still hurt.

Cinnan was extremely solicitous, unpacking one of his sleeping furs and spreading it behind a rather large boulder before taking me in his arms and lowering me gently to the ground. He was just about jumping out of his skin with the need to get on with it, but he still began by trying to make me as interested and eager as he was. I'd intended closing my shield and simply letting him do as he pleased until he'd had enough, but suddenly that didn't seem quite right. Cinnan was taking the trouble to consider me even when he didn't have to, and repaying him by giving him almost nothing more than he could have given himself wasn't right. I'd had a pretty terrible night myself the night before, so becoming aware of the wide, strong arms holding me proved not difficult at all, as easy as feeling his kisses and responding to them, as accepting his caresses and returning them. The desire in his mind was as bright as a flare, and letting it glow into mine took no effort at all. When he finally entered me I really wanted him to, and he knew it and was so deeply satisfied that he was beyond words.

There was no embarrassed rush to our time together, neither of us making unseemly haste to get it over with. When it finally did end Cinnan kissed me again, his mind filled with pleasure and delight, his eyes dancing as he chuckled softly. His chuckle was for the blush I showed around my grin, the grin that let him know I'd enjoyed myself despite my initial reluctance. It really made a difference to him that he hadn't had to force me, an added pleasure that he hadn't expected.

Covering himself was somewhat easier with the cloth pants he was still wearing, and then he got to his feet to offer me a hand up. I took the hand and let it pull me upright, brushed my *caldin* straight with a couple of uninterested strokes, then impulsively reached up and patted Cinnan's face. I couldn't have explained why I did that, but Cinnan grinned with such real amusement and enjoyment that I giggled.

"Do—I intrude?" A neutral voice asked from behind me, causing Cinnan to look up and me to turn my head. "The time has been so long that I—we—thought there might have been difficulty of some sort."

It was Tammad, of course, who stood behind me, and if he hadn't been rigidly controlling his expression I was sure it would have been very peculiar. Thick calm was stuffed over his mind like a smothering pillow, but it was an oddly green-tinged calm, as though it were holding down something like jealousy. I immediately wondered with a flash of guilt if he'd seen me patting Cinnan's cheek and was asking himself just exactly how much I *had* enjoyed myself, and then I saw what a damned fool I was being. He was the one who had given me to Cinnan in the first place, the one who hadn't thought twice about forcing me to follow Rimilian custom. If he was beginning to find something about that custom to regret, I couldn't be happier.

"Most certainly you do not intrude, brother," Cinnan assured him, expansively happy and totally unaware of the strained reserve of the man he beamed at. "The length of time taken was due to the magnificence of your *wenda*, whose like one would be hard put to find. You are a truly fortunate man, truly fortunate."

Cinnan turned away then to find his swordbelt and cast-off shirt, and Tammad's reaction to what he'd said was fascinating to see. None of it reached his face, of course, but inside he was hopping around like a bird in a worm field, not knowing which way to jump first. Cinnan's praise of me had automatically made him feel proud and pleased, but part of his mind seemed to want nothing to do with such happy emotions. That renegade part was feeling jealous and possessive, unhappy over the fact that I wasn't miserable over what I'd just been made to do. The barbarian knew that feelings such as those were irrational and was doing his best to fight them, but he couldn't seem to bring much strength to the struggle. Then some sort of idea came to him, and he walked over to me oozing sympathy—but feeling a good deal better.

"My poor Terril," he murmured, raising one hand to stroke my hair as he looked down at me. "Your pride refuses to allow you to show your hurt, yet am I well aware of its presence. The thing is now behind you, *hama*, and you must comfort yourself with the knowledge that your actions were more than honorable. I shall comfort you as well, and between the efforts of both of us, you will be assured that what you have done was fully worthwhile."

"But I feel no hurt," I replied with ruthless naïveté, giggling again just to sink the knife in deeper. "You were completely correct, *hamak*, and I was much of a fool. To be held in the arms of a man such as Cinnan is more pleasure than tragedy, and I shall not be such a fool again. I had not before realized how—capable—he is, how much of a man he is. Aesnil must have lost her wits, to run from a man such as that."

I gave Cinnan a last, secret look over my shoulder before walking away from Tammad's stroking hand as if I didn't know it was there, strolling along in a floating sort of way designed to indicate complete satisfaction and a purposeful submersion in recent, very pleasant memories. The stricken feeling in him was very sharp before he jumped on it and pushed it away from him, but that was the thing that really pleased me. So he would lend me to other men as though I were a patched and raggedy coat, would he? I didn't care how old or well-accepted the custom was among his people; by the time I got through with that mighty *denday*, the custom would be a former one.

Dallan and Tammad had already eaten lunch, so that left just Cinnan and me to attack the packs. For some reason we both had excellent appetites, and Cinnan never noticed how I kept looking at him while we ate. Of course, I didn't want him to notice, and his lack of enlightenment was perfect to keep any real trouble from starting. The man was searching for his own woman who had gone astray, it hadn't been his idea or request that had put me in his furs, and he wasn't showing the least post-sex interest in me. Those facts together kept the big barbarian who had banded me from charging over to Cinnan with blood in his eye, and that made things worse for my *memabrak*. He had bullied and manipulated me into going to Cinnan in the first place, but he had expected me to walk away as upset and miserable as I always had been until then. The fact that I was not only not miserable but was ignoring him to take secret peeks at Cinnan was driving him wild, and he spent the entire time while Cinnan and I ate pacing up and down trying to locate the self-control he seemed to have misplaced. Lending your woman to another man was fine if she came running back to your own strong arms once it was over; I hadn't thought Tammad was aware of how down I'd been when I'd left Dallan that morning, but it suddenly came to me that he'd known precisely how I'd felt, and couldn't have been more pleased.

Once the meat was washed down by drinks of water, we took to the road again. All three of the men had packed their shirts away, so every time I leaned up to look over Tammad's shoulder at Cinnan, the barbarian was more than aware of the movement against his bare back. He stood it for a good ten minutes, then flatly ordered me back to his lessons in emotional control. He was practically wide-eyed with disbelief over the way he was feeling and acting, and couldn't understand why it was happening to him. I could have explained the psychology behind his reactions, stemming from the way he'd almost lost me and the way Dallan had forced him to give me up for the previous night, but true Rimilian women didn't do that with mighty *l'lendaa*. *L'lendaa* were the ones who did the thinking and had the knowledge, and who was I to buck the system?

The afternoon lesson didn't go very well, and I didn't make any effort to explain that, either. What I did make an effort at was letting my attention wander, if not to pleasant memories then to the changing scenery all around us. By mid-afternoon we were definitely coming down out of the pass, and on this side it widened rather than narrowed. Trees and bushes and real grass began appearing, and the longer we rode, the warmer the air became. One stretch of the widened road had to be slowly and carefully negotiated because of the brown boulders and rocks strewn all about, but that was the last of it. After that we were on a road stretching through gently rolling grassland and graceful stands of trees, and the presence of animal minds returned to the background.

After a while the grassland became farmland, and there was even more traffic than us on the road. A couple of carts and one *seetar* rider passed us going in the opposite direction, but none of them stopped or even exchanged greetings with us, which surprised my three traveling companions. Apparently it was unusual for people to be that unfriendly, and Tammad frowned over what had come at him from the rider's mind. The man had been so depressed and angry that it was surprising he'd managed to get himself up and moving; he'd withdrawn so deeply into himself that he hadn't even been aware of passing us. I'd noticed a vague upset and dissatisfaction in the people on the carts, two men first, and then a man and a woman, but the feelings had been faint and undefined. The rider had been a different story entirely, and if there had been a little more strength behind the feelings, he would have been projecting instead of just leaking them.

It was getting on toward sunset when we reached the town, a place that was a lot smaller than Tammad's city. There seemed to be only a couple of streets of square, one-story buildings, with correspondingly fewer people moving about them. The stands and shops between the buildings were for the most part still being patronized, but a few were in the process of being closed for the night. Torches had been lit on the outsides of the buildings, children chased each other around with less enthusiasm than they would have if it were earlier in the day, and I could feel my curtain thickening to keep out the increased output of so many more minds. The clamor and hubbub came to the barbarian as a surprise, but then his shield of calm swirled over his mind and he forgot all about it.

"The public grounds are to the right, through that lane ahead," Dallan said, pointing to a fairly narrow opening between two buildings that was lined with shop booths. "Shall we make camp first, or shall we make inquiries first?"

"Perhaps we may do both," Tammad said when Cinnan hesitated, his choice between the options fairly obvious. "We will all choose a camping place, and then Cinnan and I shall make inquiries the while you and Terril see to our camp. Is this acceptable to you?"

"Completely," Dallan agreed pleasantly, his smile genuine. He was looking forward to filling his stomach again, and setting up camp would probably let him do it faster than wandering around asking questions. "Follow me."

This time Dallan led the way, into the opening and between the stalls. The lane wasn't very long, and beyond it was a stretch of grass and then a wide, open space, quite a few *camtahh* already set up at intervals around it. A short way to the left, closer to the open space than to the backs of buildings, was what looked like a well. The setting sun was making seeing things clearly difficult, but two long-skirted women stood by the well drawing up water.

"For what reason do we continue to camp out?" I asked, speaking softly so that only the barbarian would hear me. "For what reason do we not find—a place with rooms and food?"

Not being able to come up with a word for inn or hostel should have warned me, I suppose, but there are some things you take so for granted that warnings do not the least amount of good.

"*Wenda*, this world is not like your own," Tammad answered, also keeping his voice low. "When one visits a town or city, one shares the roof of a friend or brother. Should one merely be passing through, one camps upon the public grounds set aside for that purpose. On Rimilia, hospitality may only be given, never bought."

"On Central and other civilized worlds, no one wishes to

buy hospitality," I informed him, annoyed at his faint amusement. "It is comfort and ease one purchases, as well as hot, well-cooked meals."

"Here, one goes home for such things." He chuckled, feeling vastly superior again. Rimilian barbarians had a way of looking at things that made them right and everyone else backward, and the attitude still rubbed me completely the wrong way.

It only took a couple of minutes to reach the cleared area, and a minute after that showed us an empty section large enough to accommodate all three *camtahh*. Tammad and Cinnan unburdened their pack beasts while Dallan started a fire, and then they rode off while the *drin* of Gerleth started on his own pack beast. I stood around like a sidewalk superintendent, wishing I didn't feel so totally useless as I always do at such times, but being willing doesn't make you able. When I'd first come to Rimilia I'd hated the work the barbarian had forced me to do, not knowing what an idiot I was being. Even brushing *seetarr* is better than standing around while others accomplish something constructive, but I didn't even know if we had a *seetar* brush with us. Dallan put up his own *camtah* then headed toward a second, and I couldn't stand just hanging around any longer.

"Dallan, allow me to assist you," I said as I came up to him, drawing a brief glance. "There must be some small thing I am able to do."

"Perhaps you would care to spread the furs in the *camtahh* once they have been erected," he said, paying most of his attention to hefting the folded tent he meant to put up next. "There is very little else suitable for a *wenda*."

"Perhaps I might begin our meal," I suggested, knowing the fire was all ready to cook on. "Were you to tell me what you wish, I would be able to. . . ."

"No, *wenda*, no," he said hurriedly, finally turning to look at me with the tied *camtah* upon his broad shoulder, his mind scurrying around. "I have not yet decided what I wish for this darkness, and there is no knowing when Tammad and Cinnan will return. To offer them a meal which is overdone or cooled to tastelessness would be inconsiderate, therefore shall we not begin our meal till I am done with the *camtahh*. Then I shall allow you to assist me.''

He reached out a big hand to pat me on the head, then turned away to walk to where he wanted the tent to go, the muscles in his back, shoulders, and arms rippling when he shifted the *camtah* to the ground. He was too busy to see me turn away in misery, and probably wouldn't have noticed even if he wasn't busy. What he was most concerned with was not having his meal ruined, something that would happen without fail if he let me do the cooking with no one watching me. It would have made me angry—if it hadn't been so abysmally true.

The glare of sunset had faded to a thickening dark, soft and fuzzy around the edges and sort of bumbling, a very young dark not yet old enough to be called night. I wandered away from where Dallan was working so hard to get us settled, aware of other fires around the camping area but not really seeing them. Nothing suitable for *wendaa* to do, he had said, but when I suggested cooking he almost fell all over himself finding reasons why that wasn't a very good idea. There were women on Central who were actually ashamed of being able to cook, I knew, considering the ability too far beneath a modern, talented woman. I moved across the dust of the camping ground, watching my still-covered feet flip out the bottom of my *caldin* as I walked, wondering how it felt to be that accomplished. To be able to do something with your own hands that you could share with others, that people could enjoy and honestly praise you for. To make you feel that you weren't simply taking up space better used for a different purpose. . . .

''*Aldana, wenda*,'' a deep voice came, a voice I didn't recognize. ''Do you stroll about seeking companionship?''

I looked up in confusion with my thoughts still mostly turned inward, to discover that I'd come something of a distance from where Dallan was. There were a number of people around with tents and fires of their own, but for the most part they were solitary male people, like the one who had stood himself in my path. I didn't need more than the light of his fire to see that his *haddin* was dirty and stained, his swordbelt old and not very well kept, his *seetar* thoroughly tied and hobbled to keep it from escaping his presence and service. The man looked down at me with a sharp hum in his mind, his flat, lusterless eyes taking in every inch of me, his left hand resting on his sword hilt. He seemed different from most of the other men I'd met on that world, but not different in the right way.

"*Aldana, l'lenda,*" I acknowledged politely, wondering why he'd stopped me. "I do not stroll in search of companionship, merely do I stroll. I wish you a pleasant darkness."

I began to step around him then, but he moved just as I did, deliberately blocking my way. As soon as the hum in his mind began rising to a growl I knew what he wanted, but the revelation had arrived too late. I tried whirling fast to run back the way I had come, but that was something he was expecting. His right fist shot out and tangled in my hair, and I was forced painfully back to him.

"I mean to have the pleasant darkness you wish me, *wenda,*" he said with a chuckle, continuing to look me over. "There was another I had thought to take, yet are you a far more toothsome choice."

"You cannot," I said with difficulty, really hurting from the way he was holding me, my hands to his fist. "I am banded, and my *memabrak* will soon return to seek me."

"Do you take me for one who is bereft, *wenda?*" he demanded, tightening his grip until I cried out, his mind instantly angry. "A man may put his bands upon a *rella wenda*, yet is she scarcely of concern to him beyond her obvious value. Were you a woman a man would fight for, you would now be tending his fire and *camtah*, or accompanying him where he rode. That you remain behind and do naught is solely for the reason that you have been commanded to it, your strength conserved for your only purpose. I will give the man to whom you belong a coin in payment for your use, and he will be more than satisfied."

He pulled me around then and began heading me toward

his tent, his mind filled with desire and the intention of easing it. His grip hurt so much that my eyes were full of tears, and the sobbing that had got itself started refused to let me stop it. I was suddenly very much afraid of what would happen, but not only of what that man would do to me. I knew he would use me the way Dallan had used me the night before, but he wouldn't be at all concerned about hurting me. I could stop him from hurting me, keep him from being in the least interested in me, but to do that I'd have to turn the coldness loose again, the soullessness that had so much control and power. I was trembling and sobbing as the man dragged me along, too shaken and frightened to use my abilities myself, it would have to be the soullessness or nothing. I honestly didn't know which I feared most, being hurt or hurting someone else like that, but my trembling increased as we began to approach the verandah of his *camtah*. I didn't want him to hurt me and I didn't want to hurt him, all I wanted was for him to let me go. I tried to struggle and then cried out again when his fist shook my head hard, my mind picking up the amusement of those men who were close enough to see what was going on. They all thought it was funny that I'd been caught, and none of them would help me against one of their own kind. The sobs shook me, and the trembling, and then—

"Hold!" cried a voice, a furiously commanding voice, one that trembled more from rage than fear. I didn't understand what was happening or who could possibly belong to a voice like that, but the man holding me spun around, dragging me with him, and then I saw.

The one who had shouted for him to stop was a woman.

"Release her at once!" the woman ordered, so angry she should have been emitting bolts of crackling electricity. She stood with feet spread wide and head held high, dressed in tight gray cloth breeches and white shirt rather than *imad* and *caldin*, leather sandals on her feet, a leather band holding her long hair back. Her left hand rested on the hilt of a sword, a large sword for such a large woman, but no more the size of a *l'lenda*'s sword than she was *l'lenda* high. The big blond man holding me stared at her speechlessly for a moment, and then he threw his head back and laughed.

"You would have me release her?" he asked the woman, sounding as offensive as it's possible to be. "Surely you ask such a thing for you wish to take her place in my arms, yet must you first grow as lovely as she. A *rella wenda* this one is, dark-haired and green-eyed and softly weeping. Show me the manner in which you weep, *wenda*, and perhaps I shall choose you instead."

"You may choose me more easily than that, *gendis*," the woman returned with a snort of ridicule, looking the man up and down in scorn. "Continue to hold that girl as you do, and you shall quickly have me—just behind my sword. Remove your hand from her, else I shall remove the hand from you."

"You dare to think yourself able to face *me*?" the man snarled, wildly furious at the way the woman had insulted him. *Gendis* meant someone without a single redeeming feature, a total loss, an absolute yahoo, and his mind seethed with fury. With a single, sharp thrust of his arm he threw me to the ground behind him, then drew his sword and raised his head. "Were you truly a *wenda*, your death would be a loss," he growled, beginning to advance on the woman. "As you are not, *weerees*, there shall be no loss at all."

With the last of his words he charged the woman, sword up and swinging, fully expecting to connect with his target. The woman, however, hadn't grown furious at being called a plaything and a toy as he had expected her to, and wasn't simply standing and waiting for him to cut her down. She danced fast under his swinging blade, drawing her own weapon as she turned, fully balanced, completely unhurt, and totally prepared to meet his next charge—which came almost immediately. The man was even angrier at having swung and missed, his mind filled with the most out-of-control rage I'd ever felt, emotion rather than thought sending him forward again. He slashed again and she avoided the swing a second time, still making no effort to do anything other than make the man appear clumsier than he was. A third swing came and then a fourth, the woman dodging nimbly and the man stumbling, and the foaming fury in the man's mind almost made me ill.

I sat up on the ground where I'd been thrown, half in the dirt and half on the man's verandah, one hand to my ribs on the left where the whole side felt bruised. The woman was continuing to lead the man all over the area, her movements precise, her mind cool and controlled and not at all afraid, her thoughts busy with some sort of plan. It was fairly obvious that the man wasn't exactly the best with a sword, but he was big enough and strong enough to swing the monster thing, and if he once connected with any part of the woman, it would be all over for her. I sat and stared at the two of them, holding my ribs, wondering if the woman meant to kill the man or simply keep leading him around until he dropped from exhaustion. A couple of his swings had been so wild that he'd ended up with the woman behind him, and if she'd wanted to she could have put her sword in his back. I was sure she had been even more aware of those openings than I was, but she simply wasn't interested in them and I thought I knew why. She seemed to have contracted a disease called honor, and I sincerely hoped it wouldn't prove fatal.

The glide-and-stumble dance continued another couple of minutes, all eyes in the vicinity on it, and then came the opening the woman had been waiting for. The man was just about rabid with rage, his insane fury the only thing keeping him erect, and at last he couldn't stand being led around like that anymore. He gripped his sword two-handed and raised it high and to the right of his sweat-soaked head, screamed wordlessly to gather every ounce of strength left to him, and charged directly at the woman with the most controlled gait he'd used in the entire fight. This time he had no intentions of plowing past her, only of cutting her in half with his two-handed swing, but instead of being upset a burst of triumph flashed in the woman's mind. Although I couldn't imagine why, that seemed to be what the woman had been waiting for; she immediately shifted her stance with instant readiness in her mind, set herself, then waited. The big man came at her, closer and closer, but not until that giant sword began slashing down at her did she move, jumping back at the last instant and only just far enough. The man had committed himself to the swing, and as soon as its arc passed her she would sweep in close to him with her own sword, opening him wide before he was able to so much as think about a backswing. It was what she had been waiting for—but she'd forgotten about the spectators.

Too many of the men around there were like the one who was fighting, more uncaringly dirty than shabby, casual about possessions especially if they were someone else's, not particularly honorable and not particularly interested in being so. When the fight first started they were no more than amused, expecting the man to have no trouble with the woman. When the trouble started their amusement died, and two or three of them had gotten to their feet to urge on and yell to the man who was making them all feel like fools. When the fighter had set himself for the final charge, one of the standing men must have slipped up behind the woman in the growing dark; the first I saw of him was when he tripped the woman in her backward jump, destroying her balance and sending her down on her head. He was away again immediately, getting himself out of danger's reach, but the damage had already been done. The woman was down and dizzy from hitting her head, and the man above her didn't hesitate. He came forward with a yell of triumph and raised that monstrous sword two-handed directly above his head, gleefully ready to bring it down right into her.

I'd done a lot of agonizing up till then about what I could and couldn't do to another living being, but when I saw the woman about to die all conscious thought and decision went by the boards. Without the least hesitation I hit the man with insecurity, a hard enough jolt to make him unsure about everything, including his balance. That giant sword above his head was suddenly leaning too far back for him to have a really good grip on it—or, at least the insecurity made him believe—so all he could do was twist around as he let it fall, bringing it down safely behind him before he was hurt by it. I began getting to my feet just as he turned his head to look at the woman, his eyes gauging the distance to be sure he would reach her with a single sweep of the blade no matter how insecure he felt. I couldn't let him hurt her for trying to help me, I just couldn't, but before the problem became critical a new element was added to the scene.

"Put up that sword, else use it on one who has a similar weapon," another voice growled, and then Dallan stepped out of the gloom and approached the man standing over the woman. "Or perhaps I should not suggest such a manly thing to one who happily strikes at the helpless."

Dallan stood with his own sword in his hand, still in those tight cloth pants, bare-chested, blond-haired head up, broad shoulders back. The first sight of him had frightened the other man, but Dallan's insult triggered the man's flash-quick temper and insane anger. Rather than stopping to think about it he immediately raised his sword and charged the *drin* of Gerleth, which proved to be his last mistake. Dallan had enough body-weight and strength not to need to side-step; he blocked the swinging attack with his own weapon, then immediately moved in answer, and the man's head flew from his shoulders. My shield was already closed tight by then, so all I had to do was avert my eyes while I hurried to the woman who still sat on the ground with a hand to the back of her head.

"Are you harmed?" I asked as I crouched down beside her, quickly letting my shield dissolve. I hadn't wanted to feel that man die, but now it was over and the woman needed help.

"For the most part, no," the woman answered with a grimace, clearly annoyed with herself. "My pride, however, is seriously damaged, that and my estimation of myself as an adequate fighter. To be downed by the simplest of subterfuges!"

"You were not truly defeated," another voice put in, and then Dallan was crouching to the right of the woman as I crouched to the left, his sword already wiped and sheathed. "Had that other not intervened you would have had him, neatly and with skill. I must ask your pardon for my own intervention."

"Truly would I be a fool to berate a man who has saved my life," she said with a wincing grin, Dallan's compliment having eased a good deal of the non-physical pain she'd been feeling. "I must make the effort to recall that all people are not possessed of honor, difficult though the concept is to accept. It had not occurred to me that I must concern myself with one who would come behind. I give thanks that the *gendis* was not able to maintain his balance when first he thought to strike at me."

"Yes, a truly fortunate thing," Dallan murmured, his glance at me both brief and completely revealing. He knew I'd knocked the man off-balance, but he didn't seem to be upset by it. "You must join us at our campsite till your head has cleared, else shall you likely be faced with another of these *darayse* before you have had opportunity to recover. Once you have returned to yourself, they will be of no bother to you."

"I thank you for your offer of hospitality," the woman answered warmly, beginning to get to her feet. Her usual litheness was hobbled by the dizziness that hit her, and Dallan had to put his arm around her fast to keep her from falling again. The hum in his mind grew at the contact, but I don't think he missed the fact that the woman was still able to hang onto her sword, then unsteadily sheathe it.

"I am Dallan of Gerleth, and the *wenda* is Terril," Dallan offered, very obviously making no mention of his title and position. "Our fire is yours for so long as you have need of it."

"I am Leelan of Vediaster," the woman returned, still too shaky to notice the way Dallan was looking at her. "So the girl is yours. Has she been harmed?"

"Terril?" Dallan echoed in surprise, immediately moving his eyes to me. "In what manner might *she* have been harmed?"

"The *gendis* took her with the intention of using her," Leelan explained, glancing up into Dallan's face. As large as she was she still had to look up, but it didn't seem to bother her. "The girl was clearly unable to defend herself, therefore

157

did I demand her release. She should not have been left to walk about unescorted.''

"Unable to defend herself," Dallan echoed with what turned out to be annoyance and faint anger, his eyes just about blazing out of the dark at me. "We shall speak of this matter, *wenda*, when our guest has been seen to.''

"You would punish her for the honorless doing of another?" Leelan demanded with as much strength as she could muster while I dropped my eyes. The thought of Dallan's punishing me didn't bother me half as much as the suspicion of what I thought he intended instead.

"Calm yourself, Leelan of Vediaster," Dallan said to soothe her, his voice softer than hers had been. "The girl is mine for neither punishment nor the withholding of it, nor would I punish her in any event. She and I are *helid*, and I believe the time has come to speak sternly with her.''

"*Helid*?" Leelan repeated in great surprise while I flinched to have my guess confirmed. Dallan was going to lecture me about defending myself, and I really didn't want to go into that. "You freely admit to being *helid* with one who is female and a *rella wenda*?"

"Terril is most certainly female, yet is she scarcely a *rella wenda* as you speak of it," Dallan came back, looking down at Lellan. "Her *memabrak* is Tammad, a man who cherishes her as few women have ever been cherished, a man who would not degrade her by holding her as no more than a woman for show. Despite her great beauty, Terril is not *rella wenda*."

"You defend the girl, yet not yourself," Leelan said in nearly a murmur, smiling faintly up at Dallan in spite of the look he was giving her, a hum beginning in her mind that was both familiar and unfamiliar. "Never before have I met a man who felt no shame at being *helid* with a female. With your agreement, Dallan of Gerleth, I would learn to know such a man more completely.''

"My agreement is easily come by, Leelan of Vediaster," Dallan answered with a grin, his arm tightening the least bit around her. "Allow me to assist you to our fire, where we may take our ease and—converse."

Both of them grinned at that one, but they still started off in the direction of our campsite, happily forgetting all about me. I was using pain control on Leelan with a very delicate touch, helping along her own excellent recuperative powers rather than forcing them to the job of healing her. Even if I didn't owe her the help, I would have worked at restoring her to full health simply for the distraction she would be for Dallan. The *drin* of Gerleth had always been fascinated by women who were really free, and if Leelan's presence couldn't get me out of that lecture, nothing would.

With the former spectators of the fight all disappeared into their *camtahh*, I was able to trail a good distance behind Dallan and Leelan back to our campsite without being bothered. I might have made more of an attempt to keep up with them if my side hadn't been hurting the way it was, but probably wouldn't have intruded in any event. I had never before seen anything on Rimilia to match their mutual absorption and attraction, and it made me smile to realize that even their names were similar. Watching them stare at each other was fun, but it was bound to be even more fun when Dallan came out of it and tried telling Leelan what to do. The big woman from Vediaster wasn't likely to stand still for something like that, and Dallan would deserve whatever she did to him because of it. In the meanwhile I'd be entirely forgotten, most especially where lectures were concerned.

By the time they reached the fire Leelan was walking on her own, and Dallan glanced back to make sure I was in sight before going over to check on the contents of the large pot that hung from a tripod over the fire. He stirred the contents with a shallow-bowled wooden scoop before tasting it, then turned to Leelan with a smile.

"I feared for the stew, yet is it unharmed," he told her. "It will be a short while before it is done, however. Therefore you may rest yourself till then. I will rejoin you in a moment, when I have completed the chores left unfinished by cause of that minor distraction." Then, since I had gotten close enough, he added to me, "Best you keep a close watch on your stew, Terril. Should it burn, I will shame us all by weeping."

Leelan chuckled as she watched him walk away toward the second *camtah* that wasn't yet standing, the *camtah* he'd been just beginning on when I'd left. My talking about making the meal must have frightened him so badly that he'd left tent putting-up for later, and had immediately started the stew. Leelan turned back to look at me when I stopped by the fire, her amusement at Dallan's comment fading, then sat herself down when I did.

"You have not yet answered my query as to your well-being, Terril," she said softly, large light eyes watching me carefully. "Were you harmed by that *gendis*?"

"I am no more than bruised, Leelan," I answered, trying to manage a smile, then looked away from her. "You have my thanks for coming to my assistance, and it shames me that you were given pain by cause of it."

"Such pain is naught, girl," she said, brushing the matter aside, her mind agreeing with the words. "While training with the sword I was often given much worse, till I learned to disallow such treatment."

"Truly?" I asked, looking back at her in startlement. "It had not occurred to me that there would be difficulty of that sort given to one who wished to learn."

"How else is one to learn, save through the desire for avoidance of difficulty?" she asked, her amusement back again. She was a really big woman, no more than half a head shorter than Dallan, her body well proportioned to that height but still supple and lithe. Her long hair was Rimilian blonde and her eyes were light, and the man she had challenged had lied about her attractiveness. Her oval face had a delicate sort of beauty that was also strong with personality and character, especially when she smiled or was amused. She looked like someone who would make a good friend, which was surprising, considering where she came from.

"Terril, mind the stew," Dallan called from where he was working, his thoughts back on his stomach again. I looked at Leelan and shook my head with a sigh, making her chuckle, then got to my feet to stir the stew. When I sat down again, I decided it was time for a little truth-speaking.

"The stew, of course, is not mine but his," I admitted, forcing myself to meet her eyes. "He spoke of it as mine only to spare me the embarrassment he knows I feel at being unable to cook. That *l'lenda* was correct when he named me no more than a *rella wenda*. Few have been able to rise to my level of uselessness."

"The *gendis* was no *l'lenda*," she stated, her frown only in her mind, which left her pretty face expressionless. "Bearing a sword does not make one a *l'lenda* any more than the lack of the ability to cook makes one useless. It seems more than a matter of cooking which disturbs you, Terril. Should you wish to speak of it, I would be willing to listen."

"Before one may speak, one must first find the words," I told her with the same sickly smile I'd been managing all along. "Do not concern yourself with me, Leelan. I have been moody of late, and the incident with the—*gendis*—has upset me."

"You find it sufficient that the *l'lenda* Dallan concerns himself with you?" she asked, one brow rising toward her leather headband, her mind curious but restrained. "For what reason did he appear so incensed that a small, unarmed *wenda* such as you was unable to defend herself? Of what does he mean to speak to you, and for what reason do you appear unwilling to hear him?"

The questions were calm and undemanding, casually hung up in front of me just in case I cared to take one or two of them down to answer. Light, wide eyes regarded me in the same way, without pressure, but how do you tell anyone, even a stranger, that what's bothering you is that you'd rather be admired than feared? How do you tell them that the only thing you're really good at makes you an unspeakable monster, something that anyone with sense would avoid? Things like that sound too ridiculous and melodramatic when put into words, and saying them to yourself doesn't do any good at all. If I told her that Dallan was undoubtedly angry with me for not defending myself, she would never understand.

"How goes the stew, *wenda*?" Dallan asked as he came up, unaware that he'd interrupted anything. "But a few more moments and I will be done."

"I have myself not yet eaten," Leelan remarked, watching as Dallan checked his handiwork again. "To be frank, I found myself with little appetite for what would be produced through my own efforts. I fear that the skill of cooking is not one I may claim as my own."

"Soon there will be none upon this world save *l'lendaa* who are able to do so much as warm *dimral* in a fire," Dallan remarked back, giving the stew a final stir of satisfaction before dragging himself away from it. "To a large degree the thought grieves me, for then what use might be found for *wendaa*?"

He gave Leelan a very bland look as he headed back toward the third *camtah*, causing her to begin laughing softly but deeply.

"A man who gives as well as he gets, that one," she observed to me, still chuckling comfortably. "I am unused to ones such as he, and shall likely find this darkness of great interest. He doubted my words, yet made no effort to contradict them—nor to support them for your sake. He was aware that you had spoken the truth to me."

"He is often aware of many things," I grumbled, watching Dallan a moment before looking away from him. "I will now also likely be told that absolute truth is at times unnecessary. Should he attempt to lecture me so, I believe I shall inform him that I told you he was worthless in the furs."

"Be sure first that your *memabrak* is present," she advised with a big grin, enjoying my comment. "*L'lendaa* rarely take such light-hearted jestings in the spirit they were meant, and often become proddish from them. The matter of *helid* would be unlikely to protect you."

"Should I say such a thing, even my *memabrak* would be unlikely to protect me," I countered, still feeling down. "He, too, is *l'lenda*, and he and Dallan are close. Do *wendaa* in Vediaster have *memabrakk*?"

"Some," she allowed with a slight nod, shifting a little

away from the fire. "There are those who are unable to see to themselves, who lack even the desire to make the attempt. These are banded by men who wish such women, yet is the number of those who go unbanded far greater. We who go armed will ourselves do the banding."

"You—band men?" I said, the idea suddenly appealing to me. "As though they were *wendaa*? Do you even five-band them?"

"Indeed," she answered with a wide grin, enjoying my reaction. "Should they merit five-banding. They are most of them quite proud of the bands they wear, which show they have found favor in a *w'wenda*'s eyes."

I heard the difference in the word immediately, the rolled and doubled first letter that was usually used only for the word "*l'lenda*". I didn't have to ask what it meant, as I already knew: women warriors were not ashamed of being women.

"I commend you for the manner in which you take this news, girl," she said, still watching me closely. "*Wendaa* who are not of our country often shudder in revulsion and fear upon hearing the same, unable to so much as consider the notion. Had you been born one of us, you would likely be *w'wenda* yourself."

"Would it be possible for you to teach me the use of a sword?" I blurted without first stopping to think, pushed into the request by the inner pressure that had never really let up. "I have need of the knowledge, yet am I unable to speak of my reasons."

Her mind went so startled that she couldn't think of a thing to say, and then she lost the opportunity. The sound of *seetarr* hooves came, announcing the return of Tammad and Cinnan, and then Dallan was there by the fire with us, waiting to greet the newcomers. It wasn't the time to pursue my request—or answer it—and we both knew it, so all we did was wait until the two men had unsaddled their mounts and come to join us.

"Never before have I seen so cold and unfriendly a place," Cinnan grumbled in disgust, then realized he might have made a mistake saying something like that in front of an unknown guest. He looked at Leelan and said, "It was not my intention to give offense to one who dwells here, *wenda*. Please accept my apologies."

"As offense was not taken, apologies are unnecessary," the woman answered, a faint smile on her pretty face as she rose to her feet. "I, too, merely pass through this place on my way elsewhere, and I, too, have found it to be less than hospitable."

"And yet was it nearly the place she merged with the soil," Dallan put in, and then told the rest of the story. The barbarian was immediately furious, of course, looking at me with his mind as well as his eyes to make sure I was all right, and I finally got some glimmering of why, a long time ago, a man of that world had not raised his sword against two others he'd been traveling with when they decided to keep me rather than return me to the one who had banded me. "I shall not kill you," he had said to them as he mounted up to ride away. "That doing is the right of he to whom she belongs."

Tammad stood listening to Dallan's story with fury blazing in his mind, his outrage so strong that it nearly knocked me over in spite of the curtain protecting my mind. Part of his fury was, strangely enough, aimed at Dallan, but only in an impersonal, general sort of way. He knew Dallan had really had no choice about killing that man, so he wasn't blaming him; what he was doing was cursing the fact that there had been no choice. He wanted to have that man in front of his own sword, to be able to face him and defeat him personally, and the fact that he couldn't was so frustrating to him that his output made me tremble. It was almost as bad for me as his projections had been before we found out he was fully operational in empathy, and I was almost to the point of needing to shield when Dallan finished his story and introduced Leelan. Both Tammad and Cinnan had reacted very oddly when they'd first looked at her, their minds trying to slip out of a hum into a growl, but after the story and introduction the barbarian regarded her with something very much like respect.

"You have more than my thanks, *wenda*," he said, his

expression and voice more sober than usual. "I now stand in your debt, and shall till I am able to do for you as you have done for me. Should you ever be in need of any sort, you have only to call upon me."

"There are many kinds of need, *l'lenda*," she answered, grinning faintly as she looked him over. "One day I may indeed call upon you—should that not be too far from the circumstances you have envisioned."

"To circumscribe one's gratitude is to belittle the act which produced that gratitude," he said, aware of the way she was looking at him—and not minding a bit. "Should there ever be a need—of whatever sort—you have only to call upon me."

They were looking each other over with a good deal of approval, something I should have expected, since Tammad's tastes were a lot like Dallan's, neither one of them doing anything that wasn't done by any other Rimilians. Cinnan—and even Dallan—looked on with mild interest and polite attention, but suddenly I didn't like that free, strong, unbanded *w'wenda* much anymore. As a matter of fact I didn't like any of them anymore, especially a certain any. Without saying a word I got to my feet, left the fire, and went straight into a *camtah*.

The tent was pitch dark and without sleeping furs, but I couldn't have cared less. I crawled away from the entrance flaps and found the side wall to the right, then just sat down next to it. I hated that world and everyone on it almost as much as I hated myself, but I refused to cry about it, not any of it. I'd had to half kill myself *and* him in order to get even the suggestion of respect, but he'd given it to her almost as soon as he'd seen her. Respect and gratitude and more interest than I could stand to think about. *L'lenda wenda* he used to call me, but it was clear to everyone involved that she really was.

I had shielded completely and was sitting with my eyes closed, so it was given to my ears to tell me when I finally had company. I had been left alone for quite some time, which had made me feel even more miserable, but the entrance of someone else didn't lighten the load. There wasn't one of them I wanted to see or talk to, and for the hundredth time I wished I had a tent of my own. Whoever it was had a candle, and after the usual pause to settle it I heard the sound of someone sitting down.

"Your food has been put aside for you, *hama*," I was told, his voice even and calm. "It is no longer as good as it was when hot, yet does it retain some measure of taste."

"Thanks for the effort, but I'm not particularly hungry," I told him, hating the fact that he was punishing me again. I had walked away without saying a word to anybody, deliberate rudeness in view of the presence of a guest, so if I wanted to eat, what I'd get would be cold leftovers.

"You will eat whether there is hunger within you or not," he said, that damnable calm still completely in control of him. "The upset you were given earlier is not likely to have encouraged your appetite, yet must you eat if you wish to continue in good health."

I didn't say anything to that, and for the obvious reason. Good health hadn't been what I'd been thinking about ever since I'd entered that tent, and I didn't find much interest in it then.

"Also must we return to our own *camtah*," he continued, ignoring my silence. "It is extremely rude to keep others from their rest."

"So my presence here is rudeness," I said, glad I had kept my eyes closed and my left shoulder near the tent wall. "And here I thought I was being exquisitely polite, getting out of the way and out from under foot. I hadn't expected it to be Cinnan's turn quite so soon, not with all that gratitude you feel toward her. Why didn't you simply switch *camtahh*, and save her the trouble of having to move around?"

"You—speak of the woman Leelan?" he asked, suddenly sounding confused. "She and Dallan have gone to *his camtah*. In what manner would she affect Cinnan and myself?"

"If you're trying to say you scarcely noticed her, don't waste the breath," I said, letting my head touch the tent wall the same way my shoulder was doing. It wasn't fair for her to be so much better than me—or that he would notice. And if he'd had to notice, why had he had to do it so—openly?

"You believe I wished to take use from the woman of Vediaster?" he asked, his voice sounding odd. "You came to this *camtah* so that I might do so without hindrance?"

"Isn't that what a good, obedient Rimilian woman is supposed to do?" I said, silently cursing the burning in my throat. "Step quietly out of the picture so that her lord and master will be free to express his—gratitude?"

"*Wenda*, it was in thanks for your safety that I felt such gratitude," he said, for some reason sounding more pleased than annoyed. "The woman kept you from harm, and for that I owe more than I shall ever be able to repay."

"Don't you worry about that, she'll help you make a damned good stab at it," I answered, then couldn't help adding, "I wish she'd minded her own damned business!"

"Terril . . . I cannot reach your thoughts, yet am I suddenly possessed of a strange conviction," he said, the words slow and measured. "I had never thought to see such a thing in you, yet do I belive that you are filled with jealousy."

"I am no such thing!" I spat, still refusing to look at him, but discovering that my eyes had opened anyway. "There's not a thing to be jealous about, not a single thing! The two of you finding interest in each other is nothing more than normal on this world, nothing that would upset anyone with sense. If it doesn't make *you* jealous to give me away to all those men, why should *I* care what you do with anybody else?"

I was looking down at the shadowy hands in my lap, my head still against the tent wall, feeling so miserable that I wanted to cry. But I also didn't want to cry, and was determined not to, even if the burning in my throat strangled me. I hated everything and everyone around me, but most of all I hated that burning.

"I see now that if you had not been affected so strongly, you would not have left so abruptly," he said, and I could feel the touch of his thoughts on my shield, trying to reach through to mine. "Come into my lap and arms, *hama*, so that I might hold you."

"Don't touch me!" I told him hoarsely, shaking off the big hand that came to my shoulder. "I don't want to be held, and especially not by you!"

I should have known he wouldn't listen, he had never listened to anything *I* ever said. The hand I had shaken off came back to wrap itself around my arm, and when I pulled against it and struggled, his free arm circled my back, trying to get a better, more all-around grip. The only problem was that his stupid, oversized hand touched my side at rib height, and I couldn't keep from yelping at the pain.

"What is it?" he demanded, immediately pulling both hands off me but letting them hover. "For what reason did you cry out so? How were you hurt?"

"I must have turned wrong," I muttered, trying not to shiver because of the flashing ache. "If Cinnan is waiting to get his tent back, let's give it to him."

I began moving toward the tent flaps, intending to pass him on the right where he sat facing the wall I'd been leaning against, but he refused to let me by. He lifted me below my thighs and shoulders as he turned toward the candle, sat me gently in his lap, then started taking off my *imad*. He was very careful of my struggling while he untied ties and pulled the blouse off over my head, then began examining me with a grim look on his face. It didn't take him long to get to my side, and when he saw the large, ugly bruise his jaw tightened.

"One would find it difficult to turn in any manner which was not wrong with a bruise such as that," he said, raising cold and angry eyes to mine. "How deeply I wish that Dallan had not slain that *virenj-see*! Why did you not say you were hurt?"

"It looks worse than it is," I answered, lowering my eyes from his as I wrapped my arms around my half-bare body. "Give me my *imad* back."

"You will have it back when I wish to give it to you," he said, his voice harder than it had been. "For what reason did you not speak of this hurt?"

"Maybe because it was no one else's business!" I flared, but still didn't raise my eyes again. "Maybe because I think

168

of it more as a reward than a punishment. I took this without wanting to hurt him back, and would have taken a lot more! This is what I got for not being a monster and a thing, and it doesn't hurt nearly as much as stopping him would have! I'm learning to be human, I really am—but I wish he had killed me."

I was able to hold back until his arms came gently around me, and then I let my face fall to his chest, needing the contact desperately. It hurt my side to sit like that, but it hurt even more deep inside me. I would have done anything to be human instead of a monster, but I was afraid that somehow it wouldn't turn out that way.

"*Hama*, I cannot understand this confusion that you speak," Tammad said after a short time of simply holding me against him. "For what reason do you believe that to accept pain is to be human? And for what reason must you see yourself as monstrous when others do not see you so? Dallan tells me he believes you kept the *sadarayse* from slaying the woman of Vediaster after she had been downed from behind. Surely a doing such as that cannot disturb you."

"But don't you see that even that was wrong?" I nearly begged, raising my face to look at him. "What was the difference between what I did and what that other man did to Leelan? He snuck up on her from a place where she couldn't see him, and struck without warning; how was I seen, and what warning did I give? Using my abilities against unsuspecting people is wrong, you know it is! How many times have you told me that, over and over? How many times has Garth said it, and Len? I know it's wrong, but I can't stop doing it; I tell myself it's natural to use my abilities, foolish to wish I didn't have them. At the beginning of this trip you said I couldn't use them, but did I listen? No, I had to hurt you first, and that still didn't stop me, just the way it wouldn't stop any other monster. You have to beat me harder, and maybe then I'll learn."

I put my head against his chest again, too filled with self-hatred to do any more, and his hand came to the side of my face as he held me tighter. By rights he should have walked away from me in disgust and horror, and I didn't know why he hadn't

"I see, *hama*, that I should have given more thought and attention to you than I have," he said with a sigh, leaning down to put his lips briefly to my hair. "So deeply immersed was I in my own difficulties and intentions, that I saw no part of your own. Proper teaching should have been given you a long time past, yet did I err in seeing you as no more than a *wenda*. Sit up now, so that we may begin."

In confusion I let him urge me away from his chest, understanding nothing of what he was talking about. His blue eyes looked at me soberly where I sat in his lap, and his big hand came to smooth my hair.

"Even had you been born a *wenda* of this world, you would not have been given the teachings of a boy," he said. "You would, however, have a closer understanding of the necessary, having been taught to share your life with one who must bear the burden. In this instance is it you who bears the burden, and though I attempted to take it from your shoulders, I should have known that such a thing is impossible. It must be my duty, instead, to strengthen you for that burden. Will you hear my words and know them as truth?"

I nodded hesitantly, still not understanding, but he smiled gently, as though my agreement had been enthusiastic.

"On this world, all male children are prepared for the wielding of weapons," he said, keeping his eyes only on my face. "A number of them grow to be merchants or shopkeepers or healers who will do little with the swords they are taught to use, yet many will grow to bel *'lendaa* and some few even *dendayy*. As it is impossible to know from the very beginning what each of them will be, they are all taught the same with no distinctions. The first thing they are taught is that a weapon, any weapon, is not to be used without reason. To do so is to be less than a man, for a true man has reason and is able to distinguish between right and wrong.

"Wrong is to use a weapon merely because one is able, merely because it gives one pleasure to do so," he said. "One must think of oneself among others, and consider if one would find approval in being attacked so by another, merely because that other has greater skill. Should one find a thing wrong when it is done to oneself, it is equally wrong to do the same to others.''

"But that's what I've been saying!" I objected, the confusion I felt making me even more upset. "I've been doing terrible wrong, and it doesn't stop!"

"Hush, *wenda*," he scolded gently, briefly putting one hand under my chin. "This is but the first lesson taught a child, and although it is greatly important, it is not the only lesson.

"Once a boy's teaching with a sword has begun, he must then learn the lesson of patience," he continued. "When one bears a fine new weapon one has just begun to learn to use, one is eager to test that weapon and learning. There are many contests and trials of skill in which these young *l'lendaa* are allowed to participate, yet are they forbidden to draw sword at any other time. They are told that one does not bare a blade without using it, therefore are they made to shed a small amount of their own blood if ever they are found with weapon in hand without a proper reason for its being there.''

"You mean they're forced to cut themselves?" I asked in horror, finally distracted from my own problems. "You make children hurt themselves just for being children?"

"When one begins the lessons of manhood, one must also begin to put away the doings of childhood," he explained, looking as though he'd expected my comment. "Those young *l'lendaa* will grow quickly to be men, and as the child is taught, so does the man do. To allow the child to wave his child's sword about as he wills, is to have a man who does the same with a man's weapon. Is it not worth a few drops of blood and a wound which quickly heals, to save a life which might be accidently taken by the thoughtless sweep of an unguarded blade?''

It sounded so logical when he put it that way, but it also sounded terribly cold-blooded. I couldn't quite bring myself to agree with him, but he didn't wait for agreement.

"Once the *l'lenda*-to-be has been taught prudence, skill,

and patience, he must then be taught the reality of what he does,'' I was told. ''The contests and trials of skill are engaged in with blunted weapons, and even when one downs one's opponent, that opponent rises again after, at most, a matter of moments. From such things a boy might come to believe that his opponents will ever rise again after being downed, or that he, himself, will do so after being bested. He must be taught instead that the sword of life is never blunted, that if he should best another that other will never again rise, that if he himself is bested, he will be slain. I will not tell you now what method is used to impress this truth upon them, yet are they taught to know it beyond all possible doubt.''

I shuddered at the grimness in his voice, not about to ask any questions concerning the part he'd left out. I didn't want to know what method they used to teach boys their own mortality and the mortality of others; it had to be terribly painful, and not necessarily in a physical sense.

''Even with all this preparation,'' he went on, ''one does not truly become a *l'lenda* till one has stood in answer to a challenge and has shown one's strength and understanding. I do not now refer to skill, *hama*, for to stand victorious after challenge is a self-evident indication of skill. The strength I speak of is the strength to defend one's self and property, knowing full well that a life will be taken by that action. The understanding necessary is upon the point that one is justified in that defense, that wrong lies with the one who attempts to take what belongs to another, whether that thing is property or life itself. One is wrong to take or attack without provocation, never to defend or protect. A true *l'lenda* does not joy in bringing others hurt, *hama*, yet is he able to give that hurt when necessary. It is not only his right, it is his duty.''

He was looking at me now with an expectation of sorts, as if waiting to hear that I understood what he'd said and agreed with it. Everything was always so clear-cut and easily answered to him, so simple and understood with ease. I really did wish I could be that way, but I didn't seem to have it in me.

''Even if doing it makes him feel like an ugly, horrible

creature?'' I asked, looking up into those blue eyes that never tried to turn away from unpleasant things. "Even if defending himself makes him feel worse than anything another person could do, including killing him? Isn't it better to let other people be the monsters, even if you have to die for it? I know you don't agree with me, but I'd rather be a dead human being than a live monster.''

"You are mistaken, Terril," he said, and his continuing calm patience surprised me. "I do indeed agree with a part of what you have said. It is far easier to allow others to do as they will, far less damaging to one's self-image of nobility to merely accept harm and never to give it. One may then smugly say that he has never brought pain or harm to another, and happily accept the end of his life secure in the knowledge of his goodness. If he were not to find an end, however, he might soon discover that his goodness is not quite as extensive as he believes. He, who had the ability and skill to halt one who had no honor, chose instead to accept and allow wrongdoing for the sake of his own comfort. His great sacrifice in the name of good allows a *sadarayse*, one who is far below the level of a man, to continue on and harm others, perhaps many others before one is attempted who considers the well-being of others above his own. This one will accept the pain of bringing harm to another, so that those innocents beyond him will not suffer needlessly. It is indeed far more pleasant to accept harm to oneself, *hama*, yet at what cost? A *l'lenda* has been taught to accept his duty and not shirk it; one who shirks finds more pleasure, yet spurns the necessary. Who, then, I wonder, is truly the monster, the creature? The one who stands and fights, or the one who merely accepts what is given?''

The question, which should have been rhetorical, hung in the air between us like a palpable presence, refusing to let itself be ignored. He was waiting for an answer, demanding that I give one, refusing to let me avoid it. The only problem was that all I had was more confusion, nothing remotely like an answer.

"But you said using my abilities was wrong," I whis-

pered, wrapping my arms around myself again to keep from
shivering. "You said it more than once and so did others.
And you don't know what it's like when they're afraid of
you, when they move back to make sure you don't notice
them and *do* something . . ."

"You believe one who is *l'lenda* has never been shown
fear?" he asked, and this time there was impatient ridicule in
his tone and expression. "You have been too much among
l'lendaa yourself, Terril, where the fear is not so easily seen.
When Cinnan and I spoke to the shopkeepers of this place,
many of them trembled to find themselves faced with our
presence without the matching presence of *l'lendaa* of their
own. Had they known he and I are *dendayy*, leaders in our
own cities, their fear would have been much greater. We bear
weapons which are able to do great harm, you see, and also
possess the skill to wield them."

"But you and Cinnan would never hurt anyone without
reason," I protested, upset even more that he brought up
the same point Dallan had. "They have no cause to be afraid
of you."

"And yet they are," he said, for some reason looking
pleased. "When there is fear in a man and he fails to control
it, it soon begins to control him instead. A man in control of
his fear is aware of all danger around him; a man whose fear
is in control sees danger everywhere. The two outlooks are
not the same, *wenda*, and you were not told that the use of
your abilities is wrong. You were told that to use them
against others without adequate reason was wrong, a distinction you were then unable to make. Now you must strive
diligently to make the distinction, for I no longer forbid you
the use of your powers."

I know my jaw hit the ground, then, and from all the way
up in his lap, at that. A few days earlier I would have been
absolutely delighted to hear him say that, but right then all I
felt was panic.

"How can you say that?" I demanded, my voice suddenly
as shrill as my eyes were wide. "I'm supposed to be your

memabra, subject to you and obedient to you in all things. You can't just cut me loose that way!''

"I have not—'cut you loose,' '' he denied, and I swear I could see a grin lurking in his eyes. "You remain my *memabra* and shall continue to be obedient, yet must you see to the matter of your power yourself. I had not understood that to forbid you its use was the same as forbidding a *l'lenda* grown the use of his sword. A boy child may be made to wound himself and a girl child may be switched, yet a *l'lenda* grown must be allowed the choice of when to bare his weapon, and a woman of power must be allowed the directing of that power. I attempted to bear the burden for you, *hama sadendra*, yet this may not be. The burden of power may not be borne by any save its possessor, and that one must be strong. All I may do is aid you in gaining the necessary strength.''

"But you're not being fair," I tried, still feeling horribly—abandoned. "What if I can never be strong enough? Or what if I decide to use my abilities to get out of having to obey you?''

"You *must* have the necessary strength, therefore shall we seek together to find it," he answered, as blind and unsatisfying an answer as I'd ever heard. "And as for obeying me—do you mean to attempt *disobeying* me, *wenda*?''

The look in his eyes had hardened with the question, the sort of hardness I'd probably never be able to stand up to even if I lived to be a million years old—and got stronger every year I lived. With my shield still closed I knew he wasn't projecting at me, which meant there had to be another reason why I squirmed uncomfortably and felt the urge to drop my eyes. I wasn't afraid of him—exactly—but I also wasn't quite up to disobeying.

"Stop trying to bully me," I grumbled, but I'm afraid it came out more a request than an order. "I'm so confused right now that even this tent could intimidate me, so you're wasting good bullying.''

"Should I have *my* way, *wenda*, it will be this *camtah* especially which intimidates you," he said, surprisingly looking even more stern than he had. "Your behavior has been reprehensible of late, and I will have no more of it."

"Behavior?" I echoed, having no idea what he was talking about. "What behavior, and what has it got to do with this tent?"

"You know well enough the behavior I refer to," he answered stiffly, still mostly thunderous. "For a woman to look with interest upon a man who is not her *memabrak* is shameful, most especially when he is a man whose bands are on another. You will not again approach Cinnan's *camtah*, nor will you look upon him again in such a—a—mindless—manner. You will look only upon me so, else shall I switch you!"

His voice had by then become nearly a growl, and his brows had lowered so far that they were downright menacing. I was so delighted I let my shield dissolve, and through the curtain I could feel the heavy, ominous green tingeing his thoughts. He really was jealous, but not of Cinnan. He wanted my interest to be his alone, because that interest meant more to him than he could put into words. I loved him very much right then—but then I remembered a couple of somethings.

"I don't understand how you expect me to look at *you* like that," I said with full innocence, staring up into two dim, dangerous pools of blue. "It's been so long since it was you making love to me, that I think I've forgotten what it's like. If you keep giving a girl away, you can't blame her for forgetting."

"Such forgetting is not possible, *wenda*," he growled, really very unhappy with me. "Either a woman prefers one man above all others, or she does not. To know this when she is untouched by others, is not the same as to know it amid much other use. A man who does not fear to share his woman is one who knows well the quality of her love; to refuse to share her is to say he mistrusts her love for him."

"Well, the least you could do is remind me what you're like every once in a while," I answered in annoyance, hating the way he always made things sound so logical—when it was something *he* wanted to do. "Like now, for instance."

"No, *wenda*, I may not use you now," he denied, his mind under such strong control that it was almost like a physical drawing away. "This would not be the proper time."

"And why not?" I snapped, suddenly remembering another something else that filled me with the sort of anger that would sear anything it touched. "Can it be you have another date, one that can't be shoved aside for a while the way I can be? Are you silly enough to believe I don't *know* what you felt when you looked at her? Do you think I'll just step aside and let her lead you off by the nose? Well, do you?"

By that time I was just short of shouting, and not really noticing what must have been a fairly strong projection. Tammad's mind had winced with the desperate urge to back away, but you can't back away from someone sitting on your lap. He opted for leaning back instead, trying for distance to give him a chance to fight off my mind, and ended up thunking down flat on the tent floor with me following, leaning on his chest. He looked up at me with an echo of the thunk in his expression, one hand to the back of his head, and if it had been possible for someone with his personality to be really wide-eyed, he would have been wide-eyed.

"*Wenda*, the woman of Vediaster was not even in my thoughts," he said, looking confused. "I did no more than recall the bruise upon you, and had no desire to add to your pain."

"Oh," I answered with great intelligence, tempted to feel like an idiot, but that particular subject was too important to me. "Well, you better make sure you keep it that way. I don't want her anywhere around you, not even in your thoughts. Do you understand me, *memabrak*?"

"*Hama*, this jealousy you show is totally uncalled for," he said with the same sort of innocence I'd used, his grin pure satisfaction. "I have had *wendaa* without number since I became a man, and have thereby learned that only one holds true interest for me. What others I have now only serve to point up the truth of the matter."

"If I were you, *hamak*, I would find a safely banded woman to do any future pointing up with," I said, moving higher on his chest to look directly down into his eyes. "If you don't, the woman you find so much interest in might become somewhat annoyed."

"*Wendaa* are well known for becoming annoyed," he said, the blandness in his voice and expression doing nothing to keep his hands from spreading out on my bare back. "I have given my word in gratitude; what if I am called upon to redeem that word?"

"Why, then you'll just have to honor your word," I answered, still looking unblinkingly down at him. "While you're honoring it, though, you'd better keep firmly in mind the fact that I'm no longer forbidden to use my abilities. Other people are one thing, but you are definitely in a class by yourself. If I find you letting that—that—*female*—get her claws into you, I'm going to see how hard it is to make squished *l'lenda*"

"*L'lenda wenda*," he laughed softly, bringing his hands up to my head, feeling not the least intimidated or insulted. Loved and really wanted was what he was feeling, and it came to me then how deeply he had been hurt by all the times I'd insisted I neither loved him nor wanted him. His emotions were always so well covered that I'd never been able to reach that particular set before, but right then his mind was wide open to me. We both needed a time of stern jealousy and deep possessiveness before going back to normal interaction with other people, and that was the time we would be best off taking it before getting it out of our systems. I leaned down and brushed his lips with mine, gently and tenderly, and then had no further patience for gentle and tender. I threw my arms around his neck and kissed him with every ounce of strength I had, reaching at the same time for his mind. When he said no he usually meant it, but that time I was the one who refused to argue. I wanted him and I wanted him right then, and for once I got exactly what I wanted.

It took quite a while before it was over, and thanks to pain control I felt nothing but pleasure. When we were finally ready to leave the tent, the barbarian pushed the flaps aside to find our sleeping furs piled up just outside. We'd both forgotten about poor Cinnan, who had apparently gotten tired of waiting for us to get out of his tent. The furs had been put there to tell us we were trading tents for the night whether we liked it or not, and instead of feeling guilty we just laughed and went back inside.

7

The next few days were spent in normal boring travel, and when I wasn't giving Tammad lessons in control, I was buried deep in thoughts of my own. What I felt and what I'd been told refused to resolve themselves into something I could cope with, and being on my own as far as my abilities went was horribly unsettling. I still had the same abilities I'd had when I'd started, but suddenly whether or not to use them was entirely my own decision. No Amalgamation to turn me off when my job was over, no Tammad to tell me when I'd done wrong and punish me for it, no Garth to talk me into doing experiments, no Len to warn me about making mistakes. I'd ranted and raved about all the restrictions I'd been under, chafed endlessly and complained bitterly, but now that I had the freedom I'd wanted so badly, I was afraid to do anything with it. I kept my arms very tight around the barbarian as we rode, really wishing he hadn't decided it was time for me to grow up. I wasn't ready to grow up, and still wasn't even entirely convinced that staying with him was the best thing for *him*.

By the time we'd awakened that very first morning, the woman Leelan was already gone, not only from Dallan's tent but from the whole camping area. Afterward Dallan said that she'd told him she was on her way to take care of some unspecified business, but would be back in Vediaster's capital city about three days behind us. If we were still in the city at that time, we were all invited to share the hospitality of her house. That didn't strike me as an invitation to look forward to, but I found myself very definitely in the minority. My traveling companions thought it was a wonderful idea, but what else can you expect from men?

The pestering I'd been anticipating from Dallan never materialized, and once again it was Leelan I had to thank. The *drin* of Gerleth, back in his *haddin* as the others were, was his usual pleasant self when anyone spoke to him, but the rest of the time he was thinking, daydreaming, and fantasizing, three distinctly different efforts. Thinking usually involves facts or speculation from known quantities, daydreaming lets the mind flutter wherever it likes without direction, and fantasizing is the almost-wish for a specific event or circumstance, choreographed and dialogued to satisfy an inner craving. The thing that brought all this to my attention was the way Dallan began to fantasize, then cut it off in annoyance. Among normally intelligent beings, it's usually daydreaming that's done the least; what begins directionless is most times quickly diverted to thinking or fantasizing. Dallan wasn't letting himself fantasize, and his day-dreaming had a lot of rigidity about it.

"*Hamak*, what's bothering Dallan?" I finally asked the barbarian in a whisper, also using Centran to keep the conversation more private. "Didn't he enjoy himself with my noble defender?"

Tammad shifted in the saddle, half annoyed and half relieved that I'd interrupted the individual exercise I'd given him to do, then cast about for a way to answer me.

"He did indeed find enjoyment with the woman," I was told at last, but almost with an air of discussing things that weren't quite proper. "Any man would find enjoyment with a woman such as that in his arms."

"Then what's the problem?" I asked, ignoring that "any man" phrase he'd used. He'd been pushing away a good deal of disapproval when he'd said it, and I didn't understand why.

181

"It is not—proper—to use a woman who is unbanded and then fail to band her," he managed to get out, part of his mind bent out of shape. "That the woman offered herself to Dallan was of no moment, for she comes from a country unlike our own and the *drin* meant to have her in any event. Come the start of the new day he would have put his bands upon her, yet had she already gone. Such immoral behavior is greatly vexing to us all, yet there is little we may do at the moment to correct it."

"Immoral behavior," I repeated blankly, wondering what I was missing. "You think her having spent the night with Dallan was immoral?"

"Certainly not," he said in soft exasperation, definitely growing impatient with me. "For a man to take a woman for the darkness is natural, as things were meant to be. For a *wenda* to take herself off after such a doing, alone and without the protection of a man of her own, is completely unacceptable. What if the merging were to have begun a child? What sort of upbringing would such a child have, with no father to raise it and train it? What of Dallan's feelings, to think that a child of his might well be without protection and provision? The thing was thoughtless and highly improper, and should not have been done."

The incensed indignation pouring out at me told me I would be smart to let the whole thing drop, but that didn't mean I stopped thinking about it. It was hard accepting the apparent fact that on Rimilia it was the man who got caught if he messed around with an unbanded woman, but that was the only way I could make any sense out of it. I already knew that all the children belonged to the men and that if a woman was put up for banding by someone else the children she'd produced didn't go with her, but I never would have guessed in what direction that line of thinking could go. As long as there was a man there to claim ownership of a child, it didn't matter who fathered it; how the child turned out after it was raised was the important part. For a woman to take the chance of starting a child and then to disappear without giving the man involved an opportunity to do the right and proper thing was Rimilia's version of scandalous behavior, and somehow I couldn't help grinning at the thought. Dallan had been the victim of a hit and run, and *he* was the one worrying about whether or not that particular night would produce something unexpected.

The country of Vediaster began a few miles beyond the town we'd camped in that first night, but at first there was nothing to distinguish it from the rest of the countryside we'd passed through. Despite the fact that no one had admitted seeing Aesnil and her two companions coming through the town, we were all still certain we were right behind them. The road had widened considerably, a requirement of the volume of traffic that used it, and only short distances of that road wound through forest or uninhabited field. Most of the land all around us was under cultivation, a sign of a prosperous country, but there were also a number of sword-bearing, unbanded women on the road, most of them coming from the opposite direction. None of the three men with me did anything but nod politely in answer to their nods, but the three minds were nothing but disapproving.

We camped the third night in a stand of trees not far from the road, knowing that on the following day we'd reach the city of Vediaster, the seat of power for the country of the same name. Cinnan was distracted and almost unbearably impatient, fighting to keep himself from riding on ahead without rest, just to get there sooner. Dallan was distracted and down in the dumps, fighting to keep from watching behind us for the woman who had said she'd be coming back to the city we were heading for. Tammad was distracted with something he'd been thinking about, something pleasant but also something that was making him the least bit impatient. I was annoyed that it happened to be raining, a light, pleasant rain, but one that meant I couldn't try my hand at cooking again.

With Dallan finally thinking about something other than his stomach, I'd spent the last three days working at getting the best of our food rather than the other way around, and really believed I was finally getting somewhere. I'd cheated by watching the minds around me as I'd cooked, letting their reactions tell me when it was time to take something out of the fire or time to leave it in a little longer, what to season with and how much to use, what was tasty and what was just barely edible. The most annoying part was that none of the three seemed to notice that they weren't dying of food poisoning any longer, or that I had taken over something they hadn't even wanted me to think about. They accepted my efforts without comment and without notice, but at least *I* felt better about it.

It didn't take long before the tents were up, and once they were and the *seetarr* had been unburdened and fed, Cinnan and Dallan disappeared inside with little more than mumbled words of good night. They'd earlier volunteered to share the night watch between them, and Tammad, knowing he wasn't taking rest away from either one, accepted their offer with thanks. We both took off our rain capes and hung them on the verandah of our *camtah*, Tammad lit a candle with a small, complicated device I still considered the next thing to magic, and then we, too, went inside.

"Spread our furs, *wenda*, and then we may share this *dimral*," I was told once we were inside, the *dimral* in question, still wrapped in preserving leaf, tossed to the tent floor. The barbarian was busy settling the candle, and hadn't looked around when he'd moved through the tent flaps.

"I already have spread the furs," I pointed out with just a hint of smugness, reaching down for the *dimral* he'd brought in with him. "I did it while you were feeding the *seetarr*."

"Why, so you have," he observed with pleased surprise as he turned, his tone suggesting that the accomplishment was on a par with building a house singlehandedly overnight. "Our meals become more edible with each one that passes, you no longer consider spreading my furs a doing beneath you, and three full days have passed without a single disobedience. Truly do I believe you are at last becoming a woman of this world."

"You're teasing me for a reason," I said, just holding the leaf-wrapped *dimral* as I looked up at him, undecided whether to be pleased that he'd noticed my cooking after all, or annoyed that he was trying to get a rise out of me. "I can't tell why, but you definitely have a reason."

"Indeed I do, *wenda*," he answered with a grin, taking the food away from me before settling himself cross-legged on the tent floor. "When our meal is done, it will please me to share the reason with you."

"Why can't you share it with me now?" I asked, sitting down to watch him unwrap the meat and get ready to divide it. "I don't tease *you* without letting you know why I'm doing it."

"So I have noticed," he said, his tone dry and his glance pointed for all its brevity. "Though you insist that holding my efforts at control up to ridicule when they fail to please you will in the end aid me, I continue to find your amusement of very little aid. Ridicule is a good deal more discomforting when one is able to feel it as well as see and hear it."

"Of course it is," I agreed without hesitation, reaching for the piece of meat handed to me at the end of his complaint. "It's also something most people want to avoid at all costs, so they work hard toward that end. I've noticed that you've been working harder ever since I started laughing where you can hear it."

"I have also been thinking a good deal more upon the advisability of cutting a switch," he said, looking straight at me while taking a bite of the meat. "Before we leave these woods, you understand, and I no longer have adequate opportunity."

"You're not going to switch me," I said with only a little more confidence than I was feeling, taking a small bite of my own. "If you do you know I'll stop criticizing you, and you can't afford that at this stage. You just have to grit your teeth and take it."

"Perhaps I shall be fortunate enough to find another reason to switch you," he grumbled, chewing morosely. "Is there nothing to be found over which you would disobey me? No insult you would consider giving me before others?"

"Well, if it's that important to you, I'm sure there's

something I could find," I decided, inspecting the piece of meat I held before sneaking a look at him. For the briefest moment he forgot we were teasing each other and began straightening in indignation, his shaggy-blond head rising to the challenge, his blue eyes hardening. Then he saw me watching him and he chuckled, the amusement of a man who knew he had nothing to worry about. I'd learned the difference between teasing a man in private and insulting him in public, and wasn't about to get caught with another punishment. Very obviously and deliberately I looked around to see that we were alone, looked back to the barbarian with a smile, then just as obviously and deliberately stuck my tongue out at him. His chuckling got deeper and heavier, but he didn't say a word.

We finished our meal under flickering candlelight, the sound of gentle rain pattering lightly all around, the tent a bit on the warm side with the flaps closed. After sharing a drink of water with me Tammad replaced the skin, then turned to take me in his arms. He kissed me gently, almost tenderly, let me go briefly to remove my *imad* and *caldin* and his own swordbelt and *haddin*, put me down on his furs, then snuffed the candle before joining me. There was a strange sort of happiness in him as he put his arms around me again, that impatient excitement I'd felt earlier which didn't seem to have any cause.

"I had not meant to speak to you of this now, yet has the time presented itself as proper," he murmured out of the darkness, letting his hands enjoy me as he held me up against him. "This doing with Dallan and the *wenda* from Vediaster has brought it to mind, and I cannot rid myself of it—Terril, you do indeed become more of a woman of this world with every day which passes, and soon, I know, you will give me the final proof of it. Soon, I know, your body will fill with my child."

The words were so unexpected and shocking that I stiffened in his arms, literally struck speechless in reaction. My mind curtain kept my feelings from racing out madly and overwhelming him, causing him to misinterpret the single physical indication of response that he had.

"I do not accuse you of being remiss, *hama sadendra*," he assured me immediately, holding me more tightly to comfort my upset. "It disturbed me a great deal when I failed to put a child on you, and at last I spoke of this disturbance to Lenham and Garth. It was then that I learned of the manner in which the *wendaa* of your worlds keep themselves childless, and that this method must be renewed every so often, else will it fail. They and I calculated that soon you will no longer be held by the thing, and then we may begin the first of many children. I find myself as eager as a boy before his first woman, *hama*, and cannot wait till my love is within you. You will give me fine, strong sons, I know and, as was once told me, daughters of a beauty to steal my sleep. My love for you is very full."

And then he kissed me again, the love he spoke of flowing out of his mind and encompassing me. After that, of course, his lovemaking turned more physical, but if my life depended on remembering the time, I would be in a good deal of danger. He did what he usually did to me and somehow I responded, but once it was over and he had fallen asleep, I crept out of his furs and into mine, where I lay curled up on my side in shock.

The sleeping fur was soft and comfortable, and I didn't need to cover myself in the close, stuffy darkness. My cheek enjoyed the feel of the fur, as did my entire left side, the pain from the bruise on my ribs almost gone. My thumb moved to my lips and I thought about making myself even more comfortable and serene, in a way I hadn't used since I was a very little girl. The dark was so nice and warm, soothing and concealing, and I could stay in it as long as I liked, as long as I—

DON'T!

My mind clanged with the scream and then I was trembling and crying, still in the grip of hysteria but at least free of the terrifying beginning of catatonic withdrawal. Some part deep inside me, a calm, sad part, didn't let the terror take me again, and helped me to keep the cleansing emotional storm from waking Tammad. I couldn't face him right then, not even in pitch darkness, and the tears streaming down my face made that abundantly clear.

It took awhile before I was up to thinking again, and even then I didn't really want to. I turned onto my back in the furs with a shuddering sigh, draped my right arm over my eyes, and let the feeling of exhaustion quiet me. For once my emotions were very easy to separate, but that wasn't to say they were calm and under control. I was back to living with a whirlwind in my mind, but at least I could see the components of it.

The first and easiest part of my problem was the way I felt about being pregnant. I loved Tammad and wanted to give him everything I could, but there was something frightening and vaguely disgusting in the thought of having a child put in me deliberately. I knew people did it all the time all over the Amalgamation, but I'd always felt reluctant and repelled, and couldn't seem to shake the attitude. What made it the easier part of my problem was that I was on Rimilia, a place where women didn't have to worry about that sort of thing. I seemed to have lost all track of time, but my six-months-worth of protection shouldn't have had much more than two or three months left to go. Once it had worn off I would be immediately vulnerable, and Tammad would waste no time asking if I were ready and willing. He would take me in his arms and kiss me as he entered my body, and then it would be done the way Rimilian men always did it. There would be no pain, only overwhelming pleasure, and afterward I would be as happy as he was. I knew I would be happy—and that was my second, almost shattering problem, the one that had nearly caused me to withdraw from reality.

I took my arm down from my eyes, seeing splotches of brief, bright color before the darkness closed in again, hearing the soft breathing of my *sadendrak* where he lay asleep to my right. *Sadendrak.* The word meant someone who brought meaning to your life, someone whose absence would make that life not worth living. I would gladly die for my *hamak sadendrak*, my beloved reason for living, and sooner die than tell him I knew how happy I would be with his child inside me—because I'd already had the experience.

Toward the end of my first stay on Rimilia, I'd suddenly discovered one day that my protection had worn off without my knowing it, and that I was pregnant. At first I hadn't known what to do, and then I'd wanted to tell Tammad, but we were then in the middle of the *Ratanan*, the Great Meeting, that was so important to Tammad and the Amalgamation alike. I'd decided it wasn't the time to distract him with my news so I'd waited, but before the right time came he sent me back to my embassy, fulfilling the word he'd given on the matter even before I'd left Central. I didn't know then that he was planning to follow almost immediately and claim me permanently, I'd thought he didn't want me anymore once he no longer had need of my abilities. Almost as soon as I'd reached the embassy I'd taken a transport back to Central, and the first thing I'd done on Central was have the fetus removed from me and placed in stasis.

Tammad, my beloved, I've already been given your child—and I had it removed and put in a place where it will live forever but never grow large enough to be born, never be something to hold in your arms to love as you raise it.

How was I supposed to tell him that? It would be hard enough to say to a man of Central; how was I supposed to say it to a Rimilian?

If I could get back to Central I could have it reimplanted, but the only transport available was at our embassy, which was a long way away from where I currently was. How did I get back there without telling Tammad why I had to go, why it would be best if he didn't go with me?

What would I do if I couldn't get back, and time passed, and he made me pregnant again before I could retrieve our first child?

How did I explain that I'd given away a child that was *his*, on that world much more his than it could ever be a woman's?

What was I going to do? What could I do?

I put my hands over my face to try to hide in an even

deeper dark, but unfortunately I'd already gotten over the compulsion to hide. I knew I would have to face my number one problem head on, at some time in the near future, in a way that wouldn't make Tammad hate me forever.

The only thing I didn't know was how I was going to do that.

We reached the city of Vediaster about mid-morning of the following day, coming in from fields and forests that sparkled under the bright sun after the previous day's rain. Vediaster was as open and unwalled as Tammad's city on the plains had been, but in this new place I'd been able to find no trace of guarding *l'lendaa*, fighting men assigned to make sure the city wasn't hit with a surprise attack. I hadn't even detected the presence of *w'wendaa* in their place, which had to mean there were no guards. Vediaster was nothing but an open city, welcoming everyone who came.

The four people who rode into the city that morning were a silent group, each one concerned with his or her own thoughts. Cinnan began searching faces as soon as there were faces to search, half of him pleased there were so many females to check, half of him growing anxious and desperate at the numbers. Dallan also began searching faces, but he wasn't looking for the same one and wasn't even aware that he was doing it. Tammad was still considering what to say to the *Chama* of Vediaster, deciding what to tell the woman ruler of that country that would get her to go along with everyone else on Rimilia in their dealings with the Centran Amalgamation. The Amalgamation had been given permission to build the political complex they wanted to put on Rimilia, and in return the Rimilians were to have certain gifts. Tammad had been arranging everything, and although the leaders of my Amalgamation didn't yet know it, those arrangements were designed to give Rimilia the upper hand in all negotiations and, eventually, control of the Amalgamation itself. I didn't completely understand how that was supposed to happen, but Tammad did and he was seeing to it. Taking on the entire

Amalgamation didn't bother him in the least, nowhere near as much as *my* problems bothered *me*.

The *imad* and *caldin* I wore were too heavy for me to be really comfortable in that warm sunshine, but I soon became even more uncomfortable for another reason. When I'd first entered Tammad's city riding behind him, all of the women on the streets of that city were dressed and banded the way I was, in *imadd and caldinn* and differing numbers of small-linked, bronze indications of ownership. The crowds on the streets of Vediaster were the same, men and women and children everywhere, passing or in front of or moving in and out of the one-story stone and wood buildings and shops, but the composition and appearance weren't the same. The men were far fewer in number, and the vast majority of them weren't *l'lendaa*. The children running around playing chase games were identical, but most of the women they accompanied or played near were not in *imadd* and *caldinn*. The women wore cloth breeches and shirts and heavy sandals, and even the ones who weren't armed didn't wear *wenda* bands. Here and there a skirted figure could be seen hurrying along with head down, apparently as uncomfortable at being barefoot and banded as I was becoming. The women we passed as we rode by turned to stare at me with disapproving frowns, and if my curtain hadn't been in place and thickened, it probably would have been unbearable. The three men I rode with were tolerated, but my presence wasn't accepted well at all.

"I think we had best decide now whether to approach the palace of the *Chama* at once and openly," Tammad said suddenly to the other two men, his voice held low despite the crowd-noise and city-sounds nearly drowning him out. "To believe we will simply stumble across Aesnil upon one of the streets of the city would be foolish, even with the aid of a *seetar* who continues to feel her clearly. When she is found it will almost certainly be at the palace, yet must we decide whether to approach it openly."

"As you did in Grelana, when you came in search of Terril," Dallan said, doubling the point Tammad was trying to make. "You demanded your *wenda* from Aesnil, and were given a place in her *vendra ralle* instead."

"There is no reason to believe that the *Chama* of Vediaster will do as Aesnil did," Cinnan said, maintaining the position he'd held to doggedly for the last three days. "Should we offer courtesy of manner, we will likely receive the same in return."

"And if we do not?" Tammad asked, his mind wary with "once bitten, twice shy." "Should we be taken in this city and thrown into chains, who will there be to help free us? Who will there be to be certain of Aesnil's safety? Should we be called upon to fight for our freedom, which of us will find it possible to raise sword to a *wenda*? Are we to welcome the choice between our lives and safety and theirs?"

"What other choice have we?" Cinnan asked, his tone strong but his mind upset. "Should we not present ourselves at the palace, we will not find Aesnil."

"Merely to appear there will not immediately bring Aesnil to view, Cinnan," Dallan put in, still determined to be more practical than sympathetic. "The palace here is easily the size of Aesnil's, perhaps even larger. Do you mean to tramp up and down its halls, peering into every room? What courtesy will be found in such a manner?"

"Then what are we to do?" Cinnan demanded in a hiss, his agitation so strong that his *seetar* snorted and shook its head. "Do you propose that we take ourselves secretly into the palace in the guise of *wendaa*, hoping that those who stand guard will fail to notice us? Or do you prefer that we stand about outside the palace, telling one another amusing tales the while we attempt to see in through windows?"

"Cinnan, calm yourself," the barbarian advised softly, noticing but not looking at the people who had begun to stare at him as we passed. "We will indeed enter the palace, yet not as those who ride in search of a *wenda*. I will seek an audience with the *Chama*, and will tell her of the outworlders and what we mean to do to best them. Once she has agreed to join us, we will broach the subject of Aesnil."

Three women on *seetarr* galloped past us going in the

opposite direction while Cinnan digested that, but the dust raised by their passage didn't readily settle down. I could smell food, and people, and animals, and dust, all around and getting stronger almost by the minute. It was all giving me a not-quite headache and a queasiness in my stomach, a general sensation of not feeling really well. We hadn't been traveling long that day, but I was also feeling very tired and wishing there were good-quality accommodations nearby, someplace with an air-conditioned room, a soft, wide bed, and an excellent kitchen supplying room service. The barbarian's hard body was hot where I held him around, and I was close enough to smell his sweat.

"Such an approach would indeed be the wisest way," Cinnan grudged at last, his normal intelligence struggling to drag him away from the urge toward hysterics that he'd felt ever since Aesnil's disappearance. "This *seetar* would surely find it possible to lead me to my *wenda*, yet is the *Chama* unlikely to appreciate his presence in her halls. We three shall approach the matter as you suggest."

"Not we three," Tammad corrected, and again I could feel his mind working. "It would be best to have one without the palace, one who would either be able to aid us should ill befall us, or ride to fetch our *l'lendaa*. We know not why Aesnil was brought here, yet is it near certain that she was brought rather than merely accompanied. I had not wished to increase your distress, Cinnan, yet has the time come to speak of the matter."

"And I am the one to remain behind," Dallan said with understanding and approval, trying to help soothe Cinnan. "I shall watch carefully from afar, and should any difficulty arise, I will do what seems best."

"And I will wait with him," I said, suddenly understanding, despite the faintly vague way I felt, that that might help me with my problem. Dallan had always been someone I could talk to, and even if he yelled at me I was sure he would be able to come up with *something* I could do.

"No, *wenda*, you will continue to accompany *me*," the barbarian said at once, aiming the words at me over his right shoulder. "The *drin* Dallan must fade from sight when he leaves us, and this your presence would make more difficult."

"I would need to do no more than change my clothing and remove my bands," I protested, looking up at the face turned partway to me. "How might a man hide himself more easily than a woman in a city such as this?"

"As the clothing of a plains woman suits you best, and I shall not permit my bands to be removed from you, there is little need to discuss how your dark hair and green eyes would not go unnoticed," he answered, his voice as calm as his mind. "You will remain with the man who has banded you, and will obey him as you must."

"You're being unreasonable," I came back in Centran, more annoyed than I'd expected to be. "I can see that the people here are as blond as everywhere else, but dark hair is only unusual, not unheard of. And if necessary, I can probably find a way to cover it. Let me go with Dallan."

"No," was all he said before turning his face away from me again, absolute finality in the word. His mind was made up, and he wasn't about to change it.

Only two more streets were gone behind us before their general plans were hammered out, and then Dallan wished his two companions good luck and turned his *seetar* toward a side street leading off to the right from the main thoroughfare we continued along. I seethed in anger as I watched him go, deeply resenting the fact that I couldn't go with him. I wasn't being allowed to go with him, but no one cared how angry that made me. I was being forced to obey the man who had banded me, and that was the way things were supposed to be.

Cinnan and the barbarian engaged in very little conversation for the rest of the ride, but strangely enough Cinnan seemed to have calmed down. It looked like he found Aesnil's being taken from him easier to accept than the thought of her running away, and his mind was filled with cool planning and consideration instead of agitation. Tammad's thick calm was shielding his mind again, but beneath it I could feel his own plotting and calculating. Both of them ignored me as if I weren't there, and for them I wasn't. Even Tammad couldn't reach through my curtain to what I was really feeling, and he and Cinnan both were taking silence for acquiescence.

It was somewhat surprising to find the palace in the center of the city, only fifty feet of emptiness and a high stone wall separating it from the buildings, houses and shops surrounding it. There was a wide gap in the wall that seemed to be a major gate, guarded by a number of tall, armed women dressed in yellow, with grim, dedicated expressions on their faces; when the barbarian told them he'd come to speak with the *Chama*, we were all made to dismount. The women looked the two *l'lendaa* over with hums of interest in their minds, and although Tammad's expression never changed, his mind bulged with held-down outrage and indignation. His definition of female didn't include such behavior, and if he'd been anywhere but Vediaster at that particular time he would have let them know it. He wasn't about to jeopardize Cinnan's chances of getting Aesnil back, but the way he was gritting his mental teeth almost made me grin.

Five of the guardswomen escorted us across the ground toward the palace proper, which meant I didn't get to spend much time with the urge to grin. Every one of them considered me something low and distasteful, unappetizing in the extreme and nothing to associate with or even to walk too near. If it were jealousy or envy, emotions I'd read in other women more than once, it wouldn't have been so bad, but all those women felt was disgust and scorn. I walked barefoot across the grass behind two of them, Cinnan and Tammad to either side of me, tasting the way I was unarmed, dressed in ankle-length skirts, banded, and having been ridden behind a man. Any one of those things would have produced the disgust, but all of them together did more than that. To those large, proud women I was a lower life form, and the taste of that made me sicker and more depressed than I had been.

The sun shone bright off the white walls of the palace as we approached it, and boys came running out to take the *seetarr* leads Cinnan and Tammad held, then began leading the beasts away. The two boys wore nothing but light brown cloth wrapped loosely around their waists, definitely not *haddinn* and not meant to be, while bright rings of bronze-colored metal circled their throats. The two men watched the boys who were taking their mounts and pack beasts to be seen to until they were a good distance away, and then Tammad turned to the woman who seemed to be the leader of our escort.

"You keep boys as slaves?" he asked, the calm holding his voice neutral but only barely. "How is it possible for them to have been taken in battle, or to have committed crimes of such severity that condemnation is their lot? They are barely more than children."

"They are slaves," the woman corrected with an uncaring shrug, barely glancing at the barbarian. "Your land has its manner of enslaving, we in our land have ours. Come this way."

The woman's eyes had brushed me briefly as she turned and headed off, her meaning obvious and intended as a counter to Tammad's comment about the boys. Both men mentally brushed off the dig as foolishness, but for the first time in a good number of days I felt the confinement of the bands I wore. They had been put on by a man to tell other men that I wasn't free for the taking, but I was the one who couldn't get them off. Not having the strength to remove them meant I also lacked the choice about whether or not to wear them, and that suddenly seemed very unfair. Before banding me Tammad *had* given me the choice, but the only alternative then had seemed to be an endless series of fights that the barbarian would get into with men who didn't know I was his. He had offered to leave me unbanded if that was what I really wanted, and it had turned out not to be what I wanted at all; had that really been my decision—or merely the first time I'd been maneuvered into obedience?

The palace corridors were wide and cool, but not with the cool of marble. Walls, floor and ceiling were of a shining white rock, and underfoot it was smoother than even years of walking would have made it. Occasional hangings of silk broke up the stone expanse, along with torch and candle holders, paintings, wooden carvings, and jeweled constructions of glass and metal. I would have enjoyed moving more slowly to admire some of those things, but the female guards moved along at a brisk pace, one the two *l'lendaa* had no trouble matching. I was the only one who had to hurry to keep up.

The women led us quite a ways into the palace, then finally stopped at a beautifully carved wooden door that seemed no different from any of the other similar ones we'd passed. Cinnan had been growing anxious again, but I still hadn't let myself search mentally for Aesnil. No matter what Tammad had said or how Cinnan felt, there was no guarantee Aesnil hadn't come to that place voluntarily; if she had, I wasn't going to be the one to cause her being dragged out of it again.

"You will all wait in here," the leader of the guard said to us, throwing open the door. "Should the *Chama* agree to grant you an audience, you will be told."

"And how long a time is that likely to be?" Tammad asked, looking down at the woman instead of walking through the door. He was supposed to have obeyed her without question, and she stiffened with annoyance when he didn't. Nothing in his expression showed it, but he'd been expecting the annoyance and was enjoying it.

"It will be till the *Chama* has made her decision," the woman answered, refusing to let herself snap the words out despite the anger in her light eyes. "Enter the room or leave the palace."

Put that baldly there was nothing else to do, but the barbarian continued to look at the woman for a long moment before turning to walk through the doorway. During that moment the woman's expression hadn't changed any more than his, but the stiffness of her body was beginning to change to tension because of the worry starting to show in her eyes. If Tammad and Cinnan refused her orders there would be a fight, and somehow she knew the two men would not be easily taken. Her left palm had unconsciously caressed her sword hilt as she'd locked eyes with him, and Tammad had known as clearly as I that she would not back down if it did come to a fight. He didn't like the woman, but he did give her grudging respect; for that reason, as well as the original ones we had come there for, he turned and led the way into the room.

After all the stone of the corridor, the medium-sized room came as something of a surprise. The floor was carpeted with fur and had quite a few pillows scattered around, but three of the walls and the ceiling were hidden behind a facing of brownish rock, with nothing in the way of silk to decorate it. Large candles burned in sconces on each of those walls, throwing back the dark there would have been without them. There wasn't a sign of a window in the place, and when the guard leader closed the door behind us it made me very uncomfortable.

"This room is too close," Cinnan observed as he looked around, heavy disapproval in him. "Perhaps we should have insisted upon seeing the *Chama* at once."

"They would not have allowed it," Tammad said, also looking around from the center of the room. "There is naught we may do save wait—without refreshments of any sort."

"Barbaric," Cinnan muttered, his sense of propriety greatly offended. "*Wendaa* have no true knowledge of hospitality. Without the guidance of men, they behave as *mondarayse*."

"Best we recall that *we* are the outlanders here, not they," the barbarian cautioned, his glance at Cinnan agreeing with the sentiment but not the voicing of it. "Should the time drag on to too great a length, we will recall to them the duties of a host."

Cinnan grunted agreement without adding anything else, and the two of them chose cushions and pieces of carpeting to stake out as their own. They were getting themselves comfortable to wait as long as necessary, but for some reason I couldn't get myself to the same point of patience. I moved slowly into the center of the room, very aware of the carpeting under my bare feet, beginning to sweat in the closed-in, airless place. I didn't like all that brown rock on the walls around me, the clothing I wore hung more heavily than ever, and something about that whole situation didn't make any sense. I frowned in thought for a minute. Was it possible all people showing up at the palace to see the *Chama* were invited in to wait? Without asking who they were? Without trying to find out what their business was? Without knowing whether they were friend or foe? We hadn't been asked any questions at all, and the two men with me had accepted the lack without even noticing it. On that world women didn't question men, not unless they were asking for instructions, so Tammad and Cinnan hadn't noticed. . . . Hadn't noticed, but what were they supposed to have noticed? There was something, I'd been thinking about it only a minute earlier, but somehow it had slipped away again. I shook my head to get the sweat-dampened hair off my shoulders, trying to clear the thickening mush filling my mind. It was so hot in that room that I was sweating, and the heat and sweating were making it impossible to think.

"*Wenda*, are you ill?" Cinnan's voice came, filled with concern. "Why do you appear so strange, and why do you merely stand there?"

I looked over toward him slowly, trying to understand what he was saying, but everything felt so confused and difficult. Thinking was too hard, much too hard, and wasn't even worth the trouble. I put my hands to my head, frowning at Cinnan through waves of uncaring exhaustion, vaguely wondering what he was saying, vaguely wondering why Tammad was sitting and staring and blinking slowly at nothing. Not sitting precisely, but slumping, almost as though he hadn't the strength to sit. No strength, none at all, no will, no strength, no volition. No, nothing, none, a humming chant lulling me, the dance of Cinnan's struggle to rise flowing with the beat. Cinnan wanted to get to his feet but he couldn't, even though he was trying very hard. He didn't understand why he couldn't do it, and neither did I. Tammad lay slumped on the carpet and Cinnan struggled to rise, and I no longer had the strength of will to stay awake.

8

It wasn't waking up, precisely, not with remembering what
had happened before you'd slept and knowing what was
going on right then. I opened my eyes and was in a rather
large room, with quite a few people all around. I had an odd
taste in my mouth, knew I lay on something hard, and my
right shoulder and arm were hurting, throbbing in protest and
feeling banged and scraped. There was sunlight in the room,
and refreshing air, but with all the people looking down at me
I wasn't feeling very refreshed.

"Sit up, and then stand," one of the people looking at me
said, a large woman wearing cloth breeches and shirt, leather
sandals and headband, and a sword. It came to me then that
all of the people looking at me were women, and I didn't
understand. I didn't understand any of it, but I sat up and
then got to my feet.

"You should have been wiser than to come here so, girl,"
another voice said, also a female voice but sleeker than the
first and filled with endless self-confidence. "Your pitiful
trace of the power has given you too high an opinion of
yourself, which has caused you to reach above your proper
place. You will come to regret such impertinence."

I looked over to where the voice was coming from, and
then had to look up. At the top of a wide platform a woman
lounged upon cushions and furs, an attractive woman with

blond hair and blue eyes. She was dressed in golden silk breeches and shirt with matching silk foot coverings, and the silk was decorated with jewels and trimmed with fur. Behind the platform she lay on was an entire wall of windows, all of them thrown wide to the air and sunshine. I put my hand to my forehead as I looked at her, trying to remember what I'd wanted to say, and then I had a piece of it.

"Pitiful trace of power?" I got out, feeling a compulsion to speak the truth. "No, you are mistaken."

"Mistaken, am I?" snorted the woman, sitting straight among her comforts to look her scorn down at me. "From Aesnil's words concerning you and the comments of those who brought her I thought you the possessor of a great power indeed, yet did it take nearly as long to down you as it did to down the empty man. Even the one with the beginnings of the power succumbed more quickly, proving again that the greater the power, the greater the sensitivity—save for the greatest of all, such as myself. It is now no wonder that he has been able to make you slave to him, yet is that scarcely an excuse."

"Excuse?" I echoed, not following anything she was saying, wishing that constant buzz in my mind would go away. The room I stood in was certainly large enough, but I still felt surrounded and hemmed in.

"For one with even a trace of the power to allow any man to enslave her is totally inexcusable," I was told severely, anger and disgust obvious in the words and the snapping blue eyes. "Such a woman clearly relishes that enslavement, begging for it and then flaunting it as though it had great merit! Had you not accompanied these men, with your dark hair and green eyes and slave bands, we would not have known them, yet was such service to us scarcely voluntary. You will be given no reward for it, for you have earned something other than reward."

I don't understand, I wanted to say, unable to take my eyes off her, but her disapproval and anger had frightened me and made my lips tremble. I was going to be punished for what I'd done wrong, I knew, but I couldn't quite remember what that was.

"We must now see if there are any here who wish these two," the woman announced, looking somewhere behind me at whatever was there. "There are other matters, more important matters, I must attend to this day, therefore do I expect a speedy claiming."

"I would have this one," a voice said, also behind me, a voice filled with interest. "The *Chama* Aesnil has spoken of his ability to give pleasure, and I would see the thing for myself."

I turned slowly to find out what was going on, and saw the rest of the large room I'd opened my eyes in. All of white stone it was, with pillars of the same along both side walls and beautiful paintings and things on the walls themselves between the pillars. About ten feet behind me were two men half surrounded by large, armed women, and staring at them briefly showed them to be Cinnan and Tammad. They stood with their arms behind them as if they were tied, there were bright bronze rings circling their necks, their bodies were covered with plain brown cloth hung like very short skirts, their eyes looked unfocused, and they were unarmed. A woman about my size in yellow cloth breeches and green cloth shirt stood in front of Cinnan looking up at him, her left hand resting on the hilt of the sword she wore.

"You may have him, sister, yet must you recall the need for caution," the woman who had scolded me said, taking her turn at speaking from behind me. "You must be certain that Aesnil does not see him, for we have not as yet converted her completely to our cause. Also must he be kept well drugged, for we would not wish him or the other to escape and return with more of their sort. Our *w'wendaa* would not find it difficult to defeat them, yet would it then be known what we attempt."

"The word of the *Chama* Farian is to be obeyed," the woman in front of Cinnan acknowledged, immediately turning away from him to bow to the woman on the platform. "It shall be done as you command."

"I, too, shall do the same," said a third female voice, and a woman stepped forward from among those who surrounded the two men. "With my *Chama*'s permission, I would have the other."

"To teach him proper behavior, Roodar?" the woman on the platform asked with a chuckle, her voice amused. "It was clear he annoyed and angered you from the moment he first appeared."

"Indeed he did, *Chama*," the woman agreed with very little expression on her face, turning her head to look at Tammad. "Should you grant him to me, I will quickly teach him how great an error he has made. For his insolence he will squirm on his belly when he comes to greet me, and beg me with tears in his eyes to take pleasure from him."

The woman called Farian chuckled again, enjoying the picture the *w'wenda* Roodar had painted, but even through the buzzing mush in my mind I was disturbed. There was something about Tammad, something I had to remember, and then I had it.

"No," I said to Roodar, immediately drawing her eyes, wishing I didn't feel as though I were all wrapped up in invisible cotton. "You may not have him. He is mine."

"Yours, is he?" growled the very large woman, pacing forward to stop and stare down at me. Her cloth breeches and shirt were the same shade of yellow as all the guard *w'wendaa* wore, but hung from her neck on a golden chain was a round red disk that sparkled in the sunlight. I couldn't remember seeing it before, and wondered why she hadn't been wearing it when she'd escorted us into the palace.

"Yours, is he?" she said, still expressionless as she stared down at me. "That would be more likely the other way about, yet shall I accept the statement. As he is yours and I wish to possess him, we must face one another. Give her a sword."

I stared in mindless, uncomprehending shock as the woman stepped back to wait while one of the other guard *w'wendaa* came forward with a blade she'd just unsheathed. My hand was raised and a hilt was pressed into it, and then Roodar reached toward her own weapon.

"I shall likely do little more than wound you," she said,

unsheathing her sword as her eyes looked down at me. "Should
I take your life, my *Chama* would surely be annoyed."

I looked down at the sword that had been put into my
hand, very aware of how awkwardly wide it was to hold. It
wasn't as heavy or as long as the sword of a *l'lenda*, but
somehow it frightened me more than the larger weapon ever
could. This was a weapon meant for a woman, and already
my fingers were beginning to ache.

"I—cannot use a sword," I got out, raising my eyes again
to the expressionless Roodar. "I have never been taught to
use one."

"You are unable to use a sword, and yet you dared to
challenge me?" Roodar growled with anger and insult, looking totally outraged but still giving me the impression she'd
known all along. "You insult a warrior and sully the hilt of a
fine weapon with your touch, and dare to attempt to lay claim
to one who has taken that warrior's interest? You are nothing,
girl, far less, even, than the stone all about us, and as you
cannot face me you will face, instead, an adequate punishment for presumption."

The big woman resheathed her sword as she stepped back
again, then made a gesture with one hand. Three of the
guard *w'wendaa* came toward me immediately, two of them
grinning, the third to take her sword back with a faint but
very odd expression in her eyes. Once she had the sword she
turned away again, but the other two didn't. They already had
the ties of my *imad* open before I realized what was happening, and as I tried to struggle I wondered how they'd known
what Roodar wanted them to do. I couldn't seem to think of a
way, not even one, and then it came to me that my *caldin* had
been pushed down over my hips to the floor, and I was being
roughly pulled away from the puddle of it.

"One may easily see why these men have made you slave
to them," Roodar's voice came, a mocking drawl heavy
enough to draw my attention back to her. "You wear the
form of a born slave, girl, and truly wear it well. Few of us
here have seen such a thing before."

The mockery in her voice and eyes brought chuckling and

laughter to the other women standing around, and it finally came through to me that I'd been stripped naked in front of them! I could feel the heat of humiliation rising all through me at the impact of that realization, at the weight of all those laughing eyes on me, and my hands came up in an effort to shield myself even as I began backing away.

"Ah, no, slave, you may not retreat," Roodar said at once, bringing to my arms the hands of the two women who had taken my clothing. "You stand before us in the chains of men, a slave pretending to womanhood, and for that you must be punished. For that you *will* be punished."

She raised her own hands then, and suddenly I could see the whip she was holding. It seemed smaller and lighter than other whips I could remember, something made to hurt rather than maim or kill, but my mouth instantly went dry with fear and all I wanted to do was run. I tried to run, but the hands of the two women were still on my arms, keeping me from escaping from that terrible instrument of punishment.

"You will well recall your folly in challenging me, slave," Roodar said with horrible cold amusement, shaking out the coils of the whip as I trembled between the hands of the women. "This is but the first time of many."

Roodar stepped to one side with a nod, and then I was being thrown forward and down, to the stone at the feet of Tammad. My heart pounded and raced with the fear, increasing the pain of hitting the floor, especially in my right arm and shoulder. The stone of the floor was smoother to walk on than fall against, and I whimpered as it scraped my flesh, still desperate to run. I had to get out of there, had to get away—but how could I, when I'd be leaving someone behind? I began to look up at him, to tell him to run with me—and then I felt the first of the whip.

I screamed at the pain, screamed at the burning trail left across my back, but screaming didn't stop it from happening again. The whip cracked and my body burned, and I was forced back and forth across the floor, writhing with pain and trying vainly to escape it. It hurt so terribly that I couldn't bear it, but then it stopped as abruptly as it had started. I had been given a certain amount of pain, a measured punishment, and it had stopped because someone else wanted it stopped. Somehow doing it that way seemed worse than beating me bloody and unconscious, and I lay face down on the roughly smooth floor, hurting all over, my face hidden in my arms, crying hysterically.

"Nicely done, Roodar," the voice of the woman on the platform came, filled with satisfaction. "In time this slave will shudder in fear at the least thought of you, which is as it should be. Even now her thoughts are mere whimperings, faint and strengthless with pain and terror. She is truly nothing, and in time will become even less. Perhaps you had best take away your new possession now, for he struggles to throw off the drug and minds which hold him."

"My thanks for having been granted him, *Chama*," Roodar said with satisfaction of her own, no longer paying me the least attention. "I will take him to my quarters and begin with him at once. He clearly wished to interfere with my punishment of this slave, and for that he, too, will be punished."

I raised my head from my arms to see the man who was no longer mine, straining slowly and strengthlessly against whatever bound him, pulling weakly against the hands on his arms which effortlessly held him back. His head was moving, as though he were trying to shake it, but he couldn't manage the shake and then Roodar was in front of him. Her gesture made the ones holding him turn him and head him toward the heavy double doors at the back of the room, and I lay naked on the floor, crying and in pain, watching him walk out of my life.

"Remove that other as well," the woman on the platform said, her voice already sounding distracted. "I have wasted enough time with foolishness, for there is work and planning left to do. And take that slave to what awaits her."

There was movement among the women left in the room, and rough, hard hands came to my arms. I was pulled to my feet despite the added pain of movement, and Cinnan and I were taken in opposite directions.

*   *   *

Moving through the corridors was a blur in my memory, but every now and then I remembered that I was naked and tried to cover myself with my hands. The women forcing me along refused to allow that, though, and then I forgot about covering myself and just whimpered with the pain I still felt. I'd been punished for something and was going to be punished again, and it might not have been so bad if I could have remembered why that was being done to me. I wasn't bleeding, only covered with ugly red welts, but I couldn't remember why.

We walked a long way through the corridors and the blur, but finally there was an area at the end of one corridor that seemed to open out directly from it. I was pulled to a stop just inside the area, someone was gestured over, and then big hands were at my throat, then my wrists, and lastly at my ankles. I hadn't found it possible to follow things too well until then, but when a cold metal band was brought to my throat, I made a greater effort.

"Now you are marked as you should be," one of the women who had brought me there said, the words accompanying a solid click. "You now wear the collar of a slave, and have only to be told what your slavery will consist of."

I reached for the stiff, cold metal that had been closed around my throat, but my arms were taken again and I was forced farther into the area that widened out from the corridor. The area was all of white stone, unwindowed and undecorated, and on the floor to the back of it were neat lines of thin, uncomfortable-looking pallets. Closer to where we stopped was something I hadn't noticed sooner, about a dozen men in brown hip-wraps and bronze collars, men large enough to stand tall as *l'lendaa*, men who knelt humbly with their heads down. Not one set of broad shoulders was stiff with resentment, and I looked down at them without understanding why.

"Bless the name of the *Chama* Farian, slaves," the woman to my right told them, her voice rough and sure with command. "She sends to her serving slaves a gift this day, one who is far lower than they. This slave has allowed herself to

207

be made to serve men, and has dared to show pride for so low a doing. In consequence has the *Chama* named her slave to slaves, and may be used in any manner you each and all of you see fit. As she finds such pleasure in serving men, you may see that her every waking moment is filled with pleasure.''

I was pushed forward, then, to land on the hard stone floor on hands and knees, and behind me I could hear the sound of receding footsteps. My skin had gotten bruised and scraped from my falling that way, adding to the pain I already felt, bringing fresh tears to my eyes. I cradled my hands against me for a moment, wishing the hurt would stop, and then it came to me that I was being stared at where I knelt. I raised my head to look around, and found pairs and pairs of light-blue eyes staring down at me in wonder and confusion. The men I'd been left with were still on their knees, but their two straight lines had become a circle, completely surrounding me.

''By the Power and the Strength,'' someone to the right of me said, his voice low and filled with awe. ''Do you truly think we have been given a slave of our own?''

''Are you not able to see her there before you?'' answered a second one to my left. ''She has been put in the collar of a slave, and has been gifted to us. What are we to do with her?''

''Anything we wish,'' answered a third, kneeling before me, reaching a big hand out to shyly touch a lock of my hair. ''She is our slave just as we are slaves to the *Chama*, and she must serve us just as we must serve.''

''Yes, just as we must serve,'' said a fourth, kneeling to the right of the third, his voice uneven and his body trembling faintly. His eyes hadn't left my face, but suddenly I felt very naked in front of them all. I brought my arms up to cover myself, for some reason afraid of the very handsome man who stared at me and trembled, and the one holding my hair turned his head to that fourth man.

''Do you truly mean to do with her what you were made to do with that mistress?'' he asked, seemingly upset by the trembling of the man next to him. ''I had thought you were able to quiet the evil twisting within you, to keep it from rising up and haunting your sleep?''

"I have tried, but I cannot," the fourth man whispered in torture, his hands having turned to fists on his thighs, his face forlorn. "Three full times did the mistress put me to her service, and I have not since been able to send it from my mind. You who have never done the same have no knowledge of how it is, of how your body demands a thing the mistresses have forbidden you. Now the thing is no longer forbidden, and I shall have what has so long been denied me."

"No, you may not do this," I managed to say, half wondering what he intended, half knowing and fearing it. "I am the belonging of another, and you may not do this."

"How wide-eyed and trembling you have grown, pretty slave," he said, beginning to move forward toward me even as I tried backing away. "You have been given to us to do with as we will, therefore is there no other to deny us. You are the gift of the *Chama*, and a gift I must have."

"No!" I choked out as his hand closed on my arm, other hands holding me until he had caught me. He rose to his feet then and leaned down to pull me to mine, and then he had lifted me in his arms to carry me somewhere. My body hurt where he held me but I still tried to struggle, beating at him desperately with my fists. What he was going to do was wrong, wrong on a level he would never even understand, but if he had asked me to explain that wrong I would not have been able to call up the words.

"Do not struggle so, or the whipping you were given will grow even more painful," he advised with what seemed like real concern, going to one knee to put me down on one of the thin, neatly lined-up pallets. "You are a truly lovely *wenda*, lovelier than any other I have ever seen, and I know you will give me great pleasure. Do not fear what I will do to you, for the only pain it brings is an exquisite one."

He smiled down at me then, a warm, encouraging smile, and something inside me said, Good lord, that must be what *he* was told! A beautiful slave, a man in everything but his mind, and he'd been frightened when he'd first been called upon to serve in a different way. It must have been like raping a child, taking him and using him and then sending him back where he came from to struggle with the new feelings brought to life within him, feelings he didn't know what to do about. His big hands came to my arms to stroke them gently, his wide blue gaze consuming me, and I began to shiver again even before the mist thickened back to mush in my mind.

"No, pretty *wenda*, do not fear me," he urged, lying down next to me to take me in his arms. "I will not add to the hurt already given you, but will instead bring you very great pleasure. You will like such a thing, will you not? Only allow me to do as I must, and you, too, will be pleased."

I cried and tried to fight against his strength, not understanding what was happening, struggling to squirm loose, but he held me very tight and forced his lips down onto mine. Even in my confusion I knew the kiss was more desperation than passion, more groping inexperience than calculated heating. It wasn't a man who held me but a child with screaming needs he didn't understand, a child who rode in a man's body. I was naked in his arms and afraid of what he would do to me, and then he pushed me flat so that he could begin doing it. It hurt to struggle but I kept on doing it, even after it was too late, even with all those eyes that watched and wondered and began to think themselves about what it would be like.

9

I knelt on hands and knees and scraped at the stone floor with
the smoothing stone, hurting with every movement, the sweat
heavy on my naked body. It was hot that day, even inside the
cool stone walls, especially with the work I'd been given to
do. One of my masters was to have done that job, but he'd
been allowed to give it to the group's slave instead. There
had been quite a few of those jobs, but I couldn't remember
exactly how many. I didn't even know how many days and
nights I'd been a slave, but one thing I did know: how many
beatings I'd had. Seven, counted for me every time the
mistress came to give me another, just the way she had done
that morning. That other mistress had been with her again,
the one everyone bowed to and called *Chama*, and every time
I'd screamed and cried she'd laughed.

I sat back on my heels for a moment beside the open
terrace-doors, dragging the back of my hand through the
sweat on my forehead, tired and hurting and trembling at the
memory of those beatings. The mistress so much enjoyed
giving them to me, and each one hurt more than the last. The
mistress always came at different times, never when I was
expecting her, and seemed to find so much *pleasure* in punishing me. It was almost as though she were angry at me
about something, something I really had nothing to do with,

something that was increasing her anger with every day that passed.

A small breeze came in through the opened doors, bringing with it the smell of dusty sunshine and corrals and stables. I could hear voices outside, voices that were busy at something, voices that belonged to people happier than myself. A few lonely tears trailed their way down my cheeks at how miserable I was, but another thing I knew was something that had come to me close to the beginning of my time there. I might have been miserable, but someone else, someone who seemed to be very important to me, wasn't. He had turned around and walked away from me, and now didn't have to worry about monsters who gave away his babies. I didn't really understand even half of what that meant, but even in the mist and mush always surrounding me I knew it was a good thing. Even the beatings weren't as bad as talking about babies would have been, and that was a good thing.

If only I wasn't so miserable and confused.

The corridor I worked in was silent and empty, but someone I couldn't quite remember had promised to come back to make sure I smoothed every rough spot out of the floor, and punish me again if I didn't. I didn't want to be punished again so I reached for the smoothing stone to continue with the job, but the voices outside were growing louder and louder, much louder than was usual around that place where I was. I really had no interest in looking outside but I did anyway, and at first didn't understand what I was seeing. There were a lot of women out there, shouting back and forth in the very bright sunshine, and some of them seemed to be struggling with a *seetar*. The big black animal was being held by four leather ropes in the hands of four large women, but even so the women seemed to be at a disadvantage.

I squinted out at the glaring, sun-drowned scene, trying to understand what they were doing with the *seetar*, wondering who was supposed to ride it. It didn't have a saddle or bridle, only those ropes around its giant neck, but surely someone was supposed to ride it. Despite the fact that the women were struggling with it, it looked like a nice *seetar*, one that would be kind and considerate—and concerned. I frowned at that thought, at the strange idea that an animal would be kind and concerned, and narrowed my eyes as far as possible so that I might really *see* the beast. It was the black color all *seetarr* were, even bigger than they usually grew, and it was—

I closed my eyes for a minute and shook my head, horribly confused but desperate to understand. That *seetar* belonged to—someone very important to me, and he never would have gone off without it. I couldn't quite grasp what that meant, but I knew the *seetar* was also important to me, that it was the best friend I'd ever had. That's it, that's it, my best friend, I thought, putting one hand to my head as I looked out again. The women all around him were shouting angrily at the way he refused to obey them, the way he stubbornly refused to do just as they said. I didn't know what they wanted him to do, but they weren't simply angry about it. Even as I watched, two of the women who had left for a minute came trotting back carrying spears.

They're going to kill him, something inside me said, chilling me all the way through in spite of the heavy heat of the day. He's the best friend you ever had, and they're going to kill him. You can't let them do that, you've got to stop them.

Stop them. But how? And why would they want to kill him?

Never mind why, and you know how. Don't try to think about it, just do it.

Do it. I stared out at the scene, hurting and confused and tired, both hands to my head, and couldn't think about it. I didn't understand and remembered almost nothing, but I *had* to do it or my best friend would die. I couldn't let that happen, and I did know how to stop it.

It hurt to send my mind out, as though there were chains all around it fighting to keep it back, but chains weren't solid and neither were my thoughts. I came to the women with the spears first and took their confidence, then I took their sense of balance. The uncertainty was so strong that one fell to the ground and tried to clasp it, while the other simply fainted. The four holding the ropes were next, and deep disgust turned

those ropes into something frightful and sickening, so awful
and nauseating that to continue holding them would have led
inescapably to madness. They dropped the lines with shouts
and screams, shuddering convulsing their thoughts, but I was
already with the mind of my friend, reassuring him and
telling him he had to run. I made him know that we needed
him to help us, but the only way he could do that was to get
out of the city and stay free. In the first few seconds he tried
to refuse to go, but my assurances erased his misgivings and
then he was off, trotting through and away from the crowd of
women, a few of whom made an attempt to grab the trailing
ropes. As his speed picked up the rope ends were snatched
away from them, and then he was galloping through an
opening in the wall, scattering guards in all directions. He
was determined to do as I'd told him to and not let anyone
catch him, and my hands fell away from my head with the
exhaustion I felt, the struggle I'd had to *make* him understand. Emotional blends with highlights and connotations had
been necessary, a symphony of sense I hadn't really been up
to orchestrating, and I felt as though I had almost nothing
left.

My head hurt terribly, more than it had after the battle with
the intruder, the unvarying buzz in my mind making it worse.
I had to stop that buzz or I would be physically ill, but it was
everywhere and coming from all directions. The pain in my
knees and legs was almost smothered by that buzz and I was
being bent forward by it, my arms wrapped around my
middle against the ache. There was something I could do
about it but the memory of it was just beyond reach, hidden
in the confusion that still held me. I wanted that memory and
needed it terribly, but I just couldn't think in the middle of
that buzz. I had to block it out somehow, had to push it away
from me, had to—

Suddenly the buzz was gone, and at first I didn't understand. It felt as though something had stepped between me
and the noise, something that it couldn't penetrate, something
that shielded me—

Shield. My shield had formed around my mind, that small,

thick shield nothing could penetrate. But why hadn't it formed sooner, before the buzz had given me so much pain? Because it didn't form automatically, only when I consciously wanted it? But why hadn't I wanted it? Because I couldn't remember there was such a thing as a shield? Why couldn't I remember, and why did I feel so confused?

"What ails you, slave?" a harsh voice suddenly demanded from behind me, a female voice that drove into my confusion like a knife. "Have you finished the task which was given you, or do you seek to shirk it? Assume a properly respectful position while I make my inspection."

Without even looking up at the guard woman I immediately put my forehead and palms to the floor, a fear inside me that she would find something wrong. I didn't know what might be wrong or why I was worrying about it, and didn't understand why I felt so lethargic. It was more than just feeling tired and hot and hurting, and it didn't make any sense. Where was I, and what was going on?

"Sloppily done and almost totally inadequate," the woman muttered above me, coming back from her walk up the corridor. "To add to a slave's natural laziness is the lack of brawn in one such as you. The floor will need to be redone, again and again if necessary, till I find it satisfactory. For now you will come with me."

I straightened quickly and then rose to my feet, awash in trembling upset and dizzy with confused lack of understanding as to why I felt that way. The woman took off down the corridor, not even waiting to see if I really was following, but her confidence was justified. I was right then hurrying in her wake, part of me terrified at the thought of not being where I was supposed to be, the rest of me not arguing the point. I'd felt that way for some time, I realized, a dimly remembered but very unpleasant time, and I couldn't think of a reason for it. It came to me then that my head was still hurting from what I'd recently done, so it wasn't any wonder that I couldn't think. I'd have to wait until the headache went away.

The guard woman led me from one corridor to the next, striding along in complete unconcern, even when other women we passed grinned or snickered at the naked slave hurrying along behind her. My cheeks warmed with embarrassment when it really came through to me that I was naked, but there didn't seem to be anything to do about it. My mind put asking for something to wear on a par with not being where I was supposed to be, a feeling I couldn't argue with. I hated being naked and being laughed at, but until I could think again there was nothing I could do.

The end of a final corridor widened out into a semi-familiar square slave area, and the men in it went to their knees at the appearance of the guard woman leading me. I would have hung back if I possibly could have, but she turned and took my arm, then thrust me out ahead of her.

"Your slave has been displeasing in the task she was given," the woman announced, her amusement and satisfaction evident only in her eyes. "Which of you will punish her before she serves your meal?"

The eyes of the kneeling men came to me where I stood, most of them upset, a few of them oddly annoyed. I found that I was trembling at that mass stare, but this time didn't have to wonder why. One of them was going to punish me, and I didn't want to be punished by a Rimilian male.

"Mistress, I will punish her," one of them said, a handsome man I seemed to remember better than most of the others. "We thank you for having brought this need to our attention, and will quickly see to it."

"Quickly and thoroughly," the woman said, folding her arms as she looked at me. "You may begin now, for I have other matters awaiting my attention."

"Yes, mistress," the man acknowledged, sounding defeated, almost as though he had been hoping she would leave. He got to his feet and walked to the side of the area, picked something up, then brought it back toward me. As he came closer I saw it was a strip of heavy leather that he held, and I immediately looked up into his eyes. He was one of those who had been faintly annoyed, and I could feel my trembling increase.

"Kneel here to your master, slave," he commanded sternly,

pointing to the floor in front of him where he'd stopped, about five feet away from me. I should have hurried over but I simply couldn't, finding all but small, hesitant steps beyond me. All of the men were watching me, and the woman as well, and as I knelt on the spot I'd been ordered to I knew that I'd never in my life felt so completely stripped bare.

"Put your brow to the stone, girl,'" the man I knelt to ordered, the strip of leather now held in both of his hands, his blue eyes even more stern-looking than they had been. "I shall not punish you as the high mistress does, yet shall you be well seen to."

I put my head and palms to the stone, feeling the ache in my back as I did so. That was where the high mistress punished me, I knew, across the back and occasionally across the breasts, but that wasn't how I would be punished this time. My hair had tumbled onto the stone, some of it falling over my hands, and then I heard a faint scuff, as though the feet I knelt before moved away from in front of me. An instant later there were knees on my hair and big hands wrapped around my wrists, and then two other hands took my ankles. I was being held rigidly in place, and didn't understand why until the first stroke fell.

"Oh!" I cried, thoughtlessly trying to straighten up, or move away, or protect myself with my hands, none of which worked. I cried out again as I was struck a second time and then a third, and not long after that my eyes were full of tears of pain and humiliation. The guard woman had begun chuckling in amusement almost at the very start, really enjoying the way that leather was being applied to my bottom. If I hadn't been held I wouldn't have stayed in that position, being horribly humiliated in front of another woman, but I *was* being held and couldn't pull loose. Two men were holding me while another strapped my bottom, and the woman's laughter was filled with the knowledge that I could do nothing to stop it.

"Are you punished, slave?" the handsome man's voice came then, the sternness still in it. "Will you in future be a good, obedient slave?"

"Yes, master, I am punished," I sobbed, willing to say anything if it would make him stop, feeling my tears roll down into my hair. "I will be a good, obedient slave."

"She fails to beg you to cease," the woman watching put in, sounding as though she were giving lessons. "She must have a bit more."

"Oh!" I cried as it began again, wishing I could scream instead, my wrist and ankles almost numb from the strength of the hold on them, my head throbbing where it was forced to the stone. "Please no, master, please, no more! I will be a good, obedient slave, as good and obedient as you wish! I have been punished, master, please do not punish your slave the more!"

"A bit more will do her endless good," the woman said in a no-arguments voice as the strokes began to stop again. "You must not allow your slave to go without proper punishment, boy, else will she be quick to seek advantage over you. Does she greet you eagerly on your pallet, or must you force her to your use?"

"She—shows no eagerness for my use, mistress," the man with the strip of leather admitted reluctantly, a bewilderment behind the words. "I have not allowed her to escape her duty, yet did I expect her reception to be somewhat more—joyful."

"Once you have done with her punishment, she will be a good deal more receptive," the woman assured him, her voice full of confidence. "A well-punished slave is ever a slave eager to please."

"Yes, mistress, that is surely so," the man said thoughtfully, and then I was being strapped again, just as hard as before. I cried and screamed and begged him to stop, but it took a while before he did so. When I was finally allowed to straighten on my knees I couldn't stop sobbing, and the woman looked down at me in deep satisfaction.

"When next she requires such punishment, there will be others who will wish to witness it," she said to the man beside her, just short of chuckling again at the way I immediately dropped my eyes in mortification. "Come the time, you will inform me beforehand, do you understand? And be sure she is given her special wine before you all depart to serve the *Chama*."

"Yes, mistress," my master the slave answered, complete acquiescence in his tone. The next minute the sound of receding footsteps came, and once they were out of hearing distance my master crouched next to me and put a hand under my chin.

"How foolish you were for disobeying, *wenda*," he scolded me gently, his large blue eyes on my face. "Have you not yet learned that to disobey is to be punished?"

"Yes, master," I said with a sniff, finding it impossible to stop crying. "I have now learned that lesson."

"Clearly we, your masters, did you no service by failing to punish you before this," he said, and then he looked at me very sternly again. "Do you wish us to inform the mistress that we mean to punish you in the same way upon the next occasion?"

"Please, no, master!" I begged, horrified at the thought, putting my hands out toward him. "I could not bear being done so again, I would die of the shame!"

"So I believed, from the words spoken so often in your sleep," he said with a nod, the sternness gone again. "To avoid such a thing, will you greet the use of your masters with greater eagerness and joy? Will you accept, rather than being made to take?"

I hesitated very briefly at the question, his gaze impossible to avoid, then found the hesitation a waste of time. I had been given a choice, but I really had no choice at all.

"I will greet you eagerly, master," I agreed, lowering only my eyes when his hand refused to release my chin. "Your slave will serve you as best she may."

"Oh, excellent!" my master said with a laugh of joy, a pleased stirring coming from those others who had chosen to join him in my use. There were very few of them, I knew, but I hadn't yet discovered why. "And as our meal is not yet ready to be served, you may begin at once. There is a good deal of time before we will be called to serve the *Chama* and her guests at their own meal."

"Now, master?" I asked in dismay, knowing when his hand left my chin that I was about to be lifted in his arms, which happened just about immediately. "Please, master, not so soon after your punishment, please not!"

"What better time than when you are most eager?" he asked, straightening from his crouch and heading directly toward his pallet, his arms holding me almost without effort. "I would not have you regret your choice, therefore must I assist you."

"Master, please," I began in protest, even more upset to realize that he thought he was doing me a favor, but he had already reached his pallet and was putting me down on it. From the half crouch he slid flat to lie beside me, his arms still firmly around me, a warm, friendly smile on his face.

"Each time I look upon you, I find you lovelier and lovelier," he said, the fingers of one hand reaching to my cheek to wipe away the tears there, his big, blue eyes unmoving from my face. "You are small, and soft, and lovely and desirable, and I shall keep you forever and ever."

"Master, please," I whispered, for some reason feeling a stab of pain at his words. He was so open and vulnerable, and so clearly meant everything he was saying.

"Have no fear, they will not take you from me," he soothed, folding me in his arms and holding me tight against him. "They would not have given you to me merely to take you away again." He hesitated for a moment, still holding me close, then said, "Is it true you will please me even more because I have punished you?"

I could feel his big body trembling faintly, much less than it had the last time I could remember, but the excitement was the same, the anticipation unchanged. The child-man who held me was beginning to feel his authority over me, and also most likely the realization that he had not hit me as hard as he might have.

"It is true I will please you to keep from being punished again," I said after a moment, my hands and cheek against his chest, my body to his body. "Such a thing is not the same as what you suggest."

"In what manner does it differ?" he asked, sounding legitimately puzzled. "In either case, will you not strive to please me because of the punishment?"

"I—cannot say in what manner it differs." I was groping, feeling slightly less confused than I had, but still not completely clear. "No other thing do I know save that it does."

"I care not whether the two may differ, or whether they are just the same," he murmured, his hands beginning to move over me. "You now must please me, and greet me with a great deal of eagerness. Are you not most eager for my use?"

"Yes, master, I am eager for your use," I whispered, trying not to shudder as I spoke. It was a terrible lie I told, and it hurt me simply to speak it.

The child-man who held me heard just the words, nothing of the lie behind. His lips came to mine and I tried to respond to his kiss, but his breathing had grown a lot heavier, causing him to simply mash my efforts to nothing. He was kissing me, not trying to share a kiss, and he pressed me flat to the pallet even while he was doing it.

"Hush, lovely *wenda*, poor *wenda*," he crooned when I gasped at the feel of the rough cloth against the welts on my back, his weight keeping me from rising up again. "The high mistress has given you hurt, I know, yet shall I quickly soothe it. You wish me to soothe it, do you not? Tell me that you wish it."

"I would have you soothe me, master," I whispered raggedly, beginning to cry again. It was more than just the painful welts on my back that tore me apart inside, and I could almost remember what else it was. "Please hold me and soothe me, master, please comfort me."

"Yes, lovely one, yes," he panted, thrusting my thighs apart with his knee, but he hadn't heard what I'd asked for. The next minute he was inside me, jarring away with strength and abandon, his hands on my shoulders, using me as a substitute for his hand. His head was back and his eyes were closed, he panted heavily and the look on his face was sheer bliss and contentment. After a while he leaned down to slobber me with kisses again, but his hips never stopped moving. The tears ran down my cheeks even as I held him around, simply enduring what he was doing, realizing it would be impossible to do anything else. He didn't know how much he was hurting me, and I couldn't go back on my word by telling him.

Happily, it wasn't long before it was over, but then there were the others. The handsome child-man sat at my side, holding my hand until they were done, never knowing how much worse he was making it simply by being there. He encouraged me and the others contentedly, then insisted that I be given a moment before being made to serve them all their meal. The very plain vegetable stew had been made by one of the others, and I had to put it into bowls and then bring a bowl to each of them. When they finished eating I collected the bowls and scoops, washed them in a tub of water in one corner, then was allowed to finish what was left in the pot before washing that, too. I could remember eating every last scrap and licking the pot in the days that had passed, but that day the constant, gnawing hunger I'd been feeling was absent. For that reason I'd left almost nothing in the pot, and for that reason the almost-nothing went into the wash water instead of me. The pain in my body had increased, but the throb in my head seemed to be clearing more by the minute.

When the pot was done and put away I simply stood there and leaned my left arm against the stone of the wall, unable to remember what I was supposed to do next, my thoughts a mad whirl I couldn't even begin to follow. My stomach felt upset, and nausea was trying to get a grip on me, but the confusion in my head was worse than anything else. It was as though ten or a dozen people were trying to shout at me about different things all at the same time through a thick pane of glass, and all the while the pane of glass was getting thinner. The thinner it got the more easily I could hear them, but I didn't know which of them to listen to first.

"*Wenda*, it is nearly time for us to take our leave," a voice said from beside me, drawing me away from those other voices. "There is a thing you must do first."

I looked up to see my master standing there, smiling at me gently and encouragingly as he usually did.

"Where is it that we must go?" I asked, frowning with the effort to remember. "And what is there that I must do first?"

"No, *wenda*, it is we others, your masters, who must soon depart," he explained gently, his hand to my hair, as though he had had to say the same thing before. "The thing *you* must do is drink your wine, just as you do each day at this time."

"My wine," I echoed as he took my hand and began leading me toward the corner where the tiny supply of food-stuff was kept, the supply that had to last everyone there for three days. I didn't remember ever having had wine before, at least not there.

"You seem ever unable to recall the wine," he observed, gesturing me to my knees beside the boxes. "Also do you seem most confused at this time, yet am I told that that is as it should be. Once the drink is within you, the confusion will loose its hold."

He took a clay pitcher and a clay bowl from on top of the boxes, filled the bowl from the pitcher, then handed me what he had poured. I took the bowl in both hands and looked down into its dark, muddy gold contents, remembering a sparkling golden wine I'd had—somewhere, at some other time.

"Drink it now," the man who stood above me urged, the words gentle rather than commanding. "It will take the confusion from you, and will aid you in finding sleep. You must sleep, you know, for the new day begins early as ever, and will be filled as ever with much to do."

I looked up at him from where I knelt, the bowl held in my hands, grateful to him for having given me something that would take the confusion away. I needed something to do that, needed it badly, and now I had it.

"The time is now, slaves," a female voice announced from the entrance to the area, a place I couldn't see from where I was. "Follow me at once."

"Drink the wine," my master repeated in a hurried whisper, reaching down quickly to touch my cheek with a big, gentle hand. "When we are awakened with the new light, I will rouse you with the pleasure of use."

And then he was gone, following after the others as they all hastened after the woman who had called them. After and after and after, slaves after the master, the master a slave and the slave a master. I shook my head to dislodge the cadenced nonsense, not wanting to get caught up in it, and spilled a drop or two of the wine I was holding. The bowl it lay in was a dull pink with the suggestion of red beneath, for all the world like skinless flesh covering blood. Inside the skinless flesh was the wine I was supposed to drink, the wine I wanted to drink, but also the wine that would surely make me violently ill if I tried to swallow it. I could feel the sweat breaking out on my body and could see my hands trembling, and all I wanted to do was lie down and die. I knelt in place for another minute, struggling to control myself enough to take even a single sip, but it was just no good. I needed someone to help me take that sip, someone to help hold the bowl and coax me into it, but no one was there. The meal had been served too late, and the slaves had been called too soon, and no one had noticed that I hadn't had my wine.

I found myself on my feet without knowing how I'd gotten there, but that was more a blessing than a problem. My body hurt just about everywhere and I was getting very dizzy, so I didn't have the time to struggle to stand up. The stone floor was smooth enough, but it still hurt the bottoms of my feet as I made my way to the tub of dirty water. Bending over let the wine pour out into the water, and the muddiness of it matched very well with the murkiness. Or the other way around. A single rinse and the bowl was good enough to be put to one side; I put it aside, then went to find my master's pallet. I was allowed to sleep on the very edge of it, and that's what I needed to do. I hurt even more when I lowered myself to my left side, and then it was all gone behind sleep.

*   *   *

My eyes were open and my heart was thudding, and for a minute I didn't know where I was. I lay on my left side on something stiff and hard and uncomfortable, and the dimness around me held the soft sounds of many people deeply asleep. My first thought was, *Where the hell am I?* but if it had been said aloud rather than thought, the last words would never have gotten out. I knew where I was and also what had happened, and was finally able to appreciate the sheer luck that had broken me free.

I continued to lie unmoving on my side, but that was only physically. Inside my head my thoughts were racing, fighting with each other for priority. How long it had been I still didn't know, but Tammad, Cinnan, and I had been taken by the *Chama* of Vediaster, and I, at least, had been made a slave. I had a feeling the same thing had been done to the men, but not entirely in the same way.

My first urge was to go and find Tammad, which set me to sitting up slowly, quietly and carefully. My—master—was asleep on the rest of the pallet, and the last thing I wanted to do was wake him. It was very quiet in that slave area, the only light coming in from the corridor that led to it, the air heavy and close and too full of the scent of too many bodies. I was able to sit and maintain the sitting position, but I had to bite my lip against the pain I felt. I hurt just about all over, my energy levels felt almost entirely drained, and my insides ached with the hollowness of getting not enough to eat for too long a time. On top of that I didn't dare open my shield, not when I didn't have the strength to fight back, so how was I supposed to find someone? I'd been taken before by not realizing I was under attack; this time all they'd have to do was breathe on me, and over I would go.

I put my face into my hands and rubbed at my forehead, knowing what I had to do but hating it. The only intelligent thing was to get myself out of that palace, steal food and find a place to sleep for half of forever, then come back when I felt less like the results of a *seetarr* stampede. But that meant I would have to leave Tammad behind, still in the clutches of that—that—woman, and I knew if it were his choice he would never abandon me the same way.

I also now knew why I'd felt so strong a need for learning how to use a sword, a need that was no longer with me. The time the knowledge would have helped was already behind me, and the man who was mine now lay in the possession of another. Not for the first time I wished I had Tammad's giant strength and matchless determination, and then I wished I had it there beside me, in him with his arms opened wide. I needed him very badly right then, probably even more than he needed me, but I didn't have him and all he had as a hope of freedom was a useless, stubborn, ignorant *wenda*. One woman against how many hundreds, and I didn't even dare open my shield? If I managed to find him it would be more miracle than rescue, but I wasn't about to let that stop me. I'd worry about consequences when they were about to drop on my head—and only after I'd had a decent amount of sleep.

Just sitting there made no sense, so I forced myself to my feet and tiptoed across the area to the corridor. Behind me I could hear someone muttering in his sleep and, when chuckling followed the meaningless words, I thought I knew who it was. The slaves of that area never laughed, rarely smiled, and some had begun to express enjoyment only recently, with their new undertaking. Only one of the very few experimenters would actually chuckle, and I shuddered even as I refused to think about him. I had other things to think about first, and if we all got out of the trap that had been waiting for us, there would be plenty of time later.

The first few corridors I crept along were deserted, but the further I went the more I knew I was not cut out for the life of an adventurer. If someone had suddenly come out of one of the doorways to appear in front of me, I undoubtedly would have died of heart failure then and there. It was terrible not being able to send my mind out ahead of me and all around, but that heavy, buzzing broadcast that had knocked me over the first time was still there, so thick and strong that the air nearly vibrated with it. I wasn't feeling it but I was itching from it, understanding perfectly well why it continued on into deep night: at night peoples' defenses were at their lowest, and that was the best time to reach through to them. If I ever managed to get out of there, I intended wondering just what it was they were reaching out with and for.

I got through another two corridors of rock walls that scraped my back and tried to make me yell out loud, of high torches that illuminated me clearly no matter how small I fought to make myself, of rock floor that was whisper quiet even though I expected it to begin creaking at any moment, and then I found something I hadn't known I was looking for. A nicely carved table outside one of the closed, heavy wooden doors in the wall held something other than a vase of flowers or a well-done statuette. It looked like a pile of cloth until I got closer, and then it looked like a rain cape, only not made for the rain. It was bright red with gold trim around all the edges, and right in the middle of all that red was a neat, square-cornered tear. It looked as though it had caught on something that had ripped it, and had probably been left out by its owner so that a slave might repair it in the morning. I stared at it for a good five seconds before grabbing it up and pulling it on over my head, and that solved one of the problems I'd hoped to have. If I made it out into the city I couldn't very well wander around naked, and now I didn't have to. The thing didn't reach up high enough to cover the bronze metal band around my throat, but one problem at a time.

Making a left turn at the next corridor intersection instead of a right put me no more than twenty-five feet from my second solution. I needed to get out of that palace, and just ahead were two terrace doors in the wall, standing open with the darkness of night behind them. As I hurried toward them I heard a faint clatter coming from the opposite direction, but I wasn't silly enough to stop and turn around and look. If they were about to recapture me I didn't want to know it and, if they weren't I wasn't about to hang around and give them the chance. With heart pounding and breath rasping and legs wobbling I got myself through those doors, then let the darkness swallow me up.

It took longer than I like to think about before I was able
to stop trembling, before the quiet of the dark let me think
again instead of simply running. I sat on the grass in the
middle of that dark, well away from the torches that lit the
outside of the palace, feeling the cool night air dry the sweat
of panic from my face. The cape I had taken was keeping me
warm, but it was also urging me to lie down comfortably for
a few minutes, and I couldn't afford to do that. I was so tired
I would probably fall immediately asleep, and that would be
the end of my escape. I had to get through the wall and into
the city before I slept, through the city and out of it before I
could relax. Stopping to think about it told me which gate I
had to use, the only gate that would send me a way I had any
hope of recognizing, the main gate we had come in by. I
levered myself to my feet and tottered a moment, then staggered off to find the only gate that would do me.

Each of the gates I passed was brightly lit by torches, and
because of that I began to believe I'd never find the one I
needed. Hidden in the dark I looked at each of those gates,
realized they were too small to be the one I needed, then
forced myself to go on. It came to me after a while that I
might be moving in the wrong direction, that the gate I was
looking for might have been only a short distance from where
I began but the other way; I thought about that quite a lot, but
didn't stop moving as I had begun, to the right facing the
wall. If I started doubting myself and went back the other
way, I could spend the rest of the night going back and forth
in front of one section of wall.

When I finally reached the right gate I knew it immediately, but I took a couple of minutes to rest and think about
how I would get through it. It was gaping as wide open as it
had been when we'd first gotten there, but it also had nearly
as many armed women standing around guarding it. After a
minute or so I was able to count eight, and then was just able
to keep myself from slumping down to the grass in defeat.
Eight *w'wendaa* when I wouldn't even have been able to face
one under the best of circumstances, which that certainly was

not. I was beaten, totally defeated, and the best thing I could do was go back to the palace and give myself up.

But that would mean really deserting my beloved, leaving him in a capture that might very well be worse than death. My head came up as I realized that I didn't even know what that woman was doing to him, but it couldn't have been anything pleasant. And he was resisting, I knew he was resisting, otherwise she wouldn't have beaten me as often and as viciously as she had. I couldn't make his efforts wasted, I had to get out of there and regain my strength, and then come back for him! The thought of me rescuing a man his size was ludicrous, but I had no strength left at all for ridicule. What I did have left I needed—to get myself out that gate.

I moved as near to the opening as I could without stepping into the torchlight, then stood straight and still and clenched my fists. Every one of those women was larger than the dark-haired slave in the shadows, but it wasn't in a physical way that I meant to attack them. I still couldn't open my shield and because of that received nothing, but I'd tried once and had found that I could reach *around* my shield to touch others. I felt incipient hysterics at the thought of having done it all at once, but I couldn't let that stop me. Maybe I *didn't* know how much strength I had working that way, and maybe I didn't even know if I could split a projection effectively; what I did know was that I had to try, even if I failed.

Sending the projection out around my shield and not going along to guide it brought the sweat to my body and face again, the sweat of fear and the sweat of straining. I strained to split that projection eight ways and send each part in the right direction, and every minute of the time was afraid I was doing something wrong or simply not right enough. I stood sweating and trembling in the cool dark, watching all of the women standing exactly as they had been, and finally decided that I had to try it. If it didn't work I would be a captive and a slave again, but that's just what I'd be if I didn't get moving. I wouldn't be able to hold that projection much longer, and once the effort stopped it would be a long while before I would find it possible to start again.

Moving more like a wooden toy than a living being, I headed straight for the opening, keeping to a moderate pace. Running would have been stupid even if it had been physically possible, and creeping along would have driven me crazy. I walked through the torchlight and nighttime insect noises up to the opening, my feet making no noise on the thick grass, then held my breath as I passed between two of the women guards. If any of them had spoken or reached out to touch me I would have collapsed, but none of them was capable of doing that just then. Their introspection was so deep that they stood like statues cast in flesh, eyes down or inward, total disinterest turning them deaf and blind to their surroundings. They didn't know or care that I was passing through the gate, and that was exactly the way it was supposed to be.

Under the right circumstances, a mere fifty feet can stretch for miles; when I'd first ridden across it, it hadn't seemed so bad, but walking back was a nightmare. The sweat of strain poured over me as though it were raining, but I couldn't afford to release the projection until I was out of sight. Ten feet and my soles were bruised from the small stones and twigs on the ground, but ignore that and just keep going. Twenty feet and the red cape had grown heavier and more confining, but ignore that and just keep going. Thirty feet and you're more than halfway to the nearest dark alley, but just keep going. Forty feet and the nighttime dark has lost its breeze, but—keep going. Forty-five and it's only just ahead, a matter of steps. Even if you're staggering you can make it, just two more strides, just—

I collapsed against the side of the closed-tight stall no more than a single step inside the narrow alleyway, my forehead and palms against the rough wood and my eyes shut in the darkness. If I'd had to hold that projection even an instant longer I would have died, and that isn't a figurative analysis. All I wanted to do was fall down to the ground, and the only thing holding me up was the stall, that and the knowledge that if I let myself pass out, all my previous effort would have been wasted. I was safe where I was only until the sun came up, and after that I needed some place else. Since I had no intentions of being conscious when the sun came up, I had to find that someplace else before any of the previous happened. Whatever the hell the previous referred to.

It took three tries before I could push away from the stall side, and that included getting my eyes open again. Deeper into the alley was *that* way, away from the reflection of torches, at right angles to the stall wall. Stall wall. I was giggling before I knew it, finding that phrase hilarious, inching my way through the darkness with one hand stretched out to a wall and one clapped over my mouth. I knew I shouldn't be making any noise, but I couldn't seem to stop laughing—

Until I ran right into a large, hard body. I knew it was a body because I could feel one arm, and it wasn't simply large—it was giant. Everything funny in the entire universe died when two big hands came to my arms, and if I'd had the strength I would have screamed. I was suddenly convinced it was my master who held me, a giant male Rimilian just like all the rest, one who would carry me back to slavery and an eternity of pain-filled confusion. I mewled in terror and struck out with useless fists, and then I was being shaken hard so that very soft words would get through to me.

"Calm yourself, *wenda*, and do not struggle," I heard, no more than a breath behind each sound. "We would not wish the guard *wendaa* to find you, Terril, now that you have accomplished so excellent an escape."

Wendaa not *w'wendaa*, and he called me by name. I had just enough time to realize it was Dallan, before everything disappeared from around me.

10

I awoke with a start and the beginnings of panic, but the walls around me were a reddish-brown wood instead of smooth white stone, and I wasn't alone in the room. Not far from whatever I lay on Dallan sat in comfort amid cushions, a copper-colored goblet in his hands, his sword still belted around him. That more than anything else kept me from jumping up and running, and it wasn't until my heart had receded from my mouth that I noticed he hadn't moved. Working at keeping me off the ceiling, I thought as I lay back again and let my muscles unclench, and a damned good thing he was smart enough to do it. One move out of him and I probably would have been able to answer Garth's question about whether or not I could fly.

"*Wenda*, we must make an attempt to cease this," Dallan's voice came after a minute, sounding the least bit cautious. "I dislike finding myself at your side each time you awaken from pain-filled, fearful sleep. The practice is becoming upsetting."

"Perhaps it would be best if I were the first to make the attempt," I answered in a rusty voice, smiling faintly at his teasing. "Your part seems far easier to arrange."

"Not quite as easy as all that," he said, disagreeing, and then he was beside me, smoothing my hair back with one big hand. "So Tammad's apprehensions were correct after all. Are you able to tell me what was done to you there?''

I opened my eyes and turned my head to the man looking down at me, seeing the worry lines in his face that I'd thought I'd heard in his voice. On reconsideration I decided that sitting around waiting for someone to regain consciousness wasn't the most pleasant pastime in the world, and might even be harder than being the one who had gotten hurt.

"You may rest your mind, for I am completely recovered,'' I began at once, starting to get into a sitting position as fast as I could to reassure him, but I didn't make it. My body screamed out the demand as to whether I'd lost my mind, and then refused to let me have the ability to answer. All I managed was a croaking gasp and very little motion, and even that was swallowed up by Dallan's hand on my shoulder.

"Completely recovered, are you?'' he asked, the growl he refused to allow in his voice showing up in his eyes, his hand continuing to hold me down. "When I allow you to move it will only be slowly, and then for no more than a short time. Have you no concept of how badly you were whipped?''

As a matter of fact I didn't really, but the stiffness a portion of the pain had turned into started giving me an inkling. It wasn't going to be as easy as it had been those other times Dallan had mentioned, but it was still going to have to be done.

"I have not the time to move so slowly,'' I informed him with as much firmness as I could muster while still under that big hand of his. "Last darkness I was able to do what was necessary, and this darkness I shall do the same.''

"Indeed shall you do this darkness what was done during the last,'' he agreed, his tone, for some reason, rather dry. "Last darkness was spent by you in sleep, as well as all the day previous and half the darkness before that. It is now somewhere about mid-day, and you have so far had no more than meat broth in you, swallowed at the times you nearly awoke. I shall fetch you a meal, and then you will sleep again.''

He straightened and headed for the door in the wall to the right of where I lay, and I was too upset to protest before he had disappeared through it. It was going on two days since I'd escaped from the palace, but I hadn't done a damned thing about going back except sleep! I moved around a little where I lay, feeling the remnants of pain and the hobbling of stiffness, the strengthlessness that hadn't quite left me and the hollowness of near-starvation, and cursed under my breath. Dallan was picturing me taking a long time to recover, but he was in for a surprise. I couldn't afford to take my time, and had no intentions of doing so.

The room I lay in was rather small, but it was also rather pleasant. The reddish-brown paneling of the walls stopped at the wide window to the left of me, and a golden curtain colored the incoming light. The carpet-fur was also golden, and the pillows Dallan had been sitting among were red, all of it going well with the dark brown fur of my bed. Those furs seemed somewhat well-used, with the smell of salves or ointment to them, and once again I was naked under what covered me—but that terrible bronze collar was also gone. I thought about how I'd been stripped naked at that woman Roodar's orders and I felt the anger come, building slowly toward true fury. We had a score to settle, Roodar and I, but I would need to wait before I knew how big a score. If she had hurt Tammad she would live to regret it—that I swore by everything that was right!

I stopped the fury, saving it for the next time I'd need it. That time it had already served its purpose; although there was sweat on my forehead I was sitting up straight and had gotten that way with a lot less pain than I would have had without the strong emotion I'd used as a crutch. Anger can be very useful if you handle it properly, and it was about time I learned how to handle it.

A minute later the door opened, and I was surprised to see Dallan coming back with a tray. My stomach twisted at the thought of food, and I regretted how little I'd be able to eat.

"Have you taken to conjuring?" I asked as he closed the door before starting toward me with the tray. "I had not thought it would be possible for you to prepare provender and return so soon."

"As the mid-day meal had already been prepared and a servant was nearly here with it, I had only to take the tray," he answered, setting the thing down on my lap. "And clearly did you fail to expect so speedy a return, else you would not have been caught in so obvious a disobedience."

I was able to see the annoyance in his eyes before he turned away to begin gathering pillows from the carpet fur, but I didn't understand what he was talking about.

"What disobedience do you refer to?" I asked, taking a peek at the food he'd put under my nose. There was a thick meat soup of some kind, a slab of bread, a cup of yellow pudding that was probably pure sugar, and a goblet of what seemed to be juice of some sort.

"I refer to the disobedience of having found you sitting," he said, stuffing pillows behind my back until they were high enough to lean against. "Were you not told to remain unmoving till you had my permission to do otherwise?"

"Dallan, you continue to speak in riddles," I protested, reaching a hand out to the goblet of juice. The hand shook slightly, but I was still able to raise the goblet with only a minimal effort. "Though I look upon you with the love of a sister and feel deep gratitude for the manner in which you aid me in my need, I am not bound to obey you. I must restore my strength with all possible speed, and mean to do exactly that."

I watched him over the goblet rim as I drank, seeing the annoyance increase in his eyes as he crouched beside me to my right.

"I am greatly honored that you look upon me as a brother," he said, lacing his fingers together as he stared at me. "Also am I honored that your *memabrak* Tammad looks upon me the same, and therein lies the root of your confusion. In Tammad's absence your protection is mine, therefore are you bound to obey me as you do him. In time will your strength be restored, *wenda*, and to hurry the matter will only cause

235

you greater harm. You will rest and do as I say, and soon will find yourself in full health."

"And what harm will Tammad be given the while I lie about resting?" I asked, finding it difficult to keep my anger from flaring out. "You believe I will meekly obey you the while he remains in the hands of that—*female*? No, Dallan, do not expect it to be so, for it shall not be! I will return to that place as quickly as I am able, and woe to any who stands in my path."

"Calmly, sister, calmly," he soothed, worry having replaced the annoyance in his eyes. His hands came to mine on the goblet, gently trying to take it out of my grip, and I looked down to see the white on my knuckles. I'd obviously been trying to crush the life out of the goblet, a top-notch example of complete emotional control and stability.

"Perhaps you would do better urging me to intelligence rather than calm," I said, letting him take the stupid goblet. "To waste one's strength in anger is to throw it away before a time of true need. I shall not waste it so again, for I will soon have need of it."

"Perhaps I would do best in now speaking of other things," he replied, putting the goblet down and picking up the bowl of meat soup. "Eat as much of this as you are able, and then we will discuss what befell you."

"The *Chama* of Vediaster befell us," I said, taking the bowl while trying not to drool. "How is it you were in precisely the place I chose to make my escape?"

"Where else would I be?" he asked, rising to go after the goblet he had left earlier, and returning to sit cross-legged where he'd been crouching. "I knew well enough by what gate you three had entered the palace grounds, therefore was that the gate I took up vigilance before when you failed to emerge or send word. Knowing as you all did that I was about, I reasoned that were one of you to effect an escape it would be through there so that we might find one another. When I saw you moving unchallenged through the ranks of the guards I knew you used your power, therefore did I retreat further into the alleyway to keep from being affected. I was cautiously making my way to you when you came to me instead.''

I was too busy taking another scoopful of the thick soup to say anything immediately, and it needed to be chewed a little before it could be swallowed. If anyone had asked me just then how it was, I would have sworn it was the best thing I'd tasted in my entire life.

''I believe I should admit it had not occurred to me that you would be there,'' I said as soon as I could, reaching for the slab of bread. ''It was truly fortunate that I no longer had the strength to wield my power, for my mind had not entirely cleared itself, and your abrupt appearance frightened me badly. This place you brought me to is extremely pleasant. Have you—taken it for the time we will remain in the city?''

I'd wanted to ask Dallan if he'd rented the place or was boarding there, but the Rimilian language had no words or phrases to express the ideas. I remembered then what Tammad had said about there being no accommodations available for money, but Dallan was already shaking his head.

''I had need of a haven for you and also a healer, therefore was I unable to merely take you to my *camtah*,'' he said. ''I was not immediately able to remove that band from around your throat, which made choosing a healer at random an undertaking filled with peril. I required a healer who would not afterward speak of the palace slave who had been tended, and there was but a single way to discover one such as that. We are now both guests beneath the roof of Leelan.''

I stopped chewing almost in mid-bite to stare at him, but his expressionless façade told me nothing. I had more than a few reactions of my own to that revelation, but that was neither the time nor the place to expound on them.

''So we are guests of Leelan of Vediaster,'' was all I said, going back to my fortifying. ''And she was able—and willing—to find the sort of healer you required?''

''When she saw what had been done to you she was taken by great anger,'' Dallan said, the odd look in his eyes flickering at the admission. ''Leelan seems—disapproving—of the *Chama* and her court, and was not reluctant to give us assistance. The healer she sent for—a quiet man who seemed quite close to her—apparently felt the same.''

"We will not impose on her generosity for long," I said, pausing to take another swallow of the juice. "This darkness would be too soon for me, I think, yet the one after will surely be suitable. By then we shall have formed a plan, and will proceed to free Tammad and Cinnan.''

"Shall we indeed?" he said, sounding annoyed all over again. "We two alone will force our way onto the palace grounds, obtain entry to the palace itself, and then blithely proceed to free Tammad and Cinnan? The while those who stand guard merely look on and comment upon our progress? Or perhaps assist us?''

"You need not be so exasperated," I told him with a calm glance, paying more attention to my food than to his hysterics. "The plan will see to all of your objections.''

"A plan which has not yet been formulated, but which will no doubt contain provision for the necessity of my carrying you as well as wielding a blade," he growled, not at all happy with me. "You will not be fit to walk alone so soon, an opinion put forward by the healer which I shall, in 'exasperation,' take above your own. Do you believe me so skillful with a sword that *this* objection will be overcome?''

I took a final mouthful of the meat soup, a mouthful I was forcing on myself in an effort to more quickly increase my capacity, then finished the last of the juice. Once the goblet was down, however, I turned my head to look directly at Dallan.

"As you seriously doubt that my attempt will succeed, perhaps it would be best if you were to remain behind," I said, speaking with absolute neutrality. "The healer cannot know when I will walk, for he cannot feel what I do. Come the darkness after this next, I will walk—and succeed.''

I wonder if explosions have to gather themselves before they can go off. If they're anything like Dallan they do, and from the look in his eyes that was just what he was intending. He straightened where he sat, his eyes hard and furious, but before he was able to get the first word out there was a knock on the door. He wanted to ignore the knock, and probably would have if he were in his own house, but instead he called out, "Enter."

I don't know who I could have been expecting, but seeing Leelan walk in was something of a surprise. She hadn't changed at all in the past few days, and was wearing her sword the same way Dallan wore his; why she should have changed was something else I didn't know, but somehow I felt as though she should have. When she saw me sitting up it was her turn to be faintly surprised, but that didn't stop her from closing the door and approaching my bed.

"It pleases me to see you looking so well, Terril," she said, stopping to Dallan's right toward the foot of the bed. "The healer was quite certain you would awaken about this time."

"She is far more than awake," Dallan said, the growl even thicker, his eyes not moving from my face. "She means to attack the palace come the darkness after next, and has just informed me that, as I dared to suggest that the effort might well be extreme only for her and me, my presence will not be required after all. Perhaps you would be good enough to request the return of that healer. I would know how soon it will be permissible to beat her."

"Not for some time, I should think." Leelan soothed him with a badly swallowed-down grin while I bristled. "I cannot find it in me to fault her for wishing to return to the palace to take vengeance, however, for would we, ourselves, not wish to do the same, had we been done as she was? There are many who chafe beneath the rule of the present *Chama*, Terril, and many who would truly joy in accompanying you with bared blades, yet is there the power to consider. Farian won her place with the strength of her power, and there are none about able to match her, not to speak of besting her. No matter your determination, girl, it is simply not enough."

"You concern yourself with the *Chama* Farian's power?" I scoffed, still more than annoyed at Dallan's attitude—and the way they were both treating me like a child. "One who falls upon others from ambush cannot be truly strong, else would the ambush have been unnecessary. I thank you for your hospitality, Leelan, yet shall I follow my own advice.''

Leelan looked momentarily upset and Dallan began drawing himself up again, but for the second time the explosion didn't come off. The big blonde woman put a calming hand on his shoulder, then seated herself cross-legged beside him.

"I have not as yet heard how she and the others were taken—nor why,'' she said to Dallan when his eyes came to her. "Has she spoken of it as yet?''

"She found too great a number of other things to speak of in its stead,'' he answered sourly with a headshake, then looked at me again. "As the time of your departure draws so rapidly near, perhaps you would be kind enough to enlighten us before its arrival. We would not wish to see you gone before we were told the tale.''

"As there is very little to tell, there is scarcely a danger of that,'' I said, feeling myself stiffen in response to his sarcasm. "We rode to the main gate of the palace and requested an audience with the *Chama*, were escorted within the palace to a room where we were to wait, and once within that room we were overwhelmed. When I awoke we had indeed been taken before the *Chama*—as captives and slaves. We had all been given some sort of potion, to add to whatever had felled us.''

"What felled you was the *Chama*'s Hand of Power,'' Leelan said, her eyes angry, her right fist clenched on her thigh. "There are a number of our people with small traces of the power, incapable, of themselves, of making effective use of it. Together, however, under the guidance of Farian, five at once are frighteningly powerful. Each set of five performs only for a short time, and then is replaced with another set. They have recently begun broadcasting at a greater and greater distance from here, and that angers many of us greatly. Should it be Farian's wish to go aconquering, the sword and spear and bow should be her weapons. To use the power is dishonorable.''

"They attacked even before you had spoken with the *Chama*?'' Dallan asked with a frown, while I stared at Leelan.

So that's what that buzz was: five low-grade empaths projecting together! Even from a distance it had filtered through my
curtain, and when I was right on top of it it had just about
scrambled me. I'd known keeping my shield closed was a
protection I needed; I just hadn't known what I needed to be
protected from.

"*Wenda*, for what reason were you attacked even before
you had had an audience?" Dallan repeated, reaching over to
touch my arm. "Were their suspicions aroused, or are all
travelers done in such a manner?"

"They did not suspect, they knew," I answered with a
snort, only then really appreciating the point. "That we
sought Aesnil was not in doubt, for she had been made to
speak of the dark-haired, green-eyed *wenda* who would surely
accompany those who rode after her. It was my presence
which caused us to be attacked."

Dallan stared at me with an expression of revelation-come-
too-late, finally seeing how big a mistake Tammad had made
in not listening to me. If he and Cinnan had shown up at the
palace without me, they would have been nothing but two
large, blond Rimilian *l'lendaa*, indistinguishable from all the
rest. My presence was the equivalent of jumping up and
down waving a red flag. Of course they hadn't asked us what
we wanted there; why waste time listening to lies when you
already know the truth?

"You came here seeking someone?" Leelan said, looking
at Dallan's profile with confusion on her face. "I had thought
the one called Tammad came to speak of the off-worlders,
and you and Cinnan merely accompanied him?"

"Tammad did indeed come to speak of the off-worlders,"
Dallan answered, taking a deep breath before turning his head
to look at her. "Cinnan and I, however, have come seeking
Aesnil, *Chama* of Grelana, who was taken from Cinnan in
Gerleth, my own country. Aesnil wears Cinnan's bands, and
we knew not why she would depart Gerleth in the company
of two *wendaa* from this place."

"They mean to influence her in some manner before returning her to Grelana," I put in, digging out the memory of

what Farian had said about that. "Undoubtedly the entire matter is connected with the *Chama*'s plans of conquest."

"Again with the use of the power!" Leelan snarled, fury in her eyes. "Before Farian is done, the name of Vediaster will be despised and spat upon the world over! She fouls our honor with her every act, and we are powerless to halt her! Truly do I give thanks that my mother was spared the pain of this."

"There are others who have not been spared the presence of pain," I said, wishing I could get rid of the tray on my lap, finding that I leaned more heavily on the pillows behind me. "When I stand in challenge before Roodar, perhaps her *Chama* will attempt to intervene. Should she do so, I will see to her for you."

"You?" Leelan snorted with contempt, her usual diplomacy lost momentarily beneath her anger, but then she realized what she'd said—and how she'd said it. "Forgive me, Terril, it was not my intention to give you insult," she said apologetically, trying to throttle down her outrage over Farian. "You say you mean to face Roodar in challenge, yet Roodar is the finest sword among Farian's *w'wendaa*, and one I, myself, burn to face. Less than two hands of darknesses ago, you asked to be taught the use of a sword; this day you speak blithely of facing Roodar, and Farian as well. Forgive me, Terril, for you are a guest beneath my roof, but the words you uttered are no other thing than foolishness."

"I do not mean to face Roodar with swords, Leelan," I said, too tired for insult or for apology. "That is a thing I have already done, and the lack I felt and attempted to remedy made itself known at that time. She knew I had no ability with a blade, knew I struggled in the grip of a potion and the Hand of Power, yet showed not the least reluctance to give me pain and humiliation. For that, and even more for whatever she has done to my *sadendrak*, she will regret the day she laid eyes upon me."

"If not with swords, then how do you mean to face her?" Leelan asked, frowning, as if she groped for a memory. Dallan had been watching me rather closely; he took the tray

242

off my lap and put it on the carpeting, then rose to get at the pillows behind me.

"Terril is the possessor of a skill other than sword use," he told Leelan without looking at her, holding me up until he'd brushed the pillows out of the way, then lowered me to the bed fur. "For now, however, she is possessed even more of a need to rest and restore herself. After she has slept, we may speak with her again."

Leelan rose to her feet with her lips parted, as though ready to argue what Dallan had said, but when she saw my face the words never came out. If I looked even half as pale as I felt I was surprised she wasn't running for that healer, and I raged inside even as I closed my eyes. I couldn't afford to be sick or pale or weak, and I wasn't going to be. As soon as I got a little sleep I was damned well going to be just fine. . . .

I didn't realize how quickly I'd gone out until I woke again, finding myself alone in an almost-dark room. Outside it was completely dark, and if not for the small single candle burning in a wall holder, I wouldn't have been able to see anything.

I was lying face down on the bed furs, and once I was awake enough to think about that, I felt considerably encouraged. If I could turn over in my sleep I could do it awake, and turning over was a good start for bigger and better things. I was also feeling faintly hungry, another good sign of returning health. I thought about it for a while with my cheek to the fur, then decided to see how far it would go. The sooner I got myself up and moving, the easier I would find going back to the palace.

With that in mind I pushed my way up to sitting, but doing it didn't turn out to be easy. I'd been whipped seven times that I could remember, worked hard for long hours, assaulted by men, and kept just short of starvation level, but the worst part of all that seemed to be the day and a half I'd lain unconscious. The stiffness I felt was nearly crippling—worse than I could remember the pain alone being—and something

243

had to be done about it. I hated wasting the energy and strength, but pain control was the only answer.

I haven't often had the time or opportunity to wonder about pain control, and sitting and hurting in that small dark room didn't encourage me to start, but one thought did come to me. When I used the ability on other people their pain actually seemed to disappear somewhere, but when I used it on myself all I did was hold the pain at bay for a while. It occurred to me I'd be a lot better off if I could do to myself what I did to others, and that at least trying to do the same would scarcely hurt and would help no end if I managed to pull it off. I sat sideways on the bed furs with both arms braced to hold me up, my body covered in sweat despite the cool air coming in through the window, and began to try.

Turning your awareness inward means withdrawing it from your surroundings, so it wasn't until I blinked back out into the small dim room that I realized I wasn't alone. Not having seen Leelan come in meant she just about materialized where she stood not far from me, and I nearly jumped in startlement.

"Excuse me, Terril, it was not my intention to intrude," she said at once, raising one hand in a calming gesture. "I came to bring an evening meal, and to rouse you for it if you had not yet awakened. It had not occurred to me that rousing might be necessary even though you had indeed already awakened."

She gave me a smile with a good deal of effort behind it, trying to make light of something that had probably shaken her, and I wished I had the nerve to lower my shield and touch her mind. I was finally learning that to guess about what other people were feeling was a particularly excellent form of stupidity, but in spite of that the temptation remained.

"I was—attempting to ease the pain I felt," I said, looking away from her as I swung my legs off the bed to the carpet fur. "Surely Dallan spoke to you of the matter?"

"The *seetar* Dallan said naught," she said as I struggled to my feet, still feeling rocky and aching, but finding most of the rest of the pain gone. "He informed me that the matter was not his to discuss, and continued to maintain so despite my assurances that my curiosity was far from idle. He is stubborn and thick-headed, that one, and impossible to reason with.''

I pushed my tangled hair back from my face and looked up at her, surprised to see that annoyance had entirely replaced the uneasiness in her. And on second thought it might not have been uneasiness she'd felt, not if she hadn't known what I was doing.

"That description seems suitable for every man of this world I have ever met," I commented, feeling faint amusement for the first time in too many days. "What is it you wished to know?''

"What I wished to know," she echoed, this time embarrassed as she looked down at me. "How much more easily that question is managed, when put to another! You are a guest beneath my roof and one who has had harm at the hands of my people, and yet— What is the ability you possess, the ability spoken of by both Dallan and yourself? Do you possess a kind of power?''

She was staring at me so intently I didn't know what to think, but I was still aching too much to be bothered with hiding behind a lie. If it was the truth Leelan wanted, that's what she would get, but first I moved myself over to the tray she'd put on the carpet fur, and sat down beside it.

"I do not possess a *kind* of power," I said, taking the goblet from the tray to find more of the fruit juice I'd been hoping for. "I possess much the same power as Farian, yet am I likely a good deal stronger than she.''

"Such is not possible," Leelan protested, bringing her stare with her as she sat opposite me on the carpet fur, her hand automatically settling her sword out of the way. "Were you possessed of the power, there would have been no need of my assisting you the darkness we met. Also would I have felt the power within you rather than the complete emptiness I feel at this very moment, for I am able to know of such a thing in others. I have little of the ability myself, yet am I able to feel it in others.''

Again I was surprised, but this time at the bitterness behind the last of her words. The big blonde woman sounded as though she felt herself a disappointment to those around her, as though she were less than she should be and was manfully—or womanfully—admitting the lack even while she bitterly regretted it. I let the tangy juice wet my mouth and throat with a couple of swallows, then shook my head at her objections.

"You cannot at the moment perceive me for I have shielded my mind," I told her, reaching for the thick chunk of bread on the tray to see what the greasy-looking yellow substance on it might be. "At the time we met I was curtained rather than shielded, yet does the curtaining apparently serve to keep others from knowing what truly lies behind—and me from knowing what strength others possess save that I strive to know. I had not known of your ability before you spoke of it, nor was I able to gauge Farian when I was in her presence."

"And the reason that you required my aid?" she asked, watching me without expression while I tasted the bread. The yellow coating on it *was* greasy, but not too heavily so and was also both sweet and faintly salty. I didn't know what it was, but it certainly made the coarse bread taste better.

"I required the aid of another for the reason that I felt it wrong to harm someone with my power," I said when I'd swallowed the bite of bread and had taken another sip of the juice. "To attack from a direction none might see and protect themselves against seemed evil to me, a doing fit only for a creature entirely without honor. I would have accepted pain and hurt to keep from becoming a creature of that sort but, apparently for some, creaturehood is impossible to avoid. When once I have regained my strength I will face Roodar in such a way, and I feel not the least sense of guilt at the intention."

I finished my own confession while staring at the bread and juice I held, aware of the intense blue eyes on me but unable to meet them. It hurt quite a lot to simply admit that I *was* a monster after all, but I was tired of trying to lie to myself. If Roodar had hurt me alone she might have gotten away with it, but her including Tammad in on that had killed the possibility forever.

"I cannot believe that good fortune of this sort would smile just when it was so badly needed," Leelan said slowly after at least a full minute of absolute silence, her voice growing warmer and more enthusiastic the longer she went on. "Terril! You are surely the answer we have sought so long, yet must I be certain. You must open your mind to me, so that I may feel it as it is!"

I *had* to look up at her at that point, but looking didn't increase understanding. Her pretty face was covered with an eagerness I couldn't quite understand, and there wasn't a trace of fear or disgust.

"You would know exactly what manner of creature you consort with?" I asked, telling myself I wasn't being defensive. "You may accept my word that you are far better off not knowing."

"Do not speak foolishly, girl," she answered impatiently, gesturing aside what I'd said. "The sort of creature you refer to is well known to me, for I have known Farian for quite some time. One with the power is a creature only when she considers none save herself, only when the very meaning of honor is beyond her. To believe oneself an honorless creature is to be nothing of the sort, for the true creature cannot see herself in such a way. Now, show me the quality of your mind! It is vital that I know what strength you have!"

Her expression had changed to one of stern command, the sort I was used to seeing only in the men of that world. What she'd said had confused me, almost as much as the way she flitted from emotion to emotion. I was very reluctant to do as she ordered, but capitulation turned out to be easier than refusal.

"Ah," she breathed when I let my shield dissolve after making myself feel a need for the curtain. She was able to sense part of my mind that way, and I was able to sense the droning buzz of the Hand of Power. Knowing what it was let me analyze the buzz, and I found it to be a leakage from a concerted projection aimed elsewhere than at the city it originated from. The leakage showed it to be a roiling combination of dissatisfaction and impatience and anger with overtones of depression, and I wasn't surprised it had made me sick when I'd first been exposed to it. That sort of combination was enough to make anyone sick, especially if they didn't know it was coming at them.

"And that is the extent of it?" Leelan asked after a moment, trying not to let her disappointment show through. I could feel her mind gently reaching out toward mine, probing at the curtain she apparently couldn't perceive. She seemed to be using only a small part of herself, and although I didn't know why, she was still much too open and exposed.

"No, that is not the extent of it," I answered, bracing myself to be totally unprotected. "Pull your mind back, and lessen your perceptions a bit,"

Leelan was confused but did as she was told, and only then did I allow the curtain to leave me. If I hadn't been feeling so wildly out of sorts the caution wouldn't have been necessary, but even so the big woman winced as her eyes widened. Ever since I'd awakened the first time my mind had been raging against the inside of my shield, and I hated to think what it must look like to her.

"Mother of us all!" she gasped, her sun-bronzed face paling, one hand going to her head. "Never have I felt such strength, such range, such—Terril, you are a—a—"

"Monster or Prime, take your choice," I muttered as I snapped my shield closed again, cutting off the clanging of her shock. Since the words were in Centran she didn't understand them, but I don't think she would have heard me even if I'd spoken Rimilian.

"The others will have to be shown," she said in her own mutter, putting a second hand to her head as well. "Should I attempt to seek their belief without, they will immediately send for Hestin out of fear for my balance. No more than three of them will be able to experience her, yet together they and I will surely find it possible to convince the others. I will send for them tomorrow, at first light, and then we shall at last be able to—"

Her words cut off as her eyes finally saw me, and her grin was part embarrassment. It also came to her then that her hands were still at her head, and she pulled them down with a laugh of pure enjoyment.

"Terril, my honored guest, once again I must ask your forgiveness," she said, trying to get rid of the grin even though it didn't want to leave. "To speak of the joy you have given me would take one far better versed in our tongue than I. For now let me say only this: when you return to the palace of the *Chama*, there will be many others to stand with you. We have long awaited one who was a match for Farian, and now, thanks be to the mother of us all, we have one so far her superior that there is no comparison. Where you lead, there we will follow."

"You mean to follow *me*?" I asked in shock, feeling as though someone had switched worlds on me while I wasn't looking. "Do you mistake me for a warrior?"

"A *l'lenda*?" she repeated, laughing at the word I'd used. "No, Terril, not a *l'lenda*, yet surely a *w'wenda*, in each and every sense of the word. *W'wenda* is no more derived from the presence of sword skill than is *l'lenda*; one who is *w'wenda* or *l'lenda* will develop sword skill, yet does the calling come long before that. A warrior must first be born, and then may he or she be trained."

"I must surely have damaged your mind with mine," I told her flatly, putting the piece of bread back on the tray. "There are those about who are fit to be followed, yet I am not one of them. Were you not able to see that when I swept the curtain aside?"

"Perhaps I saw more than you know," she said, the grin now gone, calm assurance strong in her eyes as she leaned slighty forward. "What I saw was one with a very great anger in her, and one with a worry equally as great. Had Farian the strength which you possess, she would surely have already begun to claim the world. Is the world yours, or do you perhaps mean to claim it soon?"

"For what reason would I wish this world?" I asked, the sourness I felt clear in my voice. "Were it to become mine, I would have the possession of uncounted numbers of stubborn, thick-headed *l'lendaa* who are impossible to reason with. Do you think me bereft, that I would seek a difficulty such as that?''

"Truly are you wiser than I had at first thought, Terril," she said with a laugh, the grin back again. "Few would have the ability to see the matter so clearly, and then would be faced with unexpected and unsought-for largesse. You have power and conscience and wisdom; what more might be asked for in a leader?"

"The desire to lead," I pronounced, taking another swallow of my juice. "Had I not known this discussion was idle, it might well have upset me. As I shall return to the palace the darkness after this one, however, I need not be concerned over leadership. Armed forces cannot be raised so quickly." Then I eyed what was in my goblet. "And before that I must somewhere find a wine worth drinking."

"I have heard it said by those with a weather eye, that the new day will bring us rain to last throughout the darkness," she commented, looking so undisturbed that her eyes twinkled. "Also, you have not been given wine for you are not yet permitted it; first you must return to health. Eat your meal, girl, and then return to your furs; you must sleep well this darkness, for the new day will bring many occurrences."

"I had thought the new day was to bring rain?" I said, feeling more and more annoyed at all the fun she was having. "And I find that I have had enough of that meal, so the tray may be returned at any time you wish. I will, of course, seek my furs as soon as weariness descends upon me."

"Oh, of course," she agreed with a solemnity her eyes failed to share, nodding but not moving from where she sat. "Though it grieves me to disagree with a guest beneath my roof, these things cannot be as you wish them. Soon you will indeed be left to the peace of solitude, yet for the moment—" She broke off at the sound of a knock, then grinned as she immediately rose to her feet. "As ever, precisely on time."

As she headed for the door I wondered what she was talking about, then found out all too quickly. Opening the door showed two men, one of them Dallan, one a stranger, and they didn't wait to be invited in. They simply stepped through the doorway, the stranger entering first with a faint, highly perplexed frown on his face, and it suddenly came to me that I was sitting there absolutely naked! Hastily putting the goblet back on the tray, cursing Leelan under my breath for not warning me, I began to scramble to my feet to get to covers. Although there wasn't much scramble to it I did manage to stand, and then the stranger's hand was on my arm, obviously in an attempt to support me.

"What is the meaning of this, Leelan?" he asked my hostess, holding my arm to keep me from getting back to the bed. "For what reason has she been made to leave her furs?"

"She has not been *made* to leave them, Hestin," Leelan answered with continuing calm, looking up with a smile at the man who held me. "Terril has left her furs of her own accord, having felt considerably better, and now refuses the provender I have brought. Beyond two swallows of bread and three of juice, she wishes no more of it."

"Completely unacceptable," the man called Hestin stated, looking down at me with steady blue eyes while I glared at Leelan. She'd told on me without the slightest hesitation, and did no more than grin at my silent promise to get even.

"Indeed is such a thing unacceptable," Dallan agreed from where he stood to Hestin's right, between the newcomer and Leelan, his disapproval even sharper. "Now that we are here, it shall quickly be set to rights."

"There is but one thing I wish set to rights," I said, finding it difficult not to feel like a naughty child among grown-ups. "Release my arm immediately, for I wish to cover myself."

I looked at the man Hestin as I spoke, really trying to ignore the others, and was therefore able to see his surprise.

"You need not feel disturbed over my presence, *wenda*," he said, beginning to move me very slowly back to the bed. "There is no call for embarrassment for I am a healer, and have come for no other purpose than to see how you fare. Sit here now, and I will assist you in lying down."

"I need no assistance, nor do I wish to lie down," I said, pulling out of his grip as soon as it loosened, this time managing to scramble successfully. As soon as I had the cover fur over me I looked up at him again, ignoring the new surprise he showed. "What I would find joy in having is solitude for I also have no need of a healer."

"Indeed do you seem so far improved that I am amazed," he said, crouching so that his handsome face was more nearly on a level with mine. "As to your continuing need for a healer, that remains to be seen. I will first know how you truly fare, and then the decision will be made. Put the fur aside so that I may examine you."

There was a deep sense of quiet and calm in him that I could feel even with my shield closed, and his blue eyes reflected that for all the world to see. He was big and blond as were most Rimilian males and he wore a dark blue *haddin*, but above it he had on a long, wide-sleeved, open-fronted gray robe, and there was no sword belted around his waist. In calm consideration there was nothing about him at all alarming, but for some completely undefined reason I still felt vaguely uneasy.

"Perhaps you misunderstand," I said, trying hard not to be insulting. "You have my thanks for having aided me when I required it, yet I no longer require such aid. I, too, have some measure of healing ability, and prefer now to see to myself."

"For what reason does my presence disturb you?" he asked, just as though I'd spoken my feelings aloud, his calm quiet untouched and undisturbed. "There is a trembling I feel deep within you, one which was not present when first I tended you, one which has naught to do with the marking of your body. The trembling is a recognition of sorts, I believe, yet not of myself. Whom do you see when you look upon me, *treda*?"

"I see no one," I answered immediately, too deeply upset to resent being called, "girl child," trying to hide the fact that I was lying. He did remind me of someone, someone I couldn't dredge up from my memory, but someone I also couldn't forget.

"You should not have exerted yourself so far, *treda*," he said, raising one big hand to smooth my hair, his eyes unmoving from my face. "Your lovely cheeks have paled, and the trembling has now come to your hands. You must know well enough that you have no cause to fear me. I have come to bring healing rather than hurt, and shall certainly do you no harm."

He smiled then, a warm, encouraging smile, and suddenly I knew exactly who he reminded me of. I closed my eyes as the pain and illness rose high, and wished I had the ability to make myself instantly unconscious.

"The knowledge has now returned to you," Hestin said, no doubt at all in the statement, a comforting sense of support in his voice. "Lie back now, until you are able to speak of it."

I felt his hands easing me back onto the bed furs, and then I was lying flat on my tangled hair, my eyes still closed, my hands still tight on the fur spread over me. It was really too warm to be covered in furs, and the smell of ointments and salves was still more alien than familiar; right then I was more homesick for Central than I could ever remember being. On Central my abilities were usually taken away from me, suppressed by conditioning, and that's what I missed more than anything else.

"You begin to exert control over the thing," Hestin said with quiet approval, his big hand smoothing my hair. "Soon you will be able to speak of it, and once spoken of it will disturb you no longer."

"You are mistaken," I answered in as steady a voice as I could manage, opening my eyes to look at his face. Hestin did look like him, quite a bit, but the differences were what really counted. There was no true ability for violence in the healer, not the way there was in a warrior, but there was less of a difference between healer and warrior than there was between Hestin and *him*.

"Mistaken in what manner?" Hestin asked, and I discovered that his calm and quiet patience were beginning to rub me the wrong way.

"Mistaken in believing that to speak of the thing will bring forgetfulness," I said, shaking my head against his hand in an effort to make him take it away. "When the memory ceases to give me pain, it then brings anger. I would appreciate your leaving me now."

"You return to yourself so quickly," he observed, ignoring me again in favor of what *he* was interested in. "Despite the hurt given your body your spirit remains untouched, and reasserts itself as the need arises."

"What you see as spirit, I see as temper," I told him, holding his blue eyes with no effort at all. "Should you persist in remaining here to spout philosophical observations, that temper will quickly rise even higher than it currently stands. I now politely ask you to leave for a third time; should I find the need to ask again, the request will contain no politeness whatsoever."

"Terril, do not," Dallan began in upset, taking one step forward, and, "Hestin, take care not to provoke her!" Leelan said in a matching upset, and their individual but almost identical reactions finally got through to the healer the way my own efforts hadn't. He turned to look at them both over his right shoulder, his brows raised in surprise and questioning, and Leelan, after a glance at Dallan, found a shrug to send back.

"The girl possesses more of the power than any I have ever seen," she explained, sounding almost apologetic. "I feel certain she would not harm another unless provoked and perhaps not even then, and yet—I also feel that her word has not been idly given. Perhaps we would do best in leaving her now."

"How strange that I feel no least vestige of the power in her," Hestin said, turning back to put those clear, innocent eyes on me again. This time it was Leelan he was ignoring, still using that sense of mystical wisdom to get his own way, and I'd had enough of it. It looked like everyone else around him was impressed, but I wasn't.

This time I simply dropped my shield without bothering with the curtain, automatically resisting and ignoring the leakage from the Hand of Power. Doing it while flat on my back was fractionally easier, but only because I still had to pay attention in order to stay upright. Leelan drew her breath in softly, her mind excited and pleased despite her nervousness; Dallan hovered with faint disturbance, and Hestin—Hestin's eyes suddenly went wide as he stared down at me. He wasn't in any way reading or receiving me and I couldn't really tell what he *was* doing, but in some way he was even more completely aware of my abilities than Leelan.

"Are you able to feel some vestige now?" I asked, still looking up at him. "To fail to display a sword is not to imply lack of sword skill."

"Now I am not alone in spouting philosophical observations," he said, exercising that pretty smile again. "You do indeed possess a power beyond any I have ever sensed, *treda*, yet does such a power not preclude the need to be tended. You have done much toward healing yourself, yet is there only so much one may do for oneself. I would see what remains to be done."

His blue eyes were no longer wide, and suddenly I became very much aware of the mind behind those eyes—which almost caused *me* to gasp. As quiet and calm as Hestin was on the outside, that's how hard and unbending he was within him, a man whose mind absolutely refused to take no for an answer. When it came to tending the sick or hurt, he obviously considered himself the only one capable of doing it right, and that was a burden he enjoyed carrying. His easygoing outer manner seemed to be a buffer between his rigid and uncompromising inner self and the people he had to tend, something that let him do what he had to without adding to the bruises his patient might have. His mental set was pure Rimilian male, even more intense than Tammad's, and I hated to think what I'd have to do to stop him or change his mind.

"You were not raised in Vediaster," I said, knowing it for a fact. His mind was unaffected by mine, but unfortunately the reverse wasn't working out as well.

"No, I was not raised in Vediaster," he agreed, the quiet of his voice an odd contrast to what I was getting from his thoughts. "My first home was far from here, yet a healer goes where he must, where he feels himself needed. This city is now my home, and those within it my responsibility. Lie still, *treda*."

His big hands went to the fur covering me to toss it aside, and no matter how strong the power I was the possessor of, there was nothing I could do to stop him. No matter how much I hated the idea I'd been taught to obey *l'lendaa* on that world, and Leelan had been absolutely right: *l'lenda* and *w'wenda* came from within, independent of the presence or absence of sword skill.

"Do not squirm about so," Hestin said absently, his hands and attention on my right side. "To be seen unclothed by others is an inadequate cause for shame, *treda*, most especially for one such as you. Your body must surely give your *memabrak* a great deal of pleasure. Turn now to your belly."

I turned over as directed, but mainly to hide the hot flush I could feel in my cheeks. His words had brought the hum in Dallan's mind to my attention, which in turn pointed up the distracted but very definite hum that was Hestin's. To take my mind off that I tried to follow what was occupying the healer so completely, and ran smack into something I'd never seen before.

The pain control that I was capable of worked exclusively on the mind where, after all, pain is recognized and therefore felt. Hestin, on the other hand, concentrated only on the body, the place where the actual damage was, and did nothing in the way of easing pain or accomplishing healing. What he seemed to be doing was gauging the actual hurt, seeing how deep it went, and checking on whether or not natural healing had already begun. He didn't have to guess about what was wrong with somebody, somehow he knew beyond all doubt, but how it worked was something I had no idea of. He had a physical sensing ability rather than a mental one, and I wondered if all healers on that world had the same.

"Remain as you are, *treda*, for you must now be salved," Hestin said, apparently finished with the examination. It hadn't taken him long, that was for sure, but getting the salve put on wasn't nearly as easy and painless. By the time he got around to the front of me I had other things to think about besides who might be watching, and it took the actual sight of Leelan's drawn face to remember I hadn't closed my shield again. She didn't seem to understand that she was picking up my pain on her own rather than catching an accidental leakage, and I knew I'd have to talk to her about that once I'd had some rest. In the interim I let the shield form again, and tried to ignore the sweat on my forehead.

"And now, *treda*, we must speak, you and I," Hestin said after another minute, putting the salve aside and replacing the cover he'd thrown off me. "You have a great power, greater than any I have ever sensed, yet are you no more capable of true healing with your power than I am with mine. Should you continue on as you have been doing, you may well fail to survive."

Getting the salve put on was the painful part, but once it was on it took care of the pain as well as accelerated healing. By that time I was able to look at him again, where he crouched to the right of my bed.

"I am scarcely so badly hurt that I need fear for my life," I said, glad I couldn't touch his mind any longer. "The mistreatment I was given was painful, yet not permanently damaging."

"A small hurt, improperly cared for, may easily become a large one," he said, and now he was looking more stern than patient. "You have thrown off a good deal of the pain from your awareness, yet the cause of that pain remains unchanged, the hurt remains unhealed. You move about with no more than small difficulty because you have put the pain from you, not because you have begun to regain your health. Should you continue pushing yourself so, the wounds will worsen rather than heal."

"I have not the time it would take to regain my full health," I told the hardened blue eyes staring down at me, understanding exactly what he was saying but not giving a damn. "The longer I spend awaiting my own health, the less of it will be left to one who lies elsewhere. Sooner than lose him I will spend my own life, happily and without concern.

Should I succeed in freeing him and myself surviving, there will then be ample time for rest.''

"You are completely determined," he said, more observation than criticism, and then those blue eyes turned gentle again. "There are indeed certain things worth far more than life, and a man must be a fool not to acknowledge this. I, hopefully not a fool, shall not attempt to shake your determination, yet are there other matters I shall not be denied in. For the time you remain under my care you will obey me completely, and then, perhaps, there will be one who survives to rest.''

He finally straightened out of his crouch then, trailed by the stares of Dallan and Leelan as he walked to the food tray I'd abandoned; although Dallan didn't seem very happy, I couldn't tell whether Leelan was upset or amused.

"She means to return to the palace during the next darkness, Hestin," the big woman from Vediaster said as she watched the healer coming back toward me with a bowl. "Do you agree with that decision as well?''

"We shall see," he answered, stirring around whatever was in the bowl before helping me sit and beginning to feed me with the scoop. "Likely I shall not permit it, but we shall see.''

My mouth was too full of the finely chopped fish stew to put my own comments into the running, but that didn't really bother me. When it was time to go I would go, no matter anyone else's opinions to the contrary.

Hestin fed me most of the fish stew, insisted I take a little more of the bread, then brought over a cup of the same yellow pudding I hadn't been able to eat that afternoon. I really had no desire for the pudding but I got half of it shoveled into me anyway, in the process discovering I'd been right about its being almost pure sugar. About then I also discovered I couldn't sit up any longer, and I must have been out even before Hestin eased me flat.

I felt as though I'd been sleeping for some time before the soft voice pulled me out of it, and it didn't pull me out all the way. It was almost like being awake and asleep at the same time, and that was just what the voice was saying.

"You will awaken no more than is necessary to speak with me, *treda*," it said, totally undemanding yet totally undeniable. "Do you understand what I say?"

"I understand," I agreed at once, turning toward the voice without opening my eyes. There was a big, hard male body accompanying the voice just as I knew there would be, and I immediately began snuggling up to it.

"I am not the one you believe me to be, *treda*," the voice said as a hand stroked my hair, faint amusement coloring its tone. "I have come for no more than the answers I seek. Tell me of the one brought to your thoughts by the sight of the healer."

The voice was undeniable, but I didn't want to tell it what it had asked me. I suddenly felt very uncomfortable in the furs and tried to turn away from the voice, but an arm didn't let me. It held me up against the big, hard body, making sure I stayed on my left side, holding me still for the hand that continued to stroke my hair.

"You need not be reluctant to speak of it, little one," the voice pursued, understanding and compassion filling it completely. "I am already aware that you were given to men for their use, and that the use was far from pleasant. Tell me of the one whose memory brought you such pain that I was able to know of it without touching you."

"He was my master," I whispered, reaching for my throat to find what had once been there—but no longer was. "He was in truth but one of my masters, and yet he made himself the leader where I was concerned."

"And he gave you hurt because he was your master?" the voice asked, speaking gently despite the hidden edge. "He found pleasure in doing you so?"

"He found pleasure in attempting to give me pleasure, yet he knew not what he did," I answered, seeing again, behind closed eyelids, that beautiful, eager face. "He knew nothing of the strength of his passion, of the pain and frustration which was given me by his vigor. He was a child, and thought I had pleasure from him and the others. He—directed and taught the ones who desired me.''

"Directed and taught—! What manner of men were these?" Now the voice sounded confused, as confused as I had been, but confusion no longer bothered me.

"They were slaves and likely born so," I said, again feeling that terrible pain. "Born and raised to be no other thing than innocents, to be denied all knowledge and might-have-beens. They each of them held me down to use me, yet did I feel that it was I who stole innocence, I who soiled the purity of souls. Their minds, their thoughts—I could not bear it and yet I was made to bear it, to feel the pitiful efforts of those who will never be whole. They gave me pain, thinking they gave pleasure—and I knew and could not speak of it—they were forever lost and cannot be saved— Please come back to me, Tammad! Please hold me, *sadendrak*!"

"I will hold you," the voice whispered, so unsteady that I heard its raggedness even above my sobbing. It hurt so much to know that that might have been done to anyone, even my beloved or the flesh of my flesh, and the arms holding me tight were my only brace against being overwhelmed. I do not despise slaves, my beloved had once said, I merely despise those who make slaves. I, too, hated those who made slaves, hated them and wanted to see them dead. My sobbing continued for a short while, the pain most clearly shared by another, and then the voice told me to sleep, which I had no difficulty in doing.

11

The morning light was gray rather than golden, and seemed to be waiting for me as an audience. My eyes couldn't have been open for more than two minutes before the sound of rain came, heavy at first and then settling down into the steady mold of an all-day affair—and all night. I cursed under my breath in three languages, hardly looking forward to getting to the palace dripping wet and covered with mud to the knees. But then I realized it was a palace dominated by women that I was going to, and pictured the guard women standing along the corridors yelling at me for not wiping my feet, rather than attacking. The absurdity made me feel just a little better, enough so that I was able to think about getting up and taking a look out the window. There was hardly likely to be much to see, but anything was better than more of simply lying in those furs. I sat up thinking about trying to stretch gently and carefully, and that was when the door to my room opened.

"Go no farther, *treda*," Hestin the healer said as he entered, carrying a tray, the words an order despite the calm quiet of his tone. "You shall indeed leave your furs today, yet not till I have said you might."

I watched him walk over and put the tray down next to the bed instead of giving it to me, and all the annoyance and impatience I felt toward the weather suddenly had a new focus.

"And what if I should choose not to await your permission?" I asked as he gathered up pillows from the carpet fur, his intentions obvious. "I am curious to know of the manner in which you would force me to your will."

"You will obey me without the need for force," he answered, calmly setting the pillows on my bed so that I might lean on them. "You wore the bands of a man, did you not? The obedience your *memabrak* taught you will for now be given to me. Settle yourself among the cushions, and I will feed you."

"I would prefer to feed myself," I said, not quite through my teeth, watching the way he barely even glanced at me. "I am not a child, and dislike being treated as one."

"You are a *wenda*, and will do as you are bidden to do," he said, his tone so matter-of-fact that it almost seemed reasonable. He was crouching near the tray and beginning to reach for a bowl, but as far as I was concerned he'd already reached the last straw.

Once, when I'd wanted to get Dallan away from me without letting him know I was doing anything, I'd brushed him with a nervous reaction, one that caused overwrought people to think they needed to relieve themselves. Just then I didn't much care if Hestin discovered what I was doing, but I decided to see how long I could keep him going, so to speak, before he figured it out. I couldn't open my shield without warning him that I was up to something, but I'd worked around my shield before and really did need the practice.

It had taken a matter of seconds to make the decision, and once made I didn't simply brush the man the way I had with Dallan. I reached around my shield and sent Hestin the conviction that he *had* to relieve himself, leaving his own mind to supply a reason for the feeling. His hand had just touched a bowl on the tray, but that bowl never got picked up. His hesitation was so brief that it was practically nonexistent, and then he was straightening from his crouch.

"I must excuse myself for a moment, *treda*," he said,

looking like a man with muscles clenched tight. "I will return in no more than a short while."

I suppose running would have been too undignified for him, but that doesn't mean he didn't hurry as fast as possible. As soon as the door closed on him and his strangely uneven gait, I grinned, then reached down for the bowl he hadn't managed to pick up and made myself comfortable against the cushions.

The bowl held my old friend the thick, sweet, grainy mixture I'd first had in Tammad's house, and I managed to eat about a third of it before the door opened again. I thought it was Hestin coming back, but the figure that entered was Dallan.

"Is Leelan the sole person in this house who has been taught to knock?" I commented as he closed the door and came closer. I had decided that taking Hestin on was just practice for what I would have to do that night, so I could look at starting up with Dallan in the same way. Dallan, however, didn't seem to be in the mood to take offense.

"It was not my intention to intrude," he said as he seated himself among the remaining cushions on the carpet fur, sounding as though he was intent on something other than the words he was speaking. "I thought perhaps you might still be asleep, and had no wish to waken you unnecessarily."

"Unnecessarily," I repeated, wondering what was bothering him. "And now that you find I need not be awakened, you wish to speak with me."

"Indeed," he said with a nod, finally raising his eyes to my face. "It has come to me that it might perhaps be best if I were to tell you why I have no wish for us to attempt the palace this darkness. When I became convinced that you three were taken and not merely delayed, I sought out a merchant from Gerleth I had seen here when first we arrived. The man knew me as I knew him, and agreed without hesitation to ride with all haste to my father and tell him of what had occurred. In no more than a short while we will have *l'lendaa* to accompany us, therefore would it be foolish to make the attempt alone."

"In no more than a short while," I said, returning the half-distracted look I was getting. "And what might be left of Tammad to be rescued, after that short while? Should Roodar and the *Chama* find themselves under attack by *l'lendaa*, will they not deem it wiser to rid themselves of embarrassing captives, Cinnan and Aesnil included? Or perhaps they will slay those captives out of spite, should it seem to them that the palace is about to fall. Do you truly think it best that we wait, Dallan?"

"No," he growled, sounding nearly out of control, rising quickly to his feet again to pace around the small dim room. "To attack alone is likely to cost our lives, yet in honor we may do nothing else. Or perhaps I should say, *I* must do nothing else. You need not accompany me and shall not."

"And in what way do you mean to best the Hand of Power without my presence?" I asked, going back to my thick whatever without feeling insulted. Dallan was talking just to hear himself talk, and we both knew it. "Leelan has told us both of that, has she not?"

"Leelan," he growled again, staring out the window at the pouring rain, right hand on the wall, left hand on sword hilt. "Never, in all the days of my life, have I ever come across one such as she. She has refused to wear my bands, Terril, refused even to discuss the matter! Each darkness she comes to my furs and my arms, knowing me unable to refuse her, and yet she will not have my bands."

"I have never before heard of a *wenda* being allowed to refuse a *l'lenda*," I ventured, aching for the pain I knew was in him. Dallan had always seemed to prefer very free women, the freer the woman, the more he was interested. Leelan was obviously irresistible to him, but apparently she didn't see it the same way.

"Leelan is a warrior, and cannot be done as an ordinary *wenda*," he said, his voice thick with disgust. "When first I brought my bands out, meaning to close them on her, she informed me that if I attempted to do her so she would be honor-bound to face me over bared blades. Some custom of this accursed place forbids her banding, yet even this she refused to speak of. Her heart is mine even as mine is hers, this I know beyond all possible doubt, and yet she continues to refuse me.''

"Can there be another?" I asked, hesitant to bring the point up but deciding it was better said straight out. "She spoke to me once of the custom in which w'wendaa band their men. Can it be she has put her bands on someone, and cannot honorably reclaim them?"

"There are no others, even such as that," he said, turning his head to give me a look that said to stop talking dirty. "She has assured me that no other stands higher in her eyes, and yet she will not have me. Should there be a child as the result of our coupling, she has said, she will send the child to me as is proper, and yet— My mind goes to other things as well."

Like wanting to spend the rest of your life with her, I thought, sharing every bit of his bewildered hurt. He was staring out the window again, as gray and wretched as the dark, rainy day, and I wished I could think of something to help him.

"It makes no matter to her that you are a prince of Gerleth?" I asked, just to be saying something while my mind cast uselessly about, and then that suddenly became a damned good possibility. "Dallan, perhaps *that* is the reason for her refusal. Her love of Vediaster is more than great, and she cannot bear the thought of leaving it forever. Were you not a prince of Gerleth, you might well have remained with her here."

"It cannot be," he said, shaking his head against something he'd already thought of and discarded. "Leelan knows naught of me save that Gerleth is my home, nor has she attempted to suggest that I remain with her. She has given me her heart and her body, yet her soul she seems honor-bound to retain."

I opened my mouth to say that that didn't make any sense, but just then the door was also opened—by Hestin. He walked in and saw Dallan as Dallan turned to look at him, nodded politely, then brought himself over to me.

"It seems scarcely likely that I will permit your departure this darkness," he said, crouching down and reaching for the bowl I held. "Already the streets are turning to mud, and the air has taken on a chill. To court illness would be an unnecessary foolishness."

"Oh, absolutely unnecessary," I agreed, reaching around my shield again, this time with part of an extreme fear reaction. It's possible for some people to become so frightened that they lose control of their bowels and bladder, and it was this loss of control that I touched Hestin with. Not all of it, of course, only the urge toward the reaction, but the abrupt expression on his face told me that that was enough. He pulled his hand back and straightened in a single motion, turned away without a word, and this time broke into a hobbling run before disappearing. Dallan stared after him in surprise, but when he turned back to look at me the surprise was gone.

"And what would occur if I were to speak to Tammad of this once we have released him?" he asked, folding his arms across his chest in an effort to look stern. He obviously knew I'd done *something* to Hestin, and wasn't about to waste his breath simply with accusations. I suddenly felt the definite urge to squirm where I sat, and that despite the perfectly good out I had.

"You may speak to Tammad of whatever you wish," I said, leaning forward to replace the bowl on the tray. "It was he who informed me that I must decide for myself when my ability is to be exercised. I merely felt the need for a small amount of exercise."

"*Wenda*, he has only your well-being in mind," Dallan said, clearly referring to Hestin, the amusement in his eyes appearing faintly on his face. "To cause him difficulty for his concern would not be honorable."

"I cause him only small difficulty," I muttered, feeling more than ever like a child caught being naughty, paying a lot of attention to adjusting the cover fur on me. "He knows well enough that I shall do as I must, yet persists in attempting to direct me. Where lies the honor in *that* course?"

"We all of us do as we must," he said, suddenly crouching beside the bed to take my chin in his hand and raise my face. "It is a man's solemn duty to care for the woman of another in that other's absence, to see to her safety and well-being even should she wish it otherwise. That Hestin demands your obedience is right and proper, honorable as leaving you to your own devices would not be. You cannot fault him for his treatment of you."

"Can I not?" I snapped, pushing his big hand away from me with the quick outrage I felt. "And who sees to Leelan when *she* wishes it otherwise? Who is there whom *she* must obey? She is female just as I am; for what reason is she allowed freedom the while I am not?"

"Leelan is *w'wenda*," he said with a sigh, his blue eyes trying not to show that patience-with-a-child look. "You, sister, are one of those who are not, you are one who requires the protection and direction of a man. Although the bands were taken, you remain a banded *wenda*, one who must obey in all things. It was not Hestin who banded you, yet must you obey him as well."

I was just about to tell him exactly how obedient I intended being toward everyone in sight, when once again the door opening stole my opportunity. This time it was Leelan who came in, but she wasn't alone. The people behind her formed a good-sized crowd, adding to my sudden feeling that the small room had recently been declared a transport departure area. Her face took on a very brief but very peculiar expression when she saw Dallan crouched near my bed, but by the time he'd straightened and turned, it was gone.

"Forgive the intrusion, Terril, yet there are matters which must be discussed between us," she said, not even glancing again at Dallan. "There are those who have come to make your acquaintance, and they, too, have words to be spoken."

"Perhaps it would be best if I were to leave, then," Dallan said, looking at the group behind Leelan to find that it was strictly female. "Often a man is out of his depth in discussions such as these."

"We have often found it so," an older woman in the group

agreed with a downright jolly smile, stopping to Leelan's right. Most of the other women were chuckling or grinning and even Leelan seemed amused, so Dallan lost no time in bowing to them and then making his break. Once the door had been closed behind him, though, all the amusement disappeared.

"This is the one you spoke of, Leelan?" another woman asked my hostess, a woman as young as Leelan herself. Her feet were bare of probably muddy sandals, but her sword was firmly belted over the blue shirt and breeches she wore, and her frown of disapproval was set like granite. "Although rather disheveled, she would far more easily be seen as a *rella wenda*."

"To purposely provoke one of unknown abilities is scarcely wise, Siitil," Leelan answered immediately, surely aware of the way I had stiffened at the other woman's words. After what Dallan had said I was about as far from feeling charitable as you can get, and hearing that the one called Siitil had poked at me deliberately didn't do a thing to improve friendly relations.

"Perhaps we would do best to first make the girl's acquaintance," the older woman to Leelan's right put in, her tone more firm than conciliatory as she looked at the younger Siitil. She wasn't old by any stretch of the imagination, just older, and wore her own swordbelt over dark green breeches and shirt. She was smaller than most of the others despite the fact that she was one of the few who still had sandals on, and her long blond hair was just beginning to be touched with gray.

"With what are we to become acquainted, Deegor?" Siitil came back immediately, her eyes on me rather than on the woman she spoke to. "We were told there was one of power in our midst, one who was capable of besting Farian. Is it disappointment you would become better acquainted with?"

"Would I have called you all here had I not been certain, Siitil?" Leelan said with a touch of exasperation, her voice now more commanding than friendly, her eyes on the woman who continued to stare at me. "First you will do as Deegor suggests and become acquainted with Terril, and then you will be shown what I have seen.''

"Perhaps it is Terril who has no wish to become acquainted with Siitil,'' I said before anyone else could put their oar in, reaching down to the tray for the goblet of juice I hadn't yet tasted. "It pains me to be an ungracious guest, Leelan, yet do I ask you to take these others and go.''

"Siitil means you no personal insult, girl,'' the woman Deegor said as she stepped closer, taking over for a Leelan who seemed to have run out of what to say. "She and Leelan have had a comparable loss, yet does Siitil have less of a grip upon her grief. She burns to avenge those who took the lives of her mother and father, and hoped to find the means in you. As she is unable to see that you *choose* to show us nothing of ability, she is understandably bitter.''

"Deegor, you say she *chooses* to show no ability?'' Siitil pounced immediately, her rather plain face brightening with hope. "Your ability is greater than mine; what do you see?''

"I see a denial such as Farian is capable of, yet of a completely different construction,'' Deegor answered, her eyes somewhat narrowed and faintly unfocused. "She is undeniably one with power, yet how great a power I am unable to say.''

"Have you truly the power, girl?'' Siitil demanded, her stare turned blazing as it came back to me, her left hand tightened white around her sword hilt. "Should you have fully enough to decisively best Farian, I swear I will be one of those who cuts down the operating Hand of Power, though my life or reason will be lost in the doing! They will not be allowed to do *you* harm, and when you have bested Farian my blood will have been avenged! Now do I ask you in the name of decency: show us your power!''

In the name of decency. I sat sipping my juice as the young woman just stood there and waited, the burning inside her so bright I could see it with my eyes alone. I had more than half expected her to apologize when she heard I wasn't a null after all, but that didn't seem to be in her nature. What she'd done instead was swear to give up her life or sanity for me, if only

I saw to her vengeance after she no longer could. I knew I
was getting in much deeper than I could possibly handle, and
for a brief moment I felt a clenching of fear.

"Withdraw your sensing," I told her, suddenly feeling
very tired. "You will not need to strain to know my power."

"How are you able to know I——" she began, confusion
making her look even younger, but Leelan's hand on her arm
ended the words. Half of the women there seemed to press
closer while the other half drew back, and then there was a
shared gasp in a small number of voices to mark the lowering
of my shield.

"I knew you strained, for I was able to feel the touch of
your mind on my—denial," I explained, now able to spot the
other touches I'd felt. Aside from Siitil and Deegor, there
was another woman about Deegor's age but stronger of mental ability, standing at the back of the crowd where I couldn't
see her. Hers was the third active mind and Leelan's the
fourth, and everyone else was watching those four.

"By the mother of us all," Siitil breathed, staring at me
now in an entirely different way, her expression close to one
of shock. "The power—I cannot encompass it all!"

"Nor I," said Deegor, her face pale although her mind
was calm. "For what reason do you keep such strength
behind a wall of denial, girl? Do you consider it unfitting for
one such as you to share her mind with those about her?"

"I consider it unfitting to fall ill from the leakage of the
Hand of Power," I said, very briefly wondering what it
would be like to associate on a regular basis with others of
my kind. The thought was so unrealistic I couldn't even
imagine it, and didn't have the time to spend on daydreams.
"For what reason have *you* not challenged Farian?" I asked
without more than an instant's pause. "You or the fourth of
your group? You each of you have a good deal of strength,
and might well have had the best of her."

"Are we to spend the lives of those who follow us on
'might-well-have's'?" Deegor asked with a faint smile, glancing back at the momentary amusement of the woman hidden
behind everyone else. I am a *w'wenda* and might well have

risked it, yet my sister is not and she is the stronger. To be unable to raise sword beside those who follow you is a heavy burden, for it is more likely *their* lives which will be lost.''

''A consideration which Farian was untroubled by,'' the fourth woman said, coming forward from the back to stand beside Deegor. ''She, too, is naught of a *w'wenda*, yet generously spent the lives of those about her without a second thought when she took the place of *Chama*. I am Relgon, Terril, and I offer commiseration for your sensitivity. The— leakage—from the Hand of Power touches me but lightly, far too faintly to affect me as it does you.''

Her face smiled and her mind gave me welcome, and I had to smile in return when I saw that she and Deegor were identical twins. They'd kept apart as a sort of test, I saw, to find out if I could detect her presence without getting a clue from seeing her. That was before they'd felt my mind, of course, and understood that nothing short of a shield could have kept me from knowing about them.

There were ten women in the room, six of them older and four younger, and all of their minds were filled with excitement and happiness and eagerness. When Relgon finished speaking the rest of them started, most addressing and congratulating Leelan, who fairly glowed. They weren't really loud and certainly weren't boisterous, but suddenly Hestin was back, and you couldn't tell that from *his* reaction.

''Why have you all come here without first speaking to me?'' he asked in his calm way as he stopped between me and my visitors, his eyes probably just as calm, absolutely nothing like his mind. Inside he was outraged and annoyed, and I saw Deegor and Relgon wincing and sighing together. ''This *treda* has been badly hurt, and now requires rest and care.''

''Hestin, this *treda* is able to speak for herself,'' I said to his back, feeling more than annoyed myself. ''When I am weary and wish them to go, I will say so.''

''Such a decision is not yours, girl,'' he told me over his shoulder, letting me see that his eyes really were as calm and

271

easy as his tone. "You will eat considerably more from the tray I brought earlier, and then you will sleep."

Hestin didn't seem to hear the four gasps merged into one at the way my temper flared, but that was because he was being deliberately insensitive. He refused to hear anything that would interfere with his precious healing, but he couldn't say he hadn't been given the choice. Without even stopping to think about it, I touched him a third time.

Have you ever, for one reason or another, gone without food for a period of time? After a while it isn't so bad, but the first day is unbelievably hard. Once the hunger pangs get going, all you can think about is food and eating. Visions of the best meals you've ever had rise up to haunt you, and you can actually see them and smell them and taste them. Nothing you do distracts you from knowing how much you're missing and how much you want it, and it doesn't take long before you *know* you're about to starve to death. That's Hunger with a capital H, and that's what I gave to Hestin.

The big man hesitated when he felt my projection, not really understanding why he was suddenly starving, and made a sincere attempt to quiet the need and brush it aside. If the feeling had been natural he would have made it, but he didn't stand much of a chance against the power of a Prime. Pure physical hunger grabbed him by the throat and stomach and shook him, but he really was a very strong man. Instead of attacking my tray and swallowing it down whole, he simply ran out, heading for the kitchen. As soon as he was out of hearing range, Deegor, Relgon and Siitil burst out laughing together.

"Ah, poor Hestin," Relgon commiserated as the other two continued to laugh, her own amusement very much evident. "Fortunately for us all, Terril, even anger and outrage fail to bring you true cruelty. Although perhaps the healer would not agree."

"What was done to him?" Leelan asked, having felt the surge of power without being able to interpret it. "Was he harmed?"

"Not nearly as badly as a woman in his place would have

been,'' Deegor said, still chuckling. ''He was made to feel a great, overwhelming desire to consume all things edible in this house, and will be quite a while at making the attempt. He should not have given Terril such insult.''

''The fault was not entirely his,'' Siitil said, momentarily softened by the seldom-felt laughter and enjoyment she'd just experienced. ''He is a man, and men turn inexplicably strange when in the presence of a *wenda* such as Terril. His desire to have her obey him was of such a strength that even I nearly took insult.''

''The power of her is not only to be found in her mind,'' Deegor put in, glancing around at her sister in amusement. ''Also does the lack of a visible weapon affect men, as Relgon and I learned in our youth. There are few who are able to tell us apart, yet was she far more often sought after than I. In curiosity we strove to understand, and found that when she donned the weapon and I did not, it was I who stirred the interest. Men, it seems, have a great need to protect the helpless.''

''And what more helpless sight than a badly used *wenda* abed,'' I said, finally understanding why I was having so much trouble. ''Leelan, I will be greatly in your debt if you are able to provide me with a bath and some clothing. I have had enough of this lying about.''

''Terril, Hestin has said that you are not yet healed,'' Leelan protested with a frown, her mind worried. ''To leave your bed now would be foolish and dangerous.''

''And to remain in it would be even more foolish,'' I countered, not about to be talked out of getting up. ''Once before I was hurt in such a way, yet found myself quickly able to return to moving about. Hestin's fears for my safety have affected his judgment, and therefore must his opinions be ignored. Will you assist me?''

She hesitated a very long time, her mind flashing this way and that while weighing everything involved, but there were too many reasons against her refusing. Three other minds and six pairs of eyes watched her juggle, and then she sighed and nodded slowly.

"Very well," she grudged, not terribly happy about it but seeing no other way out. "You shall have your bath and clothing—provided you are able to finish the meal which was brought you. Lack of appetite indicates illness which may not be ignored."

"With the prospect of bathing and dressing before me, I will happily finish the meal," I agreed, meaning every word. Sitting around doing nothing isn't designed to rouse the appetite, and that was another reason why I had to get up.

Once we came to an understanding, everything began moving quickly. Leelan took the other women to another part of the house, and she hadn't been out the door five minutes when two women who were clearly servants carried in a big, wooden tub. Under normal circumstances I would have bathed in the kitchen, but with Hestin in there still stuffing his face, an alternate location was much more politic. I finished everything on my tray while the water was being brought in—everything but another serving of that thick, yellow, too-sweet custard—and then joined the water in the tub.

It felt so good to be on the way to being clean again that I had no trouble ignoring my aches, and had to be careful not to broadcast my pleasure. I sat cross-legged in the narrow, round tub, the water up to my breasts, my arms resting on the outside rim, my head back, my eyes closed. All the problems in the universe lose their importance and urgency in the presence of a warm bath, which is why meetings of state are held in formal board rooms around tables. If they all stripped down and made themselves comfortable, there would probably never be war again.

Much as I would have liked to take forever I didn't have the time, so after just a few minutes of soaking I washed my body and hair and then got out to dry. One of the serving women was there to help me, and she flinched inwardly when she saw my right side. More often than not the tail of Roodar's whip had caught me there, and the bruise was wide and colorful. For my own part I ignored it as best I could, and went to get into my new clothes.

Seeing the two serving women wearing *imadd* and *caldinn*—

but no bands—led me to expect something familiar in the way of wearables, but what had been laid out on my bed was an outfit like the ones my visitors had been in, breeches and shirt in light blue, with a pair of sandals on the carpet fur. For some reason I didn't much care for the clothing, enough so that I hesitated in front of it, but then I realized how much more practical it was, especially in the rain. I was going to need every bit of help I could get that night, and that was the only thing to be considered.

Getting dressed wasn't particularly involved, and the knots came out of my hair with less brushing than I thought it would take, so it wasn't long before I was being led through the house to where the other women were waiting. Wearing breeches instead of a skirt—even breeches that were tight and rather a good fit—felt odd, but my attention was distracted from that by the house I was being conducted through. By everything I saw, Leelan had done rather well for herself, with a large, well-made and well-furnished house filled with more than just the two servants I'd seen. The walls, floors, and ceilings were wood and stone, dark, light, and gray, with enough touches of color from drapes and such to bring the color level up from somber to comfortable. It was clearly a woman's house without being in the least frilly, but one part of it *was* faintly embarrassing. Leelan had male servants as well as female, and when I found myself checking them for bands, I blushed with embarrassment and riveted my eyes to the woman I was following. I hadn't found any bands, but my unthinking stares had produced a number of grins and hums of interest.

The room the other women were waiting in was a large one, with curtained terrace windows all along the back wall and a big fireplace in the wall to the right. A fire was crackling in the hearth in competition with the steady patter and pour of the rain against the windows and also had the distinction of being the only light source in the dim, not-quite-chilly room. Leelan and her guests had made themselves comfortable on the dark red floor fur among blue and purple cushions, and just about all of them were holding goblets.

When I appeared, Leelan rose and dismissed the servant, found a goblet to hand to me, then led me into the midst of still-excited and expectant minds.

"You do seem much improved now," she admitted as she looked down at me with half a frown, gesturing to me to find a scat on the floor. "Your walk and movements are not those of one who needs to be abed."

"You must learn, Leelan, not to give heed to the maunderings of men," I told her as I sat, glad she couldn't feel how achy I still was. "They have the ability to pester the life out of those *wendaa* about them, and for that reason must *wendaa* ever ignore them."

"You have more the sound of *w'wenda* to you than *wenda*," Siitil said with a faint smile while everyone else chuckled, her mind still very slightly put off by the way I looked. Siitil was more comfortable with plainer women, and if she hadn't had a damned strong reason for staying, she would have walked out a lot earlier. "We must now speak of when the attack upon the palace is to be."

"*My* attack upon the palace will be this very darkness," I answered, sipping from my goblet to find that it held nothing but juice, something the other goblets were *not* filled with. I looked at Leelan and discovered that she was already grinning at me, her mind as firm on the point as Tammad's would have been. I was up and bathed and dressed, but wine was something I'd be doing without.

"This darkness?" Siitil echoed in disbelief, her immediate outrage distracting me from my annoyance. "We could not attack this darkness even were we to begin spreading the word this very moment! Those who mean to fight beside us would be prepared, yet what of supplies to be arranged for, and healers for the wounded, and outer patrols to be seen to? The palace will not fall till we have entered it, and we will not find it possible to enter for quite some time."

"I mean to enter as I left it," I told her, sipping again at my juice. "Swiftly, quietly, and without notice I shall return, free those who are being held captive, and then withdraw again. The rain will do well in covering our escape."

"The rain will do well in increasing your difficulties," Leelan contradicted, leaning forward where she'd put herself on the carpet fur to my left, speaking above the exclamations of upset from the others. "A time of rain is ever a time of increased vigilance at the palace, for in rain one does well to expect attack. Also in rain are there a greater number of *w'wendaa* about, rather than out upon business of their own. Also, these captives will be held in the thrall of potions; how quickly and alertly will they traverse the corridors, avoiding all other living beings? How silently will they slip through the mud, making no sound for others to hear? How easily will you direct them all, and watch for unexpected attack, and defend against what attack does come? Your own escape was a combination of skill and fortune, Terril; to expect such fortune again would be the height of folly."

She sat looking at me with her mind wide open, letting me see that she believed every word she said. The buzz of the leakage from the Hand of Power was starting to give me a headache again, but I made no effort to replace my shield.

"What fortune fails to come, I will do without," I told her in a voice gone cold and unyielding, making sure I kept my mind from hers. "Should you and your followers attack the palace, there will soon be no captives to seek the release of. They hold one who means more than life to me, and I will not permit any to stand in the way of his freedom."

"Terril, please, we do not mean to prevent you!" Relgon gasped, her voice low and ragged. "Please—the pain—!"

I looked away from Leelan in surprise, then gasped in shock to see what was happening. Siitil and Deegor were collapsed on the floor fur, crumpled and boneless and looking as if they were dead. Relgon was down on her back with clawed hands to her head, and four of the other six women were pulling at their collars or moaning and writhing, while the last two looked as flat and dead as Siitil and Deegor. I snapped my shield shut immediately, so shaken that my hands were trembling uncontrollably, and Leelan grabbed my shoulder while rising to one knee.

"What has happened?" she demanded, fear and confusion

shaking her voice like an earthquake. "Terril, what has happened to them?"

"The one you mindlessly thought of as a leader happened to them," I told her numbly, feeling so sick I wanted to throw up. "You spoke of creatures as though you knew them, Leelan, yet you have never known a creature such as I."

I put my goblet aside and pulled away from her hand, then got to my feet and hurried over to the fireplace. Behind me I could hear Leelan calling her servants in to help, and then their exclamations of shock as soon as they entered. It must have looked like a massacre to them, and that was exactly what it had been. I'd been angry at Leelan while I was arguing with her, so I'd been careful to keep my mind away to be sure not to accidentally hurt her. What I'd forgotten was everyone else in the room, all the others I *wasn't* keeping my mind from. The flaring fury I'd been feeling had lashed straight out at them, and I hadn't even known I was doing it! I went to my knees in front of the fire with my arms wrapped around myself, too cold ever to be warmed again. I really was a creature, a monster dangerous to everyone around her, one somebody ought to kill so that normal people could be safe. I knelt trembling in front of the fire, hating every continuing breath I took, wishing my *sadendrak* had already been freed so that someone could come and put me out of my misery. I couldn't live with the burden much longer, not and continue to stay sane, not with the way it hurt.

It took quite a while for Leelan's servants to get everyone back to consciousness or calmed down, to get the spilled wine mopped up, to stop trying to find out what had happened. Someone had suggested calling Hestin in to check the fallen, but Leelan had vetoed the idea and it wasn't raised again. After a while I was caught in the hypnotic quality of the fire, staring at it while imagining I wasn't different from everyone else, imagining I was happy and loved and really wanted somewhere. When the fire jumped and crackled into nothing but silence I didn't know it at first, not until a gentle hand touched my shoulder. I came back to the room with a start, wondering if they'd already come for me, confused because it was still too soon. Tammad hadn't been freed yet, but after that. . . .

"No Terril, do not stiffen so," Relgon's voice came, as soothing as the arm she immediately put around my shoulders. "We have none of us been harmed beyond an aching in our heads, and the fault, in any event, was not yours."

"Then surely the fault was Dallan's," I said, looking into the fire rather than at the woman who crouched to my left. "Perhaps it would be best if he were sent for, so that all might remonstrate with him."

"The *l'lenda* is also innocent," she said, playing the game with a little chuckle. "The one who is at fault is my sister, and we all of us shall certainly remonstrate with her."

"Never before have we known a power such as yours, Terril," Deegor said from somewhere close behind me, really sounding ashamed and guilty. "It was not my intention to lead you to believe that the refusal about your mind was insulting to us, so that you would fail to replace it. One does not carry a supremely keen sword without a shielding scabbard, else is one likely to cause all manner of accidental harm and bloodshed. Had you felt free to again call up your denial, we none of us would have been touched."

"And my lack of the least amount of control means naught, is that your belief?" I asked, wondering why they were trying to comfort me after what I'd done. "For others to allow leakage from their minds is mere lack of discipline; the same from me is unforgivable."

"For the reason that you are so much better than others?" Leelan demanded, suddenly appearing to my right to look down at me. "Others are permitted error while you are not?"

"For the reason that I am so much *stronger* than others," I corrected, knowing I deserved at the very least to be yelled at, but still finding her attitude difficult. "At one time I had control of what dwelt within me, was able to direct it as I willed, yet now—I will leave at once, of course, so that this cannot occur again."

I lowered my head and tried to figure out where I could go, where I would find shelter from the rain until it got dark. I just wanted another minute in front of the fire before I got at it, but then I noticed that the people around me didn't seem to be paying attention to that part of what I'd said.

"What control might there be of strength such as hers?" Siitil asked, almost in annoyance. "Even those of us without the power were affected by the thing."

"And yet, Leelan was completely untouched," Deegor said musingly. "And we must recall what was done to Hestin."

"We must certainly recall what was done to Hestin," Relgon said from my left, where she still crouched with an arm around me. "The healer was completely unharmed from her touch, and we, who stood beyond him, were no more than aware of what had been done. It failed to come to me at the time, and yet—for what reason were *we* not given what he was?"

"Perhaps Terril might speak answers to these questions," Leelan said, sounding less angry than she had been. "Have you heard what was said, girl?"

"I heard," I replied, taking a deep breath. I'd answer their questions and then I would go. "You, Leelan, were unharmed by my carelessness for the reason that I was aware of my anger and took care to keep it from you. Foolishly I had forgotten the others, and failed to take the same care with them. As for Hestin—for what reason should any other have been affected? It was him I meant to touch, and him alone. To touch others as well would have been—"

"Undisciplined," Relgon finished softly while I groped for a word, everyone else standing in a heavy silence. They were reacting to what I'd said in a way I didn't understand, and then Siitil laughed a short, incredulous laugh.

"She is able to direct her strength," the young woman said, sounding as though she were trying to believe something too good to be true. "She is able to touch or keep from touching one out of many! By the mother of us all, she has the power of control!"

"Of all but myself," I said aloud, although it would have

been easier keeping something like that private. "And now I will take my leave to. . . ."

"Leave?" Leelan barked, back to being angry. "You would repay my hospitality by leaving us now?"

"What would be more fitting repayment?" I asked in confusion, finally looking up at her blazing eyes. "Am I to remain here in gratitude, and next time fell twice the number?"

"I believe there has been enough of such talk," Relgon said briskly from my left, tapping my arm once before beginning to urge me to my feet. "It occurs to me, Terril, that you have most often found yourself among those without the power. Am I correct?"

"What has that to do with . . ." I began in even deeper confusion, rising from my knees at Relgon's urging, but she shook her head and interrupted me.

"I have no need to hear further upon the matter of your terrible, conscienceless failing," she said, still brisk and even a bit impatient. "We will all of us sit and speak in comfort, as those who are grown rather than as wailing children. Come this way."

She began leading me to a place on the carpeting where clean pillows had been put, a place closer to the fire than the original one had been. I could understand that no one wanted to sit down again where so much wine had been spilled, but what I couldn't understand was what was going on. The rest of the women in the group looked more amused than angry or frightened, and even Siitil seemed more impatient than anything else. Relgon wasn't as big as Leelan but she was still larger than I, and I really did feel like a child among grown-ups.

"Sit here," Relgon ordered when we got among the cushions, helping out by pressing me downward. "Leelan, I believe we would all do well with wine, to replace what was so unfortunately lost."

"It comes now," Leelan answered, gesturing toward the three servants who were entering. One girl carried a tray of goblets and another two filled pitchers; the third was a man, and he carried a single goblet and pitcher. The girls went to the other guests who were seating themselves, handing out goblets and filling them, but the man came directly to me. By then I knew what was in the pitcher he carried, but was feeling too down to do more than take the goblet of juice when it was given to me.

"And now we may continue," Relgon said when the servants had finished and were leaving the room. "I have no doubt that all of you here feel as I do, yet must the thing be said aloud for Terril's sake. What occurred here a few moments earlier, the pain and discomfort we were given—this occurred for the reason that Terril wished us ill, did it not?"

"Certainly not!" one of the women said at once, her outraged voice rising above the instant hubbub of the others to startle me. "Had she wished us ill, we would likely no longer be among the living!"

"Then it was done for the reason that she is inept, and should not be the possessor of so great a power," Relgon pursued, also needing to raise her voice.

"Which of us has the choice of what power we will have?" Siitil asked with a snort of ridicule, swallowing her wine. "One does what one is able to do—and to learn to touch a single mind among many others is far from my concept of one who is inept."

"Then this *wenda* who sits beside me is evil," Relgon said among the murmurs of agreement with Siitil's comments. "She carelessly gave pain and cared naught for the doing."

"In no manner is she the same as Farian," Leelan said from my right, her voice flat with conviction, her eyes filled with annoyance. "The pain she received was greater than what she gave, a clear sign of a sense of honor—most especially as what was given was accidental."

"Then there was naught to forgive," Relgon said, reaching out to turn my face to her and away from Leelan, whom I'd been staring at. "Those without the power, those who have no concept of its existence, cannot know the agony of its possession to one of honor. We, too, have at times given uncalled-for hurt to others, and have felt as you do. Had we not felt so, we would have been as low and despicable as Farian, a thing, happily, we none of us are. Are you able to understand, girl? To feel upset is commendable, to wallow in guilt no more than childish."

She was looking at me soberly and directly, waiting for an answer of some sort, but I couldn't think of what to say. She wasn't condoning my stupidity; it was as though she were sharing it, and I seemed to remember hearing something along the same lines from Dallan about the guilt I felt. Back at the crèche on Central I'd been taught that there was absolutely no excuse for using my abilities when I shouldn't, and the memory of that training kept rising up to confuse me. I might have sat there for hours and days, simply staring at Relgon, but Siitil was too impatient to allow prolonged silences.

"I, for one, would be willing to forgive far more than an ache in my head at the prospect of possibly being able to retain my life," she said, her tone somewhat on the dry side. "Do you believe I estimate the matter correctly, Deegor?"

"I do indeed, Siitil," Deegor answered, gleeful enthusiasm moving her to a grin as she sat. "We must, however, confirm our surmise with Terril."

"What surmise do you speak of?" I asked, putting words to what a lot of the others seemed to be thinking. In some strange way I reverted to where I had been before the accident, and maybe even beyond that. Somehow I was beginning to feel as though I were one of them.

"It has come to us that one who possesses *precise* control of the power as well as great strength, will likely find it possible to save many lives," Deegor said in a comfortable way, Siitil nodding in agreement. "In order to attack the palace, one must consider the three greatest obstacles to success: the *w'wendaa* of the guard, the abilities of Farian, and the Hand of Power on duty at the time. Farian herself must be faced only after the other two obstacles have been overcome, and although nearly half the guard are sympathetic to our cause, they may not be discounted. Should the palace be attacked, the Hand of Power will send fear and doubt to the attackers and confidence and loyalty to the guard, assuring a battle in which much blood will flow, for the most part ours."

"We therefore came to the conclusion that the Hand of

Power must first be slain," Siitil said, taking up the narration while Deegor paused for a swallow of wine. "The sole manner of achieving this seemed to be a force protected against their output by a potion, led by one or two who were clear-minded and therefore able to lead. None of that force, you understand, would strike with the expectation of surviving. Those who were not downed by the Hand before they fell, would surely be done for by Farian's guard. All save those who were taken by the madness."

"Farian has taught each Hand to protect itself with an output of madness," Deegor said while I stared at Siitil with chills touching me. "To face death is scarcely difficult for a warrior, yet the thought of madness—in which one would be left alive and forced to endure—forever, should one's sisters fail to find victory— Suffice it to say that although there were those willing to dare such a fate, we others hesitated to allow the sacrifice."

"And now such a sacrifice—to the cause of all in this city and elsewhere, to the cause of deposing Farian—may be unnecessary," Siitil said with a sober happiness which seemed less personal than she had maintained it was. "To send one's output into large numbers of minds is not difficult, not for the Hand and not even for myself. To send such output precisely where it must go, into the combined awareness of the Hand, with strength enough to halt their own output—would such a thing be beyond you, Terril?"

The question hung in the air supported by the silence of everyone in the room, buoyed up by the stares of ten pairs of eyes. Even before anyone could consider facing Farian the Hand of Power had to be knocked out, and I finally understood why Deegor and Relgon had hesitated to say they could best the *Chama*. To make people commit themselves to death or insanity on anything less than an absolute certainty would have been beyond them, just as it would have been beyond me. I listened to the crackle of the fire and the dull thrumming of the rain for a moment, then remembered the goblet of juice I was holding.

"The thing would need to be done just after a new Hand

had taken its place," I said, looking down into the juice before going for a swallow of it. "As I understand it, each Hand operates for a set amount of time before being relieved by a fresh Hand, therefore would the fresh Hand have none save those already drained by previous duty to call upon for aid or replacement. Their own replacements would not yet be assembled."

"You would pit yourself against a fresh Hand?" the woman who had spoken once before demanded above a new babble, her tone more confused than accusing. "We had thought to attempt them when they were nearly drained, trusting to upset and fear to keep the new Hand from forming."

"And if their fear of Farian is greater than that which they feel for us—which it likely shall be?" Relgon countered, speaking to everyone. "No, Terril is quite right concerning the time they must be taken on, and yet— Are you certain you will find it possible to down all five of them, girl? Apart they are somewhat less than Deegor and myself, yet in concert—"

"They comprise a strength which must be overcome," I interrupted with a shrug. "Those who broadcast must have their minds opened wide, else is such broadcasting impossible. If they lack the knowledge of the manner of protecting themselves at such a time, it should be possible to overcome them."

"There is a manner of protecting oneself during broadcasting?" Siitil asked in a small voice in the middle of the new silence which had fallen, sounding more awed than at any time previous. I had the distinct impression that she wasn't really expecting an answer, and apparently everyone else thought the same. Before I had the chance to say anything everyone was talking at once, and that was only the beginning.

The eager arguments and discussions went on and on, not just allowing me to be a part of them, but demanding that I add my bit. Everyone had something to say and everyone else did their best to tear that something apart, looking for flaws in the plans rather than leaving those flaws to be found the hard way. Even what *I* occasionally suggested was attacked, and when I attacked one of Relgon's ideas, at least half the women agreed with me. I had never felt like that before, a real, true part of something that actually wanted me to be a part of it, and I think it briefly went to my head. I argued and insisted and shouted down those who disagreed with me, and nobody minded! Oh, a couple of the women threw their hands up in disgust and called me a child, but that was actually better than having the others on my side. Even after what I'd done to them, they weren't afraid to disagree with me, and that really made me feel I belonged.

"It has now become clear what our plan of attack must be," Leelan said at last when most of the shouting was over, checking her goblet with a grimace to find that it was empty. "Shall we pause first for a meal, or come first to agreement?"

"Should we come to agreement, we will have no time for a meal," Siitil said with what had to be endless impatience, already having given up on her own goblet. "Speak, Leelan, and then we shall go and do."

"Very well," Leelan agreed when almost everyone else nodded, ignoring the few grumbles, making herself more comfortable among the cushions. "The needs involved are not ours alone, therefore are we urged to now strike swiftly after having waited so long. Terril has brought us to the belief that we must indeed launch our attack as soon as we may, yet have we in turn convinced her that it may not be done this darkness. I believe the time has come to inform you that Farian herself may have set the thing for us: I have been summoned to the palace and must appear there upon the morrow, before the mid-day meal."

Surprised and disturbed muttering rose up at that, and everyone frowned at a calm-looking Leelan. On my own I wouldn't have known how to judge the revelation, but everyone else seemed to consider it more insulting than alarming.

"She means to name the one she will give you to," Relgon said after the briefest pause, her eyes hard and angry. "And you, of course, will not be able to refuse her commands."

"With all of you and half the city held hostage to those commands?" Leelan said with a snort, her own held-down anger clear. "She believes I have no choice save to obey her, yet I may indeed have a choice. We have agreed that to avoid a great deal of bloodshed, Terril and a small number of others must enter the palace first, before an attack is launched. Come the new day, Terril will enter the palace with me."

"In the light?" I blurted, still convinced that any plans including me would have to be executed at night. "When my dark hair would be seen by all who looked upon me? I might well find it possible to cause them to pay no mind to what they see, Leelan, yet the drain on my strength. . . ."

"No, no, Terril, your strength must be preserved for use against the Hand and the *Chama*," Leelan interrupted my protests, waving them aside and dismissing them. "Clearly you must be disguised and shall be, for such a thing will not be difficult. The question to be answered is this: are we to agree on that time as the one for attack, or do we require additional time which only the pledging of my word will secure for us?"

"A word which you will then be honor-bound to hold to, even should Farian fall!" one of the other women growled in disgust, strangely enough one of the two who had been completely opposed to attacking immediately. "No, Leelan, this puts a new light on the matter. You have sacrificed enough."

"Indeed," said more than one of the others, and I just couldn't stand it any longer. I substituted my curtain for the shield, made the effort to touch their minds, and found that every one of them had made the same decision.

"We are in agreement, then?" Leelan asked as she looked around, her mind filled with relief and gratitude. "We will make our attempt on the morrow?"

"We will," they all said aloud, completing some sort of formula or tradition, and then they all laughed. The agreement really was unanimous, which we discovered in the next minute.

"I, personally, will be most pleased to make the attempt

287

on the morrow," an unexpected voice rang out, causing half of us to turn around. Dallan stood just inside the room with Hestin to his left; none of us had noticed either one of them arrive.

"And in what manner do you believe you may join us, *l'lenda*?" Relgon asked, speaking when Leelan didn't. "Would it please you to raise your sword with our *w'wendaa*? Should our intentions prevail, there will be few to raise such a weapon against."

"I am honored that you would accept my sword among those of your own warriors, lady," Dallan said with a bow before beginning to walk toward us, deliberately having used the word *w'wendaa* rather than *l'lendaa*. "I, however, am bound by a previous honor, one which demands that I remain beside the woman of my friend and brother. Where Terril goes, there, too, go I."

"You cannot!" Leelan gasped, outraged, annoyed—and suddenly worried. "Your presence would alert the guard, Dallan, and even were you to be admitted you would not be allowed to walk the corridors without escort. The presence of an escort would greatly complicate our plan."

"And should any harm befall Terril, my honor would be no more," he countered, stopping to look down at the woman he argued with. "Would you ask me to compromise my honor out of deference to your need?"

All of the women suddenly flashed annoyed frustration so strongly that I could feel the waves of it through my curtain, but not one word was spoken in answer to Dallan's question. He had as much as accused them of being ready to sacrifice his honor to their cause, and that was something most of them would not find it possible to do. Dallan knew that and had been trying to get at least one of them to say he could go along no matter how out of place he would be, but Deegor spoke up before anyone could put an irretrievable foot in it.

"The request of this *l'lenda* to accompany you is the least of the matters we have before us, Leelan," she said, starting immediately to get to her feet. "We will now take our leave to see to as many of them as we may, and will send you word as to our progress. We will meet again before your departure for the palace."

Leelan nodded with a smile as she, too, rose to her feet, and in another moment everyone was following suit. Deegor had momentarily neutralized Dallan by calling his demand a request, something he couldn't correct on the spot without making himself look foolish. That didn't mean he wouldn't be a problem, but arguing it out with him could be done more easily without so large an audience. The women all said good-bye to me before heading for the door, and Leelan followed along behind them to see them out. I was drifting along too, listening to two of them making some afterthought comments on one of the suggestions I'd made, but the last of it got said without my hearing it. Just as I reached the doorway I was snagged by Dallan and Hestin both, one taking each of my arms, and the parade continued on without me.

"You seem to have been rather fully occupied, *treda*," Hestin said from my right, looking down at me calmly. "In my distraction, it had not come to me that this would be so."

"And I, too, had not realized that Leelan and the others would fail to dissuade you from leaving your bed," Dallan chimed in, his stare from my left quite a bit more on the chilly side. "A thing which was done, sister, without the permission of either Hestin or myself."

Each one of them had a big hand wrapped around the arm nearest him, and although they weren't hurting me they also weren't holding on loosely enough for me to pull free. I closed my eyes for a minute with a sigh, trying to keep my temper in check, then looked up at each of them in turn with the meager results of my efforts.

"I refuse to allow this to continue," I stated, not only annoyed but embarrassed. "I am a grown woman, and will not be ordered about as though I were a child."

"You are a grown woman who is banded, and one who was badly hurt," Dallan said with an air of repeating himself for the hundredth time, adding patience-finally-wearing-thin.

"You cannot march about as you please, disregarding everything said to you."

"And yet, what else might be expected of her?" Hestin put in, this time speaking to Dallan. "A *treda* such as she cannot be expected to behave with a full knowledge of honor, as witness her recent behavior. You blow your breath into the gale, Dallan."

"What knowledge of honor do you refer to?" I demanded at once, stung by his slighting reference. "I have done nothing dishonorable."

"*All* you have done has been dishonorable, *treda*," Hestin said in disagreement, bringing those calm eyes back to me. "A woman who has been banded by a man is more than merely his belonging, she is also the guardian of his honor. Her behavior is a reflection of the esteem in which she holds him, each action speaking loudly of her respect for him. Should she do as he would wish in his absence, she demonstrates her respect and upholds his honor before others; should she do other than what he would wish, she demonstrates the opposite. Tell us which you have done, *treda*."

"While also bearing in mind your—exercises—upon the healer," Dallan said as I stared in upset at Hestin. "It matters not that you were made responsible for your own actions as regards your power; were Tammad to appear this moment at Leelan's door and be told all of which has occurred, what would be done with you?"

I turned my head to look up at Dallan, knowing exactly what Tammad would do, but the question wasn't fair. If Tammad had been there, I wouldn't have had to do *any* of what I'd done. Beginning to feel trapped, I looked back at Hestin.

"I am a living being, an individual, not merely a reflection," I told the man, trying to keep from sounding cornered. "My actions are my own, and speak of none save myself."

"With one who is banded, that cannot be," he denied again, refusing to give an inch. "Were your *memabrak* to go out, draw his sword, then begin wantonly slaying the helpless, would *you* not be horribly shamed? In no manner would

290

you be able to halt him, yet would you continue to be enclosed in the bands of such a one. At the moment your *memabrak* is unable to halt *you*—and your lack of obedience would surely fill him with shame. Although I have never met him, I feel sure this is so. Do you believe me mistaken?"

I wanted to scream and throw something at the man who stared down at me so calmly, but screaming would have given them both too much satisfaction, and there was nothing in reach to throw. I didn't have to turn my head again to know Dallan was also staring at me, and then I got an idea for a final shot.

"Perhaps you have both failed to notice that I am, at the moment, *un*banded," I pointed out, abruptly feeling considerably better. "Perhaps what you say would be true were Tammad's bands still closed upon me, and yet they are not. I stand now as any other woman in this city, unbanded and accountable for her own actions, serenely and completely alone. And my next action, I believe, will be the finding of a large cup of wine to drink."

I started to take a step between them, certain they would have to let me go, but I'd obviously forgotten for a moment what Rimilian males were like. Their hands tightened very slightly on my arms, and I was pulled back to where I'd been standing.

"Terril, I am aware of the reason your understanding is incomplete," Dallan said very seriously, "yet does that understanding fail to alter the fact that it is indeed incomplete. You must know that to be without bands is not the same as to be unbanded."

"Indeed," said Hestin, nodding soberly. "I am told you are five-banded by your *memabrak*, a sign to all of the strength of his feelings. When the fifth band was put upon you, *treda*, was it not done with the rite of five-banding? Does that rite not continue in force, having failed to be renounced by the one who spoke it? Were the bands not taken from you by someone other than he?"

"And do you not now labor to return to his side?" Dallan

finished up, the final link in the anchor they were hooking me to. "You are thoroughly banded, sister, with bands or without."

They were both-staring at me again, waiting patiently for their words to sink in, but all I felt was furious. It wasn't *fair* trapping me like that, with roundabout alien ideas.

"I have no *wish* to obey you!" I told them both, glaring at them in turn and stamping a foot. "You cannot make me obey you!"

"No, *wenda*, we cannot make you obey," Dallan agreed with a lot of satisfaction, putting his arm around my shoulders while Hestin released his hold. "You power is far too great for us to overcome, yet is there now no need to overcome it. You will obey us, for that is the only thing you may, in honor, do. Come."

He headed me out of the room by the arm around my shoulders, Hestin following just behind, and their combined satisfaction was so heavy it set my teeth on edge. I didn't *want* to listen to them, I *didn't*, but that monstrous disease called honor wasn't giving me a choice.

It didn't take long to reach my small room at the back of the house, what had probably originally been decided on as a good hideout room. Dallan and Hestin hustled me inside, then Hestin pointed to my bed.

"Remove your clothing and then return yourself there, *treda*," he said, his eyes now more impatient than calm. "That you have been so long away from it is outrageous."

"You will, of course, grant me privacy the while I do so," I said in resignation, reflecting glumly that at least the time could be used to try thinking my way out of the trap. Hestin's definition of outrageous and mine didn't quite come together.

"You have spent your privacy upon other things, girl child," the healer answered, his voice calm and even but absolutely inflexible. "Do now as you were told."

I looked up at him immediately, reaching to his mind at the same time, and had no trouble at all discovering that I was being punished. I had gone my own way when I should have been listening to him or Dallan, and now I would pay for it. I tried to maintain an air of furious dignity while I reached down to untie my sandals then took my shirt and breeches off, but furious embarrassment was what it turned into. They both had their eyes glued to me to add to my punishment, and I couldn't climb back into bed fast enough.

"And there you will remain for the while," Hestin said as I quickly pulled the cover fur over me, his mind filled with a sense of justice. "A meal will soon be brought here to you, and then I will examine you."

He and Dallan went then to seat themselves on the carpet fur among the cushions, and I turned all the way over to my left so that I didn't have to look at them. Both the fur I lay on and the covering fur were fresh, replacing the ones that had been too full of the smell of salve and pain, but that didn't do as much as it should have to comfort me. The bed the furs covered was made up of two very large cushions, one on top of the other, different from the piles of furs used in Grelana and Gerleth but normally just as comfortable. Right then the most comfortable bed in the Amalgamation wouldn't have helped, and not only because of the way my back was throbbing. Once again I was being punished by Rimilian men, and I didn't need any of my abilities to tell me that I hadn't had the last of it.

A very short time later there was a knock at the door, which was my lunch tray being delivered by one of the servants. Dallan was the one who took it and brought it over to me, and was also the one who fed me what was on it. I hated being fed like that, as though I couldn't be trusted to do it myself and get it right, but I was still being punished. Dallan's mind hummed as he fed me, his blue eyes unmoving from my face, and that made it horribly worse.

When I had swallowed the last of the juice and handed back the goblet that had been given me, I looked up to find that Hestin was waiting his turn. I was made to lie back and the cover fur was taken from me, and then those hands were touching me and that mind was deep in the work it loved best. Only a few minutes went by before I was told to turn over, and then another few minutes passed in silence. I was too distracted and upset to notice the quality of that silence and, before I did, it was broken.

"Clearly I must now admit that I have come upon something beyond my understanding," Hestin muttered, almost to himself. "It cannot be, and yet it most certainly is."

"What disturbs you?" Dallan asked from the place he'd reclaimed among the cushions, his voice both puzzled and concerned. "Has she done that great an amount of harm to herself?"

"You speak the very point that disturbs me, man," Hestin answered, turning his head to look at Dallan. "Although she is weary from having been up and about after so long a time spent unmoving, she has not been done harm. On the contrary, despite the discomfort she feels, she is nearly well. Such a thing simply cannot be."

"For what reason do you find it unacceptable?" Dallan asked, brightening at the good news even as I turned my own head to look at Hestin with the same question in my mind. "Should we not be pleased that she is nearly beyond the harm given her?"

"Indeed," Hestin nodded in agreement, "and yet it has been no more than three days. How might she be beyond the whippings she was given in no more than three days?"

Dallan blinked at the healer without answering his question, most of the pleasure gone from his face, but I didn't understand what the problem was.

"For what reason should I not be nearly well in three days?" I asked, keeping myself flat but raised up on my elbows. "It was surely no longer than that the last instance."

"The last instance?" Hestin replied with a frown, now even more disturbed. "This has occurred a previous time?"

"I was whipped by those called Hamarda, and then escaped them," I said, shrugging as best I could. "I fled across the desert for perhaps a day, and then was found by those who took me in. When I awoke, two days later, Dallan was there beside me. I was then no more badly taken than I now am."

"She speaks the truth," Dallan confirmed, his mind showing relief that I hadn't said *why* he'd been there when I awoke, but his face was frowning and so was Hestin's. "I knew at the time she had not awakened in two days, yet I took that as the results of exhaustion—and thought that the whipping she had been given had been administered some time in the past. I had not known it had been no more than three days earlier."

"One does not recover from such a thing in as little as three days," Hestin said again, taking a pouch of salve from his gray robe. "Even with the aid of this salve. A man, perhaps, might move about despite the pain, yet would even he be far from true recovery."

"Indeed," Dallan said faintly and feelingly, his eyes showing that he remembered his own recovery time after the incident in the resting place of the Sword of Gerleth . "Even a man would not recover quite so quickly. You saw her when I first brought her here, and you see her now. What think you?"

"Can there be more than one thought to occur?" Hestin said, and this time the shrug was his. "The *treda* has the true power, and was able to heal herself."

Dallan and I both stared at him, but my stare had a groaning, "Oh, no!" behind it. All I needed was another new ability, no matter how useful it had turned out to be! But then it came to me that it wasn't new, and couldn't be if it had worked once before as far back as my escape from the Hamarda. That was long before the battle in the resting place of the Sword, so it had to be something I'd had all along. But if I'd had it, why hadn't I known about it? I found myself staring down at the arms I was resting on, for once more puzzled than upset. If empaths also had the power of healing, why didn't anyone know about it? I didn't for a minute believe that I was the only one; somehow, I knew better. So, if I wasn't the only one, why hadn't anyone said anything?

"The woman continues to be an unending surprise," Dallan said at last with a sigh, sounding no more than the least bit put-upon. "Tammad, however, will be greatly pleased, to know that his *wenda* shall be able to heal what her precipitate actions so often bring her."

"A thought has just occurred to me," I said as Hestin chuckled his agreement with Dallan, turning my head to look at the healer again. "As I am no longer in danger of harming myself, I no longer need to remain in this bed. Is that not so?"

My question to Hestin was as innocent as possible, a good girl asking permission before she got up. I was sure he couldn't justify keeping me under his thumb any longer, and I was right; the point I had missed again was that he didn't have to justify it.

"You are completely correct, *treda*," he answered, his light eyes calm—and very faintly amused. "I believe, however, that a nap will do you little harm, therefore shall you have one. To strengthen you even more against what will need to be faced come the new light, you understand."

"But I have no wish for a nap," I said through my teeth as he smiled at me, this time Dallan chuckling in agreement. "You now use your authority over me in an arbitrary manner, a thing my *memabrak* would *not* approve of. I need not remain in this bed and shall not!"

"Ah, but you shall, *wenda*," Dallan jumped in to add to the fun, leaning forward where he sat. "Above all things, Tammad would wish you to be obedient, no matter whether the command be arbitrary or to a purpose. Should he find, when he returns, that you have indeed been done as you should not have been, it will then be a matter for him to see to. Do you wish to attempt to deny this?"

"What good would it do me, you overgrown lap cat," I muttered, glaring at the man who dared to call himself my brother. I was so angry I wanted to spit, but all I could do was mutter an insult—and in Centran, at that.

"I take it you have no interest in denying the truth," Dallan said, his attitude bland with the knowledge that I wasn't about to insult him openly, thereby giving him something good to go to Tammad with. "Had it truly been our wish to give you difficulty, *wenda*, the thing might much more easily—and pleasantly—have been done.''

"What more might you do to me than hold me prisoner to your whim?'' I demanded, even more outraged that he would dare to pat himself on the back for being a good guy. "You would not attempt to beat me, I know, for in such an instance I would defend myself without hesitation—just as Tammad would expect me to. What other thing do you believe you might do?''

Rather than answer immediately, Dallan got to his feet, a small smile of amusement on his face, and came close to my bed to crouch down beside it. With him that near the hum in his mind was much clearer even with my curtain in place, and suddenly I remembered that I lay there stark naked. Granted I was belly down and my arms more or less hid my breasts, but that wasn't the point. With Rimilian men it wasn't being naked in front of them that was upsetting to a woman; it was knowing what they were all too likely to do if their interest was high enough, that nakedness would just make that much easier. Dallan reached out to stroke his hand slowly and gently down my bare back, then chuckled when I shivered.

"You forget that I know you well, *wenda*,'' he said, for some reason being careful to touch nothing but my back. "Were I to say to you that a man's duty to see to the well-being of another man's *wenda* most usually includes her entire well-being, you would find it unnecessary to ask if I spoke the truth, would you not? No longer need we consider you ill and hurt, Terril, and this state you have yourself confirmed. Hestin is a healer, one to whom I may unhesitatingly turn to assist me in seeing to my duty. Shall I ask him to learn if your body desires a man? He will do no more than touch you, and then the route of my duty will be clear.''

I lowered my face to my hands, horribly aware of Dallan's touch on my back, even more horribly aware of Hestin where he crouched beside my bare thighs. Dallan knew how well I'd been conditioned on that world, how quickly I would respond to the touch of a man like Hestin; then I would be taken in Dallan's arms, to allow him to ease me as his duty demanded. As Tammad would expect him to do. As I would hate but would be unable to refuse. I didn't want to have Dallan make love to me, most especially not then, but once Hestin touched me, the decision would no longer be mine.

"Perhaps you now feel more of a need for a nap, sister," Dallan observed after a minute when he saw I had nothing to say, his voice and mind heavy with satisfaction. "You will obey the healer and myself without question and without demurral, and perhaps I shall see my duty as already done."

Perhaps he'd see it that way. I lay with my face in my hands and my legs clasped tightly together, so furious I was ready to break. Not only was he blackmailing me, he was also punishing me again, making me obey not only Tammad and Tammad's wishes, but him and his as well! I didn't *want* to obey him, but he was making sure I would.

"The healer and I shall now leave you so that you may sleep, *wenda*," Dallan said, and a moment later the too-heavy cover fur was on me again. "Should I return and find you remaining awake, I will know that you require easing first. I wish you dreams of great pleasure."

I heard the two of them straighten up and begin moving toward the door, and a moment later they were gone. I took my face from my hands and put my cheek down on the bed fur, silently wishing Dallan an embarrassing accident of some sort, silently cursing myself for not arranging that accident. I might have been tempted to do it, but if I knew Dallan he already had someone else lined up to see to his duty if he couldn't, probably his new friend Hestin. Hestin wasn't really very happy over what I'd done to him earlier that morning, and wouldn't have minded making my punishment a little more personal. Only he wouldn't have seen it as punishment. No Rimilian male did, not even the one who'd tried to attack me. Unless they decided purposely to make it a punishment. I lay there in the dim room, wide awake, listening to the sound of the rain on the window and the splash of it as it drove itself into the ground; wishing Rimilian males could be less physical in their appetites, wondering what I was going to do when Dallan came back to check on me.

*   *   *

As it turned out, I didn't have to do a thing. If I'd tried pretending to be asleep I'm sure he would have known, but the real thing gets rid of the need for pretense. I awoke to find the day even dimmer than it had been. It was still raining out there, making the room close and damp and even somewhat on the chilly side, and I lay quietly in the furs that were no longer too heavy, sliding from sleep to thinking with no effort at all.

Only one more night had to pass, and then I would be going after my beloved, freeing him from a terrible captivity. I still didn't want to wait, was still afraid that the extra night could make any rescue attempt pointless, but the others had convinced me that to go into the palace without their support would most likely turn out badly. And even if I managed to get Tammad out, what would happen to Cinnan and Aesnil? I couldn't simply leave them to their fate, and if the plan we'd developed worked right everyone would be free, not only the three latest captives. Most if it depended on me, of course, and I almost smiled at the memory of Tammad's annoyance when I'd thought I was so important to the search for Aesnil. This time I really was important, and the feeling was anything but comfortable. So many people depending on the success of just one, when all I really wanted was. . . .

"Terril, are you awake?" a soft voice asked, coming from right near the door. I turned my head and lifted it a little to peer into the gloom, and was just able to make out Leelan, half hidden by the door edge.

"Yes, I am awake," I acknowledged, watching her come more fully into the room before closing the door behind her. "That is, I am awake only if you have come alone. Should Dallan be with you and be waiting in the hall, I am deeply asleep."

"No, it is only I," she assured me with a chuckle, stopping to light a few of the candles around the room. Once it was done the room seemed warmer and cozier, and then she brought over a few cushions for me before taking some for her own comfort at the side of my bed. "For what reason would you not wish to see Dallan?'' she asked as she settled herself on the carpet fur.

"The beast has too great a devotion to duty," I answered with a grimace as I arranged the pillows behind me, then turned back to her. "His greatest concern is for me, I know, yet I dislike the manner in which he exhibits that concern."

"Perhaps—perhaps he means to face your *memabrak* once he has been freed," Leelan suggested in an oh-so-casual way, looking down at her hands while she spoke. "He has no woman in his bands, I know, and is not a man to go long without one, and seems even closer to you than *helid* would account for, and. . . ."

"Leelan," I said, cutting into what promised to be a list of extreme length, "you believe Dallan considers putting me in his bands?"

"You are a very beautiful woman, Terril, and one who, as Deegor pointed out, bears no weapons," she said, looking up at me as though it were an effort. "You would do well for him in his bands, I know, and give him the pleasure he should have. Perhaps he will not need to face your *memabrak*, perhaps you will merely be sold to him."

"Allow me to assure you that I will not be sold to him," I said, resettling the cover fur on me while trying to decide whether or not to be annoyed. "You will need to find another for Dallan to put his bands upon."

"You mistake me, Terril," she said, flushing in the candleglow before looking down again. "I need not seek a woman for his bands, he is more than capable of doing such a thing for himself. I merely thought that perhaps, as he shows so great an interest in you—"

"That you would prepare me for being banded by him," I finished when she didn't, opting finally for curiosity over annoyance. "There is little likelihood of the thing occurring, and yet now that I think upon it there would surely be some benefit. Though his appearance is far from the handsomest his body is not entirely unacceptable, and although his talent in the furs is somewhat on the modest side. . . ."

"Far from the handsomest?" she repeated immediately,

her eyes suddenly blazing, so incensed I could feel it through the curtain. "His body not entirely unacceptable? His talents modest! Have you lost your senses, girl? Never have I seen one as handsome as he, with shoulders so broad and chest so deep! And trim, he is trim as well! And as for his ability in the furs, he is beyond comparison! To see it otherwise is to be without sight."

She had straightened to sitting instead of leaning down comfortably, and the glare she was sending was designed to fry and wither. If I'd been armed the way she was I would probably already be challenged, and that almost made me smile.

"It seems clear, Leelan, that there is already one who sees the matter in the proper light," I pointed out, doing nothing in the way of reacting to her indignation. "Perhaps *that* one would do best in Dallan's bands."

Her glare cut off as she realized what she'd said, but rather than getting flustered she seemed to slump. I could feel a small trace of embarrassment in her when I touched her mind, but mostly what I felt was hopeless resignation.

"No man would long keep a *w'wenda* in *wenda* bands, even were she to permit the banding," I was told with a sigh, watching her go back to leaning on her cushions, her eyes avoiding mine again. "And even above that, my life in that respect is not mine to do with as I please."

"Who might there be who would dare to attempt to direct a *w'wenda*?" I asked, feeling the least bit outraged myself. Leelan was free in a way I wasn't, and although I envied and begrudged her that freedom, I couldn't stand the thought of her not having it.

"There is scarcely a daring to the matter," she answered, smiling faintly as she looked up at me. "We have not spoken of this sooner for there was no need, and yet now there is no need to keep from speaking of it. The *Chama* Farian slew the former *Chama* when she marched on the palace, slaying also the *Chama's memabrak*. The children of the two were not then in Vediaster, and returned to find the deed already done. I am one of those children."

301

I stared at her without saying anything, wondering how you were supposed to express sympathy and sorrow for a loss like that in words, but she waved a hand at me and shook her head.

"You need not speak for in my mind the time now seems long ago, and soon my blood will be avenged," she said, controling her inner self even as she reassured me. "My brothers and I, upon learning of what Farian had done, were all of a mind to attack at once, no matter that our lives would be lost in attempting hers. Nearly did we proceed with the attack, yet were we kept from it by the arrival of a messenger from the new *Chama*. We were informed that our plans were known to Farian, and if we were indeed to attack, the people of the city would pay for our foolhardiness. All of our friends and *helid* brothers and sisters would follow us down to death through execution, and then would strangers and innocents be executed as well. My brothers were ordered from the city along with other *l'lendaa* then in residence, and I—I was ordered to remain."

"For what purpose?" I asked, surreptitiously helping her regain control. The memories bothered her more than she admitted, which wasn't, after all, terribly surprising.

"For my original purpose," she said, relaxing just a little more as she ran one hand through her long blonde hair. "Even had my mother lived, I would not have become *Chama* after her. To be *Chama* one must be strong with the power, and all knew I was not. Likely would one of my brothers have banded the new *Chama*, as my father banded my mother, and I would have served Vediaster as was originally meant—as mate to one whose country we wished an alliance with. To seal the bargain I would have become a *memabra* of sorts, and then would my duty have been seen to. Farian, without issue of her own, had need of one such as I for the same purpose, most especially as I was issue of the last *Chama*, who had taken the throne through the blood right of my father as well as her own power. Were she to demand that I pledge myself to the man of her choice, I would find it possible to do no other thing. Those closest to me continue to stand as hostage, and once given, my word could not be retrieved.''

''Now do I see the reason for the others having agreed so quickly to the time of attack we wished,'' I said, getting more of the overall picture. ''Were we to wait, your word would be lost to Farian on the morrow. And yet, there continues to be a thing I have no understanding of. Should we succeed in our plan against Farian, she will no longer be *Chama* and able to use you as an item of trade. For what reason will you then not be able to consort with any man you wish?''

''For the same reason as ever,'' she said with a shrug, reaching to the edge of my bed fur to tug on it gently. ''Should Farian be gone and another seated upon the throne, might Vediaster still not require relations with those about her? I shall hope that such a thing will prove unnecessary, yet should it not be, who else would there be to see to the duty? Had I sisters rather than brothers there would likely be less of a need, yet to wish for such a thing would be idle. The duty is mine as Dallan may likely never be. I would then be bound to another, yet through the will of the people of my land rather than at the command of Farian.''

''Which shall, of course, bring a good deal more pleasure to you,'' I commented as though almost in passing, finding that sort of dedication less commendable than she obviously considered it. People who were ready to sacrifice themselves for the public good, never seemed to realize that the public would probably approve of whatever they did, most especially if no member of that public was directly hurt by it. Self-sacrifice seems to make some people feel better—even while they're hating it.

''Pleasure seems to be a thing destined to elude many of us,'' Leelan said in a mutter, never noticing the undertones of my comment, and then she made an effort to pull herself out of the dumps. ''We shall, however, find a great deal of pleasure in besting Farian, and when she falls her mother may be done the same.''

Sharon Green

"Her mother?" I echoed, finding myself surprised. "What has her mother to do with this?"

"Her mother is the one who gives Farian her male slaves," Leelan said, a look of pure disgust on her face. "Never did any of us suspect that such a thing was being done, yet did we discover it when Farian took the throne. Male children were likely obtained very young, possibly through the breeding of slaves bought elsewhere, and then were the male children raised in collars, and taught their slavery from the very beginning. Surely you saw those in the palace. How else would one do the thing?"

The question was rhetorical as far as I was concerned, and definitely one I didn't care to discuss just then. I moved around a little in the bed furs, then looked at Leelan again.

"Have you thought upon how we are to keep Dallan from accompanying us?" I asked, interested in finding something else to talk about. "Have you spoken with him again concerning his intentions?"

"I spoke with him not long after sleep took you," she said, nodding sourly and with very little enthusiasm. "He is as stubborn as a *seetar,* not to speak of nearly as large."

"Then his intentions are unchanged," I said just as sourly, folding my legs under the cover fur so that I might lean forward more comfortably. "It seems we shall have to strike him over the head and then bind him in leather before we are able to depart in peace."

"You believe a *l'lenda* might be that easily struck?" she asked with a flash of deep amusement, a brief look of delighted enjoyment crossing her face at the same time. "It would surely do him no end of good, yet do I fear that he may be done so no more than a *w'wenda* might. And perhaps even less than certain *w'wendaa.*"

She gave me a wry look, obviously remembering the way she'd been tripped the time she'd come to my rescue, and then she shook her head.

"In full truth might we possibly require one or more such as he," she said, sounding as though she were admitting something distasteful. "I have heard it whispered that Farian

304

has bought the swords of a number of *l'lendaa*, and keeps them to stand her defense should the palace guard fail her. Should they truly be *l'lendaa* and not merely *gendiss*, the blood will flow even more thickly. They will see to their duty with honor, and we—we will die rather than allow them to prevail."

I remembered then what Garth had said, about how no woman on the planet could hope to match a *l'lenda* with swords, and realized that Leelan was saying the same. Skill didn't enter into it, at least not on the level they were talking about; even if the *w'wendaa*'s skill exactly matched that of the *l'lendaa*, the men would still be ahead. *L'lendaa* were bigger, stronger, and carried larger weapons which added to their longer reach, everything that would prove deadly to any woman going up against them. They would all do their damnedest to win, but it might prove to be a very costly victory.

"Then you would prefer to have Dallan with us," I said, looking at the problem from that new angle. "And yet should it beso, you said, we would surely be given an escort which would prove awkward, to say the very least."

"Indeed we would." She nodded, sending a hand through her hair again. "I, along with what few attendants I bring, am permitted to walk the halls of the palace alone for the reason that Farian wishes to give me insult. One guards against a potent enemy, you see, yet is able to ignore the harmless and impotent. Without Dallan we would laughingly be allowed in alone; with him there would surely be an escort."

"Only if it were Dallan the *l'lenda* who accompanied us," I said, leaning back again to tap my lips thoughtfully. "Was it Dallan the slave who trailed after us, perhaps there would be no escort. How many of the guard have slaves of their own?"

"Among Farian's followers?" she asked with a snort of scorn, her eyes sharply on me again. "As many as find themselves able to be granted one. You believe *they* would believe Dallan a slave, and would accept him as such?"

"If he were to appear helpless and servile enough," I said, still thinking about it. "You need to show Farian that she has naught to fear from you, that you support her and all of her doings. What better way to show her that you mean to obey her than by finding a slave of your own?"

"One, perhaps, which is to be gifted to her," Leelan said with growing enthusiasm, obviously liking the idea. "It might well arouse suspicion to say the slave was mine, for my views on the subject are widely known. That I would bring a slave to appease Farian, however, to be sure that the man I am about to be given to is somewhat to my liking. . . . Yes, my friend, the concept has a great deal of merit—should we find the magic necessary to convince Dallan of the need."

She was looking at me strangely just then, half ready to say he'd never do it, half hoping I had some trick up my sleeve to make him to it, and I couldn't help grinning at her confusion.

"It was not we who first said he must accompany us," I reminded her, an about-to-get-even feeling inside me. "Should he maintain his stand while at the same time refusing to accede to our needs, it will indeed be a sort of magic by which he is convinced."

"For your sake, my friend, there had best also be a magic by which he is later avoided," she said with a grin to match mine, strangely enough asking for no detail of what I meant, but then the amusement seemed to desert her. There had been something in the back of her mind ever since she'd first come in, and the rest of the talk we'd engaged in had really been no more than warm-up for that one particular point. She wasn't very happy about it, but it was something that had to be said.

"Terril, there is a thing you must know before we depart for the palace on the morrow," she said, the sobriety in her bringing a chill to my insides against what she might be telling me. "I would not have you taken by surprise and therefore jeopardize the plan. The time of our arrival at the palace is, as you know, to a purpose, yet are we sure to find another sight awaiting us at the same time. I have been told of this by loyal members of the guard, who speak of it as a thing which has been done upon each day already past."

Some of the ice melted at that, formed by the fear that she was about to tell me Tammad was dead, but people don't die more than once—physically, at any rate. Her news still couldn't be very pleasant, though, and when she saw my expression she hurried on with it.

"According to our plan, we shall arrive at the palace just as the first lull in the broadcasting of the Hand of Power begins," she said. "As we discussed, the lulls are used by Farian as a time when her own power may be exercised, without the need for denying the output of the Hand. We mean to locate the quarters of Roodar during the lull, wait in hiding till the Hand resumes, smash the Hand, then confront Roodar and free your *memabrak* before going to search out Farian. When the newly resumed broadcasting of the Hand abruptly ceases, those who have gathered outside the palace will attack, distracting the palace guard from us the while we seek the *Chama*."

"Leelan, I am aware of the plan," I couldn't help saying, unfortunately not very nicely. "Tell me quickly: has Tammad been given great harm?"

"No, no, not the sort of which you speak," she said at once, putting one hand out toward me in a gesture of reassurance. "Physically he has been rather well cared for, aside from an occasional light whipping. His spirit, however, must be greatly tormented, for Roodar uses the lull each day to return him fully to himself. He is well chained at those times so that he might be humiliated as Roodar wishes, and I am told he rages and shouts in great fury. When the output resumes, the potion is again forced upon him and he is unchained."

"To become again the slave of Roodar," I said, only faintly aware of the way Leelan flinched at my tone, but then I had a distracting thought. "How is it possible for her to do with him as she pleases during the lull?" I demanded. "He, too, is a possessor of power, and should surely find it possible to overwhelm her at such a time."

"I know not," Leelan said with a shrug, the wary look just beginning to fade from her eyes. "We will surely learn the

307

truth of it when we have released him. You now understand
what must be done, Terril, do you not? We must witness his
humiliation in silence and with patience, for the Hand must
be smashed before any know what we are about. You are able
to see that?''

Oh, sure, I thought as she watched me anxiously, so that if
anything happens to me when we come up against Roodar,
the Hand will already have been taken care of. Then Relgon
can tackle Farian, with a better-than-even chance of winning.
Farian was supposed to have a good deal of personal power,
but without the Hand it would strictly be one on one. Briefly
the rain beat harder at the window, a thin echo of the raging
of my thoughts against my hastily closed shield, a perfect
reflection of helpless frustration. I didn't want to do what
Leelan was nearly begging for, but I had no choice at all. I
slumped down against the cushions instead of leaning on
them, and rubbed at my eyes.

''Were I to jeopardize the lives of others and the plan itself
merely to keep humiliation from my *sadendrak*, he would
likely find it difficult to forgive me,'' I said, hating even the
words I was being forced to speak. ''He is a *l'lenda* and a
man of honor, and would surely be shamed if his welfare
were to be put before others in equal need. Once he is free I
shall likely speak harsh words to him concerning the matter
of honor, as I personally find it to be an abomination.''

''For those who consider it above all other things, it oft
times is exactly that,'' she agreed with a great deal of gentleness, putting one hand on my arm. ''And yet is it also a
manner of doing which allows one to hold her head high,
knowing she stands in the glow of that which is right, rather
than in the dimness of convenience or the dark of self-
interest. Were honor easily attained or effortlessly maintained, there would be little credit given for the exercising of
it—credit given by those who know the true weight of it. We
are each of us honored for the honor we show, Terril, a return
of sorts which may help to make the burden lighter. Do you
wish to rise now to join us for a meal? Hestin has said that
you may do so.''

A short while earlier that particular piece of news **would** have perked me right up, but I couldn't perk now from the level I'd fallen to. I got into my clothes and sandals **and** followed Leelan out of the room, then spent the rest of the evening pretending I was fit company to associate with. And waiting for the new day to arrive.

12

I was already up and standing at the window when Hestin entered my room, but I wasn't dressed. I had the cover fur wrapped around me against the early morning chill, and was staring out at the beginnings of the day I'd been waiting for. My window opened on what seemed a small back garden for sitting and taking it easy, a stone wall raised all around it to insure the privacy of the sitter. The flowers and greenery were still drooping from heavy watering, the ground underneath was still mostly mud, and even the stone of the wall was a deeper red than it should have been. Hestin hesitated when he realized, in whatever way he did it, that my mind was completely unshielded, and then he came up slowly behind me.

"You are awake early, *treda*," he said, his voice soft and even and calm, his mind not quite the same. "Did the potion I gave you enable you to sleep?"

"It enabled me to *fall* asleep," I answered, still looking out at the slowly lightening and brightening day. "I have been waiting too long for this time for the potion to be able to keep me asleep. Have the others already arrived?"

"Not as yet," he said, putting a hand on my arm through the fur. "The first meal is nearly prepared, and I wish to see you eat more of it than was swallowed by you the last darkness. This day your strength must not fail."

"I have never before found myself a participant in battle," I said with a sigh, finally turning around to look up at him. "To be successful in battle the participants must have more than mere strength, they must also have courage to see them through. My determination to see Tammad free is unflagging, yet I have not previously found as mine an overabundance of courage. Is determination a suitable substitute for courage?"

"Should it not be, you may use your more than adequate supply of stubbornness," he said with a smile, then put his arms around me and held me to him. "Do not fear that you will fail, *treda*. For your sake and ours, your *memabrak* will be freed."

"For your sake as well as my own?" I asked, confused but grateful for the arms that gave only comfort and support. "I do not take your meaning, Hestin."

"My meaning is not difficult, *treda*," he said, and I could feel the amusement he looked down at me with. "Should the *l'lenda* Dallan and I need to see to you much longer, it is we who may well find the strength lacking. You require the presence of the man who has banded you, to hold you in the place he wishes you—and to punish your excursions out of it. I am a healer and have little time to give *treda* strappings— and even less time to be tempted by the thought of it."

I leaned away from his chest to look up into his face, but didn't need to see his grin to feel it. I was letting him see that he *had* managed to annoy me enough to unsettle the doubt I'd been locked in, not enough to chase it away but enough to loosen its hold around my throat. I'd told Dallan and Hestin the night before that I would not let them beat me, and Hestin was using that to get through to me by saying the decision wasn't mine no matter what abilities I had. I might have been tempted to argue the point, but I needed all the reassurance I could get—which might *not* be gotten from an argument about strappings with a Rimilian male.

"The meal is nearly done, you say?" I commented instead, trying to sound as though that was all we'd been talking about. "Then clearly is it time I dressed. It would hardly do to miss so important a meal."

311

He chuckled as he took his arms away, obviously giving me permission to get on with it, but I didn't even realize he hadn't left the room until I was all done and turned to find him still there. To say I was distracted was an understatement, but it didn't seem to matter; Hestin was just as distracted, and I had to speak to him before he knew I was ready.

The quiet and distraction of my own room wasn't equalled in the rest of the house, something I was able to feel long before we reached the kitchen area. That's not to say the big house was noisy, because it wasn't. But it was filled with people moving briskly back and forth, getting their jobs done with efficiency and enthusiasm, their minds bulging with held-down excitement and anticipation and eagerness and every blend of holiday-morning feeling there was. Every one of them was loyal to Leelan and her group, something Relgon and Deegor had worked hard to be sure of despite Farian's attempts to slip spies into the household, and every one of them had waited a long time for that day. I'd intended using that morning to give my mind a chance to spread out, but by the time we reached the kitchen and entered it, I was already curtained.

"I give you greeting for the new day, Terril," Leelan said as she looked up from checking the contents of a pot hung over the fire, her pretty face flushed from the heat and glowing from another source entirely. "Were you able to rest?"

"With Hestin's aid, I was indeed," I said, stepping back to avoid two of the servants heading out of the room with trays. "I trust your own rest was adequate?"

"Completely adequate," she said with a laugh, abandoning the pot to a hovering woman servant who had been waiting impatiently for her to get out from under foot. "The aid I had was not from Hestin, however, and for that reason was likely even more adequate."

"Such talk is immodest and unbecoming to a woman, Leelan," Hestin said with mock disapproval, his arms in their gray robe-sleeves folded across his chest. "Also am I near to taking guest-insult."

"I offer my most sincere apologies, Hestin," she said with a laugh, coming forward to put a hand on his folded arms. "On so glorious a day as this, I would give insult to none save Farian. The meal is done, and will shortly be served. Come and join me, both of you."

We followed Leelan to the room with the windows and the fireplace, chose places on the carpet fur, then let ourselves be served. People began arriving just about then, joining us for the meal and bringing word of the fighters or arrangements each was responsible for. There was a lot of talk mixed in with the eating, but Hestin was right there making sure it went the other way around for both Leelan and myself. The others were free to starve if they liked, but Leelan and I weren't going to be allowed to do it with them.

By the time everyone but Relgon had left again, it was clear everything was ready. I hadn't thought it would be possible to raise a large enough number of fighters in less than a day, but Leelan and her co-conspirators had been organizing for longer than that. On the theory that their chance would come suddenly when it came, they had prepared in advance and had just waited, ready to set everything in motion on little more than a moment's notice. If besieging the palace had been necessary it would have taken more time for details, but our plan saw to that problem.

After breakfast it was time to get me disguised. Although I didn't know it at first, this was the part of the preparations that had taken the most effort. Hours had been spent making a wig for me of long blonde hair, and my own hair had to be spread out on top of my head before the wig could be put on. On Central, hair tinting had always been more popular than wigs and, on Rimilia, they were never used at all; with none of us having any expertise in the matter, getting the thing on and straight was a pre-battle battle. If a stray corner of my own hair wasn't showing, then the blonde locks looked crooked and somehow more glued on than grown. Leelan, Relgon, and I fought with the stupid thing until we were sweating and cursing, almost ready to say to hell with it, and then Leelan's chief house servant noticed what we were doing. The woman was a lot like Gilor, the chief housekeeper in Tammad's house, the sort of person who can be calm and efficient even in the middle of an earthquake. She joined us without waiting to be invited, tugged a little here and pushed there, then added the leather headband that Leelan and quite a few other women of Vediaster wore. I felt as though I were wearing a tied-down hood, but the mirror Leelan had produced for the occasion showed someone other than the dark-haired, useless *rella wenda* the palace guards would be on the lookout for. The thought came to me that the women of Tammad's city wore headbands for a reason other than decoration, but that was a thought I didn't have the time—or the nerve—for. Until Tammad was free it would have to wait its turn for priority.

The last part of my disguise was a swordbelt complete with weapon, fitting around my hips over the cloth breeches as though I had never gone unarmed a day in my life. It's an odd feeling wearing a weapon for the first time, and I could finally understand why it's been said that there are no dangerous weapons, only dangerous people. I could also understand why boys were made to cut themselves if they were found with their swords in their hands without having a valid reason for it. I stood looking out of one of the windows without seeing anything, my fingers to the worn leather of the swordbelt, my mind so eager to draw the sword from its scabbard that it was almost at compulsion level. I knew I couldn't use a sword, knew I didn't even have the ability to hold it properly, but having been given it made the thing mine, and somehow along with the weapon had come the conviction that if I *had* to use it I'd be able to. The idea wasn't just stupid it was downright irrational, but I couldn't seem to get rid of it. I stood staring sightlessly out of a window, and my mind and fingers itched to play warrior.

"Terril, I would not have known you," Dallan's voice came from my left, making me start guiltily. "You seem quite the *w'wenda* now, and that despite your green eyes. As well armed as you appear to be, I must be sure not to give you insult.''

He chuckled indulgently at his little joke, having quite a good time teasing me, in reality finding nothing threatening at all in me or the weapon I was wearing. It really was irrational to let his amusement get to me, but sometimes irrationality can be even more inescapable than depression.

"Should you hold to that, I shall regret not having donned a sword before this," I said, deliberately resting my left palm on a leather-bound metal hilt. "Was there some matter you wished to discuss with me?"

"Indeed," he said with a nod, grinning down at me as he otherwise ignored my first comment. "As it will soon be time to depart for the palace, I would have you know how I mean to see matters attended to. As your safety is my responsibility, you shall remain beside me no matter what occurs, or behind me should it come to sword strokes. Under no circumstances are you to take yourself off elsewhere and alone, and you will obey whatever instructions are given you quickly and without discussion. Have I made myself clear?"

"Oh, extremely clear, my *Chamd*," I answered soberly, letting him see nothing of the flaring outrage ravening in my mind. "This undertaking has become yours, then, no matter that you will likely not even be allowed through a gate onto the grounds, not to speak of into the palace itself."

"I will have a good deal less disrespect from you, girl," he growled, angered by my having called him "my *Chamd*," his finger pointing at me in accusation. "I have, till now, overlooked a good deal of your behavior out of deference to Tammad and your concern over his capture, yet shall I no longer do so. It is ever a *l'lenda* who moves first into battle and leads the way for others to follow, a thing I now do here for these *wendaa*. You shall obey me and they shall follow, and I wish to hear no more upon it."

He was looking down at me the way *l'lendaa* do, hard-eyed above broad shoulders and massive arms, his unreasonably large size straightened to the full, his mind convinced and ready not to give an inch. If I hadn't been so angry I would have been very uncomfortable but, as I've said before, anger can be a rather useful emotion. I looked up into Dallan's pretty blue eyes, at the same time letting the curtain drop from my mind, and respected his wish to hear no more about who would do what at the palace.

"Do you recall the time of our first meeting?" I asked him softly, holding his gaze while my mind began—encircling— his. "Do you recall what position you held, what commands you were forced to accept, what actions you were made to perform? You were a slave in all things save your mind, constrained to do as others bid you for Seddan's sake, held to your place by the chains of necessity. Do you recall the time, Daldrin?"

His lips parted as he continued to look down at me, possibly to answer one of my questions, possibly to protest being called by the slave-name of his own choosing, but it was already too late. My thoughts had already superseded his, telling him how he must act and the very important reason for those actions. Dallan was a man and a *l'lenda* but Daldrin was a slave, filled with self-effacement and an abso- lute lack of dignity, completely obedient and totally unques- tioning, knowing in every single part of him that the least deviation from any requirement would cause the immediate death of his brother Seddan. I'd had to really intensify his love for Seddan and the sense of dread surrounding the thought of him, but using a situation that had once actually obtained made it all a good deal easier. Dallan became Daldrin again, but this time a Daldrin clear down to the ground. He *knew* how abject a slave he had to be in order to save his brother, *believed* sincerely that there was no other way out, and was *determined* to go through with it all, no matter what. What you *know* and *believe* about something dictates your every action, and *determination* helps to keep it that way. Dallan immediately lowered his eyes from mine, went to his knees, and bowed his head.

"Terril, what have you done?" Leelan asked unsteadily from not two feet away, staring in great confusion at Dallan. "I felt the surge of your mind when you removed its veil, yet

I could not. . . . What have you said to him that he now behaves as we wished him to?"

"Words do naught with a *seetar* of a *l'lenda*," I told her, examining the results of my work critically. "He is not one who gives heed to others, therefore did I address the matter differently. For now he is to be called Daldrin, and he will do exactly as he is bidden to do. I must, however, have a few moments for him to return to himself before any swordwork is required of him, after we have entered the palace. I would not see him come to harm through the trap of confusion."

"I myself, will see that he has the time he requires," she promised, coming closer to bend and look at him with her head to one side. "How strange it seems, to see a slave where moments before stood a *l'lenda*. Are you a good slave, Dall—ah—Daldrin?"

"I strive to be a good slave, *dendaya*," my unknowing victim answered, his voice as meek and retiring as he could make it, his manner nervous at being directly addressed. "Is it the *dendaya*'s wish that I serve her?"

"Not at the moment," she answered with a look of delight, straightening up again. "How unfortunate that there is so little time left before we must depart. Would it be possible to have him so again, Terril? After the battle, perhaps, when Farian has been seen to?"

"It may be done at another time just as it has been done now," I told her, amused at her grin as much as at her question. "It must be remembered, however, that he has now been changed for a purpose, which would not be true if he were touched again. Also must it be understood that he will recall each thing said and done to him."

"Perhaps such recollection would be for the best," she mused, none of her enthusiasm dimmed, one finger tapping her lips. "He is more than stubborn, this one, and he has dared to suggest— Well, no matter. He is as aware of what was suggested as I, and this shall be my reply to it. Raise yourself again to standing, slave."

Dallan lost no time in obeying the order he had been given, but his eyes remained down, his head lowered. It didn't really bother me seeing him like that, not as much as I'd thought it would—I knew the condition wasn't permanent, and if anyone deserved being put through that, he did. I stood with hand resting on sword hilt, needing to do no more than gently support the knowledge, belief and determination in his mind, and watched Leelan move to him with deliberation.

"You do not at this time require weapons, slave," she said to him, examining him as if he were a side of beef. "Remove that swordbelt at once, and give it to me."

The slave Daldrin paled at the hardness in the voice of his mistress, and a short minute later was handing over his weapons. Leelan took them with satisfaction glowing out of her eyes and mind, and then she slowly backed away from him.

"A proper slave does not wear a blue *haddin*," she said when she had the distance she wanted, putting some effort into slinging Dallan's swordbelt over her shoulder as she continued to stare at him. "Remove the *haddin*, and then we will seek out brown cloth for you."

It most definitely would not be accurate to say that Dallan hesitated, but it was fortunate I still had an attentive hold on him. Without my support, his unquestioning obedience would probably have developed a sag in the middle. His big hands opened the *haddin* and unwound the cloth from around his middle, his embarrassed suffering clear in the darkening of his skin, and then the cloth was on the carpet fur at his feet. I hadn't realized how many people were in the room, until I began picking up reactions to that gesture.

"One is now able to see how truly well made as a man he is," Relgon said in a drawl as she came over to stand beside Leelan, her mind humming noticeably. Behind those two were four of Leelan's women servants, spread out in the room doing various things—until the unveiling. Right then they were simply standing there and enjoying the view as any normal woman would, their minds more impressed than amused, Relgon's hum multiplied by their numbers. Dallan stood with head and eyes down, but somehow I was sure he was aware of every pair of eyes on him.

"Ah, but he is not a man, Relgon," Leelan said in reply to the older woman's comment, her grin still going strong. "He is a slave who will be my gift to the *Chama*, and I now require the answer to no more than one additional question: how are we also to take into the palace his great bar of a sword which will surely be needed by him? Merely to look upon it is to know it as the weapon of a *l'lenda*."

"Yes, the sight of a *l'lenda*'s weapon is stirring indeed," Relgon murmured with a chuckle, then she looked at Leelan more seriously. "For what reason might it not also be presented as a gift? Well-wrapped in cloth and borne by the slave, who is to say what it is? And should it be necessary to reveal the gift, it might be presented as yours to the man Farian has chosen for you, precious for having been carried and used by your father's father's father or some such. There are many things one might say to the gate guard—should it be necessary."

"Which it hopefully shall not be," Leelan agreed with a slow nod. "Should those who support us succeed in being stationed at the gate. . . . Ah well, the success of such efforts will be seen upon our arrival. Let us now see to the wrapping of both of our gifts."

Relgon chuckled again as she turned away with Leelan, and the four women servants sighed as they went back to their work. Dallan still stood with head and eyes down, his trapped mind really suffering, only the determination of his need to do what was necessary making it at all bearable. I waited until Leelan and Relgon had left the room, and then I moved nearer to the man who had been given no choice at all.

"To hold another where he or she has no wish to be is often done on this world," I said in a very low voice as I looked up at him, raising one hand to run a finger through his blond chest hair. "I was forced, through a need to protect the honor of my *sadendrak*, into a place I had no wish to be. Now is it you who is similarly forced, to assure the safe release of those who are held captive, both in the palace and in the city itself. Consider, as matters progress, how great a satisfaction is yours through so noble a sacrifice; and have no fear, brother, for I shall not allow harm to come to you. I will look upon your protection as my duty.''

I ran my hand over his hard, strongly muscled shoulder and arm then turned away from him, allowing him nothing in the way of useful anger. Frustration was all the slave Daldrin could feel, that and misery at what was being done to him, outrage and humiliation forced low and into the background. He still towered over me but this time it was he who was helpless, and it would be interesting to see if he managed to get the message.

Relgon came back with brown cloth for our slave to put around himself, and a little later Leelan brought in a long, rectangular bundle wrapped in golden cloth and tied with red silk. Leelan handled it as though it had more bulk than weight, but her mind sounded a sigh of relief when she handed it over to Dallan. I stayed where I was on the carpet fur among some cushions, sipping at a goblet of juice and trying to relax. It was almost time—It was almost time—and if I hadn't had to monitor Dallan, I probably would have gone crazy.

When time drags along on one end of a wait, it sometimes has a habit of making up for it on the other end. After hours and centuries of seeing to the last necessary details, suddenly Deegor and Siitil and a couple of the others were there, and the waiting was over. I scrambled to my feet, banging my left ankle with my scabbarded sword and catching my arm on its hilt, then stood very still for a minute and closed my eyes. *Control,* I thought, taking a deep breath—*if you can't control yourself you're worse than useless.* The deep breath seemed to do more good than the pep talk, but at least I was able to wish up the curtain for my mind. I still had control of Dallan through it, but nothing else showed; no sense in warning everybody that the new secret weapon was on her way. I hadn't really noticed the buzzing of the Hand of Power that morning, but as I walked over to join the others my stomach was churning and my head was nearly pounding.

''. . . we shall soon know,'' Leelan was saying to Siitil,

obviously trying to calm the other *w'wenda* down before she went up in flames. Siitil was almost in a worse state than I was, but not from nervousness. Her burning drive to *get* to it was nearly beyond her control.

"You and those with you shall soon know!" Siitil replied in a snarl, all but the thinnest layer of civility gone from her. "We others must remain without the wall, awaiting what we hope will come! I am not made for skulking about and waiting, Leelan."

"Risking one's life is much the easier, Siitil," Leelan said, commiserating, seriously meaning what she was saying, and I couldn't stand it any longer. One person out of control in a group is enough, most especially when something can be done for the other one. I moved through my curtain and touched Siitil carefully, trying to calm her without letting her know what was happening, and happily it worked. She took a deep breath as the invisible twisting daggers withdrew from her flesh, and even managed something of a smile.

"And it is for all of us and our need for revenge that you risk that life," she said, stepping forward to put her hand to Leelan's shoulder. "Should the unthinkable occur and you fail, sister, rest easy in the knowledge that we others will find another time. For now, our lot is waiting."

With that, Siitil and the other two left, all of them feeling better than they had, giving me the absurd impression that they were characters in a play. Enter these and exit those, speak your lines and don't forget the gestures, find your mark then stumble off-stage into the wings. We all knew what was ahead but not how it would turn out, and for that I envied the playwright and the director.

"Clearly, it must be Terril," Deegor was saying to Leelan and Relgon when I returned from my trip into imagination, for some reason opening her swordbelt. "The others must be armed for their own sake."

"Clearly, what must be Terril?" I asked, moving closer to the remaining members of the group. It still made me feel odd to be the smallest one among them, but the feeling wasn't as acute as when I stood among men.

"When we enter the palace and the battle is about to begin, you must give me your sword," Deegor said, handing her own weapon to Relgon. "If it were possible I would give you mine to wear, yet are too many of the guard familiar with the look of it. I shall have to make do with your weapon."

I looked at the sword Deegor was giving up, noticing for the first time the ornate hilt of the weapon, but still didn't understand.

"In what manner will it be possible for you to reach me?" I asked her, also wondering why Relgon was now donning the blade. The only way most people could tell the twins apart was by who was wearing a sword and who wasn't. "You will be without the wall, and your sister in our midst."

"Relgon shall indeed be with you, yet only in name," Deegor said, smoothing at her gray breeches to eliminate any creases the swordbelt might have caused. "It has come to us how useful it may be, to have a *w'wenda* where none is expected. Ever has it been Relgon who has accompanied Leelan into the palace, and this time shall be no different from the rest. We need have no fear that Leelan's mind will be touched in my sister's absence."

"How excellently well all our planning has gone," Relgon observed, grinning around at all of us. "With Terril among us the thoughts fairly fall over one another in their haste to be proposed, for she is our talisman of fortune. We will succeed, sisters, I am certain we will succeed!"

The rest of us said something in agreement with that, but what, exactly, is beyond me to remember. The one thought that came crystal clear as we made ready to leave, though, was one I would rather not have had. Relgon was certain that we would win, but my talent for the future, if talent it was, remained grimly silent on the point.

The sun was high enough to be hot, but hadn't been up long enough to dry up the mud. Leelan and her escort of five *w'wendaa*, one advisor and one male slave, moved along the dirt-based street of Vediaster, avoiding as many of the puddles as possible, keeping to a decent pace, but making no effort to hurry. We didn't have all that far to go, and the people in the crowds made a point of stepping aside for us.

Leelan was being grave and silent on purpose, pretending that she was going to a w'wenda's idea of execution, all the while fighting inside to force her mind to match. Deegor walked just as silently beside her, watching the younger woman's efforts with approval, sternly keeping her left hand from searching for a hilt to rest on. I walked with the four real w'wendaa, trying to look competent and unsurprised that one of them was actually a bit shorter than I was, my mind on the alert against any sort of projections while automatically monitoring and supporting Dallan. Our poor male slave was the only one barefoot among us, or at least he had been until the mud corrected all that. He walked behind the two leaders and in front of the following w'wendaa, his large ornate burden held carefully in his arms, his awareness of the way he was being stared at giving him a really hard time. Dallan *had* to stay with being the slave Daldrin—everything inside him said so—but that didn't keep him from suffering.

When we finally got to the fifty-foot clearing between the buildings and stalls of the city and the wall around the palace grounds, Leelan ignored the guards we were approaching while Deegor casually looked them over. Her immediately suppressed flash of disappointment told me that something hadn't happened that the disguised w'wenda had been hoping for, and it wasn't long before we all found out what that was. Rather than letting us through the gate without comment, one of the guards stepped directly into Leelan's path.

"And what is it you wish here, girl?" the guard w'wenda asked Leelan, sounding polite enough but inwardly enjoying a private joke. "Do you wish to see the *Chama*?"

"I have been commanded to appear before the *Chama*," Leelan answered tightly, finding no difficulty at all in pretending to be angry and trying to keep from being insulted. "As you know this as well as I, you may now step aside."

"Ah, yes, so I do," the woman agreed lazily, standing not quite as high as Leelan but feeling a good deal larger. "You come here upon command, and for a specific purpose. For what reason is that slave not collared?''

The guard's eyes had gone to Dallan in appraisal, she obviously feeling pleased that he made no attempt to meet her gaze, but Leelan didn't bother turning around.

"The slave will be collared should Farian decide to accept him," she answered, this time working a little harder at sounding stiff and angry—rather than just short of upset. "He is a gift I have brought for the *Chama*, one I believe will please her. Do you mean to keep us standing about here till darkness has fallen?''

"By no means," the woman answered, and then she deliberately brought her eyes back to Leelan with a nasty grin on her face. "I would not be the cause of delaying the *Chama*'s pleasure, girl, for she is eager indeed to inform you of which country she will very soon make an alliance with. The gift you bring is certain to sway her not in the least—which is a great pity for you. You may now enter.''

The woman stepped back, still grinning her amusement shared by the rest of the yellow-clad guard *w'wendaa*, and just for an instant Leelan didn't move. Her mind was so clouded with fury that I was sure she was about to draw her weapon, but apparently some people are stronger than their emotions. After the instant of hesitation she simply started forward through the gate, and the rest of us came after her. Dallan was treated to the sort of caress he wasn't used to getting as he passed the woman who had been doing the talking, but all his startlement did was increase the laughter around us. We left the wall behind as we moved across the grounds toward the palace, some of us noticing that the sun had grown so warm we were sweating, and once we were out of earshot of the guard *w'wendaa*, Deegor put her hand to Leelan's shoulder.

"There is but one thing you need bear in mind, sister," she said in a voice low enough to carry to Leelan and us but not beyond. "That is the gate through which Siitil and her wild ones will enter.''

Leelan's mind flared with such savage delight, that I nearly

flinched back behind my curtain. After that her anger seemed
to settle down, and the rest of us could go back to breathing
normally again. Or, at least I could; no one else in the group
seemed bothered that we'd been *that* close to starting the
fighting early. The fact that I alone was unable to use a sword
undoubtedly had nothing to do with the way I felt; the fact
that I might have had to use one anyway was more to the
point.

We were nodded through into the palace itself by another
couple of yellow-clad guards, but this time Deegor's mind
was pleased to see them. That a good number of the guards
were on our side would mean nothing if the Hand of Power
wasn't knocked out, and it came to me with a shock that their
almost-constant buzz hadn't been chipping at me for a while.
We only had a short time to get to where we were going, and
then it was all up to me. Being in the middle of the four
w'wendaa kept me from slowing down, but it didn't keep the
wig and headband I wore from suddenly growing tighter and
more confining.

We took our parade up and down corridors and halls,
constantly oozing the attitude that we were only where we
belonged, and the most notice we got was a glance or two
from those we passed. I couldn't decide if walking about
openly was less nerve-wracking than sneaking around alone
in the dead of night, but another revelation suddenly came to
me. The first time Leelan had asked me to head that revolu-
tion, I'd refused, and she had never asked again. Somehow I
seemed to have almost—floated—into the place I then was, a
very familiar feeling on that world. Rimilians didn't seem to
take no for an answer, a trait obviously common to male and
female alike.

We came at last to one corridor more deserted than the
others we'd been through, one that made everyone else almost as tense as I was. No one went into the corridor who
didn't belong there, and getting caught would have meant
trouble. Deegor immediately went down to one knee and
began messing with the strap on her left sandal, an excuse for
our standing still outside one particular door. Three of our

four *w'wendaa* had already gone through that door, and we couldn't follow until they'd checked things out.

After what couldn't have been much more than a minute—but seemed like an hour—later, one of the three was back at the door, gesturing us inside. We lost no time in getting through the doorway, and once the door had been closed behind us I looked around at our temporary refuge. White rock made up the walls and ceiling, but under our feet was white fur carpeting. Yellow silk draped part of the walls and curtained the windows, the small tables set here and there were beautifully carved dark wood, and the various decorations hung at a few points on the walls were also dark. The room was expensively done up for someone of supposedly refined taste, but something seemed to be missing.

"As this apartment is and has been untenanted, none should arrive to disturb us," Leelan said, making no effort to look around. "Roodar's apartment lies beyond the wall of the sleeping room, more accessible to us than she knows. Once the Hand is seen to, we will begin by calling on her."

I realized then that Leelan was talking primarily to me, and also suddenly understood what her words really meant. Tammad was right then no more than a room away from me, close enough to be helped, close enough to be freed. Without even thinking about it I was abruptly facing the dark wood door in the right hand wall that undoubtedly led to the apartment's sleeping room, but Leelan's hand came to my shoulder before I could take a single step.

"Terril, you must recall that it may not be done yet," she said very gently, surely knowing what I was thinking, compassion clear in her every word. "Should Roodar learn of our presence before the Hand is seen to, she may in some manner succeed in alerting the guard. There are not a sufficient number of us to adequately protect you against concerted attack, and should you go down without having seen to the Hand—"

Then the game was over for everyone, Tammad included, I finished in my mind when she let it trail off, my eyes still held by that dark wood door. You might be able to blast the first half dozen or so to come at you, Terry, but what about the ones behind them? The idea of dying is only somewhat upsetting, but what if you die before Tammad is safe? Giving your life for him would be no terribly great sacrifice, but being patient is absolute hell, isn't it? You've talked a lot about the need for self-control and how well you thought you were progressing with it; how about giving one short, decisive example of what you think you've accomplished?

"You all of you are here for no purpose other than to assist me in freeing my *sadendrak*," I said after a minute, still staring at that door. "The Hand might have been seen to from without the wall about the grounds, had there been none within requiring protection. You all risk your lives on my behalf, a thing I am well aware of. There is surely no more than a short while to wait till the Hand is again assembled."

"That is surely so," Leelan said with a lot of warmth and support, the relief showing no place other than in her mind, her hand patting my shoulder before leaving it. Then she hesitated, her thoughts wavering over a decision, but once considered, she felt she had to speak. "Terril," she said slowly, "we may not enter Roodar's apartment at this time, yet may we see within it. Would you—wish to do such a thing?"

I turned at last to look at her, wondering what she was talking about, and the expression on my face made her gesture at the room we stood in.

"This wing was meant to house those of high standing who visit the court of Vediaster," Leelan explained, sounding as though she were trying to distract herself as well as me. "Certain of the apartments here were prepared so that those of questionable motive might be closely watched, and it was one such apartment which Roodar was given by Farian. As neither knew the true purpose of the apartment, those guard *w'wendaa* who remained loyal to me were able to keep watch upon Roodar without her knowledge, the purpose being to discover for what reason Farian treats her so well."

"For what reason should she not?" I asked, wondering if there was any ruler anywhere who didn't spend most of his or her time worrying about everyone around them. "She is a loyal supporter of Farian and, as you yourself said, the finest sword among the *Chama*'s *w'wendaa*. For what reason should she not be rewarded?"

"Roodar is given far more than simple reward," Deegor put in, moving closer to where Leelan and I stood. "She was unknown among us before Farian's attack, yet now lives higher than any save the *Chama* herself. Should she wish a thing she need only request it, and Farian immediately makes it hers. It was Roodar, we know, who took the life of Leelan's mother the *Chama* when Farian's power proved stronger, for Farian is not *w'wenda* and does not wield a sword. Beyond that we know naught of her, and naught of the reason Farian values her so highly."

"And that despite the constant watch kept upon her," Leelan said, clearly disgusted. "Her value to the *Chama* has never been spoken of in her own apartment, yet were we able to learn other things—such as her doing with your *memabrak*. In truth we *should* resume the watch post—yet only one or two need do so. As the sight may well be painful for you, you need not feel that you must accompany them."

She and Deegor watched me carefully as they waited for an answer, and for a moment I truly didn't know what to say. I was fairly certain I could control myself if I didn't actually *see* what they were doing to Tammad—but what if we found them just about to really hurt him? Nothing would be able to keep me from acting then, and that could well destroy the entire plan. But was the plan worth having Tammad really hurt, maybe even dead? Not to me it wasn't, and that was one selfish stand all the talk of honor in the universe couldn't move me from.

"Leelan, I thank you for your concern," I said at last, raising my eyes to look directly at her. "It may well prove painful to look upon my *sadendrak*—yet I must."

"And we all do as we must," she agreed with something of a nod, then glanced around to gather everyone up. "Let us all take ourselves to the sleeping room, then, and recall that absolute silence will be necessary."

Deegor led the way into the sleeping room, and the last *w'wenda* through the door closed it behind her. Our male slave was put to his knees by Leelan just beside that door, his burden on the carpet fur beside him, and after patting him on the head and whispering something in his ear, she left him where he'd been put. The sleeping room was large, and furnished just the way the reception room was, and I happened to notice that some of the white carpet fur was being marked by the remnants of mud we'd brought in on our sandals. The thought crossed my mind that we'd be lucky if mud was all that stained the carpet fur, and then I was carefully watching what Leelan was doing.

The wall of the room directly opposite the door was of white stone as were all the walls, but hung on that wall between yellow silk drapes was a very wide and intricate carving in dark wood, the white stone behind it showing through the gaps in its graceful but meaningless pattern. The carving stretched down the wall almost to the floor, but it was the left side of the thing that Leelan ran her hand over. The sleeping room was dim enough to make us all move closer to see what she was doing, but we were all able to hold back on the gasps when she took hold of one part of the carving and swung it out away from the wall. The carving was really a door, and with a gesture telling us to follow, Leelan led the way into the wall.

The space behind the carving was wider than I'd thought it would be, and it was almost dark when Deegor entered last and pulled the hidden door closed behind us. Leelan, moving without sound, continued on to the right a few paces, waited until we were all in a line next to her again, then groped at something in front of her. A minute later what seemed to be a narrow strip of the wall now in front of us was silently folding upward, Deegor apparently handling the other end of it, and faint light was coming through to the darkness we stood in. The open strip behind was positioned so that someone Leelan's height would have to bend down a little and someone my height stretch up a small distance, which meant it was essentially eye level for just about anyone. What looked like white curtaining hung over the opening, and stepping forward showed that it could be seen through with very little difficulty.

Very little difficulty if you don't count what there was to be seen. The room we looked in at was also a sleeping room, decorated in green, tan and white, and wasn't as empty as the one we'd just passed through. I'd been deliberately keeping my mind well behind its curtain, more than half afraid of what I would find if I reached out, but it wasn't quite as bad as I'd imagined it. Aside from the normal furnishings of a sleeping room Roodar had added a heavy frame of wood in front of the wide, sunshiny windows, two posts linked to each other with wooden ties at top and bottom as well as a wide, steadying base of minimal thickness, an arrangement that made sure anyone standing on that base in the frame would not be able to knock the whole thing over. The one standing there right then was Tammad, of course, his thick wrists held high by the chains coming from the two posts, his braced legs kept wide by chains on his ankles, his face set in a grim, determined expression. It was easy to see how difficult knocking the frame over would be, because Tammad was trying, his fists clenched in their manacles as his giant body sought to break the posts and send them down in splintered bits to the carpet fur. It looked like he'd been trying for quite some time, but although the posts creaked against the ties holding and bracing them, he couldn't seem to get either of them to splinter. His naked and collared body was covered with sweat over welts that looked painful and he appeared a little leaner than usual, but aside from that and a desperation in his attempts to break free, he was mostly unharmed.

Relief was too debilitating an emotion for the time and place I was in just then, not to mention somewhat premature, but I still found myself leaning on the wall below the opening rather heavily, my hands flat to it rather than to the body of the man I wanted so desperately to go to. He was far less injured than I had dared to hope for, and it was only a matter of a short while before he would be free. I wanted to laugh and cry in sheer joy, both at the same time—and then a door in the far wall opened to admit two *w'wendaa*.

Tammad's struggles stopped almost immediately at the sound of the door opening, and he watched the two women approach from his left with narrowed eyes. The two newcomers were talking together and laughing as they came in, and the laughter didn't stop when they halted in front of the captive *l'lenda*.

"It is nearly time to resume your duties, slave," one of the two said to him, letting her eyes move intrusively over his body. "Should Roodar not have returned by then, it is we who shall see to the matter. You will, of course, give us absolutely no difficulty."

Tammad stood in the chains holding him and stared down silently at the woman, his jaw set grimly, his hands again turned to fists beyond the manacles. He wasn't verbally disagreeing with the woman, but his light eyes had developed a stubborn look which the woman didn't miss.

"I will hear from your own lips that you mean to give no difficulty," she pursued in a harder voice, stepping onto the frame base to move closer to the man she looked up at with such cold authority. "Must you be reminded once again of the pretty little slave brought here by you, and what her lot has been for your past refusals? She weeps so well when the lash is put to her, that Roodar may soon begin to *hope* for difficulty from you. We, however, prefer an obedient slave to the sight of a dark-haired *weerees* writhing upon the stone in pain, therefore do I demand words from you. How will you have it, slave?"

Tammad's lips parted slightly to show teeth clenched against a snarl of rage, but I could see that his eyes were wild with a sick, twisting worry that kept the snarl from being voiced. So that was the way they held him while he was lucid, I thought with shock and outrage, not just with chains but also with threats against *me*! They must have told him about it every time Roodar had whipped me, making him believe that the pain I was given was because of him! Not until Leelan's hand came to my shoulder to steady me did I realize I was trembling,

331

and the rage inside was something I had to hold down by main force.

"I—will give no difficulty, *dendaya*," Tammad said then, his voice forced out unwillingly between his teeth, a faint tinge of fear edging it. "You will have no reason to give the girl greater pain, pain which should have been given instead to me. I—was also told that I might perhaps be allowed to see her. . . ."

"Were you indeed?" the woman interrupted too pleasantly, enjoying the way his stumbling words immediately cut off. "An obedient slave may perhaps be rewarded by his mistress, yet must he first be proven truly obedient. Are you an obedient slave, slave?"

"I—am an obedient slave, *dendaya*," her victim answered, looking down at her helplessly. The shame and humiliation he felt were terrible pain, but it was something he had chosen to accept in order to get what he had to have.

"How pleasant to have an obedient slave before one," the woman said with a purr while the second one laughed, her hands clasped behind her back as she looked upward. "I find you quite attractive, slave. Ask that your *dendaya* touch you, beg that she honor you."

There was something of a hesitation, but the victim held chained in place had very little choice. If he wanted what had been promised him, he had to obey.

"I beg you to honor me with a touch, *dendaya*," he choked out, his eyes no longer able to meet those of the woman, his voice faint with self-disgust and loathing. He knew what would happen when he said the words, and when the woman put her hand on him, intimately, possessively, his eyes closed entirely with the bottomless humiliation.

"Ah, yes, you find that the touch of your *dendaya* causes you to tremble, does it not, slave?" The woman laughed, the movement of her hand leaving him in no doubt as to what she held to. "You had best hope that when Roodar returns, she finds interest in the thought of your use. Once the potion is again down your throat, you will cringe and whimper and snivel until you are seen to."

"I believe it is time that the potion be fetched, sister," the other woman said, interrupting her own laughter for the purpose. "Roodar will not return for a time, now, yet must he be prepared against that return."

"And once prepared, I may perhaps use him myself," the first woman murmured, both hands high to caress the chest and shoulders that couldn't avoid her touch. "Fetch the potion, sister, the while I allow the nearness of this slave to stir me."

The second woman chuckled in amusement and obligingly headed for the door, and I suddenly discovered that Leelan's hand wasn't simply on my shoulder any longer. One of her hands held my right arm in a grip that should have been painful while her other hand patted and smoothed my hair, very soft sounds urging me to silence and calm coming from her throat. Somehow Deegor had appeared at my left to do almost the same thing, both of them surely able to see the way my fingers held claw-like to the opening we'd been looking through. I could feel their anxiety and upset surrounding me without having it affect me in the least, but then Deegor's lips came to my ear, and I could just make out the breath-soft words.

"The Hand of Power, Terril!" she whispered, somehow managing to put urgency into words that were almost soundless. "The output of the Hand has begun again, and they may be seen to in no more than a matter of moments! Hold fast, girl, for it is nearly time!"

I don't know how often the words had been repeated before I understood them but, once I did, things became worse instead of better. The curtain over my mind had been on the verge of collapse from inner pressure when Deegor distracted me, something both she and Leelan seemed to understand and were trying to keep from happening. I still wanted to explode out at anything in reach, first and foremost against the woman who now stood behind Tammad, trailing her fingers over him, but Deegor was right. The Hand had indeed started broadcasting again, and all I had to do was wait about five minutes to be certain that everyone was prepared and in their place before I stopped it. After that it didn't matter *what* I did to the woman, but to touch her before then could ruin everything.

Five more minutes and Tammad would be free—but they were going to make him take that slave drug again.

I ignored the hands on my arms and continued to look through the opening, this time using my hold on the wall to keep me erect. Five minutes and he would be free—but if they gave him that potion it would be another whole day before the effects of the drug left him. Someone who had never been subject to that drug would also never understand how terrible it would be for him, but I'd had experience with that—*potion*—and I *knew*. Another whole day of living hell, confused and beaten down and almost afraid to breathe, another day of something worse than death that he would accept without struggle for *my* sake! I held to the wall and tried to *will* the time into moving faster, tried to make it all elapse before the second woman came back—but time rarely lets itself be coerced.

When the figure moving slowly with a filled bowl in her hand appeared in the doorway, she should have, by rights, heard the shriek of denial in my mind. She was already back but it was still too soon, and he would swallow it all without a single murmur, thinking he was helping *me*! I found my back pressed into the unopened back wall of the passage, my fists to my head, so close to losing all control that I thought I would die. If I had to let him swallow that drug I would be useless afterward against the Hand, I knew I would! I had to keep him from accepting it without letting anyone know we were there, had to make him know that I was already free and safe beyond anything they cared to try—

Out of desperation came the answer to my need, and I pulled away from the two Rimilians trying silently to calm me, and went back to look through the opening. The second woman was halfway to the frame, the first now simply standing and awaiting her, and there was no time to lose. I had to tell Tammad I was free, in a way that he couldn't doubt, in a way that no one else could detect.

It seemed like months or years since I'd done it last, but very deliberately I reached around my curtain to touch my beloved with a kiss. It had been almost a joke between us, a private gesture that no one else was aware of, and all I could do was hope that he would notice and remember. It was so light a thing, and his mind was in such a turmoil, and I couldn't let my curtain go so that he would be able to feel me there. That second woman had known when the Hand had begun broadcasting again, which meant she was sensitive enough to detect my presence if she were to feel my un-shielded mind. All I had to work with was a kiss, and I could feel the soundless scrape of my sword hilt as I pressed my body harder against the wall that separated me from every-thing that made life worth living.

At first, Tammad didn't seem to notice the sensation of lips on his as he stood there with his eyes closed, but then, just as the second woman reached the frame, his head came up and a frown took him. I kissed him again, afraid to put too much strength into the sensation to keep it from registering as something other than what it had to be, and this time his eyes opened to show shocked disbelief. I could feel his mind darting around searching for me, the hope rising inside him— but my curtain was still in place and the woman with the drug had already reached him.

"Drink it now, slave!" the first woman ordered in an ugly voice as the second raised the bowl high enough for him to reach, both of them displeased with the way their victim was apparently ignoring them. "Drink it this instant, else shall Roodar have the dark-haired slave brought here, and whipped to crimson ribbons before your eyes!"

The woman's viciously spoken threat brought the agony of fear to a man who had never before felt fear over anything, and he immediately lowered his head to the bowl and started to drink it down as commanded. There was nothing I could do to stop it, nothing at all—and that's exactly what I did. Frantically I hit Tammad with absolute denial, hard enough to rattle his teeth, loud enough to make him think someone had screamed, "No!" at the top of their lungs, right into his ear.

His head jerked up again as he cried out with the ringing ache, startling the two women, and that was all I had been waiting for.

Stripping the curtain from my mind, I flashed my thoughts and will and feelings right straight toward the strongly droning Hand of Power. Five minds awaited me where they sat, hands linked together to help with their thought link, five minds opened wide in a pentagram of projection. They really were strong together, much stronger than individual power could account for, but my blast of hatred and fury and frustration and rage hit them so hard and so unexpectedly that they instantly blanked from all sense of perceiving. One instant they were there and the next they were gone, to what fate I had no idea, nor did I care. I'd done what had to be done, and now was free to do as I pleased.

"Leelan, now!" Deegor said excitedly as I looked through the opening at the two guards again. "The Hand is no more! Open the way!"

With a burst of triumph Leelan pushed at the wall in front of us, and then we were stepping out face-to-face with the two shocked guards. The first woman paled and drew her sword, but the second, the one with the bowl, just stood there staring at me, wide-eyed and shaken. My mind was totally unshielded and she could feel the strength and fury in it, and then she felt something else. The first woman had come toward her and put a hand on her shoulder, and then that first woman dropped her sword and snatched the bowl out of the second woman's hand. The raging thirst she was feeling would let her do nothing else, and before the second woman could shout a warning, the first had already swallowed what she had so desperately needed.

There was a puzzled silence among those who stood with me as the first woman happily wiped her mouth with the back of her hand and the second watched in horror, but that was only because the people with me didn't know what the drug would do. And then the woman who had been so thirsty frowned, one hand lifting to her head, her eyes widening, her whole body trembling. She was beginning to be very confused and very unsure of herself, and the fear was starting to creep into every part of her, making all the rest of it that much worse. She had seemed to have a very good opinion of the drug while it was still in the bowl; once it was inside her instead, she slid to her knees and began trying to make herself very, very small.

"Amazing," Deegor breathed from beside me, watching the kneeling woman trying to melt into the carpet fur. "I felt a stirring in the air a moment before the Hand was done, and with this one was aware of no more than that she had been touched. Never before have I seen such precision of control, Terril."

"Leelan!" the second guard breathed, finally dragging her eyes away from her former companion and bringing them to the leader of our group. "What has happened to the Hand of Power? What do you do here?"

"What has become of the Hand of Power, I am as yet unable to say," Leelan answered with a shrug, looking at the other woman coldly. "As for the meaning of my presence, that should surely be obvious. Farian's time as *Chama* draws to an end."

"You will not find it possible to best her," the woman said, making the effort to pull herself together. "With Roodar beside her, Farian will not be taken even with the aid of one such as *that*."

The last word the guard spoke clearly referred to me, but I hadn't been paying more than token attention to conversation since the first woman had gone cringing to her knees. I'd been moving toward someone who'd had his eyes on me the entire time, and by then I was standing in front of him and gently reaching around his body to hold him as tightly as I'd been dreaming about so long. My mind spread out to smother him with the love I was feeling in the same way my body tried to smother his, drawing a wide, fuzzy-edged feeling of love in response, and the only way it could have been better was if he'd been freed of the chains so that his arms could hold me as well.

"You believe Farian's power to be a match to Terril's?"

Deegor asked the woman, her voice sounding amused. "The *Chama* will no more find it possible to withstand her than your sister was able to do."

"And now we must see to you," Leelan told the woman, drawing her eyes again. "There are things we must be about, therefore have we little time to dally. We will have your surrender, else will we have your life."

"To surrender is not done by a true *w'wenda*," the woman answered, drawing herself up. "Have at me, then, all of you, in the name of battle against the *Chama*."

"We are not Farian, to fall upon a single blade in numbers," Leelan said disgustedly, her eyes unmoving from the woman, the entire tableau visible to me where I stood. "You shall be given the honor due a *w'wenda*, and may choose which of us you will face."

"As I now have your word upon the matter, I shall do exactly that," the woman answered, her smirk so clear I could see it even with her back to me. "It will please me a great deal when your honor is compromised, O daughter of a dead *Chama*, for you shall have to do no other thing in order to save the life of one quite close to you. I have been told I might face any among you, none excepted, and to withdraw the offer would be to show dishonor. The one I choose to face is Relgon."

The woman's voice rang out triumphantly, her mind viciously delighted that she had found it possible to strike so hard a blow at the opposition. If Leelan honored her word she would lose a close friend and adviser; if she saved her friend's life by refusing, she would be soiling her own sense of the proper. The woman had it all figured out, and therefore felt nothing but continuing delight when Leelan and her "friend" exchanged looks of surprise.

"Do you mean you wish to face *me*?" Leelan's "friend" asked the triumphant guard, the wall of innocence in her mind hiding what was behind. "You would draw a weapon against one who is unarmed?"

"For what reason should I not?" the woman retorted, standing with her left palm resting on her sword hilt. "As I am to lose my life, it will give me great pleasure to be accompanied by another. Take a weapon and face me, woman, else shall your noble friend be forsworn."

"There is naught else for it, my friend," Leelan said to the older woman, working hard to feel resigned as she put a hand to her shoulder. "You may use my sword to face her."

"Very well, Leelan," the answer came—much more successfully resigned—along with a sigh. "I will be honored to accept your sword. When one is challenged, one must answer."

The sword in question was solemnly handed over and as solemnly received, and then everyone else stepped back. The guard woman was faintly surprised that Leelan was going to let it go on, but she was also much too satisfied to complain. One way or the other she was determined to hurt Leelan, and she drew her blade with a good deal of relish, anticipating some fun before she had to give up her own life. It didn't bother her in the least that she was about to slaughter someone who was helpless, but she did feel a bit puzzled when her opponent stopped in front of her and lowered her point.

"Before we begin, I feel I should correct one small misconception on your part," the helpless victim said in a very mild way, looking at her opponent with steady blue eyes. "We and you know that you are unable to match Leelan with a sword, therefore do you seek to give her harm in another manner. One who would do such a thing is a craven, and totally without honor, and were my sister here even she would have little difficulty in besting you. *I* shall have no difficulty whatsoever."

"Your sister?" The woman laughed, still not getting the point, her fist tightening around her hilt. "Your sister is not one I would care to face, yet is it you I have before my blade, Relgon. Your days of accompanying Leelan are done."

"My days of accompanying Leelan are merely beginning," the older woman said with a faint smile, tossing her head to rid her shoulders of long blond hair as she raised her point again. "And Relgon is the sister I so recently referred to. *I* am Deegor."

I couldn't see if the guard woman's face paled, but her

mind certainly did. Deegor was now allowing her grim pleasure to show through, and her opponent was surely able to
feel it. The next instant the guard attacked, trying to get with
surprise what she couldn't get with skill, but Deegor was
ready for her. Effortlessly the *w'wenda* blocked the attack,
drove the guard back with hard, slashing blows, then knocked
her weapon aside and ran her through. I had already shielded
against such an end, so I was able to watch the body crumple
to the floor fur without doing more than tightening my hold
on Tammad just a bit. There was momentary silence while
Deegor looked down at her erstwhile opponent, and then we
all heard a voice we hadn't heard in quite some time.

"What occurs here?" the voice demanded, causing us to
look around or over toward the wall we had come through.
Dallan stood there with his sword in his hand, some small
amount of confusion still in his eyes, but for all intents and
purposes back to his original self. The sword looked strange
with him still in a slave wrap, but no one felt the urge to
laugh.

"I see you have released him, Terril," Leelan said in
approval while everyone else began moving purposefully in
different directions, Deegor to clean the sword she had just
used. "It will save a good deal of time we are now badly in
need of. We must reach Farian before she attempts to flee."

Dallan began again to demand to know what was going on,
but then he saw Tammad where he still stood in his chains,
and understood that explanations would have to wait. He
came over to stand with us while Leelan's women moved
around the room, two of them grabbing the drugged guard
where she cringed against a wall, then forcing her to show
them where the keys to Tammad's shackles were. Happily the
key was right there in the apartment, hanging on a peg under
the spot where Tammad's sword had been mounted on the
wall, and it took only another minute to get him loose.
Although he didn't actually stumble, he was a good deal less
steady on his feet than he should have been, but when he
wrapped those mighty arms around me that was all I could
bring myself to care about.

340

"How do you fare, brother?" Dallan asked him while the women took off again on errands of their own. "Later you must certainly rest a good while."

"Later I shall certainly rest," Tammad answered, his mind vaguely curious. "For what reason are you clad so, brother? I had not known that they had taken you as well."

"I was not taken," Dallan answered, giving me a low-browed scowl where I stood with my cheek against Tammad's chest. "More accurately, I was not taken by those who first took you. We shall speak of the matter—at length—when the attack has been successfully concluded."

"We will speak of the matter then," Tammad agreed, still seeming understandably confused and vague, but that was all the time we had for talk. Leelan's *w'wendaa* brought over Tammad's sword and the dark green *haddin* they'd found, and Deegor and Leelan pulled me bodily away from the arms I didn't want to leave.

"Terril, we must now hurry on," Leelan said without giving me the chance to do more than make a single sound in protest. "Your *memabrak* must dress and join us, and then we shall seek out Farian. There are no others of her guard remaining in this apartment."

She seemed rather disappointed at that, something that made Deegor grin, but I was forced to admit I understood how she felt. I now had what I wanted, but there were others who didn't.

So I stood and waited while Tammad dressed himself and added his swordbelt, during which time Dallan returned briefly to the other apartment to retrieve his own swordbelt. It didn't take long before everyone was ready, but when Tammad came over toward me and said, "Terril," Deegor stepped between us and raised a hand in his direction.

"You may not have her," she said in a firm but kindly voice as she looked up at him. "There are others who now need her more, as you can surely understand. There is a battle to be fought and won."

"Yes, battles must be won," Tammad agreed, terribly disappointed but feeling no urge to argue. He was struggling

341

weakly against the confusion he still felt, but everything was happening so fast around him, and he was so tired after all he'd been through.

"For what reason would it be detrimental to our battle if I were to simply walk beside him?" I asked, annoyed that I was being positioned between Leelan and Deegor as we began to leave the apartment. "Are you of the opinion that your efforts toward my safety would be greater than his?"

"His great fatigue aside, certainly not," Deegor said with a distracted nod of agreement from Leelan, a reassuring touch on the shoulder coming from the older woman. "Were the matter one of your safety alone, you might certainly walk beside him. Fortunately or unfortunately we shall likely find fighting in the corridors, and you are the one who bears the only sword I might use. I would take it now to free you of the necessity of remaining beside me, yet might we well require again the belief that I am Relgon. The time should not be long."

The time should not be long. It seemed to me I'd already had to wait far too long, but I couldn't really argue with Deegor's need. I cast one longing look back at Tammad where he followed with Dallan, then let the two *w'wendaa* from Vediaster navigate me through the door.

The corridor we exited into was empty, but all of a sudden we were able to hear the sound of swordplay, an unguessable distance off. The battle really was on, but inside the apartment we hadn't been able to tell. Despite the way all of me had wanted to concentrate on nothing but Tammad, I'd still kept a good portion of my mind alert for any attempt to replace the Hand of Power. Now I realized consciously what I'd known all along: that there hadn't been even a whisper of a try at replacing them, no matter who had or hadn't been there when they'd gone down. Their room was located some-where in the center of the palace, I'd been told, and they must have had guards around them—or maybe not. Siitil had thought they were guarded, but maybe it was only from the outside of a room. Inside—who could hurt the Hand of Power?

I was tempted to ask what the exact arrangements were, but Leelan and Deegor were too busy looking around carefully as we moved along the corridor for me to distract them. Leelan and her four *w'wendaa* had their swords out and Deegor was practically on top of me to my left, but Dallan and Tammad followed along with their swords sheathed. The men were only there as a just-in-case, I remembered, and somehow they seemed to accept that; if the battle was waged by *w'wendaa* alone, they would not try to involve themselves.

The next few minutes were enjoyable only if you like nerve-wracking experiences; for those like me who tend to prefer more peaceful circumstances, the best thing to be said about the time is that we weren't attacked. We moved from corridor to corridor, Leelan, for the most part, leading the way, but the fighting we could hear continued to be found elsewhere. I had the distinct impression I was the only one who appreciated that fact, though, and tried to imagine how I would feel if I could actually use the weapon I wore. Most of the minds around me were eager to get into the thick of things, eager to come face-to-face with the enemy, and that was an outlook I wasn't used to. Avoiding difficulties was more the Centran way of doing things, and despite my former penchant for kicking up a fuss, I'd spent most of my life doing the same.

We finally reached one particular corridor that wasn't empty, but rather than get upset my companions were elated. There were unmoving, yellow-clad bodies on the no-longer-white stone floors, more yellow-clad bodies still up and moving, and a good deal more breeches-clad figures standing around with them. Although swords were out no one was fighting, and after a moment I realized the women before us were all on our side. They were gathered in front of intricately-carved dark wood double doors, and as we came up to them, Siitil stepped out of their midst.

"Leelan, the battle has gone well," she said at once, looking almost unrecognizable with all the agitation and frustration gone from her. "When the Hand ceased its output we attacked at once, yet have we now been halted for a time in our forward progress. The usurper is behind these doors, and we are unable to open them without a ram. As I have already sent for one, it should be here momentarily.''

"Excellent," Leelan answered with a very cold smile, looking at the doors rather than at Siitil. "It should not be long, then."

At first I thought Leelan was simply repeating what Siitil had said, but then it came to me that the wait she was referring to was the one necessary before she might face Farian. Her mind was a good deal colder than her smile, and I might have considered shivering if the ram hadn't been brought up just at that moment.

Four *w'wendaa* carried a heavy metal table, four others having gone along to guard them, and everyone else moved out of the way to give them room to do what they had to. I wanted to spend the waiting time next to Tammad, but Deegor and Leelan were still flanking me, and a number of *w'wendaa* had positioned themselves around and behind us all. The women began swinging the table at the doors, immediately ruining the carvings and producing a loud, grimly insistent cadence, and the eagerness in the minds all around me began building again.

No one can tell me that the thoughts of the people in that corridor didn't do as much as that table to force open those doors. If the building anticipation had gone on even one more minute I would have had to shield, but the doors turned out to be more fragile than my reluctance to blind myself. They crashed open with the sound of snapping wood, the women with the metal table were quickly gotten out of the way, and then we were all moving into the room they had tried so hard to keep us out of.

The room itself was rather larger than I had expected, with a big oval platform directly ahead in front of the far wall, and although there was a door in both the left- and right-hand walls, there were no windows. Rows of candles illuminated the white stone of the walls, ceiling, and uncovered floor, and made seeing the three knots of almost motionless women very easy, as though it were a picture we were looking at

rather than reality. To the right stood those who were unarmed, one almost on top of the next, their minds running the
gamut from excited elation to petrified fear, their faces showing the same. To the left were at least a dozen yellow-clad
w'wendaa, their swords in their fists and their minds grim,
their faces showing nothing but determination. The *w'wendaa*,
it appeared, were just as motionless as the first group, most
likely due to the fact that we outnumbered them more than
two to one, which made attacking us not the best of ideas.

The third group was the smallest of all, but that, most
certainly, was the one that got the greatest amount of attention.

Standing on the raised platform amid the silks and furs and
cushions were six people, two of whom were Farian and
Roodar. The other four were *w'wendaa* who seemed to be a
bit more prepared to fight than the ones standing on the floor
to the left, and a brief but intense burst of disappointment
came from the back of our own group. With not a single
l'lenda in sight Dallan knew he was out of luck as far as any
fighting went, and he was probably cursing that luck in a
silence to match the rest of the silence around us. There
wasn't a single sound in that entire room—until Leelan stopped
our advance with a gesture, then moved one additional pace
forward alone.

"Your time as *Chama* is done, Farian," she announced
in ringing tones, grim satisfaction and pleasure filling every
part of her, her head held high and proud. "Surrender to us
now, and you shall be permitted to live a short while longer."

"Shall I, indeed," the woman Farian murmured in return,
cold fury in the light eyes looking down at Leelan, her whole
bearing set into regal outrage. "I am unsurprised that you call
for my surrender, girl, for in no manner would you find it
possible to best me without it. You are, however, destined for
disappointment in your demands. I have no intentions of
surrendering."

The woman stood tall and straight in her rose-colored silk
shirt and breeches, her slender body giving the impression
that she was unarmed more through choice than due to lack of
skill, and I finally understood why I had no memory of the

strength of her mind. She was the first Rimilian I had come across who was capable of shielding, undoubtedly the "denial" which had been mentioned in relation to her. There was something odd about the shield—I could see that immediately—but defining exactly what the oddness was was something I didn't have the time for just then.

"Honor demanded that the offer be made," Leelan came back immediately, projecting calm regality of her own. "Those with honor shall ever display it, even to one such as you. Which of these do you choose to stand for you?"

"With a sword?" Farian asked, suddenly showing spiteful amusement. "It was my understanding that you meant to challenge *me*, girl; have you discovered an understandable reluctance for a doing such as that? You will attempt to beat me with the weapon which bested my Hand of Power?"

"You will be bested with precisely the same weapon, *woman*," Leelan answered, stressing the word *wenda* just as Farian had been stressing the word, *treda*. She saw as we all did that Farian didn't know what had knocked out her Hand of Power, which meant she hadn't detected the fairly tight beam I'd used. "It was merely my intention to allow you a form of defense which will be useless to you after personal challenge has been given. Should this, however, not be in accordance with your wishes. . . ."

"It happens that such a thing is exactly in accordance with my wishes," Farian said with a smirk, her anger at being called *wenda* quickly swallowed. "You think to face my good right arm, and then allow Relgon there to strive to her utmost against *me*. What will truly occur, however, is that first my good right arm will strike *you* down, decisively yet no so far that you will be unable to see me best your chosen power, and then the two of you will be slain. After that those others will be taken, and will be clearly taught the consequences of the folly they engaged in. Let it begin now."

Farian raised her arms in a theatrical gesture designed to look more impressive than ridiculous, and when Roodar immediately began descending the steps toward Leelan, that was the way everyone took it. The gesture said it was the *Chama* who was allowing the fight to start, and no matter how angry that made Leelan, there was nothing she could do about it but step forward and draw her sword.

Roodar unsheathed her blade a good deal more slowly, at first looking at everyone in our group except Leelan, her expression completely calm and unconcerned. There was no recognition in her eyes when her gaze swept past me, but when it touched Tammad she smiled very faintly, as though pleased that someone had thought to bring something of hers along. Deegor's hand on my shoulder showed me I'd actually taken one step forward in mindless rage, but no one else seemed to have noticed, especially not Roodar. She had already turned her full attention to Leelan, and so had everyone else. All I could do was stand there with fists clenched, staring at that so-called *w'wenda*, wishing with everything inside me that it could have been me facing her with swords instead of someone else doing it.

The someone else named Leelan, however, was more than pleased with the arrangement. She and Roodar were both big women, and the swords they held in their fists were held with strength and skill. Roodar wore the yellow of the guard and Leelan was dressed in shirt and breeches of green, but that seemed to be the only difference between them. Both were young, both had long blond hair held back with leather headbands, both stared at one another with blue eyes, and both were eager to get down to cases.

Almost no time at all was spent in circling before the first ring of blades came, a vicious overhand cut initiated by Roodar. Leelan blocked it and swung in answer, and Roodar was the one who had to move fast to keep from getting chopped. The yellow-clad *w'wenda* retaliated with a series of blows designed to get through to her opponent with speed and strength, but Leelan stopped the attack with strength and skill, then began an attack of her own. The two were very well matched, but the elation in the thoughts of the people around me led me to believe that it was clear, even in the few minutes the fight had been in progress, that Leelan was Roodar's superior and would soon prove it.

Which turned out to be a conclusion reached by someone other than the people who were on Leelan's side. I, like everyone else, was so intent on watching the fight that when Leelan stumbled and almost dropped her guard, all I could do was gasp in dismay, expecting to see the fight ended immediately but in the wrong way. Roodar moved in to attack without hesitation, almost as though she'd been expecting something like that, and if Leelan had been any slower she would have died. She'd gone to one knee to catch her balance, her mind clanging with confusion and lack of understanding, and managed to bring her sword up barely in time to keep her head from being opened. She took two or three blows like that before being able to regain her feet, and the minds around me were no longer as confident as they had been.

I suppose it was the confusion in Leelan's mind that first made me suspicious, a confusion that said as clearly as words that there had been no real reason for the *w'wenda* to have lost her balance. Leelan was shaken by not understanding why it had happened, and that made me take my attention away from the fight to look around, something no one else was doing. For that reason no one else noticed that some of the guard *w'wendaa* to our left seemed to be just regaining their own balance, as though what had happened to Leelan was a sickness that had struck them as well. For a moment I couldn't understand at all why that should be, and then it suddenly came to me that they had been in a direct line behind Leelan when she had been struck. That fact still made no sense—until I remembered how impressed everyone had been over my being able to touch Hestin without also touching the people behind him.

My eyes went to Farian then, where she stood with languid ease watching the ongoing fight, a faint smile on her pretty face and anticipated victory in her eyes. Her shield still seemed to be firmly in place, but I was ready to bet any amount named that it had dropped briefly to allow her to touch Leelan—with a spillover onto the people behind her target. Farian was no more capable of precise control than anyone else on that world, and was determined to win no matter what had to be done to guarantee it.

I stirred where I stood next to Deegor, angry but also confused. The way the guard *w'wendaa* were acting showed the spillover clearly, but if Farian had so little precision control, how had she missed Roodar? Her "good right arm" had been directly in the line of fire, so to speak, so whatever had happened to Leelan should also have happened to the other woman—only it hadn't. There was something there that I was missing, something I wasn't taking into account—and then a very unpleasant thought occurred to me. I moved my eyes from Farian to Roodar, the woman I'd so wanted to face, and couldn't keep from shuddering.

Roodar was still completely engaged with Leelan, and when I reached out to touch her mind, she wasn't any more aware of it than her opponent was. I could feel a very faint play of thoughts in her mind, the sort that were usually accompanied by any number of emotions, but in her case the accompaniment wasn't there. Roodan wasn't incapable of feeling emotions, at least not the stronger emotions like hate and envy and desire and pleasure, but wherever she felt them, on whatever level of her mind, it wasn't a place accessible to empaths. Roodar was a null, and totally untouchable by mind power.

I put an unsteady hand to my head as I continued to watch the furious exchange between the two women warriors, just as shaken as I'd been the first time I'd touched a null. There weren't many of them, happily, but to an empath that was still much too many. Nulls seemed to live on a different plane from everyone else, to look at things with alien eyes, and I'd never been able to accept their differences with anything even approaching calm. Even as I stood there I felt a terrible sense of impending disaster, a conviction that something horrible was going to happen, all no doubt due to my aversion to nulls. It was no longer any wonder why Tammad had been unable to touch her during his lucid periods, and no longer odd that Farian treated her the way she did. Roodar had to be the one who had helped Farian overcome the former *Chama*—

and the one she expected to help her overcome her present challenger. It came to me then that *I* was that challenger, and that if Roodar bested Leelan, the most skilled *w'wenda* among us, the next target for the big guard woman's sword would be me.

Or, worse than that, she would simply treat me the way she had the last time, making me a slave who could never get free. The thought of such a fate made me tremble uncontrollably, giving me a sense of nakedness and helplessness despite the breeches and shirt I wore, despite the weapon at my side, despite the strength of my mind. If Leelan fell then I did too, much lower than to mere death, and that wasn't something I could allow to happen. I was afraid, very much afraid, and found to my surprise that sometimes fear gave you a strength that was only supposed to come from courage.

I turned my attention back to Farian, just in time to see that the *Chama* wasn't pleased with the way Leelan had recovered her balance and confidence. Her frown recognized the fact that Roodar was visibly losing ground and points, and might soon lose the final and most important point. Her shield somehow—flickered—as though it were opening and closing faster than anyone could detect, and I instantly became aware of the heavy uncertainty being sent toward Leelan. As soon as that uncertainty hit the *w'wenda*, Roodar was sure to try to do the same—possibly more successfully than the first time.

I wasn't quite sure how it happened, but without any conscious effort on my part my mind was suddenly between Leelan and that bolt of uncertainty, my shield up to protect both of us. The projected emotion hit my shield and clung to it, trying to soak through, but it had less chance of doing that than a cupful of water had to penetrate marble. The unsupported emotion began sliding off then, weakening and dissipating, and the fight went on without Leelan knowing anything had been attempted against her.

But Farian knew. The woman who called herself *Chama* straightened in shock, not understanding why Leelan hadn't been affected, and suddenly there was another touch on my shield. When the same lack of response happened Farian tried a third time, but by then it was too late. Even as the touch slammed into my shield Leelan was furiously beating aside Roodar's sword, and then the null lost all need to ever feel anything again. Leelan's blade was buried in her chest, directly between her breasts, and her own sword slid from lifeless fingers. Right to the end Roodar had shown almost nothing of emotion, and that was the way she died. Leelan withdrew her weapon with a jerk, and a dead, calm-faced Roodar slid to the once-white floor.

"And that, I believe, sees to that," Leelan said in a short-breathed but triumphant way as she turned to a pale-faced, disbelieving Farian. "And now, O *Chama*, we must see to you as well."

"See to *me*?" Farian breathed with instant fury, drawing herself up again as outrage flashed in her eyes. "There are none among you *capable* of seeing to me, and that I will prove with every bit of my strength! Step out to face me, Relgon, and we will soon see which of us remains beyond the last of it!"

Farian was glaring at Deegor, too wildly out of control to think about what had happened to Roodar any longer, too far into the mists of rage to realize that what had protected Leelan was not something to be expected from Relgon. The older woman who stood beside me smiled very faintly, then shook her head.

"Were my sister here, she would surely accommodate you, Farian," she drawled, still feeling a twin's amusement at being mistaken for her sibling. "I, however, am Deegor, and scarcely the one you were meant to face."

"Who, then, has been chosen?" Farian demanded, glaring around with even more confidence than she had previously shown, indicating clearly that Relgon's strength had likely worried her a little. With Relgon elsewhere, though, her confidence was returning to bolster a bravado based on anger.

"The one who has been chosen to face you is here," Leelan said, putting a hand out to gesture me to her. As I stepped forward Farian's eyes immediately glued themselves to me, and her frown was one of disdain mixed with confusion.

"Your chosen champion is a small, odd-looking *w'wenda*?" she asked as nastily as it's possible to do, obviously trying to make me feel out of place and not very capable. "The power would be shamed to find itself in a vessel such as that. Has it ever been given a name?"

"It has indeed been given a name," I said before Leelan could reply, at the same time reaching up and pulling off the wig I'd been wearing. "Its name is Terril."

Farian narrowed her eyes as I shook my hair out, a faint worry touching her as memory of me returned, but then she remembered what she thought she'd seen of my ability and she laughed.

"You come here behind one who was previously able to do no more than flee in terror?" she said to Leelan, delighted taunting clear in her voice. "I have only to best one who is nearly empty, and then I may do with the rest of you as I please? I am truly well-served, Leelan, by your not having been slain. It will now be possible to have you watch the slow deaths of your closest sisters before you, yourself, are sent to the one I have chosen to band you."

As the last of her venom-filled words ended, her shield flickered again, and what was being thrown at me was the terror she'd mentioned a moment earlier, thickened and edged with vindictiveness. I had just enough time to see that before my own shield snapped closed, protecting me from the attack and surprising me all over again. I hadn't willed the shield, hadn't had the time to do so any more than I'd had the time when Leelan had been the target, but the shield was there anyway. It seemed that I'd finally developed what I'd always wanted, an automatic shield that appeared when I needed it, and if I'd had the time I would have been elated.

What kept me from having the time was Farian's continued attack, four further bolts when the first clearly had no effect. I had the impression from the impacts that the woman was beginning to tire, and when the raging attacks suddenly stopped I wasn't surprised.

"What is it that you hide behind?" she demanded, just short of frothing at the mouth, her fists clenched as she leaned toward me. "To hide is not to stand and fight, for victory may not then be yours. Strip away the covering as I have done, girl, and let us meet mind to mind."

Her challenge was filled with mockery, daring me to show her what I had. I looked up at her for a very brief moment, then shrugged my shoulders.

"You have not before truly seen my mind, Farian," I said, feeling more than a touch of spiteful enjoyment. "Learn now what lies behind the curtain."

With that I dropped my shield, and had the very great satisfaction of seeing Farian pale and drop her jaw. The woman's unshielded mind was strong all right, probably about as strong as Relgon's, but it was immediately clear that it couldn't compare to mine. Farian's sudden trembling showed that she knew it, and then her shield was abruptly back in place.

"I declare this challenge now done," she said in a rush, her voice uneven despite her attempts to steady it. "It cannot be denied that I bared my mind to hers, yet did she fail to best me. In accordance with the laws of this land, I continue to be *Chama* and shall continue to be obeyed. Lay down your weapons, and submit to binding."

The uproar that broke out at that was nearly deafening, almost as bad as the dismay and misery and gasping horror in the minds around me. The knot of guard *w'wendaa* raised their swords again with grins of delight, and although the group I stood in front of moaned in agony, none of them raised swords in answer.

"What is it?" I asked Leelan, suddenly afraid of what was being felt by our *w'wendaa*. "What does she mean, and why do you not prepare yourself to resist?"

"In what manner may we resist?" Deegor demanded as she came up behind us, nearly shouting to be heard over the others, her mind almost as frantic and defeated as Leelan's. "Did Farian not answer our challenge, just as she was bound to do? She bared her mind to you, Terril, and you failed to strike. By the law of our land she now stands victorious, and we, ourselves, honor-bound to obey. In the name of all you hold dear, for what reason did you fail to strike?''

The question was filled with more bewildered hurt than I would have expected from the older woman, and I couldn't have felt it more if she'd underscored it by plunging a dagger into my chest. I felt the same from Leelan, who had turned away to keep from having to look at me, and from the others behind us, two of whom were crying, and the shocked knowledge that I'd failed them brought to my own mind the desperate need to defend myself.

But no one said I had to *do* anything to her, I protested in the silence I couldn't seem to break, throbbing under Deegor's continued stare. They never told me I had to *strike* at her!

What did you *think* they wanted you to do? another part of my mind countered, disgust dripping from every word. Did you think besting someone meant showing off what a pretty glow your mind has, and leaving it at that? They trusted you, Terry, and they depended on you, and after everything they went through they can now thank *you* for their failure.

But I'm not a warrior! I nearly wailed, more sick to my stomach than the Hand of Power had made me. All the breeches and all the swords in the world won't make me one, and they should have known that! They should have known better than to have their very lives depend on me!

The inner voice didn't have anything to say to that, but not because there wasn't anything to say. My sense of time suddenly shifted so that everything around me slowed nearly to a standstill, giving me all the opportunity I needed to finally admit that my failure hadn't been one of lack of knowledge. I'd known they'd expected me to do to Farian what I'd accidentally done to that original group of conspirators, but that was the whole problem. It was *Farian* they wanted me to do it to!

I closed my eyes with the terrible ache I felt, knowing that if it had been Roodar instead, I would have been able to do anything necessary. I'd hated Roodar and still did, for what she'd done to me and what she'd done to Tammad, and striking at her would have been easy. Farian hadn't exactly been sweetness and light, but although I detested everything she stood for and disliked her personally, she wasn't even responsible for raising those male slaves. I didn't like her, but I didn't hate her!

Isn't that somewhat childish? the something inside me asked, this time sounding slightly more patient. An infant has to have an emotional reason for doing or not doing something, but adults know how to deal with abstracts. And know how to accept the responsibility for their actions, without needing an excuse to point to. Farian has to be stopped for everyone else's good, no matter how much pain-of-conscience it gives you to do it. No hate to fly along on, no grudge to blind your awareness, just the need of the people around you. Have you grown up enough to do it on that basis, with your eyes wide open and your mind free of uncertainty?

That terrible question hung in front of me, so direct that all I wanted to do was look away, and then I thought of a way out. If I let that emotionless, uncaring state take me over the way it had when I'd faced Tammad, everything would be done the way it had to be. The coldness would see to it that Farian was bested, and I wouldn't have to get involved at—

It didn't take the inner voice to stop that thought, and I was suddenly more ashamed than when my "master" had strapped me in front of the guard. If I let the coldness take over there would be nothing to worry about, nothing but my absolute inability to take responsibility for my own actions. I would continue to be the coward who ran away from everything, the child who always had to have someone else to blame for what she did. Tammad had given me permission to make decisions about my abilities, but not because he had continued to think of that decision as his to make; *I* was the one who had needed it to be spelled out, who had had to be forced away from the crutch. No one can or has to give a *l'lenda* permission to do anything, and at long last I really understood what that meant.

I finally looked up from my inner dialogue, and was somewhat surprised to see that no more than a minute or so could have passed. Deegor was still staring at me with pain in her eyes, the women of our group were still torn apart by the thought of what their adherence to honor was about to make them do, and turning around showed Farian well on the way to full restoration of her usual arrogance. Triumph shone out of her eyes as she began congratulating herself on her brilliant stroke, but the congratulations were just a bit premature.

I can't honestly say I was fully confident, but there was no uncertainty in me when I projected a strong, general blast of static designed to reach everyone in the room. Silence descended faster than any amount of shouting would have accomplished, giving me a backdrop against which I took one step forward toward the woman on the platform.

"You are mistaken, Farian," I said with something close to true calm, seeing her immediate shift to petulant anger at being disagreed with. "This challenge is not yet done, for my failure to strike was an attempt to allow you to surrender without being harmed. Should you refuse to accept this offer upon the moment, it will then be withdrawn."

"Ah, I see," Farian answered with a ridiculing smirk, her brows raised in amused revelation. "You failed to strike when my mind was bared, solely out of a sense of honor. Now that I have again raised denial to protect me, you call for my surrender else shall I be struck. You are a fool, girl, and shall soon be an enslaved fool. I refuse to surrender, therefore you are invited to strike."

Her smirk was really outstanding by then, a sign of her absolute confidence in how safe she was, emboldened even further by the mutter of surprise and confused dismay coming from my own people. Farian was convinced that nothing could get through her shield, just as convinced as everyone else was, but I was betting they were all wrong.

I sent my inner sight right up to her shield just as I had done with Len, but found it considerably more of a shock than his. The oddness I'd noted when we first got to the room resolved itself into something I'd never seen before, something clearly developed by people who weren't from Centran stock. Rather than being a sphere, Farian's shield was more like shifting diagonal lines, fast-moving lines that seemed to allow no way through them. They weren't really solid any more than my shield or Len's was solid, but the overall effect of the lines made them very difficult to look at. Causing mental eyestrain seemed to be one of the ways the shield protected its possessor, and very briefly I nearly felt outclassed and defeated.

But only very briefly. What I'd thought of as the coldness was suddenly there supporting me, calming and smoothing my own emotions so that I could work without being distracted. I knew then that *that* was its purpose, a way of controlling myself when I really needed the control, not something that took me over and dehumanized me. It was there to be used, not allowed full control, the master of a child but the tool of an adult. I didn't know how far I'd moved along the road toward adulthood, but a tool like that was something I truly needed right then.

Getting my own emotions out of the way let me really look at the shield, and it was then that I became aware of the time interval of the shifting. Matching the shift was the key to getting through the shield, that rather than trying to go around it. I didn't think it was possible to go around a shield like that, and thinking about the time interval immediately set my mind into an attempt to shift in the same direction and at the same speed that the lines did. The coldness continued its support as my mind moved faster and faster—and then I was matched to the interval and sliding through.

After giving me her permission to strike, Farian had herself struck a pose, a languid stance of derision and insult meant to rub her untouchability in my face. The couple of minutes it took me to match up were enough to increase her confidence even more, and she had just begun a sneeringly dirty laugh when I passed her protection and touched her mind. If not for the coldness I would have pulled back immediately in disgust and horror, utterly repelled by the peculiar brand of madness she possessed. Farian had never been denied anything in her entire life, and rather than set her own boundaries and learn necessary self-denial where others were concerned, she had opted for going after and getting everything there was in reach. No matter what she had to do to get it. No matter whom she had to hurt. The ultimate spoiled brat who would never stop until she had it all.

Supported by the coldness I retained my touch, and Farian's laugh turned instantly into a scream, her hands going to her head as though she thought she could physically thrust me away. Absolute silence returned with that scream, a shocked and disbelieving silence, but one that seemed to understand exactly what had happened.

"No!" Farian screamed again, her eyes wild with fear, her hands still at her head. "I cannot bear to be hurt! I give you my surrender and you must accept it!"

Her mind really was frantic, mainly due to the lack of self-confidence she'd always suffered from, but I could see that surrender was a weapon to her, a way of protecting herself from someone stronger until she had the opportunity to knife them in the back. That was the way she'd always used to get out of paying for the things she'd been caught doing, but if I let her get away with it I'd be as guilty of her next viciousness as she was.

"The opportunity to surrender was given you earlier, just before your rejection of it," I said, wishing I could simply let her go but knowing it wasn't possible. "The option was then taken from you, and will not now be restored. You chose to give misery and pain and deceit when you could have given happiness and easing and honor; as you gave, so shall you get."

She screamed again when the misery and pain hit her, two things she had never really felt before. Wide-eyed and hysterical she fell to her knees, her mind screaming louder than her throat, and then she found that she hadn't yet had the worst of it. I sent a hint of remorse and pity, leading her to believe I was going to relent, and then hit her even harder instead. Deceit always made the ultimate betrayal even worse for the victim, and she choked and foamed at the mouth before collapsing face down on the platform. Her mind was now clanging with shock, her shield long gone in uselessness, and that was when Deegor slowly mounted the steps of the platform to stand over her, a sword in the *w'wenda*'s hands. She looked down at Farian less with pity than with a sense of justice having been served, slowly raised the sword two-handed above her head, then brought it whistling down. I had just enough time to break my contact with Farian and throw up my shield before the sword found its target with a sickening "thwunk," and then it was all over and I was left standing there and trembling, my duty done but my soul sick because of it.

"Terril, you have given us our victory!" Leelan said as she suddenly came up beside me, quickly putting an arm around my shoulders in the abrupt bedlam. She was absolutely euphoric at having won after all just when defeat had looked so certain, but she was also aware of how hard it had been for me, and not due to inadequate mental strength. It was true I was beginning to feel really tired, but she knew my problem had had nothing to do with that.

"All of Vediaster now owes you its thanks," she said, her voice and eyes gentle as she looked down at me. "It was you alone who had the ability to free us, and this you did despite the pain it gave you. Naught save a true sense of honor could have seen the thing done, for we know you likely could have saved yourself alone. All shall honor the one who has so truly earned it."

I looked up at her with a small frown, but what she'd said was entirely accurate. With Roodar dead there wasn't anyone around who could have made me a slave again, and I'd known it even if the knowledge hadn't been conscious. I could have gotten Tammad and myself out of there but hadn't, finding it more necessary to stay and free everyone else as well. Thinking about Tammad caused me to begin to turn to look for him, but that was when Deegor made her way back to us.

"And now we have only to install the new *Chama* in her place," she said, having noted with approval the way her *w'wendaa* were disarming and tying the guards who had served Farian. The knot of unarmed women to the right weren't being bothered, and a good many of them seemed overjoyed.

"It has not occurred to me to wonder who has been chosen to be *Chama* in place of Farian," I said, taking a deep breath in an effort to put it all behind me until I had the time for solitary consideration. "Surely Leelan has the greatest claim, for it was she whose mother was the rightful *Chama*."

"Leelan cannot be *Chama*," Deegor said with an incredulous laugh, staring at me in a very odd way. "Our *Chama* must be possessed of the power, which we all know she is not. Also is there another matter, as fully a part of our laws as that. Surely you know. . . ."

"Deegor, you must allow *me* to explain," Leelan said, interrupting, looking for all the world as though she'd been caught in a high-spirited prank that others might not consider very amusing. "Well might it be looked upon as dishonorable to have failed to speak of the matter more fully at an earlier time, yet did I hold no single thing back and indeed brought most of it to your attention, Terril. It was very much a matter of need, therefore did I. . . ."

"Leelan, please," I interrupted in turn, suffering almost as much from her discomfort as she was. "You need not go on in such a way, for our lives will not continue forever. As there is a thing you wish to tell me, you need do no more than speak of it."

"Perhaps you are correct," she said, glancing guiltily at a frowning Deegor, and then she squared her shoulders and plunged into it. "Terril, the laws of Vediaster demand that she who bests the current *Chama*, be made *Chama* in her place. It is a thing known to us all and expected."

"A thing known to you all," I echoed, briefly wondering why each shock I got had to be worse than the one before. "Known to you all, yet never quite mentioned to me. Now that all matters of battle are seen to, I am lightheartedly informed that *I* am the new *Chama*. A pity this was not mentioned earlier, for I have no desire to be *Chama*, nor shall I be. You must find another for the honor."

"Terril, you cannot refuse," Deegor said quickly, putting

a restraining hand on my arm as she cast a look of daggers at a supposedly shamefaced Leelan. "You most certainly should have been told of this sooner, yet does the lack do naught to change matters. By law you are *Chama*, and *Chama* you must remain."

"You have given so much to Vediaster," Leelan added with a corner of her hidden satisfaction showing, her expression one of smooth urging. "Surely you will not refuse to allow Vediaster to give to you in return?"

"I will not be *Chama*," I repeated with all the calm I could manage, looking up at each of them in turn. "This country is not mine, nor do I mean to remain in it. You must find another to be *Chama*."

"We will discuss the matter," Deegor said in a soothing way, her hand patting my shoulder, and then she had to turn away because of a sudden disturbance between some of the prisoners and their captors. Leelan glanced at me then hurried after the older *w'wenda*, not about to leave herself in a place where she might have to answer any awkward questions, and that left me technically alone. I knew I didn't want to discuss anything with anybody—and then I turned to find Tammad's eyes on me, from where he stood just a few feet away. Why he hadn't come closer I had no idea, but rather than worry about it I went to him.

"Did you hear that nonsense?" I asked him softly in Centran, putting my arms around his body as he gently folded me in his own arms. "If they think I'm staying here to be *Chama*, they're out of their minds. You're the only thing I'm interested in, and you're the one I'm staying with."

"I may not have you," he answered in an oddly calm voice, oddly calm because of what he was saying. "There are others who now need you more, and such a thing must be understood and accepted. Battles are meant to be fought and won."

"You battled with the desire to keep me, and that's the battle you won?" I asked in shock, looking unbelievingly up into his expressionless face. "Just like that, it's all over between us, and you have nothing more to say about it than that you understand and won't argue? You never hesitated to give me away temporarily because of your sense of duty and honor; you can't possibly mean you're now going to do it permanently?"

He looked down at me with his usual calm and not the least trace of denial, just short of a frown as he groped for the right words to say what there couldn't be any right words for, and that was when Dallan came over, followed by Hestin. I didn't know where the healer had suddenly appeared from, but he wasn't the only new arrival. People were streaming in through the doors we'd broken down, and the noise level would probably soon be out of control.

Hestin began by not saying a word, but instead let his hands do their job. He touched Tammad on the chest, on the back, and finally put his fingers to his head, then turned to Dallan.

"Your suspicions were entirely correct," he told the *drin* of Gerleth, his tone merely disapproving but his mind outraged. "This man has been so badly abused that he is near dropping from exhaustion and pain. We must lose no time finding a place where he may rest."

"Let us all seek such a place together," Dallan answered, stepping to Tammad's other side to reach for his arm. "Should any attempt to dispute your choice, *I* shall see to persuading them."

Hestin was pleased with Dallan's grim promise, and between them they gently disengaged Tammad's arms from around me, then began leading him out of the room. Although he turned his head once to look at me before disappearing through the doors, he made no attempt to resist the urgings of the other two men, or to change his mind about what he'd said. I stood staring at the doorway long after they were gone, too numb to feel anything, too numb to think.

After a while someone, Leelan, I think, found me just standing there, and immediately decided that I could probably use some rest. I was led to a very large room with a wide bed of costly furs on it, my swordbelt was unstrapped from around my waist, I was helped onto the bed and my sandals were removed, and then I was left alone. It was very pleasant in that extremely large room, the furnishings were in very good taste, and even the predominantly golden decor wasn't tedious. It came to me that that was probably the *Chama*'s bedroom, and I suddenly realized how important I'd become. I was the center of attention there, the hero of the hour, and no one would ever look down on me again.

I turned to my left side on the bed furs, still too deeply lost in the massive folds of shock to be anything but disbelieving, that and somewhat bewildered. After everything that had happened between us, after all the talk of love, how could he just decide to give me up like that? Because he wasn't saying he didn't love me, only that he couldn't have me? Was that supposed to make it bearable and acceptable? Was that supposed to erase the terrible need I had to be beside him, to be held in his arms, to share his limitless strength, to be deeply loved even as I loved in return? Most of the women in Vediaster were the independent sort, and although I had envied their freedom at first, I had finally come to know that "freedom" wasn't what I wanted. I wanted—and desperately needed—the deep involvement I'd been a part of, a relationship that had rarely been calm and comforting, but had been starting to get that way. It's rather melodramatic to say you can't live without someone, but what that really means is that you haven't the will to live without them. I'd lived most of my life knowing I couldn't depend on anyone around me even for a minute, had met a man who had supposedly changed all that, and now, because of the sense of honor that had *made* him so very dependable, I was groping again for a step that wasn't there. He loved me, but honor and duty always came first.

I turned to my back again in the very comfortable furs, then almost smiled at another realization. The terrible problems I'd had, about having Tammad's children and telling him of the one I'd given away, were suddenly no longer problems. They were completely solved and no longer had to be worried about, and that was definitely a benefit I hadn't expected. I closed my eyes in order to get the rest I really did need, feeling very proud that I hadn't broken down and cried like an infant. I continued to be proud until I fell asleep—and then my dreams were made of tears.

13

When I finally woke up I discovered it was the next morning, which meant I'd slept through the rest of the previous afternoon and all of the night. Golden sunshine streamed into the very large golden room, and I was able to lie unthinking in the furs until someone peeked in and found me awake. Very quickly after that I was surrounded by servants and assistants, diplomatically rousted out of bed, then shown to the apartment's bathing room. I had help getting undressed, help getting washed, help getting dried, and help getting dressed again in fresh breeches and shirt made of silk. The clothes were a surprisingly good fit, but that was the only surprisingly good part of any of it. When a tray of food was brought in and someone tried to help me eat from it, I finally decided I'd had more than enough. I quietly told them all that I'd take it alone from there, and anyone who didn't instantly disappear from the room would instantly regret it. Even if most of them hadn't been there for my fight with Farian, they'd all heard about it, and about half an instant later I was the only one who hadn't disappeared.

I was quietly brooding over the observation that obsequious behavior from those around you tended to encourage outrageous exercises of power and position, when a knock came at the door. Since I knew who it was I didn't bother answering, but that made no more difference than it ever did. When

Dallan got no response he simply opened the door and walked right in, then came over to me where I sat among lovely gold cushions.

"You appear well-rested and refreshed from your labors," he observed, picking a section of floor fur for himself. He was back to wearing his blue *haddin* under his swordbelt instead of a brown slave-wrap, and seemed extremly pleased over the change. "I have come to see how you fare, for Hestin tells me Tammad will continue to sleep for some time yet. The sleep has been encouraged by a potion, of course, yet is it necessary to enable him to return to himself. Until that occurs, I will do as I have done till now."

"And keep watch over me," I said with a nod, then gestured toward the tray of food that had been brought for me. "You may help yourself if you wish, there is sufficient for many more than just one."

"You have my thanks for your generosity, *wenda*," he said, but the words just covered the sudden, close attention he bent on me with a frown. "I will be honored to share your provender—after you have spoken of what disturbs you."

"I am attempting to speak of a thing which will disturb you as well," I said with a faint smile for his usual perceptivity, looking into his pretty blue eyes. "Dallan—your duty to watch over me is no more, for I have been told I am no longer the belonging of Tammad. Honor demands that I retain my place here as *Chama* for there are many who need me, and honor may not be denied even by one who nearly begged to be allowed to do so. To a *l'lenda* honor is all, and no matter that I, myself, am not *l'lenda*. I am no longer permitted to love one who is."

"Terril—he said this to you?" Dallan asked, the shock and dismay in his mind so great that it reflected on his handsome face. "I cannot believe he would do such a thing— Perhaps you are mistaken?"

"He said he might not have me, for there are now others who need me more," I answered, strangely enough trying to be gentle for Dallan's sake. "How is it possible to be mistaken when told a thing such as that? I was not told that he no longer loved me, only that he would no longer have me. Do not be overly upset, brother. I have seen at last that what occurred is for the best.''

"Sister," he said, tragedy in his eyes and in his thoughts, but I shook my head before he could go on.

"Dallan, you know what difficulty I had living in this world," I said, trying to explain it to him as I'd worked it out for myself. "His beliefs have never truly been mine, and a thing such as this was bound to occur at some time if not this one. Never have I been able to put his welfare and happiness after any other thing, yet honor and duty have always stood first in *his* thoughts. I do not fault him for this for he is *l'lenda*—yet I am not, nor do I wish to be. I am done with him now, and oddly relieved to have it so."

He stared at me with such pain that I was tempted to soothe it down for him, but that was the sort of temptation I had to learn to resist. There's very little separating the urge to help and the urge to "change just a little," and that was a fork in the road I had no intentions of traveling. If people left me alone I would do the same for them, and then maybe the road would get easier.

Dallan was busy trying to accept what I'd told him, when another knock came at the door. This one was a mere formality, however, because Dallan hadn't closed the door when *he'd* come in; most of the small crowd was already in the room, and the knock had just been to get my attention.

"We give you greetings for a new day, Terril," Relgon said for all of them, her mind considerably calmer than those of Deegor and Leelan. Eight of our original group of ten were there, and they all seemed agitated but determined.

"And I give you the same, Relgon," I answered politely, then gestured at the multitude of cushions. "Will you not come in and join me?"

They all perked up at the unexpected invitation, possibly having anticipated being thrown out the way my assistants had been earlier, and immediately began coming farther into the room. All of them felt better—with the single exception of Leelan, who had very quickly noticed Dallan's presence there. I had the feeling she was trying to decide just how *long* he'd been there, but once they were all settled on the floor fur, Relgon gave her no time to even consider asking.

"We have seen to a number of things for you, Terril," the older woman said at once, her mind faintly amused with the knowledge of what Leelan was feeling. "First and foremost have those who were members of the various Hands of Power been taken and separated, and their fate may now be decided at leisure. Also has the palace guard been reorganized, although a number of its former members remain to be examined. Many served Farian merely through necessity or a sense of duty toward the office, and these should not be punished with those who served willingly."

"And what became of the Hand I struck?" I asked, not really wanting to know but still compelled to ask. Relgon didn't avoid my eyes, but her mind offered me comfort even before she spoke.

"There was no need to separate that Hand," she said, a compassionate understanding in her at how I would take the news. "They—received the power of your thrust with their minds wide, and likely were gone before any pain was able to touch them. The guards who stood beyond their chamber were completely unaware of what had occurred."

I nodded without saying anything, feeling the admiration in the minds of the others over the fact that I'd been able to kill five people at once without even disturbing the guards who had been no more than feet away. That, of course, was why Tammad, Cinnan, and I had been put in a room alone when we'd first gotten to the palace. The Hand had strength but not control, and they'd simply saturated the entire area in order to get us. The mountain stone on the walls of the room had to act as reflectors and magnifiers—which explained why I'd felt as I had while we were traveling through the mountain pass. The walls of rock had been picking up the broadcasts of the Hand, reflecting and magnifying it and then passing it on to me. I wondered then if the white stone of the palace didn't have some sort of magnifying abilities of its own: I hadn't been able to even begin questioning what was happening to me as a slave until I managed to close my shield. I realized then that thinking all those thoughts was actually helping to divert me from what I'd done to the Hand, so the best thing I could do was go on with the diverting.

"What of Cinnan and Aesnil?" I asked, ashamed that I hadn't thought to inquire sooner. "Have they been greatly harmed?"

"The *Chama* of Grelana was in no manner physically harmed," Deegor put in, temporarily taking over for her sister. "Her mind, however, is greatly confused, for Farian had been attempting to make a loyal follower of her. The confusion will pass, we believe, for the *Chama* does not seem one who takes easily to following others. The man Cinnan, on the other hand, was not well treated in his capture, and now rests in the care of Hestin. When learning of his presence, the *Chama* was quick to go to his side."

"Which will surely aid in his mending," I said with another nod, then looked around at them. "Are there any other matters which require discussion?"

"We have not yet spoken of the most important matter of all," Relgon said, her light eyes calm as she broached the subject no one else seemed to want to get to. "I am told that inadvertently a knowledge of our laws failed to be fully shared with you, and you were caused upset through the lack. We all wish to offer our apologies, and hope that you now see the need for such a law. As our *Chama* must be one with the power, to merely slay her does not allow another to take her place. The *Chama* must be bested with the power itself, and the one to best her then becomes *Chama* in her place."

"I am aware of your reasons, yet are you mistaken upon one of the matters referred to," I said, then moved my eyes to Leelan. "The law was not inadvertently kept from me, the omission was deliberate. I had informed Leelan that I had no wish to lead your group and she was unable to shake my resolve, therefore did she allow me to believe that I did no more than agree to be a part of it. I was kept ignorant of the fact that I strove to be *Chama*, for it was known that I would not wish the place. How foolish she and you are, to accept an unknown stranger as ruler of your country.''

"We would be foolish indeed, were it an unknown stranger who was accepted,'' Leelan said at once, before anyone could react to my deliberate attempt at insult. ''You speak truly, Terril, when you speak of my actions, yet must you see the matter through my eyes. Not only were you willing to give the aid we required, you also wished no more for yourself than assistance in freeing your *memabrak*. Such a one is to be considered unfit for the place of *Chama*? With the power you possess, another would have sought and demanded all she might, also would it have been naught to her what became of others. Have you proven to be such a one? Your concern and sense of honor mark you, girl, and truly pleased am I that your rewards are greater than those you sought.''

Leelan sat leaning comfortably on a cushion, her pretty face showing a very satisfied expression, her mind gleeful over the way she'd made everything come out right. I suppose I could have controlled myself if she hadn't used the word ''honor,'' but that was one word that made me feel rather touchy.

"How nice that you are pleased, Leelan,'' I drawled, getting more comfortable against my own cushion. ''As you consider it self-evident that one with concern for a country and its people will make a fine *Chama*, you will undoubtedly be even more pleased to know that my first official act will be the consummation of an alliance with the country of Gerleth. I am acquainted with Rellis, the *Chamd* of Gerleth, who has fathered two sons. Rellis will surely agree to having his younger son band a personage of Vediaster, one who was daughter to the former *Chama*, and in such a way will you, too, aid your country. Do you believe the alliance likely to be accepted, Dallan?''

I turned my eyes to the *l'lenda* where he sat not far from me, pretending not to see how devastated Leelan was, and found that the man was finally understanding why Leelan had until then refused his bands. Under other circumstances he probably would have told her immediately who he was, but something in the tenor of his thoughts hinted that he was remembering what Leelan had said and done while he was an involuntary slave.

"I have lived in Gerleth all my life, and know the *Chamd* well," he said at last, also pretending not to see how upset Leelan was. "I am of the opinion that Rellis will find the alliance eminently acceptable, and the banding as well. This personage of Vediaster will be very fortunate. . . ."

Hearing Dallan himself seal her fate was just too much for Leelan, and she was up on her feet and running out of the room even before he'd finished. He watched her disappear with a definite pang of guilt over the way he'd gotten even, then rose himself and strode after her. Everyone else was silently upset at the goings on and the goings out, and once Dallan was out of sight and hearing Relgon decided to comment.

"For one of compassion, your first act as *Chama* was rather cruel," she observed, looking at me with a bit less calm. "Surely you have no intentions of seeking any such alliance? Leelan would naturally bow to the need, yet would she then also need to put forever from her thoughts the one who has just followed her. Would you take what life they might have together, in an attempt to be revenged for the great harm she has done you?"

Relgon's gesture meant more than just the room and what was in it, and it was accompanied by murmurs of agreement from the others. I looked slowly at each of them, and smiled a nasty smile.

"The alliance will be made exactly as I have said," I informed them firmly and deliberately. "How well stands now your opinion of one who is a stranger? How easy will be your lives beneath the sway of such a one? And how easily will you find one of greater power to best her? Truly are you fools for what you have done."

I stood up then and turned my back on them and their anger, strolling slowly toward the wall that was all windows. How pretty the golden sunshine was, coming in through golden curtains to turn gleaming everything it touched. I had no idea what was beyond those windows, and very little interest in finding out. If my new associates got angry enough life could become painful again, but that was a small price to pay for the freedom I needed. I had to leave Vediaster as quickly as possible, preferably without anyone rushing after me in concern, getting out of there before. . . ."

"Terril."

The single word and hand on my shoulder made me cringe involuntarily, but nothing came after that. The anger I had hoped for was conspicuous by its absence, and compassion stood in its place.

"Truly, girl, you have lived too long among those without the power," Relgon said gently as she and Deegor each put an arm around my shoulders. "One who means others ill thinks the same, the venom of her envy or hatred or despising clearly there to be felt."

"Also does such a one take care not to turn an unguarded back upon those with weapons," Deegor added, like an echo with a separate soul. "Had your mind been set between us and you, we would have known that as well. No more was there within you than a great deal of unhappiness, so clear that we all were able to perceive it. Have we forced upon you so great and terrible a burden, then?"

"No, no, the position is merely unwelcome," I quickly reassured their deep upset, inwardly sighing over having forgotten that they'd be able to tell how I felt. "I shall remain for a short while to assist you, yet during that time a new *Chama* must be found."

"You are determined and will not be swayed," Relgon said, looking down at me with partly narrowed eyes. "All these riches mean naught to you, and you yearn greatly for another place. You mean to return with your *memabrak* to his own country, then."

"No, I shall not go with the one who was my *memabrak*," I said, looking away from her penetrating gaze and back to the windows, feeling the pain despite my resolve not to. "There is a road of my own I must follow, and I am most eager to begin the journey."

The arms of the two women tightened briefly around me then, trying to soothe the pain they could feel. They could tell I didn't want to talk about it and respected my wishes, and for that I was very grateful.

"And, of course, there will be no alliance with Gerleth which Leelan must be committed to," Deegor said after a minute, taking her arm away. "Although an alliance with so strong a country would be beneficial to us here, the price of it would be far too high."

"The price of it will seem as though no cost at all," I countered, bringing my gaze back to see the startlement on both of the twins. "I am rather fond of the younger prince of Gerleth, and that despite his penchant for constantly antagonizing me. His name, should you find it of any interest, is Dallan."

Seeing two identical faces gaping at you open-mouthed from left and right is the least bit unsettling, but then they and the others were laughing, as well as congratulating me on the way I'd gotten even with Leelan. Everyone had a grand old time, and then it turned out that they had a number of jobs that only I could do. *Of course* they were going to begin looking for a new *Chama*, most likely applying the law used when the *Chama* died of natural causes, but first there were these jobs. . . .

Hours and hours disappeared with the doing of those jobs, and finally I'd called a halt so that I could be alone for a while. There was no longer the sound of battle as I walked along the corridors, and I gratefully acknowledged that fact as I rubbed at my temples with the fingers of both hands. I wasn't overtired and I didn't have a headache, but I couldn't ever remember working so hard with my mind. There had been quite a number of guard *w'wendaa* and members of Farian's court whose loyalty no one had been able to determine for sure, and that had been one of my jobs. There were no more nulls, thank goodness, but even without them the time had been unpleasant, forcing woman after woman to feel and speak the truth. So many of them had been delighted with the former *Chama* and her intentions, and most of them, when caught in the lie of swearing allegiance to the victors over her, cursed me for what I had done. Being screamed at like that didn't bother me, but the memory of what their minds had been like—

"Terril!" The call drew me out of my own thoughts, but was welcome. Dallan came up to me from one of the cross corridors, and smiled down at me with an expression I'd rarely seen before.

"I was told you walked alone to clear your mind of the thoughts of others," he said, reaching out one big hand to smooth my hair. "Is my presence an intrusion?"

"*Your* presence, no," I said, returning his smile. "It is female minds I must escape for a while, as the others were well aware. I had not known how pleasant it would be to state a need to those who are capable of doing as I do. I had only to give my assurance that I would defend myself should the need arise, and was then able to go off without even the presence of guards."

"There should be little danger for you here in the palace," he agreed, following along beside me as I began walking again. "I sought you out for I wished to thank you for the offer of an alliance between Gerleth and Vediaster. Although the formalities are yet to be completed, the incidental banding has already been done."

"You told her then," I said, smiling even more at the sense of blissful completion in his mind. As long as I'd known him there had been a sort of questing after something deep inside, and the feeling was no longer there. Leelan made Dallan whole, and he was very much aware of it.

"I did not speak as quickly as I had thought I would," he answered, grinning at the memory. "When first I entered her apartment, meaning to ease her upset, she threw insults at me for having dared to support your betrayal. She had no wish to be mated with this prince of Gerleth, she said, telling me in such a way that *she* was the personage referred to, and then stated that I clearly had no true feelings for her, else I would speak against the alliance.

"I considered it best to grow thoughtful at these revelations, then at last shrugged them off as of no consequence. I informed her that the younger prince of Gerleth was widely known as one who should have been born *wenda*, and once his bands had been closed for a short while on his new *memabra*, I would challenge him for her. Leelan was aghast at my words for, as she quickly informed me, the younger prince of Gerleth was indeed widely known, yet as a greatly able *l'lenda*. If I were to challenge him, I would more than likely fall.''

Dallan was chuckling by then, his eyes twinkling as he shared his amusement, and I grinned and nodded for him to go on.

''I immediately assured the woman that I most certainly would not fall in any meeting with the prince, then became determined to show her how deep my feelings truly ran. Rather than be the one to challenge, it would be I who would need to be challenged, for it would be I whose bands were upon the woman in question. Leelan grew horrified when I produced those bands, then attempted to keep me from my intention as she had once said she would. She is a woman of great skill and adequate strength, yet is she still *w'wenda* rather than *l'lenda*. When my bands were upon her despite her objections, when she fully knew the man who had claimed her, I then told her what name he was known by elsewhere.''

''At which point she either laughed in relief and delight, or sought your life and privates,'' I said, still as amused as he was. ''Shall I attempt to guess which?''

''As you are acquainted with Leelan, there should be little mystery to the matter,'' he answered, more than delighted himself. ''It was necessary that I point out to her how undesirable it was for a woman to contemplate such doings with her *memabrak*. She in turn pointed out that she had attempted rather than contemplated them, therefore the matter should surely be acceptable. I find it quite fortunate that one seldom laughs alone, else would she have gotten a good deal of her own back.''

''You will likely need to guard yourself for some time yet,'' I observed, amused at the thought. ''And in what manner did a *w'wenda* look upon having the bands of a *l'lenda* closed on her?''

"She was far from pleased." Dallan sighed, immediately both annoyed and disturbed. "A single band about the wrist is customary in Vediaster, I was told, with a matching band upon the man. I cannot see my woman as anything less than five-banded, and certainly cannot accept a band of my own, but I feel the matter is not yet settled between us.''

"Undoubtedly it one day shall be," I said, giving him what comfort I could. "To the satisfaction of you both." I stopped again, short of the next cross-corridor, and smiled up at him. "You have my thanks for having shared the time with me, brother. I shall wish you nothing more than all the happiness the world contains.''

"A happiness which I wish might be shared with you, sister," he said, his eyes showing hurt again. "We must make the opportunity to speak together, for there are surely many men who would wish to band a *Chama*, and just as surely one at least who would be acceptable.''

"I will be certain to seek a time," I assured him, not bothering to mention that seeking was a good distance from finding—or reminding him of what he'd taught me about how it would be for me with a man other than Tammad.

"And now you wish to return to solitude," he said, probably seeing the need in my eyes. "Perhaps you would care to take the meal later with Leelan and myself.''

"It would give me a good deal of pleasure to do so," I said, really meaning it. "Later I must see Aesnil to aid in the removal of the confusion given her by Farian, and perhaps she, too, will wish to join us.''

Dallan thought the suggestion a good one and then we parted company, he to go back the way we'd come, I to continue on up the corridor. By the third step I was deep inside myself again, this time trying to calm my impatience to get out of there. I had the feeling Relgon and Deegor were going out of their way to show me what it was like to be with others of my own kind, hoping that I might then be persuaded to stay. Under other circumstances I probably would have been tempted, but not under those circumstances, and certainly not with—

The hand closed on my arm so hard and so unexpectedly that I cried out, but by then I was already into the cross-corridor where I'd been pulled, a cross-corridor dim with the light of a single distant torch. I immediately reached to the mind directing the hand that had pulled me in there, then stood frozen in shock while two massive arms crushed me to a broad, bare chest.

"Where have you been, girl?" his voice demanded in a fierce whisper, rocking emotions making it tremble. "You were given to *me* as a slave, and should not have been taken by any other! Had I not heard your voice I would not have found you again, to return you to your place at my side. You shall not again be allowed to leave me!"

The slave held me to him with a desperate relief that flowed over me like a tide turned savage by a storm, pushing me under where I would likely drown. He was so *glad* to have me back, and so afraid he might lose me again, and I shuddered in his arms, not strong enough to pull free, totally incapable of striking at him with my mind. He was so innocent, and had been hurt so much, and the feelings he had for me—

"Release that woman at once!" another voice snapped, far from a whisper, and then I knew that Dallan had heard me cry out and had come back to help me. The slave stiffened and his painful fear was a rake of claws through my insides, but he didn't let me go.

"But this slave is mine!" he nearly begged, the words echoing in the warm chest my cheek was against. "She was given to me, and you have no right to take her! And you cannot have her in any event! When the mistresses see that weapon you bear, they will end you! Slaves are not permitted to bear weapons!"

Dallan was silent for a moment, his mind shocked and struggling to make sense of what had been said to him, and all I could see was the thick arm in front of my face, indistinct in the dimness of the corridor. That arm was one of

the two that held me, gentle in spite of everything, warm and
alive and—

"You are one of the male slaves of this palace," Dallan
said with dawning comprehension, his voice less harsh than it
had been and accompanied by the sound of his sword being
returned to its scabbard. "I was told that your whereabouts
were a mystery, and it was feared that you were in some
manner done away with. Are the others with you?"

"My brothers and I were commanded to remain in this
corridor until we were returned for," the slave answered,
now sounding bewildered. "The others are at the far end and
I alone crept to this one, hoping to find one who would allow
us to leave. We have had neither food nor drink since we
were brought here, and. . . ."

"By the Sword of Gerleth!" Dallan spat, frightening the
slave even more. "They brought you here knowing full well
you would be unable to leave if they failed to return, for this
was meant to be a final, vicious stroke against those who
condemned them for their love of slavery. Eventually your
bodies would have been found, and it would be known to all
that it was their very victory which slew you. Had they not
been victorious you would have been returned for, rather than
left to starve and die of thirst! What a pity their plans have
now come to naught. Gather the others, for the time has come
for you all to leave here."

"But—we cannot leave!" the slave whispered, trembling
at the idea. "We have not been given permission to do so by
one who is free, and therefore. . . ."

"*I* am free," Dallan interrupted with pity in his voice and
mind, hating the need to be so gentle. "Such is the reason I
wear a weapon without fear. No longer are there slaves in this
palace, for all have been freed. Come with me now, so that
you, too, may know freedom."

"Freedom," the slave whispered, trembling even harder.
"We will now be made to know freedom. I will fetch the
others at once."

He released his two-armed grip as he began to turn, but he
still kept one arm firmly around me as he got ready to go

back to the others. I was his and not about to be turned loose, but suddenly Dallan was there, taking his arm off me and stepping between us.

"No!" the slave cried, trying desperately to pass Dallan, but although he was nearly the *l'lenda*'s size it was as though a half-grown boy fought with a man. "Please! The female is mine!"

"The woman is free," Dallan told him, still speaking gently even as he kept him from reaching me again. "She is free and therefore cannot be claimed as a slave by you. When you, too, are free, you may present yourself to her as one free person to another."

"I may do such a thing?" the slave asked, still upset but somewhat diverted. "I shall be free, and I may present myself to her?"

"Indeed you may," Dallan assured him, patting his shoulder as he urged him toward the darkened far end of the corridor. "And the others may do the same with other *wendaa*. Let us fetch them now, so that you and they may be fed and begun upon the road to freedom."

"Yes, let us begin," the slave agreed, filled with a fearful enthusiasm, and as they made their way up the corridor I backed a few steps in the opposite direction, stumbled and nearly fell as I turned, then ran as fast as I ever had before in my life.

I have no memory of the corridors I passed through, but there must have been quite a few of them. The first thing I do remember is coming to a pair of open terrace-doors, stopping a moment to drag in uncounted, painful gasps of air, and then plunging wildly through them. Outside it was a warm, bright early-afternoon, with very few people around and an air of peace overlying everything. I stopped again to look around, the sweat dripping down my face and spotting my shirt and breeches, my heart pounding, and slowly it came through to me that I'd left the palace at a point near the stables. I was panting and still wanted to run, but I forced myself to a more normal pace and that way covered the rest of the distance to where the *seetarr* were kept.

It was much dimmer inside the stables, but the boy had no trouble seeing me. He came up anxious to be of service, terribly proud of his new green *haddin* and uncollared neck, and in just a few minutes I had a *seetar* complete with saddle and bridle. I had to use a block to mount him, but once mounted he responded well to my mind and carried me to the nearest gate. The guards there were startled to see me riding through all alone, but before they could protest or try to come with me, I was already across the open stretch and moving into the city streets.

It took me awhile to find the main street that led out of the city, but once I did I followed the road a short distance before finally turning off into a quiet stand of trees. A small breeze moved the leaves overhead as I dismounted, and my *seetar* snorted in contentment at having been allowed to stop in such a pleasant place. I sat down in the grass in front of one of the white-barked, narrow-boled trees, folded my legs in front of me, then buried my face in my hands. The urge to run was still inside me, and I didn't have to wonder why.

"I almost did it," I whispered to myself, so sickened and horrified that I couldn't picture ever being tranquil again. "Because he thinks he loves me, I almost let him claim me. When he puts his arms around me, it felt *good*."

And that was the part that tortured me the most, the fact that the slave's arms had felt good. Tammad hadn't said that he didn't love me, but how do you give up someone you love? I needed to be loved, needed it so desperately that I'd almost been ready to accept it from a man with the mind of a child, but he wasn't the one I wanted to love me. I wanted the man *I* loved to love me, but honor and duty meant more to him than I did. He was better off without me, I knew he was, but that didn't work in the reverse no matter what I'd said to Dallan. I needed him more than I needed my life, more than I needed my eyes or mind or heart, but the disease called honor had come between us, an incurable disease.

I was crying by then, the sort of crying that comes from a hurt that simply won't stop. The man I loved and needed didn't love or need me, at least not as far as I could see, and there was no other way to look at it. Once he rode away his memories of me would begin to fade, until one day I would be gone entirely, replaced by whatever woman he banded next to laugh with and make love to. I loved him too much to do anything but wish him happiness with her, more happiness than he'd found with me. As for myself, I'd made that decision some time ago; all I wanted was the nothingness of the end of life and the end of pain. The loneliness seemed to hurt more than ever, more than it had before I learned what it was like to live without it.

I leaned back against the narrow tree with my eyes closed, my knees raised to support my elbows, my hands to my now-aching head, my body shuddering from the crying. Being all alone is not the same as being lonely, which you can be even if you're not all alone. I suppose it's easier to take if you're big and strong, but I wasn't big and strong and didn't want to be. All I wanted was—

I heard the twig snap at the same time I felt the startlement of my *seetar*, and it was all I could do to keep from sending my mind out. Very few things are able to startle an animal as large as a *seetar*, and if one of those very few things was close by, I didn't want to chase it away. I had come close to being killed by something once and it had been horrible, but the worst part had been touching its mind. If I made sure not to touch its mind it should all be over before I knew it, me getting what I wanted and a wild beast getting a good meal. I wanted that trade with everything in me, but I still began trembling when my *seetar* rumbled a warning and backed off just a little. It was coming closer, it had to be coming closer, and then it was—

I couldn't feel much of anything and I couldn't move or open my eyes, but somehow I had come partly awake. It was strange to know that that was what being dead felt like, and then I became aware of someone speaking.

"... lucky can you get?" an unfamiliar male voice was saying. "There we were, all ready to gas everyone in that palace to get her, and she practically stumbles into our laps."

"We wouldn't have known she was that close if I hadn't checked the transponder *you* were supposed to be watching," another male voice countered, sounding annoyed and short-tempered. "Did you at least remember to turn her off after giving her the gas?"

"Are you kidding?" the first voice demanded in outrage. "Of course I did. You don't think I want an awakened Prime anywhere near me, do you? Even if we don't bring her out of it before we get back to Central, I'm happier with this one turned off."

"We're not taking her back to Central," the second voice said, this time sounding faintly distracted. "Our employers decided some time ago that they needed her in their special program, but that barbarian they loaned her to refused to give her back. Now we have her whether he likes it or not, and she goes straight to New Dawn."

"What's on New Dawn?" the first voice asked, full of curiosity but beginning to fade out just a little. "I thought it was a frontier world with nothing but savages."

"It's a frontier world with open spaces, savages—and the special-project breeding farm," the second voice answered with a chuckle, also sounding a good deal fainter. "They raise the best of the male Primes there, and also give them the best of the females they want bred. She won't be ready for it for a little while, but they'll be after her as soon as they see her. I wouldn't mind doing it to her myself."

"Yeah, and me," the first voice agreed, so low I could barely hear it, and then it all went away.

DAW

Presenting JOHN NORMAN in DAW editions . . .